THE RANGER
BY
RHONDA NELSON

AND

HOT-BLOODED
BY
KAREN FOLEY

MILLS & BOON

Check out what *RT Book Reviews* is saying about Rhonda Nelson's heroes in—and out of—uniform!

"This highly romantic tale is filled with emotion and wonderful characters. It's a heart-melting romance."
—On *Letters from Home*

"Wonderfully written and heart-stirring, the story flies by to the deeply satisfying ending."
—On *The Soldier*

"A highly entertaining story that has eccentric secondary characters, hot sex and a heartwarming romance."
—On *The Hell-Raiser*

"A highly romantic story with two heartwarming characters and a surprise ending."
—On *The Loner*

THE RANGER

BY
RHONDA NELSON

First published in Great Britain 2011
by Mills & Boon, an imprint of Harlequin (UK) Limited,
Eton House, 18-24 Paradise Road, Richmond, Surrey TW9 1SR

© Rhonda Nelson 2010

ISBN: 978 0 263 88067 0

14-0611

Harlequin (UK) policy is to use papers that are natural, renewable and
recyclable products and made from wood grown in sustainable forests. The
logging and manufacturing processes conform to the legal environmental
regulations of the country of origin.

Printed and bound in Spain
by Blackprint CPI, Barcelona

For Amy Weaver, my BFF and
quintessential cool chick.

A Waldenbooks bestselling author, two-time RITA®
Award nominee and *RT Book Reviews* Reviewers'
Choice nominee, **Rhonda Nelson** writes hot romantic
comedy for the Blaze line. With more than twenty-five
published books to her credit and many more coming
down the pike, she's thrilled with her career and
enjoys dreaming up her characters and manipulating
the worlds they live in. In addition to a writing career
she has a husband, two adorable kids, a black Lab and
a beautiful bichon frise. She and her family make their
chaotic but happy home in a small town in northern
Alabama. She loves to hear from her readers, so be sure
to check her out at www.ReadRhondaNelson.com.

Dear Reader,

Thank you so much for picking up *The Ranger*. It's the sixth book in my Men Out of Uniform series, and I can't tell you how much I enjoy writing these unrepentantly male badass heroes. They're all Southern gentlemen, so they know how to treat a lady—when they find the right one—and they're honest and noble to the core. Toss in a wicked sense of humor to go with an equally wicked smile and these guys are lethal. And Will Forrester is no exception…

Will's first assignment for Ranger Security, though a bit bizarre, seems harmless enough. Find Theo Watson, an elderly gentleman who is looking for the Watson family jewels, which were, according to family lore, hidden right before the Union soldiers marched on Atlanta during the Civil War (or the War of Northern Aggression as some still call it down here.) But when Rhiannon Palmer arrives on the scene determined to "help" Will, things take a completely unexpected turn and soon all Will wants to do is *help* Rhiannon…right into bed.

Be sure to look for Chase Harrison's story, "The Prodigal," in *Heroes Welcome* next month and Tanner Crawford's in *The Renegade* in August. Nothing warms the cockles of my heart more than hearing from my readers, so be sure to check out my website at www.ReadRhondaNelson.com.

Happy reading!

Rhonda

1

FORMER SOLDIER Will Forrester pushed through
the double doors of the sleek Atlanta high-rise that
housed Ranger Security and prepared to meet his
new destiny.

For the first time in his adult life, as a civilian.

His fingers involuntarily twitched at his sides,
betraying the slightest hint of unease. Though he
had always thought highly of the gentlemen who'd
started this company—finding better soldiers than
Brian Payne, Jamie Flanagan and Guy McCann
would be damned near impossible—Will had nevertheless never imagined that he'd be working for
them.

In fact, if anyone had told him three months ago
that he would be anything other than in service
to Uncle Sam, he would have asked them to hand

over their crack pipe and would personally have escorted them to rehab.

But that was before the…incident.

Will determinedly closed the door on that line of thinking before any of the horrific images could form. One, in particular, haunted him.

Knobby knees, thin limbs, a bloodied, tattered teddy bear…

He squeezed his eyes tightly shut and swore under his breath. Dammit, he had to get a grip. He couldn't afford to blow this. He had been especially grateful to Colonel Carl Garrett for making the recommendation for this new career. Frankly, when he'd decided he had to get out—that he no longer had the stomach for war—Will hadn't given much thought to where he would go or what he would do. He just knew that he couldn't do his job anymore, that he'd never be able to do it again.

As for the men who were with him that fateful day, Chase Harrison and Tanner Crawford, who knew what they were going to do? Chase seemed to be dealing with the tragedy much better then he or Tanner had, so Will figured he would ultimately continue in service. Tanner, however, was more than likely on his way out. He sincerely hoped Garrett would extend the same recommendation for Tanner that he had for him. Tanner deserved it.

On some level Will had imagined that he'd go

home to Mockingbird, Mississippi, a quaint little town nestled in the heart of the Delta. His grandmother was still there, after all. Gardening, quilting and sipping iced tea. Having lost his parents and little brother in a car accident when he was ten, Will had been raised by his paternal grandparents.

His grandmother had kept him well loved and well fed and his grandfather, who'd passed five years ago, had taught him the benefit of fewer words and more action, the advantage of hard work and patience and, of course, how to treat a lady. The thought made Will smile. God knows John Forrester had loved his "Miss Molly" and had treated her accordingly. He missed him, Will thought now, and knew his grandmother did, as well.

It felt like a lifetime ago that he'd been home, that he'd put his feet under her table and enjoyed a home-cooked meal and good company. He actually should have gone to see her before coming here, but Garrett had insisted that he was needed *now*.

Besides, his grandmother would ask probing questions—ones he didn't want to answer at present—so this was truly for the best. He'd go and see her as soon as he got this new job in order—first things first always—and he'd make sure to call more often in the interim.

"Will Forrester?" a slim, no-nonsense gentleman asked from behind a remarkably tidy desk.

Will nodded, startled back into the present.

"I'm Juan-Carlos," he said briskly, extending his hand. "The Triumvirate are expecting you. Follow me, please."

The Triumvirate? Will thought, feeling his lips automatically slide into a half smile. That was definitely a unique way to describe the owners of the elite security company. And the hint of droll humor he'd heard behind the description was especially puzzling.

Juan-Carlos led him down a carpeted hall, past several offices into a large lounge area that looked more like a man cave than any sort of business room. A flat-screen television was anchored to the wall—currently tuned to a Braves baseball game— and a well-used pool table overlooked downtown proper. A stainless-steel refrigerator—no doubt stocked with the drinks and snacks the three of them were currently enjoying—stood against another wall. Various bits of technology—laptops, cell phones, MP3 players and the like—lay scattered over the battered coffee table, along with their feet.

Seated on dark leather furniture, the three men stood when he entered. Brian Payne was easily recognizable with his blond hair and penetrating ice-blue eyes. Nicknamed the Specialist, Payne was notorious for his ability to always do things right the first time. Much like failure, half-assed wasn't an option.

Equally impressive with his supposed genius-level IQ, Jamie Flanagan had dark curls that gave him a boyish quality, but the set of his shoulders and the line of his jaw let a man know that the Irish-American former soldier was a force to be reckoned with.

Guy McCann rounded out the rest of the Triumvirate, with a reputation of recklessness and luck that bordered on the providential. McCann's smile was a little irreverent, but the shrewd green gaze currently sizing him up felt anything but flippant.

It was Payne who spoke first. "Forrester," he said, striding forward to shake Will's hand. "Welcome to Ranger Security."

Flanagan grinned, plopped back onto the couch and shoved a potato chip into his mouth. "The perks kick ass."

"Ignore him," McCann piped up, snatching the remote control out of Jamie's reach. "We do actually work," he drawled.

"On occasion" came the long-suffering voice of Juan-Carlos as he quietly shut the door.

Guy glared at Payne. "He's getting a little too mouthy for a secretary."

"He's an office manager," Payne corrected. "And he's indispensable. Which he knows."

"If he continues to smirk at me, what's not going to be indispensable are his teeth," Guy threatened. "He's a subordinate. He should act like it."

Will wondered if they knew he referred to the three of them as the Triumvirate, but decided not to mention it. He didn't want Juan-Carlos to lose any of those pricey porcelain veneers on his account.

"Can I get you something to drink?" Payne offered, jerking a thumb toward the refrigerator.

Will shook his head. "I'm good, thanks."

"Have a seat," Jamie told him, gesturing toward one of the empty chairs. "We're pretty informal around here."

He actually liked that, Will thought. These guys were obviously just as comfortable in their own skin as they were with one another. It was the sort of familiarity that took countless hours and inherent trust and he instinctively found himself wanting to be a part of it. To share in the easy camaraderie. Though he'd been happy about the job—about having an alternative at all to the military career he'd envisioned—for the first time since he'd officially walked off base, Will instinctively knew he'd found where he belonged.

This was going to work. He felt it.

"How's my grandfather-in-law?" Flanagan wanted to know.

Will smiled and tried to frame a diplomatic response. Colonel Carl Garrett was an old warhorse with a piss-and-gravel voice that had been honed on the battlefield and fired in the boardroom. Will had a lot of respect for the man, but he'd ruffled more than a few feathers through the years. Of course, no one could be in the colonel's position without pissing off a lot of other people. It was the nature of the career.

"Well," Will finally managed. He waited a beat. "The same as always."

"So he's still an interfering, egotistical old bastard on a power trip, then?" McCann said. He snorted. "Figures."

Payne laughed. "Careful, Guy. That interfering, egotistical old bastard is responsible for some of our best help—" his cool gaze slid to Will "—and our newest recruit." He lifted a brow. "You've reviewed the employment package?"

He had and was still astonished. "It's generous."

And that was putting it lightly. In addition to the salary, the benefits were beyond amazing. Preferring that specialists lived in close proximity, Payne had purchased the entire building and renovated the upper floors into apartments. Though Jamie and Guy lived in Atlanta only part-time, Payne was in residence at all times in the penthouse suite. Considering he'd been in the service since college, Will had little in the way of personal belongings and even less in the home furnishing department. That he would be able to move right into an out-fitted apartment was a perk he could genuinely appreciate.

"You'll earn it," Payne assured him. He handed him a laptop, a cell phone and a Glock 9 mm. "Tools of the trade. All of the software you'll need to interface with our programs here at the office have already been loaded onto the computer. Numbers are programmed into the phone and your permit to carry concealed is in the laptop bag." He shrugged. "Doubt you'll need a weapon for this first case, but better armed than not, in my opinion."

He wouldn't need a weapon for his first case? What exactly did that mean? Will wondered.

"Do you need a car?" Payne asked. "I've got a couple in the garage."

Will shook his head. He'd actually just traded in his old Jeep Wrangler for a new Black Rubicon.

"Here are the keys to your apartment," Payne said, tossing them lightly to him. He released a small breath. "That covers everything but the briefing on your first assignment."

McCann slid a folder across the coffee table to him. "It's a bit unusual," he said, and the small smile playing over his lips did little to inspire confidence.

Will flipped open the file and quickly scanned the first page. Theodore Watson, seventy-six, missing from his home for the past few days. He read on and immediately understood McCann's grin.

"A treasure hunt?" he asked dubiously, glancing up at Payne.

Jamie chuckled. "In a manner of speaking. Mr. Watson is looking for his great-great-grandfather's treasure. According to his family history, this particular grandfather had amassed quite a fortune in jewels. Afraid that the Union troops were going to seize his possessions, like many other people who lived in the South who had any wealth, he hid them. Unfortunately, he died before he recovered them from his hiding place and hadn't shared their whereabouts with anyone else."

"Or he could have, and that lucky soul kept it for himself," McCann pointed out. "The Watsons are practically royalty in the small burg of Begonia, Georgia. They're old money. Lots of land."

Will frowned. "So it's his family who've hired us? Is Mr. Watson a danger to himself? Got any health issues that make his disappearance particularly disturbing?" Granted the man wasn't exactly a spring chicken, but from the looks of this file he lived by himself, which would indicate that he was relatively healthy, at any rate.

Payne, McCann and Flanagan shared a look. "Tad Watson, Theo's son, is more concerned with keeping up appearances than his father's actual safety," McCann explained with a twisted smile. "From what we've been able to discern, Theo has been looking for this treasure for more than sixty years, and is a bit on the eccentric side. Tad doesn't approve."

"He's an embarrassment," Jamie said, pulling a shrug. "Tad wants him found so that he can do damage control."

"He's throwing around words like *senile* and *dementia* and *diminished capacity,*" Payne said. "Laying the groundwork to have him committed, or at the very least put into an assisted-living facility."

Though he'd never met Theodore Watson in his life, Will found himself inexplicably annoyed on his behalf. What the hell was wrong with people? he wondered. Whatever happened to respecting your elders? Furthermore, this was the South. Eccentricities were typically celebrated. Crazy, so long as it wasn't harmful, was charming down here.

"The senior Watson is much more philanthropic than his son would like him to be," Jamie added with a grimace. "If he managed to put his father into a home, he'd be able to control the family finances."

In other words, he was greedy. Impossibly, Will liked Tad even less.

"At any rate, the son has provided us with a list of probable locations his father could be," Payne announced after a significant pause.

"He hasn't looked himself?" Will asked, surprised.

Another uncomfortable look. "Tad is actually out of the country."

"Flying over the Atlantic right about now, wouldn't you say, Jamie?" McCann remarked. He tossed a handful of M&M's down his throat.

Atlantic? Right now? Will frowned. "Let me get this straight. His father is missing, so he's concerned enough to hire one of the premier security firms in the country…but he's *not* concerned enough to postpone a business trip?"

"Actually, it's a vacation," Payne corrected, his voice chilly. "Italy. He'll be checking in periodically and wants to be notified as soon as his father is located."

How considerate, Will thought, utterly disgusted. He grimaced. "Right."

"There's also a list of acquaintances in there, people he might have contacted before he left," Jamie said.

Will looked up. "He didn't mention he was leaving to his son?"

McCann snorted. "I sure as hell wouldn't, if I was the old guy, would you?"

He supposed not. Still…

"We know this isn't exactly an exciting or glamorous first assignment, but it's what pays the bills," Payne said.

He didn't give a damn about exciting or glamorous, and after a minute he confided as much. "I'm just…thankful to have a job, to have a place here. It's more than I could have hoped for, particularly considering I made the decision to leave abruptly."

Payne's calm gaze found his. "We know exactly what that's like. It's why we're here, you know."

And he did know. Garrett had given him the abbreviated reason as to why Payne, McCann and Flanagan had left the military. They'd lost a dear friend and comrade, Danny Levinson, and each of them felt as if they were in part to blame. Couldn't be any easier to live with that than what he was currently struggling with, Will thought.

Help me, he heard again, for what felt like the

thousandth time. The tiny, faltering voice. Fearful yet trusting and so, so weak…

"It gets easier," Jamie said, his eyes grave with understanding.

Will merely shrugged, hoping like hell that was true. It sure couldn't get any worse.

"THIS ONE IS STAYING," McCann announced as soon as Will Forrester disappeared around the door frame.

"Ordinarily when you make predictions like that, I think you're completely full of shit, Guy, but in this instance I think you might be right," Jamie agreed.

Brian Payne silently concurred. Though they'd lost their past two employees to other career paths—and women—Forrester seemed different. There was a sadness, an ownership to Will's grief that he recognized, as well. Hell, who was he kidding? They could all identify. Innocent blood on your hands was something they could all empathize with. Though Payne had realized that it wasn't completely his fault that Danny had died, there was a part of him that would always feel responsible for his death all the same. Like Will, it didn't matter that the intel was faulty, that he'd done everything he was supposed to do.

He'd lost a man.

And Will Forrester, according to Garrett, had had a child die in his arms.

Terrible stuff, that.

"What do you think?" Jamie asked. "You think he's going to have any trouble making the transition to our way of life?"

Payne shook his head. "Not at all. You've read everything I've read. He knows what he's doing. Was one hell of a soldier who simply lost the stomach for war."

"With good reason," McCann said. "Damn, how do you find your happy place after something like that? How do you move forward?"

Jamie passed a hand over his face. "I don't know. Women and children, you know? That's the stuff of nightmares."

Though Garrett had been very vague with the details of Forrester's last mission, Payne knew that it had involved the accidental death of innocent civilians. Payne had willingly fought terrorists without batting a lash because he'd been fighting for the greater good against an enemy who wasn't above killing innocent women and children. Conscienceless zealots bent on revenge and power. But if he was ever involved in a mission like Forrester's, which had resulted in the death of those they were trying to protect… He didn't know how he would cope and, frankly, was thankful that he'd never have to try.

"I liked him," Jamie said. "My gut says he's a good guy."

"If we're going to start talking about feelings, then I'm outta here," McCann said, purposely lightening the moment.

"Kiss my ass, Guy," Jamie told him, hurling an empty plastic soda bottle at his head. "You know what I mean."

"Do you think we should have mentioned the chick?" Guy asked, shooting Payne a look.

The chick in question was Rhiannon Palmer—good friend to Theo—who was hell-bent on finding him, as well. Having been told by Tad—her ex-boyfriend—that Ranger Security was on the case, Rhiannon had already been in contact many times asking for updates. A local elementary guidance counselor specializing in emotional intelligence, she was pushy, feisty and had all the tenacity of a bulldog.

"She's on the list of acquaintances," Payne said, and smiled.

And she was now Will Forrester's problem.

2

RHIANNON PALMER GLARED ominously down at her cell phone as she absorbed the last text message from her miserable, sanctimonious ex-boyfriend and felt a low growl build in the back of her throat.

Butt out. It's under control.

She fired off a final go-to-hell message, then sank back against the cushions of her porch swing and tried to plan her next move. Her dog, an Australian shepherd named Keno, determinedly nosed her palm and Rhiannon gave her an absentminded rub.

"Oh, Theo," she moaned aloud. "Where the hell are you?"

Honestly, if she hadn't been so worried about

her dear friend and mentor, she could quite happily have throttled him. He'd purposely waited to make his escape while she'd been finishing up the final class in emotional intelligence, a course she taught at the local community college during the summer. August through May, she was the guidance counselor at Begonia Elementary School, a job she genuinely loved.

Rhiannon could perfectly identify with so many of the kids who walked through her door. She'd been the shy, insecure little bookworm with the added freakishness of being able to accurately read people's moods. Hidden things, even, which weren't readily discernible on the surface.

With the exception of Elizabeth Alston, her best friend, it had made her an outcast on the playground, and had made adults a little too uncomfortable around her. Of course, having a child pick up on your secret crush on the assistant principal— particularly when you were married to the basketball coach—couldn't have been easy, Rhiannon thought, remembering that particular incident with a small smile.

At any rate, it wasn't until she'd met Theodore Watson, a local librarian with plenty of money and too much time on his hands, that Rhiannon had been made by an adult to feel anything other than odd. Even her parents, bless their hearts, hadn't been quite sure what to make of their daughter, a fact that she'd been aware of from the time she was a toddler.

But Theo… Theo had made her feel *special*. He'd looked at her and seen potential, and she'd loved him ever since.

As a semi-empath himself and possessing a keen interest in emotional intelligence—or EI—Theo recognized her unique ability and had quickly made her feel more at home in her own mind than she'd ever been in her life. Not only had he helped her hone her skill at recognizing others' emotions, but he'd taught her how to use her own to influence the people around her. Despite her admittedly hot temper, Rhiannon could be quite soothing when she wanted to be. She glared at her phone again.

Right now she wasn't in the mood to soothe anyone, even herself. She was enjoying her irritation.

Stupid Tad, she thought. Moron. Idiot. Gigantic ass.

Though she'd dated Tad only to make Theo happy, Rhiannon nevertheless bitterly regretted the decision. It had taken less than a minute into their first meeting for her to realize that a love match wasn't in their future, but Theo had been so happy—so overjoyed that Tad had asked her out—she hadn't been able to refuse.

Unfortunately, much like the first date, the relationship had quickly ended in disaster. Though she'd been ready to pull the plug from the get-go, Tad had beaten her to the punch, evidently sensing her uninterest, and had dumped her publicly on Facebook.

Mortified didn't begin to cover it.

In addition to dumping her, he'd complained loudly to anyone who would listen in their small town about how "clingy" and "needy" she was, which was absolute bullshit. Rhiannon was many things, but clingy and needy weren't among them. Thankfully most people were well aware of her true character and Tad's penchant for self-importance, but it hadn't lessened her irritation or humiliation all that much.

Furthermore, that had been three years ago and Tad still had the audacity to act as if she was stalking him and couldn't get over him.

She couldn't get over him because she'd never been *on* him to start with. There was nothing to get over. She saw Tad only when she absolutely couldn't avoid him.

Unfortunately, no matter how much it irritated her to have to be in contact with him, Rhiannon didn't see any other choice. Tad had taken off for his Italian vacation, certain that his father had merely gone off on another relatively harmless search for the Watson treasure. He was embarrassed by his father's continued obsession with what he thought was a "ridiculous old story manufactured after one too many shots of moonshine."

Rhiannon didn't agree with Tad in the least and trusted Theo's instincts. He was a brilliant man who wouldn't have wasted sixty years of his life looking for something if he hadn't genuinely believed it was there. Because his family had wearied of listening to him go on and on about the family jewels, they'd actually talked at length about it many times.

If the jewels were real—and she, too, suspected they were—then she knew beyond a shadow of doubt that Theo would eventually find them. He'd actually called and left her a message the day he'd left.

"Rhi, I think I've got it!" he'd crowed. "Matthew 6:21. 'For where your treasure is, your heart will be also.' Don't you see? I've been looking in the wrong place. All this time and it's been right under my nose. Don't worry, dear. I'll be in touch."

But he'd been gone three days—plenty long enough for him to have found what he thought he was going to find if it had been where he thought it was and…nothing. Ordinarily, Rhiannon wouldn't have been worried. Theo was a youthful seventy-six, fit and relatively healthy.

But recently Theo had been diagnosed with

diabetes and, just like a typical man, he wasn't taking it seriously enough. He didn't monitor his blood sugar the way he should and routinely got too caught up in his research to eat regularly. Skipping meals in any circumstance wasn't healthy, but was particularly harmful for diabetics.

Theo had made her—and his physician—promise not to tell Tad. Due to his father's notoriously generous philanthropy, it was no secret that Tad was just looking for an excuse to move him into an assisted-living home and attempt to garner power of attorney over him. Furthermore, Tad and his father had different dreams for Watson Plantation, ones they'd been having increasingly frequent arguments about.

The Watson Plantation was unique in the fact that the family had never sold a single inch of land from the original plot. It was eighteen hundred acres of rich soil, and Watsons had been farming it for almost two hundred years. Through Theo, Rhiannon knew that they rotated the crops to keep the earth in good condition. She loved it most when they planted cotton, seeing that sea of fluffy white bolls nodding in the breeze.

True to his heritage, Theo was determined to keep farming the land and keep the old home place in the family, to preserve it for future generations of Watsons.

Tad had visions of trendy subdivisions, strip malls and fast-food restaurants. Or more accurately, the money that would be garnered as a result of selling off each bit of the estate acre by profitable acre. As an only child, Tad had no interest in maintaining the family legacy. He just wanted to line his pockets and travel the world, preferably with a supermodel at his side. He had no time and even less respect for his father, which annoyed the sheer hell out of Rhiannon.

Rather than skip his vacation and look for his father himself, Tad had hired a security company out of Atlanta to do the job. Though it had taken quite a bit of swearing, Rhiannon had finally managed to get the name of the company out of him and had called them many times over the past twenty-four hours. According to Brian Payne, the gentleman she'd been speaking with, their operative would be in town and on the case today and, being as close to Theo as anyone else, she fully expected a visit.

And then she would make sure she got to tag along, because there was no way she could continue to sit here and do nothing. Though taking off on her own had occurred to her, the agency's resources were better and more advanced than hers. They could track phone calls, credit cards and the like. If she had a general idea which way he had headed, Rhiannon thought Theo had given her enough information over the past several years to figure out exactly where he was going.

And the sooner she found him, the better. Considering the diabetes and his poor attitude about it, she wasn't going to be able to take an easy breath until then.

She might as well be breathing where it would do her some good.

Or she could not breathe at all, Rhiannon thought as the best-looking man she'd ever seen in her life suddenly loped up her sidewalk.

Sweet God.

She almost swooned.

Every bit of the moisture in her mouth promptly evaporated and the tops of her thighs tingled with heat that had absolutely nothing to do with the mid-morning sun. A line of gooseflesh marched up her spine and camped in the back of her neck, making her entire scalp prickle with awareness. A violent full-body blush stained her skin from one end to the other and, though she knew it was simply her imagination, she could have sworn she heard the faintest strands of porn music as he stepped fully into view.

Six and a half feet of rock-hard, splendidly proportioned muscle and bone stood in an open-legged stance in front of her, showcasing long, lean legs and a crotch that instantly captured her gaze.

Probably because she was practically at eye level with it, Rhiannon thought faintly.

He wore a black T-shirt that hugged every rippling muscle and a pair of trendy sunglasses she instantly wished he'd remove. Confidence straightened his shoulders and shadowed the angular curve of his jaw, and a small cleft she had the almost irrepressible urge to lick bisected his chin. His hair was a golden-brown and shorn into a military cut that made him look all the more like a badass.

His mouth, possibly the most sensual thing she'd ever had the pleasure to gaze upon, shifted into a smile, and the simple rearrangement of his lips made something in her middle go all warm and squishy.

Hell, even her dog was panting.

He removed his glasses, revealing a pair of eyes that were a pale misty gray—almost disconcertingly clear—and lined with sinfully thick dark brown lashes.

He was sex incarnate, Rhiannon thought.

And she instinctively knew she was in trouble.

"Rhiannon Palmer?" he asked, his voice a husky baritone that put her in mind of rumpled sheets and massage oil. She tested the mood around him, and several things hit her at once—interest (gratifying, of course), confidence (also attractive—he knew what he was doing) and a sadness so deep and profound she almost gasped when she felt it. A frown worked its way across her brow. *Loss, regret, shame.* She could feel them all now. A tangled mess of remorse and misery so heavy she was surprised he could walk beneath its burden.

Denial was a powerful thing, though.

Rhiannon stood on wobbly legs and struggled to find her focus. "You've found her."

He smiled again. "I'm Will Forrester with Ranger Security and I'd like to talk to you about Theo Watson."

She'd thought as much. "Ah." She sighed. "I've been expecting you."

He blinked. "You have?"

"I've been speaking with your associate," she explained. "Brian Payne."

"Right," he said, though something in his gaze shifted. Irritation, perhaps? Intriguing. "Do you mind if I ask you a few questions about Mr. Watson?"

"Only if you don't mind if we go into the house," she said, ducking around him to get the front door. "It's getting a little hot out here."

And with him tagging along, she didn't think she was going to get any cooler, but she thought she'd fare better with the benefit of climate control. Honestly, she'd never had such a visceral reaction to a man before. It was as terrifying as it was thrilling. She tried to tell herself that she'd simply been too long without sex—more than a year, shamefully—but knew better.

It was him. Every beautifully proportioned inch of him.

"Sure," he said, left essentially without a choice.

She clicked her tongue for the dog and watched the shaggy creature promptly go and sprawl across one of the air-conditioning vents.

Having seen Keno's antics, as well, Will Forrester chuckled. The sound seemed rusty, which she found unaccountably sad. This was a guy who should laugh. "Smart dog."

"Too smart," Rhiannon agreed. "She can open the refrigerator, too."

He shot her an impressed, slightly disbelieving look. "Seriously?"

Rhiannon nodded once. "Seriously. She knows better than to take anything out, of course, but has to do it a couple of times a day just to let me know that she can." She gestured toward the couch. "Have a seat, please. Can I get you something to drink? I'm going to have a glass of tea, so…"

He nodded his thanks. "In that case, yes."

Rhiannon made her way to the kitchen, which was open to her living-room, dining-room combo. "Lemon?"

"Sure."

While she fixed the drinks, she watched him covertly. His keen gaze quickly noted everything in the room, from the pictures on her mantel to the slightly crooked throw rug in front of her couch.

He straightened it, and in that lone, impulsive gesture, she was able to size him up.

Will Forrester liked to be in control.

Pondering that, she felt a small smile slide over her lips as she returned to the living room. "Here you go," she said, handing him the glass.

He accepted with a grateful smile and took a sip, then sighed. "Thank you. That hits the spot."

One of them at least, Rhiannon thought, suppressing a laugh. Good Lord, had she ever seen a more beautiful man? Had she ever gazed at such masculine perfection in her life? He was criminally handsome. Even his ears were sexy. They had to be; otherwise she wouldn't be fantasizing about breathing into one of them right now.

He stared at her and a small grin played over his lips, as though he knew exactly what she was thinking. Impossible, she thought, and resisted the urge to press the glass to her forehead.

She took a chair opposite him. "So how is the investigation going so far?" she asked. "Have you had any leads?"

He winced. "Not exactly. I've been making calls during the drive over and so far I haven't found so much as a trace of him. He used his credit card to fill up with gas at Big Bo's Gas Mart on Friday, withdrew a sizable amount of cash from the local ATM and has completely fallen off radar."

Rhiannon grimaced. He must have known that Tad would hire someone to find him, she thought. Otherwise, why bother with using cash? "When you say a sizable amount of cash, just exactly how much are we talking about here?"

"Two thousand dollars."

"Eek," she said. "That'll buy a lot of gas, greasy food and cheap motel rooms, won't it?"

"If he's careful, a week to ten days," Will confirmed. "Do you have any idea where he might have gone?"

"He's looking for the treasure, obviously," she said, then shook her head. "The Watsons are originally from Philadelphia and they slowly migrated to the south, but that leaves a lot of territory, doesn't it?"

He nodded, jotting down a note in a small book. "It does…and it looks like it's my job to cover it. That's a start, at any rate." He stood and handed her his empty glass. "Thank you," he said. "I appreciate—"

Startled, Rhiannon stood, too. "You mean, you're leaving now? Right this second? For Philadelphia?"

He paused, and those shrewd gray eyes caught and held hers. She repressed a shiver. "I'm going to talk with a few other people in town first—friends, coworkers, the staff at the Watson Plantation—but if nothing comes of any of that, then yes, I'll be leaving shortly."

Good thing she'd already packed, then, Rhiannon thought. She'd actually thought they'd do a bit more poking around in town first, but this guy was obviously quite efficient. She'd been right not to strike out on her own. This would go a whole lot faster and a whole lot easier if they combined forces. The sooner she could make sure that Theo was okay—that he hadn't passed out from low blood sugar and tumbled down a stairwell or Lord knew what else—the better she'd feel.

That was her top priority at the moment, her only concern.

And then once she found out he was okay, she was going to verbally abuse him until he wished he hadn't been found. Damn him for making her worry like this. Didn't he know how important he was to her? Hadn't he known she'd be a wreck? Particularly given the diabetes? Couldn't he have invited her along, or at the very least let her know exactly where he was going?

She wasn't Tad, dammit.

More determined than ever, Rhiannon nodded once. "Okay," she said briskly. "Let me get my bag."

3

HER BAG? What the fu—

Before he could form the question, the beautiful—and evidently demented—creature darted from the living room and down a hall. Her bare feet slapped against the hardwood as she made her hasty retreat, bringing to his attention her curiously painted toes—hot-pink with silver stars.

No two ways about it. Rhiannon Palmer was quite possibly the sexiest woman he'd ever met in the flesh, or seen between the pages of a magazine, for that matter. She had long black hair that fell in wavy disarray around her elfin face, wide violet eyes and a mouth that put him in mind of sex. Though she wasn't what one could call classically beautiful, she had a memorable, unique face. That visage paired with an especially soft, curvy body and an ass that was ripe and lush sent her sexy quotient through the roof.

He'd taken one look at her and gone uncomfortably hard.

While he had to admit that wasn't a first, it was the first time since he'd left puberty behind.

Had he met her in any other circumstance, he would have been all over her like white on rice. He would have made a play for her faster than she could say *condom*.

Unfortunately, charming and witty aside, she didn't appear to be dealing with a full deck, and that point was never driven home more clearly than in that instant, when she strolled back into the living room with a rolling suitcase at her side. She'd put a pair of enormous sunglasses on her head and sparkly flip-flops on her feet and a bag big enough to house China over her shoulder.

"I'm ready," she announced, as if he should have been expecting this.

Will blinked. "Ready for what?"

"To go with you, of course."

He laughed uncomfortably and looked away before finding her gaze once more. "Er…that's really not necessary. I'm perfectly capable of—"

"I know that it's not necessary," she said. "It's expedient. You and I both have the same goal—to find Theo. It'll go quicker if we help each other."

He hated to point out the obvious, but… "I don't need your help."

Nor did he want it. In the first place, she was obviously…different. The word seemed a lot more charitable than *crazy*. In the second place, this was his first assignment for his new job and he'd just as soon not be distracted. In the third place, she was too damned sexy for his own good. And in the fourth place—damn, this was a long list—she unnerved him.

Will didn't like being unnerved.

Her laugh tinkled between them, and that sexy sound settled around his loins. "Yes, you do need me. You just don't know it yet."

Definitely crazy, Will thought. More's the pity. "In that case, I'll call you if I need your assistance." He smiled reassuringly and backed toward the door. "Don't worry. I'll find him."

Her smile turned a bit hard and she expelled a patient breath, as though he were the one being unreasonable. "Look, Mr. Forrester, you seem like a smart man, so I hope that this doesn't sound too patronizing, but…you don't know who you're looking for, and I do. Theo has been over every aspect of the Watson treasure story with me backward and forward. It's quite possible that you'll stumble upon a lead and not even realize it."

Will paused, looking for a flaw in her logic. He

supposed even sexy, crazy people had moments of lucidity. "True," he admitted. "But if that's the case, then why haven't you been out looking for him?"

"I have looked around here, in all the usual places," she said. "But he's not in town. If he was, I'd have found him by now. Furthermore, if he was staying close to home, he wouldn't have needed the cash—that says road trip to me—and he wouldn't have left me a message telling me not to worry."

Will's senses went on point and he felt his gaze narrow. "He left you a message? When? Do you still have it?" He wasn't aware of any contact with anyone after Watson supposedly disappeared.

"Of course," she said. She walked over to her answering machine. "He left it three days ago. That's the last I heard from him." She pressed the play button.

"Rhiannon, Tad here. Please stop harassing the Ranger Security people. Finding Dad isn't going to score you any points with me—"

She flushed and skipped over the message to the next.

Ah, Will thought. So that was her game, eh? From the sounds of things she and Tad had had a falling-out and Rhiannon was interested in helping find Theo Watson in order to put herself back in his good graces. He found himself unreasonably disappointed.

"Ignore him," she said, her voice throbbing with anger. "He's an ass."

Sour grapes, then? Had Tad taken a woman with him to Italy? Will wondered. His initial impression of Tad painted the man as a selfish, disrespectful boor. Crazy or not, he would have figured she'd have better taste. The thought made him slightly nauseated.

"Rhi, I think I've got it!" an older male voice said over the machine. "Matthew 6:21. 'For where your treasure is, your heart will be also.' Don't you see? I've been looking in the wrong place. All this time and it's been right under my nose. Don't worry, dear. I'll be in touch."

Excitement and affection rang in every syllable in Theo's voice and it was quite obvious that he adored Rhiannon Palmer. The fact that he would leave her a message advising her not to worry, but didn't bestow the same courtesy on his son told Will that he either didn't care whether Tad worried or not, or didn't expect him to be concerned in the first place. And considering that Tad was in Italy and Rhiannon was here, determined to go with him to help find Watson…

Well, clearly the older man was an excellent judge of character.

Nevertheless, it didn't change the fact that she couldn't tag along with him. Granted, he was new to the security business, but he didn't think that was proper protocol at all. After more than a decade of following orders and procedures, Will had learned to appreciate not only the chain of command, but the boundaries it put into place.

She was over the line.

"Does Tad know about this message?" Will asked. "He didn't mention it."

She lifted her chin. "No, I didn't tell Tad. He thinks his father is a ridiculous old fool and has evidenced his true concern by not changing his vacation plans." She crossed her arms over her chest. "I don't owe Tad anything. Furthermore, if Theo had wanted to call him, he could have."

"True." He considered her thoughtfully and finally asked the question that was driving him nuts. Ridiculous. He ought not even care. It didn't matter. And yet… "So you and Tad are a thing?"

She snorted and rolled her eyes. "I went out with Tad because Theo had grand dreams of me being able to turn his spoiled, shallow son into some sort of a redeemable facsimile of a man. The minute Tad realized that I was not going to fall into bed with him, he dumped me—via Facebook—and has continued with the false delusion that my greatest desire is our reconciliation." Her brows formed a straight line. *"It is not."* Her expression softened with genuine affection. "I do, however, utterly adore his father—he's been a better father to me than my own—and I am desperately worried about him."

Maybe she wasn't on medication after all, Will decided. Maybe she was just a little odd. Charmingly so, he had to confess. Charming + sexy = Trouble, he thought, tearing his gaze away from her ripe mouth. Another thought struck.

"My information says he's of sound mind and in good health. Is that wrong?"

She hesitated long enough for him to notice. "It is."

He waited. "But…" he prodded.

Her shrewd gaze probed his, evidently deliberating how to answer him. "Are you obligated to pass along any information I give you to Tad?"

A warning bell went off in his head. She was hiding something from him. Something that he instinctively knew was crucial to his case. "That would be at my discretion, of course."

She winced, disappointed. "That's not the answer I was hoping for."

Will leveled a gaze at her. "If there are extenuating circumstances that I am not aware of regarding Mr. Watson, then I would urge you to tell me."

"Only if I can trust you not to mention this to Tad. The last thing he needs is more ammunition to try and put his father into a home." An ominous expression settled over her face, putting him in mind of an angry kitten. "I won't give it to him."

Senile and *dementia* and *diminished capacity,* Will thought, Payne's words coming back to him.

"He's fine, really," she said. "He's just..." She trailed off, seemingly unwilling to finish.

"I will not mention this to Tad," Will said, hoping he wasn't going to regret making that rash promise. For reasons that eluded him, he wanted her to confide in him.

She melted, and the relieved smile that slid over her lips made him feel as if he'd just battled a dragon on her behalf. "He's recently been diagnosed with diabetes and isn't taking it seriously," she confessed. "He's prone to skip meals and not check his sugar. It makes me a nervous wreck," she said, her brow clouding with concern. "Obviously he doesn't want Tad to know. It would just be one more reason to try and get him into a home where he could be 'properly looked after.'" Bitter sarcasm coated her last words.

Will frowned. This changed things. His grandmother—he made a mental note to call her later—was diabetic and Will knew firsthand how quickly things could go south with the illness. He'd had to get her a hard candy or a quick glass of orange juice more times than he cared to count.

She bit her bottom lip. "I'm sure he's probably fine, but knowing that he could let his sugar drop too low, that he could fall or get hurt and not knowing where he is…" She made a low, frustrated noise in her throat. "It's driving me crazy. I could throttle him, truly. So you see, that's why I have to go. I can't just stay here. I *can* help you. I know you don't think so right now—I can tell," she added with a small knowing smile that completely unnerved him. "But I can."

While he understood her concern and knew it was genuine, Will shook his head, albeit more reluctantly. He was relatively certain taking her along was against company policy, and even if it wasn't, it would be better for his sanity if she remained here. She was too damned tempting and, though he'd always prided himself on his self-control, there was no point in putting himself through hell to hang on to it. "Ms. Palmer—"

"Rhiannon, please."

"Rhiannon, I'm going to level with you. This is my first assignment for Ranger Security—"

Her eyes widened. "Then you definitely don't want to screw it up."

"*And* I really don't want to risk it by allowing you to accompany me. I'm sure you understand." *You also scare the hell out of me,* he silently added. *And it's been too long since I've properly bedded a woman and you are too tempting by half.* Note to self—get laid ASAP *after* this assignment.

She drew back and leveled a long look at him, one that felt as if she was probing the hidden recesses of his mind. It made him distinctly uncomfortable.

Finally she released a fatalistic sigh. "The hard way, then?" She nodded once, as though agreeing with herself. "Fine."

Charmingly unhinged, Will thought again.

But he'd won.

For the moment, anyway.

SHE SHOULD HAVE BEEN a private investigator, Rhiannon thought as she watched Will Forrester disappear into the bank. This "tailing" thing was ridiculously easy. And he'd even gotten a head start. She'd had to make sure Keno had enough food and water until Elizabeth came by to pick her up, lock up the house and load her things into the car.

Of course, she'd imagined that he'd go straight to the Watson Plantation and she'd been right. She'd merely waited for him to come out—twinkling her fingers at his astonished face as he'd made his way back to his car—then followed him here. She glanced at the clock and winced when her stomach growled. One o'clock. She hoped he got hungry soon. She could use a bit of lunch, and the special today at Willie's Diner was meat loaf—her favorite.

In the meantime she decided to give Elizabeth a try again. Her friend was a gymnastics instructor, and the only time she could catch her during the day was between classes. Thankfully, this was one of those times.

"Twinkle Toes," Elizabeth answered. The sound of rowdy children and dance music bled through the line.

Rhiannon dug through her purse until she found a granola bar. "Hey, it's me." She tore into the packet with her teeth.

"I saw where you'd called earlier. Sorry I missed you. Any news on Theo?"

"A little," Rhiannon told her, and relayed the information she'd gotten from Will. "He's definitely on the move. The eternal question, of course, is to where?"

"You would know better than anyone else," Liz said.

Rhiannon rolled her eyes. "Why don't you tell that to Mr. Security Expert? He wasn't exactly receptive to my join-forces plan."

She chuckled. "He's a man. Did you really expect him to be?"

"I expected him to be logical."

"He's got a penis. He's incapable of being

logical." A bitter undertone colored her voice and Rhiannon instantly became annoyed on her friend's behalf.

Her lips twisted. "Speaking of dicks, any word from Mark?"

"Not one," Elizabeth replied.

She *tsked* sympathetically. "Sorry, Liz. He's a total idiot. You know that, right?"

She chuckled sadly. "True," she said. "But I was the bigger fool for ever falling for him to start with."

"Nah," Rhiannon said, though in truth she quite honestly had never understood Mark's appeal. He was relatively handsome, she supposed, but left a lot to be desired when it came to intelligence. Then again, though she was a bit of an expert when it came to emotions, Rhiannon had never fully understood love.

Of course, considering she'd never actually been in love, how could she possibly understand it?

To be completely honest, the emotion sort of terrified her. She'd seen people do strange things, completely lose their own identity, sacrifice their self-respect, their dignity over the puzzlingly powerful emotion. And the jealousy it inspired? Sweet hell, she never wanted to deal with that.

Her own parents had an extremely volatile relationship—screaming and crying one minute, kissing the next. It was a roller coaster of emotions that had completely drained her as a child and young adult…and she'd just been a bystander. She genuinely didn't know how they stood it. How they bore that kind of emotional upheaval all the time. And for what?

Love.

Well, no thank you, Rhiannon thought. She would pass. At least on romantic love. She had experienced the other sorts. The love of friendship, for instance. Like Elizabeth. Like Theo. And she loved her parents, as well, but there was a small part of her that was thankful they'd retired to Florida and taken their emotional maelstrom with them.

That was the problem with being an empath— she felt everything much more strongly. The good *and* the bad.

Though she knew Theo and Elizabeth worried about her, Rhiannon was quite content on her own. When she wanted sex, she had sex. She was choosy, of course, and didn't invite just any old guy into her body. But she always purposely chose men who were interested in the same thing she was—a brief physical relationship only. No strings, no expectations, no declarations of undying love.

That was precisely what she was trying to avoid.

Rhiannon was secure enough in her own skin and happy enough with her own company. Did she occasionally experience a pang of longing to be in love and loved in return? Yes. After she watched a romantic comedy or when she passed nuzzling couples on the street. But the sensation quickly passed, or it used to, rather.

Much as she loathed admitting it, those bouts of longing for a deeper connection to another person were growing more frequent of late. She wasn't exactly sure what was bringing on the desire and, while a big proponent of EI—which was, in part, learning to identify and deal with your emotions properly—Rhiannon found herself a little reluctant to tap too fully into that part of herself.

Will Forrester exited the bank, and his step faltered when he saw her car. His gaze tangled with hers and the strangest sensation fluttered through her middle—expectation, maybe? Desire, definitely. But something more. Something she couldn't readily identify, which was almost more disconcerting than the feeling itself.

"You're sure you don't mind keeping my dog for a few days?" Rhiannon asked Elizabeth distractedly, though she knew the answer.

"Not at all," she said. "I'll pick her up this afternoon when I leave the studio."

"Thanks, I appreciate it."

"So…if he won't let you come with him, then what exactly are you going to do?"

Rhiannon smiled as she watched him make his way to his car. She could feel his irritation rolling at her in annoyed waves of displeasure. "I'm following him. It's driving him nuts," she said cheerfully.

Elizabeth laughed. "What? How do you know?"

"Because he keeps glaring at me." She got the impression that Will Forrester was used to calling the shots and hated having his plans thwarted. She pegged him as a methodical list maker who balked at the idea of spontaneity. He was too regimented, too controlled, and she had the irrational urge to shake him up.

Liz chuckled again. "Intimidated?"

"Not in the least."

"I didn't think so. So tell me about this guy. I'm picturing Columbo. Short, stocky, bad suit, needs a shave."

Rhiannon's gaze lingered on Will's mouthwatering ass, and another grin slid over her lips. "Er… not exactly. Go look up tall, dark and handsome," she said. "His picture will be there."

"Oh, really?" Elizabeth replied, an ooo-la-la in her voice.

"Pure eye candy, Liz. Utterly gorgeous." And

that was putting it mildly. He was magnificently handsome, sinfully sexy. While she'd never been strictly in love, she'd been in lust a few times.

The tingly heat that had flooded her body the instant she'd laid eyes on Will Forrester was completely out of the realm of her experience. Even the bottoms of her feet had buzzed.

"Deets," Elizabeth demanded. "I need details. Hair?"

"Brown. Short. Classic military high and tight." Aha, Rhiannon thought. The hair, the demeanor, the attention to detail. He was probably former military. That sure as hell made sense. She could certainly see that in his character.

"Eyes?"

How to describe them? she wondered. "Pale gray, but not flat. More silver I would say."

"Ooh, those sound nice."

They were. And when he looked at her… Man, her insides turned to mush.

"Body?"

Rhiannon grinned. *"Amazing."*

Elizabeth chuckled. "Ass?"

"Mouthwatering."

"Poor you," her friend remarked with faux sympathy. "Having to follow that guy around."

Rhiannon sighed dramatically. "It's a tough job, but somebody's got to do it."

She cranked her car and slid out into traffic behind Will. Her cell suddenly beeped, indicating a call waiting. She frowned. "Hey, Liz, I'm getting another call."

"Keep me posted," her friend said.

Rhiannon hit the flash button. "Hello."

"How long are you going to keep this up?" he asked, glaring at her from his rearview mirror.

She smiled brightly. "How did you get my number?"

"Same way I got your address. From the agency's file. How long?" he growled. Strangely, that was a turn-on. She wondered if he made the same noise in bed.

"For as long as it takes. Indefinitely. Forever. Whichever comes first. Why? Am I starting to get on your nerves?"

"No."

"Liar." She laughed. "I can see you scowling from here."

"Shit," he muttered, but she saw him smile. And oh, that smile…

"All of this could be avoided if you would simply let me help you."

"What part of *no* don't you understand?"

"I understand the word," she said, relieved when he pulled up in front of the diner. "It's the reasoning I'm having trouble with."

He sighed. "You're going to drive me crazy, aren't you?"

She fluffed her hair in the rearview mirror. "Only until you see sense."

4

RHIANNON PALMER SLID into the booth across from him and blithely snagged a menu from behind the napkin holder. "I'm so glad you finally stopped for lunch. I was starving."

Will chewed the inside of his cheek, reluctantly admiring her tenacity while simultaneously annoyed beyond reason. "Glad I could accommodate you."

She perused the menu. "I'm used to eating on a schedule, you know. I get cranky when I get hungry."

He moved the salt and pepper shakers to the middle of the table and arranged his silverware. "You're diabetic, too?"

"No," she said, popping the menu back into its place. "School. I'm the guidance counselor at Begonia Elementary."

Will snorted. "Guidance counselor?"

She straightened and those violet eyes narrowed fractionally. "My profession amuses you?"

"No, but imagining you as a guidance counselor does."

"Why?"

"Because my guidance counselor was a soft-spoken, bun-wearing cat lover who gave out 'Kindness Pays' stickers and cherry suckers." He purposely let his gaze drift over her. "You don't exactly fit the stereotype." Furthermore, weren't guidance counselors supposed to be soothing?

Rhiannon Palmer was anything but.

She was a live wire. One touch and she would fry him senseless, render him unable to form complete sentences. She was a red-hot mess—and despite better sense and a relatively keen sense of self-preservation, he was utterly fascinated by her.

He did not have time to be fascinated by her.

New job—one she was seemingly determined to ruin for him—missing old man with diabetes; the list was endless.

Honestly, when she'd made the "hard way" comment, he'd had no idea what to expect. He'd actually thought she meant that *she* was going to have to do things the hard way. Like, by herself. It had never occurred to him that the unpredictable beauty would *follow* him.

But that was exactly what she'd been doing all afternoon. He'd come out of the Watson Plantation manor—gorgeous, but ultimately unhelpful—and there she'd been. Sitting in a little hybrid SUV sporting a bumper sticker that said, "Well-behaved women rarely make history." And she'd actually waved at him, as though this were completely normal. As if they were old friends.

Bizarre.

"Afternoon, Rhi," the tall, thin waitress said. "I was beginning to wonder if you were going to show up today."

Rhiannon sent Will a pointed glare. "Unexpected delay. Please tell me you put a plate back for me," she wheedled shamelessly.

The waitress smiled. "Of course."

Her face brightened. "You're a peach, Wanda. Thanks."

"Tea?"

She nodded once. "Yep."

Wanda's attention swung to him. "And what can I get for you, sir?"

"I'll just have what she's having."

Wanda made a moue of regret. "Sorry. We're out."

Rhiannon smiled at him and offered up a small shrug. "Sorry. Have the open-faced roast beef," she suggested. "It's excellent."

"What are you having?"

"Meat loaf."

Dammit, he loved meat loaf.

"We should have gotten here earlier," she said, seemingly sensing his irrational displeasure.

Feeling like a total idiot, Will purposely schooled his expression into one that didn't make him look like a moron and simply nodded. "The roast beef, then," he said.

She widened her eyes in exaggerated wonder after Wanda walked away, and looked out the window toward the street. "Looks like I'm not the only one who gets cranky when he gets hungry," she remarked in a significant voice.

"I'm not cranky," he said. "I'm annoyed. There's a difference."

Another fatalistic shrug, as though this was all his fault. "You wanted to do it the hard way."

Though there was absolutely nothing dirty about what she'd said, his imagination nevertheless immediately leaped in that direction, which only served to irritate him further. Actually, he'd rather not do it at all, but he couldn't say that to her without fear of innuendo.

Will rubbed the bridge of his nose. "Please tell me that you aren't going to do this—follow me—all the way to Philadelphia."

Her gaze sharpened. "So that's where we're headed?"

He swore and leaned back.

"Watch your language," a little old lady in the booth directly behind him snapped. "I've got my grandson over here."

Rhiannon snickered as Will flushed beet-red and turned to offer an awkward apology.

Bloody frickin' hell.

Wanda returned with their plates and he stared broodingly at her meat loaf. She speared a bite and popped it into her mouth, then sighed with pleasure. The way her lips closed around her fork was particularly sensual and it didn't take much to imagine her mouth around another, increasingly hard part of his anatomy. Sweat suddenly dampened his upper lip.

She was going to be the death of him.

"You can't keep following me," he said, gallingly hearing a note of desperation in his own voice.

"You're right. It would be better if we traveled together." She sipped her tea. "We should take my car, though. It uses less of the world's finite resources."

Will dredged his soul for another ounce of patience. "That's not what I meant, and you know it."

She took a deep breath and set her fork aside for

the moment. "What is it about me going with you *exactly* that you object to?"

He blinked. "What?"

"Why *exactly* would it be so terrible for me to help you?"

It was a good question, Will would admit, and he wished he had an equally good answer. In all fairness, if she were going to trail after him—and he knew she was—it did make more sense for them to travel together. She had more knowledge about his target than any other person, and particular intel on the so-called treasure Watson was after. Logically, it made sense.

But…

He drew back and lifted his shoulders in an unconcerned shrug. "I've already told you. This is a new job. My first case. I may be new to the agency, but I've read the handbook—"

She gave an it-figures eye roll, which—while irritating—he chose to ignore.

"And *you* are against the rules." Strictly speaking, that was a lie. The handbook hadn't covered how to avoid irritating women hell-bent on "helping" him. "I can't afford any distractions," he finished.

"I would *not* be a distraction. I would be helpful."

Helpful or not, she would still be a distraction. A

beautiful, sexy, charming distraction he didn't have time for. Ranger Security was paying him to find Theodore Watson, not for trying to seduce the old man's friend. And Will knew himself well enough to know that he wouldn't be able to resist her. It had been too damned long since he'd been with a woman and she was too tempting by half. Human nature. Sexual chemistry. He'd seen a flicker of awareness in her eyes, too. It didn't take a genius to see where this would ultimately lead.

Bed.

And as wonderful as that might be—and he instinctively knew she would quite literally rock his world—this was not the time or place for it.

Furthermore, there was something about her that made him slightly…uneasy, for lack of a better description. Interesting behavior aside, there was something almost compelling about her. He could feel her drawing him in, and he had the most irrational urge to confide in her. To simply blurt out the truth. To tell her he couldn't afford to fuck up this job, that it was the last damned thing holding him to a career he used to love. That tied him to a past that, despite years of good deeds, he could no longer be proud of.

It was tainted with death.

Help me…

She leaned forward, laid her hand over his and smiled softly. "Are you okay?"

Predictably, her touch sizzled through him, chasing the images away with the flame of instant desire.

Will essayed a smile and was surprised at how easily the lie rolled off his tongue. "Of course." He paused. "But you still can't come with me."

HE WAS SUCH A LIAR, Rhiannon thought, and she was more than prudently intrigued by whatever was haunting him. The pain she'd felt settle around him like a shadow was positively debilitating and yet he'd merely smiled and managed to shrug it off. Not completely, of course, and there would come a point when he would not be able to do it, but…

It was none of her business.

Seriously. None of her concern. He was here to find Theo and that was all.

Furthermore, she instinctively knew—and didn't need any sort of EI to know this—that he would not welcome any interference on her part. Denial was getting him through whatever horror was haunting his soul and it was not her place to point out that it was futile. That a reckoning would eventually come.

Even if she wanted to.

Even now she could feel herself leaning toward

him, trying to draw him in and thereby draw out whatever was hurting him. She'd always been an emotional magnet, had always felt compelled to help people process their feelings, but even Rhiannon acknowledged this was more potent than anything she'd ever experienced before. She'd been telling him repeatedly that she could help him, but only now realized the secondary truth in her own statement.

Whether he knew it or not, Will Forrester needed her.

Unfortunately, she could tell that he was still as hell-bent as ever that she not come along with him. She didn't have to be able to read his mood to know that. It was written in every line in his face—the implacable gaze, the hard angle of his jaw, the determined firmness of his distractingly sexy chin.

Perhaps a new tack was in order. "Okay, fine. You win."

He blinked at her seeming capitulation and his gaze grew suddenly suspicious. "What do you mean I win? I win what?"

"I won't ask to come with you again. I'll just follow you, if you don't mind." She sighed heavily and played her trump card. "I'll feel safer."

Total crock of bullshit. She'd driven across the country alone when she was eighteen for the hell of it. Because she'd wanted to see the Pacific Ocean. She'd spent three months backpacking across Europe, staying in hostels and the like. While she wasn't exactly fearless—spiders scared the hell out of her—she was no shrinking violet and never would be.

But if playing one got her what she wanted, then so be it.

"Safer?" he deadpanned. "How so?"

"Oh, you know. A woman traveling alone. Without protection. Easy target for serial killers and rapists."

He snorted. "I think you are perfectly capable of taking care of yourself."

She inwardly preened at the comment, but purposely furrowed her brow. "I hope so," she said. "I've got some mace." And a taser and a brown belt, but he didn't need to know that.

His cheek creased with a smile and he leaned back and crossed his arms over his chest. "You should send a thank-you to your local drama teacher," he remarked, that gray gaze lingering on her face. "You're quite good."

"I don't know what you mean." Her lips betrayed her with a twitch and he didn't miss it.

"Aha! See, there we go. You're bullshitting me."

"Language," Rhiannon reminded him with a

significant nod over his shoulder. "Mrs. Parker will wallop you next time."

Still grinning, he leaned forward. "Give it up," he said. "I don't have time for this. Every minute I spend arguing with you is another minute I could be looking for Mr. Watson."

"You're having lunch," she said innocently. "I'm not wasting your time."

"But you will," he muttered ominously.

"Sorry?"

"I'll call you," he promised. "I will keep you apprised."

She shook her head. "That's not good enough. I have to help. I have to find him. He's like family to me." Her voice broke at the end and there was no drama intended. She didn't know what she would do without Theo. He was her rock, her very best friend.

Something in his expression shifted, softened, and Rhiannon took the opportunity to press her advantage.

"Have you been to Theo's house yet?" she asked.

"No." He grimaced. "Tad was supposed to leave me a key, but forgot. I can get in, of course, but I'd rather not have to break a window or screw up the lock."

She grinned. "I have a key."

"Have you been over there already?"

"Of course." She waited, forcing him to ask her what he wanted to know.

"Well?"

"Well what?"

He exhaled mightily. "Did you notice anything unusual? Check the messages on his machine? Was anything missing?"

No, she hadn't thought to check the messages on his machine and she wasn't altogether certain anything was missing, other than Theo. He had watered his plants, though, and stopped his mail. Martha, their carrier, had told her that. She should probably go back with him, Rhiannon realized. Much as it pained her to admit it, there were things he would likely think of that she wouldn't.

She thoughtfully chewed the inside of her cheek, then gave a brisk nod, deciding. "I did not check his messages," she said. She told him about the plants and the mail. "He would have taken copies of his grandfather's journals, I would imagine, though I didn't look to see if they were gone. We also need to check his luggage. See if he took the big case or a smaller one."

"We?" he drawled.

"We," she insisted. "Key, remember?"

"Fine." He relented. "I'll admit you'll be useful in this instance, so I will allow you to accompany me."

She rolled her eyes and picked up the check. Control freak. "Bet that high-handed attitude doesn't get you laid much," Rhiannon said, sliding out of the booth.

A startled chuckle broke up in his throat. "I don't need the attitude to get laid," he said, falling into step behind her.

She could feel his gaze on her ass and couldn't repress the smile sliding over her lips. "Yeah, you're right," she agreed with a lamentable sigh. "Probably best if you keep your mouth shut."

He guffawed. "I'll keep that in mind next time."

Rhiannon presented her check to the cashier. "Enjoyed it, Willie," she called back toward the kitchen.

Wilhelmina Malone lumbered into view, her dark face wreathed in her usual smile. "Glad to hear it, child. You get a piece of pie?"

"Better not," Rhiannon said, smacking her hip. "It'll end up right here." Or on her sizable ass, she thought.

While she never really dieted—she liked food too much for that—she nevertheless tried not to be a glutton. She could easily stand to lose ten to fifteen pounds, but the extra weight didn't bother her enough to motivate her to try. She actually liked being a little curvy. Women were supposed to be, dammit, despite what the current issue of *Vogue* said.

"Nonsense," Willie told her. "Help yourself and get a slice for your friend there, too." She looked Will up and down. "Looks like he could use a good piece of pie."

Between her telling him how to get a piece of ass and Willie telling him he needed a piece of pie, she was beginning to wonder if Will was starting to feel a bit abused.

"Thanks," she said, then shot Will a look over her shoulder as she made her way to the pie case. "Chocolate, lemon or pecan?" she asked.

"What are you having?"

"Chocolate."

"Then that's what I'll have."

Rhiannon peered into the case and *tsked* regretfully. "There's only one piece of chocolate left."

His lips twisted wryly. "Figures."

"You can have it," she told him. "I'd rather have the lemon." She put the slices of pie into a carton and snagged a couple of plastic forks from the cup on the counter.

He sighed. "I'll take the lemon. I'm not going to steal your pie."

He held open the front door for her and she

caught a whiff of some woodsy cologne. Nice, Rhiannon thought. The fragrance suited him.

"You can't steal it. It's a gift." She handed the carton to him.

He popped the lid and carved off a piece. "Being nice to me isn't going to do any good. You're still not coming with me."

Rhiannon took a bite of her own, savoring the meringue. "I wonder how many times you're going to have to say it before you start believing it?"

He stared at her mouth, seemingly distracted, then reached out and caught a piece of the fluffy dessert on her bottom lip against his thumb. Her gaze tangled with his and she carefully licked it off.

"You've got it backward," he said, his voice a bit strangled. "It's not how many times am I going to have to say it before *I* start believing it. It's how many times am I going to have to say it before *you* do."

Still rattled from the feel of his thumb against her tongue and how much she'd like to lick other parts of his body, Rhiannon grinned up at him. "In that case, you should save your breath."

He swore again.

5

THOUGH STILL OF ANTEBELLUM architecture, Theodore Watson's house was nothing like the grand Tara-like mansion his son called home. Built in the early 1820's, this was a simple white clapboard house. Four rooms downstairs, each boasting a single fireplace and divided by the customary wide hall, and three rooms upstairs.

Theo was a master gardener according to Rhiannon. The grounds were shaded with huge live oaks and magnolias, lots of creeping ivy and ornamental grasses. Rhododendrons and roses bloomed, adding a splash of color, and an entire area had been devoted to nothing but bird feeders, houses and baths.

The scent of dusty books, Old Spice and cherry pipe tobacco hung in the air and, while Will had never met Mr. Watson, something about the way

the older gentleman cared for his surroundings—
and the creatures that orbited through it—put him
in mind of his grandfather. John Forrester had been
well-read and had also had a soft spot for his feath-
ered friends.

Will wandered over to the fireplace and checked
out the pictures on the mantel. You could tell a lot
about a person by the images they chose to put on
display. A faded wedding photo was placed prominently in the middle.

Rhiannon drifted to his side and nodded at the
picture. She stood so close that he could smell her.
Something light and orange. "That's Theo and
Sarah," she said, smiling. "He was a handsome
devil, wasn't he?"

Examining the happy couple, Will supposed he
was. He wasn't accustomed to making judgments
on manly looks. Nevertheless, the bride wore a
radiant smile and there was no denying the pride,
adoration and love in Theo's youthful expression.
Staring at the image—the pure emotion in their
eyes—made something strangely like envy curl
in his chest. *Ridiculous,* Will thought, batting the
feeling away like a pesky fly.

In truth, Will had always been so focused on his
career he'd never truly considered having a wife
and family—the whole dinner-at-five, church-on-
Sundays scenario. Had he ever been in love before?

Yes, once, in college and it had ended badly. She'd wanted a ring and he'd wanted to wait. He hadn't been ready to say I do, had been so engrossed in his career even then that he'd recognized on some level that it wouldn't have worked.

He'd balked and she'd bailed.

Since then he hadn't been with a woman who hadn't known going in that he was not interested in anything more than a little mutually satisfying recreational sex. He knew plenty of other soldiers who'd managed to make the marriage thing work, but had always known himself well enough to realize that, were he to have married, either the career or the marriage would have suffered, and that was unacceptable.

He'd chosen the career. *A smear of blood, a tiny hand...*

He swallowed hard and with difficulty, beat the images back. They were coming at him more frequently lately, Will realized with some dismay. He'd actually thought he was getting better at dealing with it, but...evidently not. He cleared his throat, aware that he'd been quiet entirely too long. He could feel Rhiannon's gaze on his face, examining him with those curiously perceptive eyes.

"And Sarah?" he asked. He expected he knew the answer to this question.

She inclined her head. "She died when Tad was eight. Aneurism." Her gaze lingered on the picture. "He never remarried. Said so long as his heart beat it would love her and it wouldn't be fair to another woman to only give her what was left." She smiled. "And believe me, lots of women tried. There's no telling how many book clubs were formed at the Begonia Public Library with the express purpose of putting its members in closer proximity to Theo."

That's right, Will thought. Watson had been the local librarian, as well, and he wondered how he'd found the time, particularly when he was also at the helm of the family business. Evidently he had good help in place—otherwise there was no way in hell the older man could get it all done. Especially with a miserable excuse of a son like Tad, who didn't appreciate the hard work, blood, sweat and tears that had gone into his heritage. Sheesh. Will liked that the plantation had stayed true to its roots and farmed almost all of the land. The fields were presently full of cotton, blanketing the earth in white.

Though it was his understanding that Tad was next in line to assume the CEO position, he could see where Watson wouldn't want to relinquish the reins to a greedy son who, apart from the house, had no interest in preserving his family's legacy and wasn't interested in helping worthy causes.

According to Rhiannon, Watson funded a local no-kill shelter, and offered numerous scholarships to aid local high school students who needed a little help to attend college. The parks and library had benefited from his benevolence, as well. Will grimaced. No doubt Tad would put an end to that if he ever got the opportunity.

His gaze skimmed along, looking at other pictures, then stopped short when he recognized a familiar face. Younger, of course, and sporting braces, but...

"That's you," he said, smiling. She'd been awkward, a bit shy looking, but the promise of beauty was there, even then.

"No cracks about the metal mouth," she warned him primly. "The end justified the means."

"You've known Theo a long time," he remarked. When she'd said he'd been a better father to her than her own, he'd just assumed she'd meant as an adult. He hadn't realized she'd known him since she was a child. Of course, that would explain the bond. He could tell that she genuinely loved the older gentleman.

"I have," she confirmed with a nod. "I was a bit of a freak growing up and spent a lot of time at the library. Theo and I shared a common quirk, which made me feel less like an outcast, and—" she sighed "—the rest is history."

She was being purposely vague, which naturally cued his curiosity. "A common quirk?"

"It's not important," she said, dismissing the question as though it wouldn't interest him. "The answering machine is in the kitchen. I'm going to check the messages, see if there's anything significant on there."

Now, that was odd, Will thought. The same woman who'd told him his attitude wouldn't get him laid often didn't want to share a "quirk"? Was she hiding some sort of physical flaw? A third breast? A sixth toe? His brooding gaze slid over her, making his pulse trip with desire. Wouldn't matter, Will decided. She'd still be the sexiest woman he'd ever laid eyes on.

Damn.

Had he had any idea that he was going to be presented with this sort of temptation, Will would have made a little time for sex before starting his new job. How long had it been? he wondered. Two, three months? Too damned long, obviously; otherwise he was certain he wouldn't be having this reaction to Rhiannon. He wouldn't be mentally stripping her naked and imagining her toned legs wrapped around his waist, her sexy mouth feeding at his. The mere scent of her wouldn't be driving him crazy and the riddle of her supposed quirk wouldn't spark his intense curiosity.

It was a pointless distraction, Will told himself, and futile, as well. He didn't have any business puzzling over her reticence to share her quirk, much less allowing himself to feel the desire currently sliding through his veins.

Theodore Watson had flown the coop, and it was his job to track him down.

The fact that he had to remind himself of this only irritated him further. Will ordinarily had the focus of a cobra and the tenacity of a bulldog.

It was her, he decided. She, with her hot-pink toes and delectable ass, was interfering with his ability to think.

Will abruptly decided that he needed to check in with the Triumvirate—damn Juan-Carlos for sticking that term in his brain—and see what proper protocol was for his present situation. He was supposed to make daily reports and, while he could simply forget to mention that Rhiannon Palmer was intent on following him to Philadelphia, it was a lie of omission he'd rather not have come back and bite him on the ass.

He unclipped the cell from his waist and hit number one on his speed-dial list. Juan-Carlos answered, of course, and he asked for Payne.

He seemed the least likely to rag his ass over his gorgeous, irritating little problem.

"How's it going, Will?" Payne asked by way of greeting.

"Slowly," he admitted. He brought him up to speed. "I'm at Theo's house now, poking around, but other than the fact that he's taken a small suitcase and copies of his great-great-grandfather's journals, I'm not having any luck. The family actually originated in Philadelphia and, considering the cash he took with him and the message he left Rhiannon Palmer, I'm assuming that he's headed there, or somewhere in between."

"You've met Ms. Palmer, then?" Not a trace of laughter betrayed his voice, but Will heard it all the same.

Will ducked into Theo's bedroom. "A little warning would have been nice, Payne," he hissed, annoyed that his new boss seemed to have purposely withheld some key information. Will liked having all the facts, dammit. How was he supposed to make good decisions without them? "I can't shake her," he admitted, swallowing the gall. "She's been following me all over town and is hell-bent on either tagging along with me or tailing me all the way to Philly."

Payne coughed to cover a poorly disguised

chuckle. "I was afraid she might become an issue."

"Issue, hell," he said. "She's a pain in the ass. How am I going to get rid of her? What's the protocol?"

"Are you sure you need to get rid of her? She knows your target and is familiar with this so-called treasure he's looking for."

Will leaned around the door frame to make sure she wasn't listening, then drew back. This was unexpected and he found himself strangely— stupidly—thrilled. "You think I ought to let her come with me?"

"I don't see what it could hurt. If she follows you, then she's just going to be a distraction. You take her with you and you can at least control the situation." He paused. "I've been in a similar position, Will." He laughed softly, seemingly remembering. "Take it from me, you're better off allowing her to come with you than her mucking along in your wake, screwing with your ability to focus."

Will barely repressed a snort. Either way she was going to screw with his focus. Even now, though she wasn't anywhere near him, he was still keenly aware of the fact that she was in the house, that she was close. He could *feel* her, as though her very heartbeat had the ability to ping him like sonar.

Theo and I share a common quirk.

That little mystery was going to drive him bat-shit crazy.

He swore, causing Payne to laugh.

"That bad, is she?"

"She's a beautiful nightmare," Will said honestly.

"And it would have been easier if she made a dog point?"

"Definitely." He couldn't impart enough dread into that one word.

"I see."

Good, then that made one of them.

"Regardless, my advice doesn't change. You're still better off taking her with you than allowing her to follow you. She could be useful."

Will exhaled mightily, stared at an Audubon print on the wall. "You're right, of course."

"Keep us posted."

"Will do," he said, then disconnected.

Damn. He was so screwed.

CHUCKLING UNDER HIS BREATH, Payne set the cordless phone back into the base and looked at the two expectant faces on the men whose attention had previously been on another Braves game.

"Let me guess," Flanagan said. "It's a woman."

"Rhiannon Palmer," Guy guessed correctly. "I knew she was going to be trouble."

"She's been tailing him," Payne told them. "Keeps insisting that she can help with the investigation."

"Can she?" Jamie asked.

"Possibly," Payne conceded. "I just think it's a little ironic, don't you?"

Guy lobbed a paper napkin ball at the trash can and gave a little *boo-yah* when it hit the mark. "What do you mean?"

"Seems there's an interfering woman involved in every case we've taken lately."

"True," Jamie admitted.

Guy released a tragic sigh. "And yet we keep marrying them."

SITTING IN THE PASSENGER SEAT of Will's Rubicon, Rhiannon inhaled the new-car scent and studied the atlas she had open on her lap. Since he'd finally come to his senses and gruffly announced that she could come with him—no idea what brought that on, but she didn't care because *she'd won*—she'd decided not to make taking her little hybrid a sticking point. She was just grateful to be doing something, to be contributing to the cause.

They'd stopped at a convenience store to stock a cooler—sodas and orange juice—and to snag a few snacks for the road. Will was a butterscotch Life Savers fan, and though there was absolutely no reason to find this little fact endearing, she did. She rolled her eyes and tried to pretend that she wasn't keenly aware of him, that she wasn't marveling over the strength in his hands or the competent way he handled the wheel. Both elicited a shiver.

Needing a distraction, Rhiannon pulled out her cell and dialed Theo's number again.

Will slid her a glance. "Who are you calling?"

"Theo," she said. Predictably, it connected to voice mail. She decided to leave another message. "Theo, you'd better call me the instant you get this. Please," she added. "I'm worried about you."

He quirked a brow. "Do you have caller ID?"

"Yes, why?"

"Did he leave the message on your machine from home or from his cell?"

"His cell, I think."

He merely nodded, snagged his own phone and placed a call. "What's his number?"

She rattled it off and he shared it with the people on the other end of the line. "Right," he said. "Let me know if you get any hits."

Ah, Rhiannon realized. He was tracking Theo's cell, trying to see which tower his last call was routed through. She nodded, impressed. "You're pretty good at this for someone who just started."

She watched his eyes crinkle at the corners with an almost smile. "Thank you."

"So were you in the security business before you started with the Ranger guys?"

"I guess you could say that," he replied, but didn't elaborate and, though he didn't so much as bat an eyelash, she felt a tenseness settle around him.

She chuckled, determined to draw him out. "That was a very vague answer."

He tapped his thumb against the steering wheel. "You'd know all about those."

She knew exactly what he was talking about, so didn't bother being coy. He'd been quite curious about her "shared-quirks" comment regarding her and Theo. While Rhiannon was a relatively vocal proponent of EI, she didn't exactly go around advertising her personal experiences with it.

Men, in particular, seemed unnerved by her special insight into their emotions, and intuition told her he'd be more spooked than the average guy. Probably because he wasn't just bringing along a little rolling case of baggage—he had a massive trunkful of it. Even now she could feel the weight of it pressing in on her, and she marveled at his ability to function at all.

Furthermore, she recognized this particular weight—it had all the hallmarks of death. The regret, the grief, the oppression. But who had he lost?

Rhiannon wondered. And better still, why did he blame himself?

"Truth uncomfortable for you?" he asked.

"Not at all," she said, shooting him a smile. "I let it drop, didn't I?"

"Surprisingly, yes. Only makes me more curious, though."

She grinned and pushed a lock of hair away from her face. "I know that feeling, as well."

"I was in the military," he said. "Army. A Ranger."

So she'd been right. He was military. And a Ranger? Those guys were usually in service for life. Too much time spent training to simply change their mind. Something must have happened, Rhiannon decided, studying him from the corner of her eye.

And that something was directly related to his pain.

"The hair was sort of a tip-off," she said. "Well, that and the fact that you're bossy."

He chuckled. "I'm used to giving orders."

"*I'm* not one of your soldiers."

His gaze lingered over her legs, drifted along her hip, slid over her breasts and ultimately settled on her mouth. A bark of ironic laughter rumbled from his throat. "Believe me, I am well aware of that."

Holy hell, Rhiannon thought as the tops of her thighs caught fire. Her nipples tingled and she felt short of breath, as if the heat between them was sucking all the oxygen out of the car. She'd been feeling that off him, too—the desire—but clearly he'd been trying to control it, as well. And when that control slipped...

Damn.

"S-so you're happy with the career change?"

"I will be so long as you don't get me fired," he muttered.

"I will not get you fired," she promised him. "I'm here to help you."

He merged onto the interstate, headed north and heaved a fatalistic sigh. "So you've said."

"Haven't I been helpful so far? Didn't I let you in Theo's house and tell you everything that I know?"

"You have."

She settled more firmly against the seat. "You'll see," she said primly. "We're going to make an excellent team."

"Rah, rah," he cheered with bored enthusiasm. *Smart-ass,* she thought, reluctantly impressed with his humor. Probably because it was similar to her own.

"We should probably go through Chattanooga," Rhiannon told him. "Theo's great-grandmother was from Soddy-Daisy."

"Soddy-Daisy? You just made that up, didn't you?"

"Of course not." She showed him the map. "It's right here. See?"

A pained expression settled over his gorgeous face. "Why do I get the feeling we're going to have to dismember every limb on Theo's family tree in order to find him?"

"Probably because we are."

He harrumphed. "What's the significance of the Bible verse?"

"Ah," she said. "Mortimer Watson was a very devout man and his diaries are littered with his spiritual reflections and various Bible verses. The significance of Matthew 6:21 is that its only appearance is two weeks before the Union troops marched through Begonia on their way to Atlanta."

Will inclined his head. "I see."

"Theo has known that the verse was a significant clue and we've scoured records and diaries trying to find any reference to the word *heart*."

"And you didn't find anything?"

"No…but evidently Theo has."

A thought struck. "And wherever he's gone, he's taken his metal detector with him. It usually sits by the back door, and it wasn't there when I went to check the messages on his machine."

"So he's digging, then?"

"That's my guess. Lord knows he's practically taken the house apart and dug from one end of the Watson Plantation to the other." She chuckled. "Tad nearly had a fit when Theo tore up the hearth."

Will's incredulous gaze found hers. "You're kidding me, right?"

"I wish." She closed the atlas and tucked it into the side pocket of her door. "It was a relatively common hiding place, you know? People would bury their valuables beneath the hearth, mortar back over it and then their goods were safe in the event of fire." She smiled, remembering. "Theo had thought *heart* and *hearth* were close enough in spelling, so he took apart every fireplace on the lower floors."

"He's determined, isn't he?"

"He's always been convinced it was real. He's been actively searching for more than sixty years."

"That's dedication."

She smiled fondly, picturing her friend's lined, dear face. "That's Theo."

"Wonder why he didn't tell you where he was going?"

She'd wondered that, as well, and could only assume that he'd left in such a hurry he hadn't wanted to wait until she'd finished her class for the day. As she'd just said, he'd been looking for this for sixty years. Waiting another moment would have been impossible for him.

She shared as much. "I don't think there was any real purpose behind not telling me. I think he just got excited and went directly into treasure-hunter mode." She gazed out the window, stared at the passing scenery. "And if it weren't for the diabetes, I wouldn't be concerned at all. I know that he's avoiding Tad and I'm a mere casualty of that. But I just can't shake the feeling that something terrible could happen to him and no one would be there to help him, you know?"

Will was silent for a moment. "We'll find him," he said reassuringly.

We, she thought, glad that he was finally coming around. Her heart warmed.

"Thanks. I needed to hear that."

"So where do we start?" Will asked. "What are we looking for in Soddy-Daisy?"

"Relatives, old family home places and graves," she said.

"That covers a lot of ground," Will remarked, staring straight ahead.

"But it makes sense, given the cash he took with him. He's looking for family treasure. It only makes sense that he'd go where his people were from." Or at least it did to her.

He nodded and shot her a resigned smile. "So how much farther to Soddy-Daisy?"

6

THIS WAS PRECISELY WHY he didn't want her tagging along with him, Will thought as he finally settled into his rented bed for the night. Rhiannon was in the room next to him, and though he knew she was probably still fully clothed and not doing anything particularly sexy, he nevertheless knew she was there.

So he pictured her naked.

As if on cue, her shower started.

Bloody hell.

Sleek, wet skin, back arched into the spray, rivulets of water cascading over the heavy globes of her breasts, clinging to rosy nipples. Dark hair tangled down her back, darker hair between her thighs...

He shifted as he went uncomfortably hard, then determinedly began to translate the TV Guide into

Spanish to try to occupy his mind. When Spanish didn't work, he moved to Russian. He'd just finished the eleven-o'clock listings when her shower finally—blessedly—went off.

But she was still naked, still wet, and he knew it.

His dick jerked hard against his zipper and he speared his hands through his hair and gave a sharp tug.

It was at that precise moment that he heard a tentative knock on their adjoining door.

Shit.

He scrambled up and tried to think of a convincing way to cover up his hard-on—his dick was practically peeping out the top of his jeans. Then, in a moment of inspiration, he quickly untucked his shirt and hoped that it wouldn't betray him.

He opened the door, and the scent of warm oranges abruptly washed over him. "Yes?" he asked in a voice that wasn't altogether steady.

She was partially hidden behind the door, her hand securing the towel behind her back. Unfortunately—or fortuitously, however one decided to look at it—her bare, heart-shaped rear end was reflected in the room's slightly foggy mirror, giving him an unobstructed view of the most beautiful ass he'd ever seen. He instantly imagined his hands on her rump as he pushed into her from behind, the smooth indentation of her spine.

"I forgot to pack toothpaste," she said, wincing. "Do you mind if I borrow yours?"

Water clung to her eyelashes and her nose was shiny. It was small, he realized now. Quite possibly the most petite nose he'd ever seen. How had he missed that? And why in God's name did he find that so endearing?

"Er...sure," he said, trying to untangle his thoughts. He darted to his bathroom and pulled a travel tube from his case. "Here you go," he said, handing it over.

"Thanks," she said. "I'd wait a few minutes before I showered if I were you. The hot water's a little iffy."

He nodded. "Noted."

"I'll give this right back, if you want to leave the door open."

For reasons he didn't understand, she seemed reluctant to leave. "Sure," he said, for lack of anything better.

She grinned again, then partially closed her door. Seconds later he heard the telltale sounds of the rest of her evening routine.

Will blew out the breath he hadn't realized he'd been holding and sagged against the wall, the memory of her ass still clinging determinedly in his mind. He massaged his temples, valiantly holding on to what remained of his sanity.

Damn. This was *so* not good.

He could *not* act on this attraction. It would be the pinnacle of stupidity, the absolute height of idiocy. New job, first assignment. He couldn't afford to fuck it up.

Too important. No place else to go. He'd be rudderless, without a purpose. The thought terrified him.

While not strictly a part of this investigation, she was a crucial key to whether or not he was able to see it through.

Distance, Will told himself. He had to be with her when they were in the car—he was trapped. But his evenings had to be his own. And the next time they booked a hotel room, he'd make sure they were on a different damned floors, not in adjoining rooms. He couldn't keep torturing himself by listening to her bathe, wishing he could join her. Imagining filling his hands with her breasts, filling the rest of her with himself.

"Here ya go," she said, handing the tube of toothpaste back. "Hey, I'm not exactly tired. Wanna watch a movie on pay-per-view later? After you have your shower maybe?"

"Sure," he said, wondering if he could cut his tongue out with a blunt object. Hadn't he just resolved to stay away from her? Hadn't he just determined that she was too much temptation? That he'd go through hell trying to resist her if he didn't stay away from her?

Yes, he had.

And it hadn't made one whit of difference.

She smiled at him, her unusual eyes lighting up. "Great. I'll pop over later, then."

Rather than lie on the bed and brood about his own stupidity, Will labeled the small thrill of anticipation dread and climbed into the shower. It was a movie, he told himself. Harmless enough, right? They'd watch the film—he'd purposely choose something he knew she'd hate, like *Blood 'N Guts IV*—then he could send her on her way. She'd go back to her bed. He would stay in his. He would keep his hands to himself and everything would be fine.

Ten minutes later Rhiannon came strolling into his room with two of the pillows from her bed, a couple of soft drinks she'd snagged from the vending machine, two bags of chips and two packets of M&M's. She quickly made her nest on his side of the bed, then handed him his portion of the snacks.

"I'd rather have popcorn and chocolate, but the chips will do in a pinch," she said, as though they did this all the time. She sighed happily and tossed him the remote. "What's that cologne you're wearing?" she asked, sniffing the air appreciatively.

"Bulgari," he said, startled by the abrupt subject change.

"It's woodsy," she said. "With a hint of pepper. Nice."

He hadn't given it much thought beyond the fact that he liked it. "Thanks." He settled in next to her, careful to keep a pillow between them. She wore a pair of striped boxer shorts and a little tank top. No bra.

His mouth watered.

She'd pulled her hair up into a giant knot on her head and looked completely relaxed and at ease. Clearly she was not as uncomfortably aware of him as he was of her, Will thought, annoyed once again.

Was she attracted to him? Yes, gratifyingly, he knew she was. He'd seen her eyes darken with interest, had watched her gaze linger over his mouth. She was equally intrigued...but obviously had better control.

It infuriated him.

He was *always* the one in control.

Because he was incapable of thinking rationally, he removed the pillow and slid an inch or so in her direction, purposely tilting the mattress until she leaned toward him, as well.

Her breath gave a little hitch and he smiled, marginally mollified.

"So," he said, aiming the remote at the television, "what do you want to watch?"

"Doesn't matter," she said. "I'm not picky."

He selected *Saw III* and waited for her reaction.

Because she was the most unpredictable creature he'd ever met, her eyes lit up. "Ooh, a horror movie. Blood and guts. My favorite." She popped a chip into her mouth.

He laughed and shook his head. "You are one odd girl, you know that?"

"I'm unique," she corrected. "*Odd* makes me sound like a freak. *Unique* means I'm charming."

"Can't you be a charming freak?"

She shushed him. "The movie's starting."

He laughed, surprised. "It's the previews."

"I know. I like them."

"We're not going to talk at all?"

She heaved a put-upon sigh. "No, because we're watching a movie," she said with exaggerated patience, as though she were explaining this to a half-wit.

"Then why didn't you just watch it alone? What's the point of watching it together?"

She looked over at him and smiled. "So that we

can share the experience, then talk about it when it's over. That work for you?"

He chewed the inside of his cheek to keep from smiling. "Yes, it will."

She nodded. "Good."

Only it didn't work, because thirty minutes into the movie she was sound asleep, curled up on her side, her delightfully distracting rump pressing into his hip.

Will groaned.

Her breath came in even little puffs and a single strand of hair had fallen down and curled over her smooth cheek. He was suddenly hit with the almost overwhelming urge to tuck it behind her ear, but was afraid that if he touched her, he wouldn't be able to stop. She was quite honestly the most compelling person he'd ever been around in his life. Sexy and open, outrageous, charming and, yes, odd.

Rhiannon Palmer was different.

He couldn't exactly put his finger on what made her so special, but he knew it all the same.

She was an unknown quantity. Dangerous.

And if he didn't keep his distance, he was doomed.

With a reluctant sigh, Will carefully rolled away from her, snagged one of the pillows and let himself into her room. The scent of oranges still hung in the air and her lacy bra dangled from the doorknob. He shook his head, settled into her bed and then looked heavenward.

"I'd better get points for this," he muttered. "Because this is *not* funny."

"SORRY ABOUT RUNNING YOU out of your bed last night," Rhiannon said as she sprinkled golden raisins over her oatmeal the next morning. "I must have been more tired than I realized."

She had to have been; otherwise she would never have fallen asleep like that, particularly when she'd been so miserably aware of him. Honestly, she'd taken one whiff of that cologne, aftershave or shower gel—who knew which one?—and had become strangely intoxicated with the scent. It had made her want to slowly stalk him to the bed, then lick him all over. Between the scent and his own personal magnetism she'd been a basket case within seconds of walking into the room.

Then he'd gone and moved that pillow, forcing her slightly against him, and her arm had practically caught fire. He was quite frankly the sexiest man she'd ever been around in her life, and the need hammering through her blood with every beat of her heart was simply relentless.

She wanted him.

With an intensity that walked the fine edge of dangerous and debilitating.

Ordinarily when Rhiannon wanted something—or in this case some*one*—she didn't hesitate. Life was too short for regrets, and happiness too often was fleeting. While she wouldn't call herself a total hedonist, she nevertheless wasn't accustomed to denying herself.

But for whatever reason—self-preservation, maybe?—she was hesitant to act on this particular attraction.

There was an edge here, an intensity she wasn't altogether certain of, and that peculiar sensation coupled with her unusual instantaneous fondness for him made her slightly…leery. Factor in the haunting sadness emanating from him and she was certain she could become entirely too involved, or at the very least, involved on an unfamiliar level she had no desire to tread.

She could easily see herself getting…attached to him.

In the first place, she didn't want to be attached. Too much emotional insecurity in investing personal happiness in another person for her comfort. And in the second place, were she to develop any sort of lingering interest in him, she instinctively knew she'd scare him to death. Like her, she sensed he wasn't looking for anything permanent.

Which should have made him perfect. And yet she hesitated.…

Having consumed enough eggs to send his cholesterol into the danger zone, Will merely leaned back and shook his head. "No problem," he said. "Same bed, different room."

"Any updates this morning?" she asked. "Any news on that cell tower?"

He nodded. "He was still in town."

"Damn."

"Any other hits?"

"None," he said. "Which means he's probably turned it off."

She grimaced. "Or let the battery go dead. He's horrible about that. But at least we know we're on the right track," she reminded him.

The freshly cut flowers they'd found on Theo's relatives' graves yesterday had his signature thoughtfulness written all over them. The ground was unbroken, indicating that he hadn't found what he was looking for there, but she had no doubt that it was he who had placed the relatively new blooms on those plots.

And then there'd been the penny, of course.

She smiled, remembering. Because he shared his thoughts with people whether they asked for them or not, Theo always had a pocketful of pennies to give to those with whom he shared his opinions. Sarah's headstone, in particular, was always covered in pennies.

"So what do you think our next move should be?" Will asked her.

She blinked with exaggerated wonder. "You're asking me?"

"I wouldn't have had any idea to look for Theo in Soddy-Daisy, much less that the flowers and coins left on those graves were his doing." He took a sip of water. "So, yes, I am asking you."

Self-satisfied pleasure expanded in her chest. "Because you need me?" she pressed. "Because I am helpful? Just like I said I would be."

"You're a helpful distraction," he conceded, his cheek lifting in a too-charming half smile. She couldn't get over his eyes, Rhiannon thought, once again struck by their unique shade. A bright silvery-gray.

She chuckled and leaned forward. "How exactly am I distracting you? By offering my assistance? By being your navigator? By telling you that you're eating too many eggs and not enough fiber?" She determinedly scooped up another bite of oatmeal, setting a good example for his benefit.

She knew exactly how she was distracting him, of course. She was equally distracted, and for the same damned reason.

Lust.

He frowned at her plate. "Oatmeal is nasty. I'd rather eat a cardboard box."

"We should pick up some fiber bars when we stop for my toothpaste."

"I don't mind sharing," he said. There was an undercurrent to his voice she didn't fully understand.

She shook her head. "I prefer my own brand."

He snorted and rolled his eyes. "Why am I not surprised?"

"There's nothing wrong with yours," she said. "Most people like their breath minty fresh."

He slid her a sardonic look. "And you don't?"

"Mint makes me gag. I prefer oranges and cloves."

"Mint makes you gag?" he asked, slightly incredulous. His lips twisted. "Bet that made for some interesting kissing sessions, huh?"

Her gaze involuntarily dropped to his lips and she felt her own mouth tingle in response. She'd bet he was one hell of a kisser. "Only when a guy dosed up on something strong. Usually the taste is too faint to trigger the reflex."

"Little favors, eh? That could definitely give a guy a complex. Finally build up the courage to make his move and you gag on him."

She chuckled at his analogy. "It's not like I can help it, you know," she said. "It's just…too strong."

"It's supposed to be," he told her. "How else is one supposed to fight bad breath?"

She narrowed her gaze in playful censure. "Are you saying my breath is bad because I don't use minty toothpaste?"

He fought a grin and his gaze drifted over her lips. "I won't know until you've tried it, will I?"

"Fine," she said drolly. "Tonight after I brush my teeth, I'll be sure to breathe on you."

This line of conversation could *so* get her into trouble. It felt too much like flirting and not enough like harmless banter.

Naturally she found it thrilling.

The grin that tugged at his lips? *Pure sin.* "I'll look forward to it."

Perversely, so did she.

7

"THEO WAS HERE a couple of days ago," Mimi Watson said. "I was surprised, of course. Haven't seen him in years."

"Was he just visiting, Miss Mimi, or was there a specific reason he came by?" Rhiannon asked the elderly woman.

Mimi's faded blue eyes were warm as she worked the crochet needles between her arthritic fingers. "Oh, he just wanted to chat. Said he was working on a genealogy chart, a new hobby of his, and wanted to pick my brain about some of our relatives."

Rhiannon sent him a significant look. "Really? Which ones was he interested in?"

She corrected a bad stitch. "All of them, really, but he was particularly interested in where Mrs. Amelia Watson was buried. Oh, and little Winston, of course." She *tsked* under her breath. "The infant mortality rate was terrible in those days," she said sadly. "Moving south was not an easy journey for old Uncle Mortimer. Buried a wife and child on the way. The child first, of course. The pox. Amelia grieved herself to death. She's buried in Kingsport, I believe. Wasn't sure about Winston, but like I told Theo, I think they lost him somewhere around Roanoke."

"That's terrible," Rhiannon commiserated softly, and Will could tell the news affected her on a deeper than ordinary level. Almost as if it was her own family.

A puzzled frown wrinkled her forehead. "Theo has shared a lot of your family history with me over the years. So Mortimer must have been married before then? Sophia was his second wife?"

"That's right. He missed his family terribly, you see. The story I've always heard was Miss Sophia was a very jealous woman and destroyed all the pictures of Mortimer's late wife. Guess she knew that Amelia would always have his heart, that she was the substitute wife."

Always have his heart, Will thought. That certainly sounded like a significant clue.

And once again he had to hand it to Rhiannon. She'd spent several minutes going over the atlas this morning, searching for places along their route to Philadelphia that Theo had mentioned. She'd hit pay dirt with Sweetwater, pulled out her BlackBerry and used the mobile phone book to pull up all the Watsons. She'd found Mimi and instantly recognized the name as one Theo had mentioned.

Mimi Watson had at least a decade on her nephew, but lived alone in a small cottage downtown. She wore a trendy sportswear outfit in shades of lavender and her snowy-white hair was set into a sweeping, puffy style. Her lined cheeks were powdered to perfection and bright pink lipstick painted her mouth. Her white tennis shoes didn't show the faintest scuff and gleamed against the green indoor-outdoor carpeting covering her front porch. She epitomized a genteel Southern lady and, though they didn't have the time, he could have listened to her tell stories in her lovely drawl all day long.

Rhiannon laid her hand on Mimi's knee. "Mimi, thank you so much for all your help. It's a relief to know that Theo was here and was fine."

"Silly boy," she said, disapproval coloring her tone. "He should have let you know where he was going. People tend to worry when their old folks just vanish. Poor Tad must be a wreck with nerves," she fretted.

Rhiannon delicately avoided answering by asking instead, "He was here day before yesterday, you say?"

"Yes. I insisted that he stay for dinner, of course, and you know Theo." She gestured to a vase of flowers. "He's always so thoughtful."

Rhiannon grinned. "Yes, he is." She nodded once. "Well, Miss Mimi, we'd better be on our way."

"Good luck finding him, dear. I'm sure he's fine. You let me know when you run him to ground, you hear?"

"Absolutely."

Rhiannon gave her a quick hug and, feeling strangely out of place, Will merely nodded once.

"Okay," she said with a heavy breath when they were once again in the car. "We've got our next destination."

He backed out of the drive. "Kingsport."

"Yes." She pushed her hands through her hair. "But I don't think we're going to find him there."

Will didn't, either. They were only about three hours from Kingsport and Theo had left almost two days ago. If he'd found what he was looking for in that town, then they would have heard from him by now. Clearly he hadn't, and he had moved on.

"So you'd never heard of the first wife? Amelia?"

She shook her head. "Not that I can recall."

"Do you think Theo knew of her?"

"I don't think so," she said, her tone thoughtful. "He must have found something. He's been going through some old boxes, had found them tucked away in the corner of the attic in the cottage there on the plantation. It was the first house, you see. The temporary home while the plantation home was being built."

Will considered that. "Then why doesn't Theo live there? Why move to town?"

She leaned her head against the back of the seat and rolled her neck toward him. A smile played over her ripe mouth. "The official reason? Because his estate manager needs to live on site. The real reason? He's convinced it's haunted."

Will chuckled. "Haunted? But wouldn't he be related to this particular ghost?"

"Doesn't matter," Rhiannon said. "He still gets spooked."

"Who is it?"

"Interestingly enough…it's Sophia."

A bark of laughter rumbled from his throat. "But she sounds like such a sweet, understanding lady."

Rhiannon scowled. "She sounds like a bitter old bitch to me, but what do I know?"

His lips twitched. "Don't hold back. Tell me what you really think."

"Do I strike you as the kind of person who holds back?"

Will shook his head. "You absolutely do not," he admitted. "You're frighteningly…honest. It's refreshing, actually." And he meant it. No doubt a person never had to wonder where they stood with her. Furthermore, though he'd laughed at the fact that she was a guidance counselor, he could easily see how kids would readily warm to her. She was frank without being cruel and there was a comforting quality, despite her obvious energy, that literally compelled a person to want to be close to her. To confide in her.

Mimi was a perfect example. Rhiannon had never met the woman before in her life and yet within three minutes of being in her company, Mimi had acted as if they were old friends. Rhiannon had been able to garner the older woman's trust with enviable ease. Had he been asking the same questions—alone—Will didn't think he would have fared so well. Just another reminder of how much she was genuinely helping him.

Distracting him, too, of course. He could never forget that. Take now, for instance. Her warm citrusy scent—it must be in her shampoo, too, Will thought—swirled around his senses and the yellow-

and-white checked top she wore showcased her pear-shaped breasts to absolute perfection. She wore a denim skirt that was long enough to be appropriate but short enough to make him sweat, and a silver chain loaded with star charms dangled around her ankle.

Because he was a nosy bastard, he'd taken a cursory look at her toiletries in her bathroom this morning and realized that she hadn't brought a single bit of makeup, only a small tube of tinted organic lip balm. Hell, she'd gone to sleep with her hair in a damp ball on her head and woken up this morning looking as though she could have shot a shampoo commercial. She was effortlessly sexy, and something about that made her all the more appealing.

And minty toothpaste made her gag. He laughed under his breath, remembering.

She shot him a look. "Something funny?"

Just you, he thought.

And clearly he was an idiot…because while she'd been stocking up on fiber bars and bagged popcorn—she'd had a craving—at the drugstore this morning, he'd snuck to the photo-center cash register and purchased a new tube of toothpaste.

One that wouldn't make her gag.

And a box of condoms.

FINDING AMELIA WATSON took a bit more effort, but after a vital-records search using various spellings of Amelia's name, they finally got a hit.

Rhiannon stood at the foot of the grave and felt a pang of regret for the woman who had grieved herself to death over the loss of her child. Theo's flowers—only slightly wilted this time—were nestled against the chalky, weathered headstone.

"Another penny?" Will asked. "Is this the quirk you were talking about? Do you and Theo leave pennies on headstones?"

Half of her mouth hitched up in a grin. "Nice try, but no."

"Damn."

"Theo likes to share his thoughts, whether he's asked for them or not," she explained. "He's just being courteous."

He arched a skeptical brow. "You mean he talked to Amelia's marker?"

She studied the headstone. *Beloved wife and mother.* "In a manner of speaking."

"No wonder you're so close to him. You're both—"

She shot him a glare, silently urging him to re-think what he was about to say.

"Unique," he finished, smiling.

She nodded primly. "You're learning."

"We're closing the gap," he said. "Getting closer."

Which was true, yet she could still feel an unexplained sense of urgency. Rhiannon was by no means psychic—clairvoyance was not her talent—but she knew well enough to trust her instincts, and those same instincts now were telling her that she needed to find Theo before something terrible happened. An unexplained ball of dread sat in her belly, a constant reminder that they needed to push on.

"So he obviously didn't dig here," Will said, inspecting the undisturbed grass.

"No need if the metal detector didn't give him any indication there was a reason to."

"True," he conceded. He inspected the sky, in particular the low orange ball of sun sinking to the western horizon. "We're less than three hours from Roanoke. We should probably get on the road."

He was right, she knew. They would need to get an early start tomorrow. She'd also done an online search for Winston Watson's marker—or records of any sort—and hadn't found the first thing. Of course, she'd done only a cursory search. It didn't mean nothing was there—it just meant she hadn't had time to look properly.

Unfortunately, if finding Winston's marker was easy, then she suspected she would have heard from

Theo already. He'd had at least a thirty-six-hour jump on them and obviously was still searching. Poor record keeping, lost or destroyed documents... there were so many things that could have gone wrong over the years.

Rhiannon let go a small breath. "This is going to be like looking for a needle in a haystack."

"Yeah." He passed a hand over his face. "And Mimi said 'around Roanoke.' That leaves a lot of ground."

Yes, it did. And Rhiannon wasn't entirely sure where they should start.

Will stooped, picked a dandelion from the ground and twirled it between his fingers. "Theo was a librarian, right? He knows those systems better than any of the other more advanced technologies out there now, I would assume?"

She considered him. "Yes."

"Then he's probably relying on old obits from newspapers stored on microfiche."

She brightened. "You're right. He's competent on the computer, but he is much more at home in the library."

"So we start with the libraries on the fringes of Roanoke and tighten our circle. Work from the outside in."

She smiled at him, impressed. "That's an excellent plan."

His lips lifted with droll humor. "I do have them on occasion." He laid the bloom on the headstone. "Are you hungry?"

She gave him a duh look. "Do you even have to ask?"

His chuckle was low and sexy. "We need to find a sandwich bar with Wi-Fi," he said. "Get a list of libraries and start mapping our route."

Rhiannon headed for his Jeep. "You're on a roll."

"Smart-ass."

Twenty minutes later Will had his laptop open and had begun the search. He'd ordered an enormous sandwich and waffle fries and was periodically taking bites between searches.

He grimaced. "There are a lot of little libraries around here," he said, scrutinizing the screen.

Rhiannon popped a bite of artichoke into her mouth. "How many?"

"More than twenty on the fringes, and that's not including the city."

"No wonder we haven't heard from Theo."

"Yes, but I think we can gain some ground. I imagine he's just wandering from town to town making inquiries and checking cemeteries along the way. We have a plan."

"Are we going to check the cemeteries, as well?"

He shrugged. "It couldn't hurt. There are a lot of deaths that never make it into the obituaries. Particularly if they weren't local and were simply passing through, you know?"

Rhiannon's eyes widened significantly as she digested that. "We're going to be spending a lot of time in your car."

His eyes twinkled and he cocked his head. "Mine might not be as economically friendly as yours, but it's got more legroom."

She couldn't argue there. And he was an excellent driver. He expertly negotiated traffic and, though it was ridiculous, she'd found her gaze riveted on the way his hands rested against the steering wheel—the large palms and long, blunt-tipped fingers, the masculine muscles and veins that made his arms so very different from hers. A breath stuttered out of her lungs as she imagined them wrapped around her, his skillful hands on her body.

"It's nice," she said, trying to distract herself from that line of thinking. "And really new. When did you get it?"

"A couple of days ago."

"So you would have wanted to drive regardless."

He made another notation on the map and added

an address. "I would have wanted to drive even if I'd been in a tank."

She grinned. "He who has the keys has the power, eh?"

"Something like that," he admitted, still focused on his task.

"So how much longer are we driving before we settle in for the night?"

"I thought we could put in another hour on the road. You up for that?"

"Sure." Though she was a bit worn out. The endless time in the car, the stress of worrying over Theo and the unceasing attraction—being constantly aware of and in tune with every move he made, every breath that entered and exited his lungs—was beginning to get to her. She needed a little distance. A chance to regroup. To possibly desensitize herself.

As if that would help, she thought fatalistically.

She was hopelessly in lust with him, had been fantasizing about him all day. In bed, against a wall, in the shower. Didn't matter. She just wanted, and there was nothing tender or gentle about the sentiment. She wanted the hot, desperate, mindless sort of sex that resulted in frantic disrobing, torn underwear and whisker burn. Her skin prickled with heat and she squirmed in her seat as her sex tingled with warmth.

"Are you okay?" he asked, looking up at her.

"Sure. Why?"

"You look a little flushed."

Busted. "My sandwich is hot."

He smiled, the wretch, as though he knew she was lying. "Want me to blow on it?"

"With your minty breath? No, thank you."

He laughed and his gaze drifted slowly over her mouth. "Still going to breathe on me?"

"Yes," she said, her toes curling at the thought. "If for no other reason than to prove to you that mint isn't the only option when it comes to fighting bad breath. We've been brainwashed with advertising to believe otherwise, I know, but—" she sighed as though it were a tragic injustice "—it simply isn't true."

His lips twitched. "I'm surprised you haven't mounted some sort of campaign," he said. "Launched a Web site or blogged about it."

She tossed her napkin onto her plate and grabbed her purse from the back of the chair. "How do you know I haven't? Now, if you'll excuse me, I'm going to brush my teeth."

8

Three chain hotels later, they finally found one that passed muster. Hotel number one had a surly desk clerk who displayed poor personal hygiene and hotel number two had, according to his companion, "smelled funny."

It would not do.

This one, however, boasted the clean scent of lemon cleaning solution and had a huge vase of purple irises—her favorites, she'd explained—on the check-in counter, and she was certain it would do nicely.

Will watched her lean over and sniff the blooms, and the small smile that captured her lips made his own inexplicably slide into a halfhearted grin. For someone with such high standards, the littlest things made her happy. She was a conundrum, Will thought, with more facets to her personality than the most complexly cut diamond.

"I love this shade," she said, fingering a bloom as the desk clerk located their rooms. "It's the color of my bedroom."

"Purple?"

"More lilac I would say," she told him, as if he would understand the difference. She lifted her foot and absently rubbed the back of her calf. Her long curly hair was once again pushed away from her face and secured with her ridiculously large sunglasses. They swallowed her face and looked especially bizarre with that tiny little nose.

Naturally, because he was quickly losing any perspective—provided he'd ever had it to start with—he found it charming.

"You're in luck," the desk clerk said. "We've got one room left."

Rhiannon blinked and her mouth rounded in a little O of surprise. She looked at him, then back to the clerk. "Only one?"

"Oh, you're not together?" the clerk asked.

"We're traveling together," Will explained before this could get any more awkward.

She smiled regretfully. "I'm afraid it's all I've got. It's a double," she said. "If that makes any difference."

To his amazement, Rhiannon merely shrugged.

"I'm cool with that, if you are," she said, as though sharing a room with him wasn't the least bit disconcerting. "It's late and I'm tired."

"I'm fine with it," he said. He slid a credit card to the desk clerk. "I just didn't expect you to be."

She blinked up at him, her eyes innocently surprised. "Why not? I'm much more logical than you."

An incredulous laugh broke apart in his throat. "You are *so* full of shit."

She *tsked* under her breath. "Cursing again. You've got a terrible mouth."

He grinned at her. "But it's minty fresh."

"You're on the second floor," the clerk told him, handing him the key card. Her lips twitched. "Elevators are just around that corner. Continental breakfast is served from six to ten. Enjoy your stay."

He nodded his thanks, then slung his bag over his shoulder and reached for Rhiannon's.

"I've got it." She grabbed it and they headed toward the elevators. "Honestly, it's on wheels."

He depressed the call button. "I was trying to be nice."

"I know." She sighed as though it were a bad thing. "You open doors and pull out chairs and everything. A girl could get used to that kind of old-fashioned courtesy."

They stepped into the elevator and his gaze slid to her once more. So the guys she typically dated weren't always as polite? Interesting…

"Courtesy doesn't ever go out of fashion," he said. An image of his grandfather sprang to mind and he smiled. "At least, not according to my grandfather."

The doors slid open and he waited for her to pass. She looked at him over her shoulder. "Sounds like he's a smart man."

"He was," Will confirmed. He scanned the hall for their room number.

Her gaze softened and a sympathetic frown lined her brow. "I'm sorry."

"Cancer." He sighed, slipping the key card into the slot. "Damned miserable disease. We lost him five years ago." He was glad he'd made the time to call his grandmother today. She'd been thrilled to hear from him, her familiar voice damning him when it broke on the verge of tears. Though she was smart enough to know that something terrible had sent him fleeing from the military, she didn't know what; and Will was determined never to tell her. It was hard enough living with it himself. He'd be damned before he off-loaded it on her.

"Both of my grandparents died when I was very young, so I never knew them," she said. "I was always envious of people who did."

Will flipped on a light. "Mine raised me," he told her, for reasons he couldn't begin to explain. This wasn't something he ordinarily talked about. Not because it was painful or he had anything to hide—he just never felt the need to share. It was her, he realized again. She just had that way about her.

She rolled her bag up against the wall, dropped her purse on the low dresser and turned to face him. "Really?"

She didn't ask why, just left him the choice as to whether or not he wanted to tell her. He liked that. "Yeah," he said, rubbing the back of his neck. "My parents and little brother were killed in a car accident when I was ten."

She gasped. "Will, that's horrible. I'm so sorry."

"It was a long time ago."

"Were you in the accident, as well?"

"No. I was at school. David, my little brother, had a doctor's appointment that day. Asthma," he explained. "A truck ran a light and hit them."

Her face crumpled. "Damn."

Because he couldn't stand the sadness on her face, he purposely laughed to lighten the moment. "Who has the potty mouth now?"

It worked. She smiled. "Yes, but at least it's not polluted with mint." She gave a delicate shiver.

He shook his head and gestured toward the beds. "Which one do you want?"

"The one farthest from the door, if you don't mind. You can have the death bed."

His eyes rounded and he knew he was going to regret asking, but couldn't help himself all the same. "The death bed?"

She plopped down on her bed and leaned back, testing the mattress. "Yes," she said. "If we're attacked in the middle of the night, more than likely the intruder will come after you first because you're closest to the door." She sat up again and her hair settled around her shoulders. "And that will give me the opportunity to escape."

Will felt the edges of his mouth tremble. "You've given this a lot of thought, haven't you?"

She kicked off her shoes and happily flexed her toes. "No more than anything else."

"And you wouldn't try to save me? You'd just run?"

She considered him for a moment, then released a small sigh. "I would probably try to save you," she admitted grudgingly. "I've grown quite fond of you."

The unexpected declaration caught him completely by surprise, but more bewildering than the announcement was the way it made him feel. His heart lightened and a certain sense of manly satisfaction expanded in his chest, making him feel ridiculously—amazingly—happy.

It had been so long since he'd known true joy, the sensation almost knocked the breath out of him. She was a blip on the radar of his life, a passing thing, a fleeting character who would disappear from his world as soon as they located Theo... and yet her casual revelation left him with the certain impression that she was going to reverberate through his universe much longer than she'd be a part of it.

"You don't have to look so frightened," she teased, thankfully misreading his thoughts. "I'm fond of the bag boy at my local grocery store, too, and would probably try to save him, as well."

He feigned disappointment. "So I'm not special after all." He sighed.

She laughed at him. "Oh, please. If I did think you were special—me or any other woman, for that matter—you'd be gone faster than I could say commitment phobic," she said.

Intuitive, too, Will thought, though naturally he was going to argue with her. "So that's the quirk, is it? You're psychic?"

"No," she said. "But I am very good at...reading people." She lingered over the phrase, as though there were something significant that he was missing. His intuition flared.

"Reading people? How so? What do you mean?"

She sucked in a breath through her teeth, hesitating. "I already know how you're going to react," she said, more to herself than to him. "And you already think I'm weird."

"Not true. You're unique," he said, proving that he remembered her correction.

She chewed the corner of her lip, still seemingly undecided. She finally released a long breath and gave a what-the-hell shrug. "Have you ever heard of emotional intelligence?"

"Vaguely," he admitted, and a finger of unease nudged his belly.

"It's the science of learning to identify, control and manipulate the emotions of yourself and others. Learning to change harmful emotions into helpful ones." She tucked a leg under her bottom. "I actually teach a class on it at the local community college. Theo and I are keenly aware of other people's emotions, of what other people are feeling. When I was younger, I would just get…bombarded with feelings that didn't belong to me and I didn't know how to process them." Her troubled face was suddenly transformed with a soft smile. "Theo understood me—is probably the only person who ever has—and helped me learn how to cope with it."

The longer she'd talked the more tense he'd

become, and right now every muscle in his body felt as if it had atrophied. She could *feel* his emotions? All of them? The irritation, desire? God help him, the grief over what had happened? Did she feel that, too?

Help me...

Her ripe mouth curved into a knowing smile. "Relax," she said. "I haven't asked you a single question, have I?"

Yes, she had, Will thought. At the diner. When the crushing sadness had settled around him and he'd had to work a little harder to shrug it off. She'd put her hand on his, had asked him if he was okay.

He'd lied.

Hadn't he known there was something different about her? Hadn't the memories been worse since he'd met her, coming more and more frequently? Hadn't he been compelled to confide in her? He hadn't bared his soul, but he'd certainly been a hell of a lot more chatty with her than he'd ever been with anyone else. Her apparent ease with Mimi... It all made sense.

"Why don't you take a shower," she suggested. "Let the hot water work some of the knots out of your back."

He arched a brow, equally impressed by and terrified of her ability. It was intimidating to think that she knew his emotions, that she could feel them emanating from him. No secrets, stripped bare...

On the other hand, there was no point being coy about wanting her, Will decided.

She knew. No doubt had known all along.

"Reading my emotions?" he asked, lifting a brow again.

She chuckled. "Those, too, but your face is what's giving you away." Her eyes twinkled. "I've spooked you."

"It's...unnerving," he admitted, shooting her a look.

"It's not a cakewalk on this end, either," she said, grimacing significantly.

No, Will considered thoughtfully, he imagined not.

WELL, THAT HAD GONE about as well as she'd expected, Rhiannon thought later as she took her own shower. Will's scent still hung in the bathroom, flooding her senses and making that ever-present sense of longing curl tighter in her belly. Men were more careful of guarding their feelings than women were and any inkling of perceived weakness that went along with that was sure to rattle their cage.

Whatever Will was battling was substantial— she'd recognized that from the beginning. She'd felt it the minute he'd made the connection—the trepidation, the anxiety of her knowing that he wasn't quite as together as he appeared. He wanted to be in control, to govern his own thoughts and feelings, and he damned sure didn't want to share them with her.

No doubt he was waiting for her to ask what had happened, what had made him leave a career he'd obviously loved, what sort of horrific event haunted his soul.

But she would not.

Feeling other people's emotions—things that were private—was invasive enough. She would not compound the unintentional intrusion by prying, as well. Besides, she'd never had to pry. People typically wanted to share with her. Provided they had enough time, she suspected Will would, too.

And though she knew it was dangerous—that any sort of emotional bonding with him would be foolhardy—she wanted to know. She wanted to soothe him. To try to help him heal. All of that would simply invest her further into a relationship she neither wanted nor needed—it was too close to that unmanageable emotion known as love for her liking. But she couldn't seem to help herself. Something about Will Forrester, other than his potent sex appeal, called to her on a deeper, frighteningly unfamiliar level.

Furthermore, though he had hadn't said as much, she'd felt his surprise that he'd told her about his parents and little brother. How terrible, she thought again. To lose your entire family in one fell swoop. Thankfully he'd had his grandparents and he seemed to hold them both in very high regard. Love and admiration had rung in his tone when he'd spoken of them, and she hadn't been kidding about getting spoiled with his courtesy.

Will Forrester was part of a dying breed—an authentic Southern gentleman. He said *please* and *thank you,* held open every door, including the car, and never failed to make her feel like anything but a lady...even when he was burning her up with one of those less than subtle I-want-to-fuck-you-blind looks.

It was thrillingly hot and made her equally so.

Even now, smelling his aftershave, knowing that he was in the other room—shirtless, a pair of low-slung shorts on—lying across the death bed made her nipples tingle and her sex quicken. Her belly clenched and an indecent throb built between her thighs.

Rhiannon turned off the shower, snagged a towel and quickly went through her evening routine. She moisturized, she partially dried her hair—it would take too long to do it properly and she didn't have the patience—then slipped into a pair of cotton shorts and matching cami.

Then she brushed her teeth.

Two minutes later she strolled back into their room and stowed her things. She felt Will's brooding gaze linger over her breasts, skim over her hips and settle on her ass, caressing her with the heat of that heavy-lidded stare. She could feel his desire— it was practically arcing off him, sparking against her own. In a minute, if she had her way, they were going to blaze out of control.

A dry bark of laughter rumbled from his chest. "Just out of curiosity, can you feel what I'm feeling now?"

She bent over—purposely allowing her shorts to ride up—and stowed her cosmetics bag in her suitcase.

She straightened slowly, then turned and looked at him. "I can," she admitted. "But not for the reasons you think."

He laced his fingers behind his head, doing his own little torture trick as his abs rippled invitingly. "I'm afraid I don't follow."

She sidled forward. "Luckily this isn't an intelligence test."

Another sexy laugh. "Explain, please."

Rhiannon sat on the edge of his bed and slid a finger deliberately down his belly. His unsteady breath hissed between his teeth, making her smile. "My feelings mirror your own, so they're sort of... tangled up. I can't tell which feelings are yours or which feelings are mine. I'm just doubly—" she bent forward and put her mouth a hairbreadth from his "—hot," she breathed.

She drew back and quirked a brow. "Well?" she asked.

Will's silvery-gray eyes darkened into a magnetic pewter shade and the grin that pulled at his lips was quite possibly the sexiest thing she'd ever seen. "You tell me," he said. "I bought a tube of your brand this morning, too."

Before she could laugh, he flipped her onto her back and his mouth was on hers. Hot, warm and demanding, his lips moved masterfully over her own. His tongue tangled around hers, probed the soft inner recesses of her mouth.

Her blood suddenly felt as if it was boiling and moving too damned slowly through her veins. She wriggled closer, thankful that he hadn't bothered with a shirt. His skin was smooth and sleek, supple muscle and perfect bone. She slid her palms over his shoulders, up into his hair and arched against him, gasping as the feel of her sensitive breasts met the weight of his chest. His shorn locks tickled her palms and she felt the long, hard length of him against her thigh.

Warmth abruptly pooled in her center and the throb she'd felt earlier pulsed with every quickened beat of her heart. Her breath came in desperate puffs and the overwhelming need to feel him inside her—to feel him pushing in and out, filling her up and laying her bare—all but obliterated every other sensation. She was a slave to the desire, a prisoner of the longing. The room could crumble into ruin around them and as long as he and the bed remained, she'd be fine.

She'd never felt this sort of intensity before, this absolute single-minded drive to have a man inside her. It was new and wondrous and just a little bit frightening, but the fear heightened the experience. She shifted, opening her legs, and gasped as he settled against her.

Rhiannon felt her eyes roll back in her head and a shaky, euphoric laugh rattled her chest. "Oh, sweet heaven," she said, pulling her thighs back and anchoring them around his waist. "This will be *so* much better when we're naked."

9

FOR ONCE THEY WERE in agreement, Will thought as Rhiannon's greedy thighs clamped around his hips. Her impatient hands slid over his back, down his ass and gave a determined squeeze, which sent him flexing against her once more. She bucked beneath him, not the least bit shy about what she wanted.

Him.

The knowledge almost set him off and he hadn't even fully had her yet.

He would.

He was going to map her body with his tongue, read her like Braille. He was going to fill his mouth with her pouting breasts and feast on her sweet sex until she came.

Then he was going to make her come again.

He left her mouth and licked a path down her

throat, savoring the taste of her on his tongue. She was sweet and tangy and he wanted to bury himself so far inside her that it would take some sort of nuclear weapon to blast him out.

Need hammered through his veins, blotting out everything to the exclusion of her. She was all he wanted. She was all that mattered. He found the crown of her breast through her shirt and suckled, and her little gasping purr of pleasure made him harden even more.

"You have been driving me crazy," he told her, slipping the straps of her shirt aside. Ah, perfect, Will thought. Heavy globes, rosy nipples puckered for his kiss. He laved her first, sampling, then suckled deep, giving a sharper tug.

Her breath hissed out of her mouth and she shifted her hips more provocatively against him. She bent forward and nipped at his shoulder, then licked a determined path up his neck and sighed hotly into his ear.

"Likewise," she said. "And you thought I was crazy before."

He smiled against her. "No, I didn't."

"Liar." She laughed, slipping a hand over his hip. She shifted and cupped him through his boxers, making what was left of his breath completely flee.

Small, capable hand stroking his dick, a sweet,

perky breast in his mouth and a woman who was clearly an uninhibited, enthusiastic bed partner beneath him.

Life could not possibly get any better.

Unless…

He dragged her little shorts off and was pleasantly surprised. "No panties?"

"You're gonna talk during sex, too? There are *so* many better things you could be doing with your mouth," she said, slipping a finger along the engorged head of his penis. A single bead of moisture leaked from the top and she swirled it around him with her thumb in a mind-numbingly distracting little circle.

"Like w-what?"

"Later," she said enigmatically. "When we have more time." She bucked against him. "Right now I want you to take me."

He had never in his life had a woman say that to him before, had always thought it was something that happened only in porn movies. But the fact that this woman had just said it to him made him absolutely want to beat his chest and roar. It was direct and sexy and, dammit, fucking fabulous, and he'd never—*never*—wanted another woman more.

Thankful that he'd had the forethought to buy the condoms when he'd gotten the new toothpaste, he snagged one from beneath the phone book, where he'd hidden it earlier, and quickly tore into it with his teeth.

She saw it and laughed. "Confident, were you?"

"Hopeful," he corrected as she dragged his boxers over his ass.

Her eyes darkened to a midnight-blue as she feasted her gaze on him. She licked her lips and took the protection from his hand. "Let me," she said.

A second later he was fully sheathed in the condom and a mere half a second after that, fully sheathed in her. He took her hard, plunging into her heat, and the gratified smile that slid over her lips as he finally filled her up triggered his inner caveman. His lips peeled away from his teeth as he pushed into her, harder and harder, almost savagely, and the more firmly he seated himself, the more she seemed to like it. Little grunts and groans of pleasure slipped past her carnal smile, and she raked her nails lightly over his back and gripped his ass. She drew her legs back, anchoring them around his waist, and met him thrust for thrust.

The headboard banged repeatedly against the wall and, while he knew the hotel was full and they were surely disturbing someone on the other side, he didn't give a damn.

Couldn't.

Her greedy muscles tightened around him with every thrust, holding him in, causing an exquisite draw and drag between their joined bodies. It was hot and hard and dirty, with an elemental primal intensity to it that made it hands down the best sex he'd ever had in his life.

And he hadn't even come yet.

But he was about to.

Could feel it building in his loins, gathering force as his balls tightened and the urgent, insistent tingle built in the root of his dick.

A little laugh tittered out of her throat, her eyes fluttered shut and then she suddenly went wild beneath him. Everything seemed to tighten around him—her legs, her arms, her sex. She bucked beneath him, forcing him to up the tempo.

"You are— Holy hell— I'm— *Damn.*"

She went rigid beneath him as the orgasm took her. Her mouth opened in a long soundless scream that suddenly became a long, low moan of pleasure. Her toes curled into his ass and for whatever reason, that was what set him off.

The climax blasted from his loins like a bullet down the barrel of a gun and with every greedy squeeze of her body around him, another wave of sensation shuddered through him, milking his body of all it had left. Wringing him dry. He angled deep and seated himself as firmly into her as possible, felt his back bow beneath the stress of the pleasure and heard his own strangled cry in his ears.

Breathing hard, he lowered his head and looked down at her. Her wild dark curls were fanned out on the muted gold tones of the bedspread, her cheeks were flushed, her lips plump and swollen and her eyes knocked the breath out of him. She was wantonly beautiful, unrepentantly sexy, and the satisfied smile curling her mouth made him feel as if he'd conquered the world.

Or at the very least, hers.

She slid her hands over his back, tracing his spine with the tip of her nails. It felt delicious. "We're going to have to do that again."

He was still inside her, he could still feel her fisting around him and she was already game for more?

Crazy, unique, weird, odd…whatever.

She was officially perfect.

"So I'm good enough to sleep with, but not good enough to sleep with?" Will teased the next morning when Rhiannon, still satisfied and drowsy, opened her eyes. He sat on the edge of his bed. He wore navy blue boxers—no shirt, amen—and an endearingly sexy smile.

She stretched and let go a long groan. "I thrash

around a lot," she lied, not wanting to hurt his feelings. She'd deliberately waited until his breathing was slow and deep and she was certain he was asleep before getting up and sneaking back to her own bed.

He inspected her bed, which was curiously undisturbed, and merely arched a brow. "I'm going to take a quick shower," he said. "Do you need it first?"

She shook her head. *Always polite,* she thought as he headed for the bathroom. A conscientious worker, a fabulous lover. Were she in the market for a permanent sort of man, he would definitely be a contender.

But she wasn't, Rhiannon reminded herself, and ignored the unwanted sense of melancholy that accompanied the thought.

Permanent went hand in hand with love and she'd decided long ago that she didn't want any part of that weakening, unpredictable emotion. She'd seen the damage it could do.

No, thank you.

And she was happy, dammit. Content.

So why had she wanted to linger long after the sex was over? Something she'd never had any desire to do before. Why had she wanted to feel his arm snugly around her middle, his breath in her ear, and why had it been so damned hard to leave his warm, curiously comfortable side and get into her own cold, lonely bed?

Better still, why did her bed feel lonely, when it never had before?

Quicksand, Rhiannon thought. If she wasn't careful, she could so easily sink.

The minute she'd felt her reluctance to move away from him, she'd made herself do it just to prove that she could. That he really wasn't different. She sighed.

But she knew he was.

Off-the-charts, otherworldly attraction aside, something about him made her simply go all gooey on the inside. He was smart and funny, interesting and wounded. And he was good, Rhiannon decided. If there was one thing she'd learned with her ability to read emotions over the years, she'd learned to be a good judge of character. So often people's emotions were tied to their motivations. After a while it was simple to pick up on false concern, a greedy heart, a malicious spirit. Will had none of those things.

He was unequivocally…honorable.

The adjective seemed out of date and old-fashioned, but it fit him all the same.

And right now he was doing all he could to survive, to put his world back together. She could feel the desperation behind the determination, could sense the ever-heavier cloak of grief, guilt and despair tightening around him. And she could just as easily feel him pushing against it, resisting it.

This was not her problem, Rhiannon knew, yet she longed to help him. To ease a bit of his burden. Unfortunately, she knew her assistance would not be welcomed. Because Will still believed he was fine.

The truth was coming, though, whether he wanted to face it or not.

The only thing that remained to be seen was whether they would still be together when that reckoning came.

Probably not, she thought, and her spirits sank like a spent party balloon.

Ridiculous, she countered, sitting up. She was a believer in EI. She would just not permit herself to feel this way. She crossed her legs and concentrated on getting her emotions under control, into channeling them into a healthier, prudent direction.

Will chose that moment to stroll out of the bathroom.

"Sorry," he said. "I didn't realize you were praying."

Her lips twitched. "I'm not praying right now," she said. "I'm...working on something."

"It looks unpleasant."

She kept her eyes closed, but still grinned.

"Could you shut up, please? You're interfering with my focus." Oh, who was she kidding? He'd blown it all to hell and back.

She felt him approach, and his soft breath drifted over her face. Oranges and cloves. "I actually like this toothpaste," he whispered. "You've converted me, and I'm brand loyal. You should be proud of yourself."

She opened her eyes. "And how much of your conversion is directly related to wanting to kiss me again?"

His eyes twinkled and dropped to her mouth. "A significant part."

"And will you go back to your minty toothpaste when I am no longer around?"

"Possibly."

"Traitor."

He kissed the tip of her nose, causing an unexpected rush of emotion coursing through her. "You wound me."

She harrumphed under her breath. "You are so full of shit."

"That's what I like about you," he said. "You're so careful with your opinions. Such a delicate little flower."

An image of her riding him for all she was worth suddenly materialized in her mind's eye and her stomach involuntarily tightened with longing at the reminder.

Hot, warm skin. Gleaming muscles. The feel of him buried deep inside her. His knuckle pressing against her clit as his mouth fed at her breasts.

He didn't treat her like a delicate little flower, thank God. He treated her as if he couldn't control himself, as if he couldn't take her hard enough, fast enough or completely enough. It made her feel wanted and feminine and womanly. She loved the way he suckled deeply from her breasts, not only taking her nipple into his mouth, but as much of the globe as he could, as well. As if he couldn't taste enough of her. It was raw and uninhibited and surpassed anything she'd ever experienced.

"I hate to rush you," he said. "But we should probably get moving. We've got a lot of ground to cover today."

Thankful for the subject change, Rhiannon reluctantly stood and stretched. "Has Tad even checked in?" she asked. She'd heard Will on the phone with Payne last night, but hadn't caught much of the conversation.

Will grimaced. "No. However, per our employment contract, he has been apprised of what we're doing."

She toyed with a strand of her hair. "Does he know I'm with you?"

"No."

"Good," she said, gathering her toiletries. She rolled her eyes. "You heard that ignorant message. The moron would assume that I was simply trying to help find Theo to further our reconciliation."

"You know you want him," Will teased.

"The hell you say," she shot back, feigning offense. "He's an ass."

He slid into a pair of worn denim jeans, but didn't bother to zip or button the snap while he looked for a shirt. Effortlessly sexy, she thought, her gaze tracing the fine line of hair that disappeared beneath the waist of his shorts. "But there has to be somebody, right?" he asked.

The question was casual, but she sensed more than curiosity behind it. She purposely kept her voice light. "No, there isn't. I'm happy with the status quo."

Her answer seemed to surprise him. "Really?"

She nodded once. "Really." That ought to put to rest any lingering fears that she would become clingy. "What about you?" she asked just as lightly, though his answer was ridiculously important to her. "Any girl waiting for you back home in—" She frowned. "Where did you say you were from originally?"

He shrugged into his trademark black T-shirt. "Mockingbird, Mississippi," he told her. "And no."

His gaze tangled with hers. "I, too, am happy with the status quo."

"No ring, then?" she asked, snapping her fingers with feigned regret.

He merely laughed.

"Where is Mockingbird, Mississippi?" She wanted to know. It sounded quaint, much like Begonia.

"Heart of the Delta," he said. "Two traffic lights, one grocery store and ten churches." He flashed a grin. "Much like any small Southern town."

He'd certainly nailed that. "And your grandmother is still there?"

"She is." He zipped his suitcase and set it on the floor, then collected his laptop bag.

"What's her name?" Names were important. She could always conjure a face to go with a name, even if it was wrong.

"Molly."

Dark hair and eyes, a plump face and a smile that was kind and slightly mischievous, Rhiannon thought, instantly picturing his grandmother.

"Any other relatives?"

He sighed. "Just the assorted aunts, uncles and cousins I only see every few years."

Sounded like her. And she actually lived close to most of her family.

"What about you? Surely you're not in Begonia all alone."

"Not exactly," she said, gathering her outfit for the day. "My parents are in Florida and are regulars at Disney World. They do their part to contribute to the local economy."

He chuckled. "That's admirable. What about the rest of your family?"

She sighed. "Like you, they're scattered around town, but I rarely see them. We're not close." She frowned. "Theo is really the closest thing to family that I have, and I chose him."

"He's lucky," Will said, surprising her with the sincere comment. Something shifted behind his eyes, but it was gone before she could make an identification.

"We both are."

She jerked her hand toward the bathroom. "Speaking of which, I should probably hurry." She gathered her things. "I'll only be a minute."

"I'll time you."

She laughed. "Two, then."

"You've got ninety seconds."

"Kiss my ass."

"I'm willing to adjust our schedule if you really mean it," he said silkily.

His voice sent a shiver of longing through her that settled warmly in her womb.

She was so, *so* in over her head, Rhiannon thought. And simply drowning no longer seemed like such a bad alternative.

10

WEAVING THROUGH the libraries and cemeteries around Roanoke was long, tedious work and at the end of the day, other than being able to cross several smaller towns and half a dozen libraries off their list, they had little to show for it.

The strain, he could tell, was beginning to get to Rhiannon. There was a new tightness around her eyes and, though she was still the same charmingly strange, smart-assed girl he'd come to know over the past few days, there was a hollowness to her laughter that hadn't been there before.

She genuinely loved Theo Watson and, though Will didn't want her to love him—he was rebuilding his life right now and didn't have time for anything other than fleeting companionship—he was suddenly more envious of that old man than he'd ever been of anybody.

It completely defied logic, and he'd been trying all day to convince himself that it wasn't true, but Will grimly suspected he knew better. He envied Theo her unconditional affection. He envied him that place in her life. He envied him the right to enjoy her company.

Refreshingly, he hadn't even had to make the disclaimer to Rhiannon, because he knew she was only interested in the same thing.

So why had he asked her if there was a guy in the picture? Will wondered. And why had his guts twisted and hadn't released until she said no? Honestly, what was it about her, specifically, that had gotten him all snarled up in knots?

Furthermore, why had he felt a thrill of a challenge flare in his belly when she'd quite plainly let him know that she was happy with her status quo? He was happy, too, and yet he wanted to be her exception to the rule. He inwardly snorted.

He was acting like a chick, he realized, and the knowledge promptly soured on his tongue.

She was seriously knocking him off his game, Will thought, one he grimly suspected he might end up losing.

And then there was the other issue, the one he'd been trying not to think about, the galling knowledge that she could feel the pressing weight of regret that shadowed his every move…and it was only getting worse. Will had thought that leaving the military would help, that the distance would do him good, and to some degree he'd been right.

Unfortunately he'd walked right out of that nightmare into one with a woman who seemed to be some sort of emotional astringent, and every minute he spent with her—every sexually satisfying, curiously enjoyable second—he could feel himself losing ground, could feel everything he'd managed to keep locked down boiling up inside him.

Skinny, scabbed knees, Spider-Man T-shirt and blood. So much blood...

He squeezed his eyes tightly shut and beat the images away, replacing them with her smiling face, the way she'd sunk her teeth into her bottom lip as he'd plunged into her, that little grin she'd worn when she'd smelled those flowers last night. Happy snapshots of memory, and he realized too late the significance that they were all of her.

Shit.

Presently they were sitting in another dingy back room in another tiny library, flipping a page at a time through the microfiche records. The little octogenarian in charge with a pack-a-day voice had let them know in no uncertain terms that she would close promptly at five and all records had to be returned to their proper place. She'd checked on them a few minutes ago and had told them that she was stepping out back to have a smoke. Big surprise there. They had fifteen minutes.

Rhiannon closed the final file, returned it to its slot and sighed as her shoulders sagged.

"Another dead end," she said. "This is going to take forever."

"Not forever," Will corrected. "But it is going to take time."

Frustration laced her tired voice. "Don't you feel like we're running out of that?"

"Not at all," he said. "We're actually making good progress, better than Theo, I'd wager. We *will* find him. I am certain of that."

"I wish I was as optimistic," she said, leaning her head against his shoulder. The innocuous gesture smacked of familiarity and trust, things he wasn't accustomed to feeling with a woman, and naturally, burned through him like a wildfire. He had tried to act like a professional today—he *was* working, after all—but it had been damned hard.

All of him, he thought darkly.

For what felt like the thousandth time today, he wondered if his "relationship," for lack of a better term, with Rhiannon would get him fired. He wasn't altogether sure that they'd sack him for it, but he could hardly blame them if they did. He sincerely doubted screwing around with someone directly involved in his *first* case—he resisted the pressing urge to snort—was considered good form. He'd intimated as much to Payne, though, and the man had still advised him to take her along. Of course, Payne probably thought he had enough sense of restraint and self-preservation to resist her.

His gaze slid to her once more—the elfin face, that especially cute little nose and lush, pink mouth. His dick stirred, readying for sport.

Clearly he did not.

He turned and wrapped his arms around her, meaning to simply comfort her. That was all. He could control himself, he thought, even as her soft body melded against his as though it had been made especially for his arms.

Comforting her worked for a moment, then he felt her lips on his throat and soothing her suddenly was no longer his primary objective.

Getting into her again was.

It was madness, sheer and utter insanity, but he couldn't seem to help himself…and didn't want to.

Without the slightest bit of hesitation, he found her lips and breathed a sigh of relief into her mouth when he tasted her again. She made him crazy. Absolutely wrecked him. A need that was never fully sated reared up at the slightest provocation and pulled him under. His muscles tensed, his loins burst into flame and the desire to plant himself between her thighs again obliterated every other thought.

It didn't matter that they were in a tiny little library in the middle of nowhere with a librarian who was more a warden than a book lover. It didn't matter that he could potentially lose his job—he was damned either way now anyway, right? Sinner or saint, he was still going to hang.

He just wanted her. God help him, had to have her.

"I can't keep my hands off you," she confessed, as though it were a mortifying weakness.

"Good," he said, setting her on the table, thankful that she'd worn another skirt. He freed himself and pulled a condom from his pocket, then swiftly rolled it into place. "I like it when your hands are on me."

He nudged her gratifyingly damp panties aside, then he pushed into her and his world fell back into place. Everything settled into its rightful position and the breath he'd been holding leaked out of his lungs in a sigh of relief that felt dredged from his very soul.

He rested his forehead against hers and smiled, silently admitting to himself that he was doomed.

She sighed, as well, as though she needed him as much as he needed her, then scooted forward, wrapping her legs around his waist and her arms around his neck.

"Take me," she said once again, his own personal porn star.

And he did.

THE DESPAIR and frustration she'd felt only seconds ago seemed like a distant memory, Rhiannon thought now as Will's big warm hands settled on her hips and he pushed into her.

She sighed, savoring the sensation, and clamped her feminine muscles around him. He was hot and hard and completely filled her up, chasing away an emptiness she hadn't known existed, would have sworn she'd never felt.

She wrapped her hands around his neck and held on as he repeatedly plunged into her, in and out, in and out, harder and faster. Her breath came in labored little puffs and her nipples tingled with every thrust of his body into hers.

"I've been thinking about this all day," she confessed. "Wanting you all day."

And it was true. Every cell in her body had been keenly aware of him, practically singing with his nearness. She'd looked at his mouth and gone wet, let her gaze linger on the smooth column of his throat and something in her belly had gone all hot and muddled.

And his hands…

Damn, how she loved his hands. Big, capable, wonderful on her body. They made her feel small and feminine, safe and protected, enflamed and unbelievably alive.

He smiled down at her and nuzzled her ear with his nose, sending a wave of gooseflesh racing down her spine. "You could have said something. It's been hell keeping my hands off you."

"I was…trying to be…good," she said, leaning back so that he could get better access. She shifted forward, aligning their bodies so that she could feel his balls slapping against her sensitized flesh.

It felt *wonderful*. Positively wicked.

She bit her bottom lip as pleasure bolted through her, felt her neck grow weak and her head heavy. The flash of climax ripened in her womb, building and building, growing heavier and more insistent with every frenzied stroke of him deep inside her.

"I like it when you're bad," he told her. "It's sexy."

"I was waiting on you to snap," she said. "Your control is impressive."

And it was true. She'd been trying to make him crack all day. Little touches, a heavy-lidded look, double entendres left and right, and yet he'd deter-minedly clung to his self-control. It was infuriating. She'd wanted to make him give in first today—for reasons she'd couldn't begin to fathom, that had seemed vitally important—and then he'd wrapped his arms around her and the affection she'd felt in the gesture had been equally bittersweet and terrifying.

Affection wasn't supposed to be a part of this, and worse still, she wasn't supposed to want it.

And then, because she'd needed a distraction—a reminder of what they were supposed to be, that this was casual and nothing more—she'd given in and kissed his neck, knowing that it would set him off.

He chuckled. "You weren't the only one trying to be good," he confessed. "I *am* supposed to be working."

Her gaze tangled with his. "By law you're sup-posed to get a fifteen-minute break every four hours." She felt a cry of pleasure build in her throat and swallowed it back. She fisted around him, holding him to her. "You're good."

Something in his expression changed, his eyes smoldered and, without warning, he lifted her off the table and backed her against the wall. The shift in her weight and their positions was absolutely eyes-rolling-back-in-her-head perfect.

She gasped as he managed to hit a hidden spot deep within her, nailing the supersensitive flesh with each brutal thrust into her body. She wrapped her legs tighter around his waist and, catching his rhythm, worked herself up and down on him. She tasted his neck, slid her fingers into his hair and gave a little tug. He growled low in his throat and pounded harder, pushing into her with relentless, reckless force. Knickknacks on a shelf wobbled ominously and the sound of her ass and back hitting the wall reverberated like a gunshot repeatedly through the room. She was breathing too loudly, making too much noise, and she buried her face in his shoulder in an attempt to drown out her own cries.

"Come for me," he said.

And she did. On command. The orgasm broke over her with enough force to make her spine go rigid. Sparklers danced behind her lids and her vision blackened around the edges. She couldn't catch her breath and then stopped trying—oxygen seemed overrated at the moment compared to the cataclysmic storm of sensation whirling through her sex. She fisted around him and with every forceful spasm, another almost unbearable bolt of feeling swept through her.

Will pistoned in and out of her, pounded into her as though he couldn't take her hard enough—rough and thrilling, elemental and raw—and little masculine growls of pleasure slipped between his clenched teeth.

Her orgasm seemed to trigger his own and he suddenly shuddered against her, angling high and burying deep, seating himself as far into her as he could. A low, purely masculine cry stuttered out of his mouth and his hands tightened against her rump, holding her utterly still as the force of his release rocketed through him. She could feel him pulsing inside her, sending another shudder of sensation racking through her.

Breathing hard, spent and fully sated, Rhiannon pressed a kiss to his temple. "You need to be bad more often," she said.

He grinned. "Likewise."

A bell tinkled in the distance and her eyes widened as that significant sound registered in her foggy brain.

Will chuckled. "Can you stand?"

She nodded, not altogether sure that was true. "If not, I'll just lean here," she said. "And try to look normal."

He carefully set her down, snagged a tissue from a nearby box on the table—evidently dust was a problem in this airless little room, she thought—and quickly disposed of the condom.

When she was sure her legs wouldn't give way,

Rhiannon pushed tentatively away from the wall and dragged her skirt back down over her hips into its proper position. Meanwhile Will tucked his shirt back in and zipped his pants. They were presentable, she realized, but the scent of sex hung heavy in the air, betraying their latest activity. Rather than have the librarian wander in and assess the situation, she quickly grabbed her purse and his hand and darted from the room.

Just in time, too. Mrs. Marcus was on her way back. "I'm closing," she announced without preamble. She smelled like menthol and mint, and the scent instantly triggered Rhiannon's gag reflex. "If you didn't find what you were looking for, you can come back tomorrow. We open at nine."

"Thank you," Will murmured, nodding his goodbye—ever the gentleman, Rhiannon thought.

She covered her mouth, gagging again, and he quickly propelled her out the door, quiet laughter shaking his shoulders. "Are you okay?"

Rhiannon pulled a cleansing breath into her nose and glared at him reprovingly. "Yes," she said. "Don't make fun. I told you I can't stand it. Ugh. That was strong. My nose is still burning."

He still chuckled. "Minty breath, your Achilles' heel." He threaded his fingers through hers and tugged her toward the Jeep. "You got any other quirks I should know about? Anything else that might make for an awkward situation?" He opened the door for her and waited for her to climb in.

She pretended to think. "I cry during credit-card commercials, I'm afraid of clowns and spiders, I am anti-pumpkin pie and am Begonia's current watermelon-seed-spitting champion." She paused and slid him a look. "I have no desire to be spanked, but a little light bondage sounds intriguing."

His eyes glazed over comically and she laughed. "You okay?"

He determinedly closed her door and joined her in the car in record time, then cranked the engine and quickly darted out onto the highway. "In a hurry?" she asked, unable to hide her grin. "Where are we going?"

He tapped his thumb against the steering wheel and slid her a smoldering look. "To a hardware store. We're going to need some rope."

11

"So you're afraid of clowns?" Will asked, taking a draw from his beer. They'd found another hotel for the night—the same chain that had suited her before—and had settled in at a little Irish pub. The music wasn't too loud, the beer was cold and the food was delicious. His gaze slid over Rhiannon.

And naturally, the company was above par.

She sipped her whiskey—Jameson, so he had to approve—and her eyes twinkled with warmth. "*And* I'm the watermelon-seed-spitting champion," she reminded him. "I thought you'd be impressed with that. I beat out several men for that auspicious title."

There were lots of things that about her that impressed him, but that didn't necessarily make his list. Still…

He nodded, chasing a bead of moisture down

the side of his bottle with his finger. "You're an impressive woman."

She rolled her eyes. "You thought I was crazy."

"I never said that," he told her.

She tapped her temple. "Didn't have to, remember?"

He thought about lying, but no doubt she would pick up on that, too. "I thought you were…different," he admitted, somewhat reluctantly.

She laughed, the sound hearty and uninhibited, much like her. "That's a politically correct description if I've ever heard one."

He took another drink. "More diplomatic, I would say."

Her dark blue gaze caught his and she seemed to be considering something. "Actually, it was the gentlemanly response." She tipped her glass at him. "I like that about you. It's refreshing."

So she'd said, Will thought as another one of those increasing urges to bare his soul whisked through him. His hand tightened around his bottle and he determinedly beat it back.

She grinned and quirked a knowing brow, but didn't ask. She never asked, and after a moment he wondered why. He knew she had to be curious, had to wonder what haunted him.

"What?" he asked. "No questions? You're just

going to arch your sleek little brow and give me that I-know-your-secrets look?"

"I don't know your secrets," she said. "I only know the pain."

Her expression grew thoughtful and she seemed to focus on something he couldn't see. It made him unaccountably nervous and he belatedly wished he'd kept his thoughts to himself.

"Regret," she murmured. "Loss. Shame. And something else," she said, her gaze tangling with his once more. "Something elusive that I can't put my finger on."

More disturbed by her assessment than he could ever have imagined, Will felt an uncomfortable laugh rattle out of his throat. "Well, if you can't figure it out, I'll be damned before I try."

She hesitated again, then leaned forward, drawing him in once again. He could feel his center of gravity shift, inexplicably pulling him closer to her. "The feeling of someone else's private emotions is intrusive enough," she said. "I can't help it, but it doesn't negate my accountability. So stop worrying that I'm going to ask you about it. I have my suspicions, of course." Her lips twisted. "I've been me for a long time, you know, and there are certain markers for particular emotions." She reached across the table and laid her hand on his. As always, her touch sent his heart into an irregular rhythm and sizzled through him. "But I will not add insult to injury by asking you to explain it to me."

Wow, Will thought, impressed by her compassion and conscience. She was...simply remarkable. If he were as emotionally attuned to other people, would he be so magnanimous? he wondered. Would he resist the urge to mine those emotions and the impulse to interfere?

He cleared his throat, uncertain what to say. "Thank you," he finally murmured.

"Thank Theo," she said, leaning back once more. "I didn't used to always be so sensitive."

He chuckled. That fit, actually. It was the logical, compassionate response to her gift. He could see her wanting to help, to soothe. It was her nature, after all.

She folded the edges of her napkin. "I didn't used to appreciate the fact that just because I could pick up on a person's emotions it didn't mean that I *owned* them. I had no claim to them, though I felt them, as well."

He studied her. "Sounds like that would be confusing."

"It was, in the beginning." She blew out a breath. "But like I said, Theo helped me. He is much more empathetic than I am. He can pick up on subtle nuances I can't even detect."

"I imagine that's more curse than blessing," Will remarked.

She merely smiled. "It comes in handy."

He grinned, but it faltered. "So you said you had your suspicions," he stated in a leading way.

Her expression grew cautiously still. "I do. Are you asking me to share them?"

"I'm curious as to how close to the mark you are," he murmured.

She considered him another minute, testing the atmosphere around him, he imagined. "All right, then," she said. "The weight I feel around you... It's enormously heavy. The grief, the shame and the regret feel like death to me, like you blame yourself for it."

He locked every muscle in his body to stem the shudder trying to break through him and she must have felt that, too, because she suddenly reached across the table and took his hand again. Her smile was sad.

"When I consider the fact that you were a Ranger—underwent all that training to achieve the goal—then that tells me you had planned to make a full career out of the military. That you never intended to leave. You're focused, driven and loyal. Quitting would never have been a part of your plan."

He gave a little breath and smiled at her insight.

"Which means you lost someone close to you—a comrade, maybe?"

The silence lengthened between them as Will struggled to block the images her stunningly accurate words conjured. *Crumpled little bodies, slain women, and the boy...*

The one he'd tried to save, but hadn't been able to.

Help me...

Blood was a common enough occurrence on the battlefield, but he couldn't seem to get the stench of that child's out of his nose no matter how hard he tried. He stared at his beer, followed a flurry of bubbles up the side of the bottle and gave his head a small shake.

"Frightening close," he finally admitted to her, tightening his hand around his drink to hide the shake.

She winced with regret. "I'm sorry."

"Bad intel," he told her, the words welling up inside him. "Women and children." *Bloodied teddy bear, stained shirt.* "A boy. I...couldn't save him." And he'd felt that child take his last breath in his arms. The cloak of dread that had been stalking him for months suddenly settled over his shoulders and he couldn't shrug it off. It clung to him determinedly, tightened around his neck, making him feel as if he was choking. The grief, the despair, the failure. It hurt to feel it, and the pain made him feel weak. Irrational, he knew, but it didn't change anything.

Her hand squeezed his. "I'm so sorry," Rhiannon again said softly. "When you say bad intel…what does that mean? Your information was wrong?"

He tried to focus, struggled to find the words to explain. "Yeah," he murmured, remembering. "Insurgents were supposed to be in the area. They'd set a trap. Waited from a distance as we moved in, then remote detonated, you know?" Bastards, Will thought. "We retaliated, of course, and by the time we realized our enemy wasn't there…it was too late."

"And you feel responsible?"

"My team," he said. "I was point."

"And the people who died, the boy, you're certain it was your weapons that killed them?"

His lips twisted into a bitter, cynical smile. "Does it matter?"

She looked away and made a small face. "No, I guess it doesn't."

Once again the silence swelled between them and Will gave a shaky, hollow laugh. "You're good," he said. "Even the shrink couldn't get me to talk about this and yet you—" his gaze searched hers "—you don't even ask and I spill my guts."

Unreal, he thought. And like a boil being lanced, the relief was instantaneous. It still ached, the pain lingered, but the reprieve was nice. It wouldn't last, of course. He was a marked man—the experience had changed him. He'd never bc able to fully let it go, but it would be nice to know he was going to be able to function.

She pulled a sheepish shrug. "I'm a magnet," she told him.

"A what?"

"That's not an official term, just my own," she said. "But I basically have that effect on people. I draw them out, so to speak. I always have. Total strangers have been known to spill their guts to me in the checkout lane and once during my pelvic exam my gynecologist told me that she was tired of her unattentive husband and was leaving him." She winked and tipped her beer into her mouth. "Interesting conversation."

Will chuckled and shook his head. A magnet, eh? That sure as hell made sense…because he'd be damned if he could stay away from her.

And he was quickly losing the will to try.

RHIANNON STARED at her reflection in the bathroom mirror in Madigan's Irish Pub and wished the little four-leaf clovers pressed behind the glass in the frame would truly bring good luck. She needed it right now.

She'd known that the grief Will had been carrying around was substantial—had felt that all along—and even though her suspicions had been damned close to the mark, having them confirmed in his stilted Southern drawl while the agony rolled off him in waves was almost more than she could bear.

Though she'd wanted to point out that this was not his fault—on any level—she instinctively knew that he would never completely relinquish ownership of the blame. It was still too fresh, the horror too vivid in his mind to even consider releasing any personal responsibility.

Does it matter? he'd said, with that heartbreakingly sad smile.

Ultimately, it did not, and Rhiannon knew in his place she would no doubt feel the same.

On the plus side—if there were a silver lining to this conversation—she'd felt the first vestiges of the gloom lift a bit off his shoulders and she desperately wanted to believe that she had played a key part in that. Helping him had become almost as important to her as finding Theo, and she hadn't realized that until she'd had to excuse herself to the bathroom where she could take a moment to simply weep.

For him.

Because she knew he wouldn't do it.

Finished now—she hoped, at any rate—she took a bracing breath and splashed a bit of cold water on her face. Her eyes were slightly puffy, her nose a bit red, but she would fake a sneeze when she returned to their table and tell him that the air freshener had set her off.

She took another deep breath and shook the tremors off her hands. Dammit, she had to get hold of herself. She was beginning to care too much, to feel too much when she was around him. Wonderful sex aside, there was a niggling feeling that she was sliding down a slippery slope and if she didn't dig her nails in now and cling to the side of the cliff, she'd fall right off into the murky unknown.

Love.

The very word sent a dart of panic right into her heart. Fickle, unpredictable, uncontrollable emotion. Made fools of smart people, made the strong weak and rendered all other emotions virtually useless. It was the trump card, the boss, and up until now she'd never been the least bit tempted to dip her pinkie toe into its vast pond.

And she wasn't now, Rhiannon tried to tell

herself, squeezing her eyes tightly shut. He was just an especially nice guy with great hands, who had the singular ability to unleash her baser instincts. He could draw an orgasm out of her faster than she could do it herself—which was saying something—and he made her want to climb right out of her skin and into his. Her heart fluttered with sweet anticipation and a strange sort of release when he kissed her, and her sex sang when he put those wonderfully large hands on her body. It was new and different, even special, she would concede.

But it wasn't love.

It couldn't be.

Will raised a brow in concern when she sat back down at their table, and she sighed.

"Damned air freshener in the bathroom," she complained with a beleaguered huff of annoyance. "As if we're not breathing enough chemicals in the air, let's add some that are pine scented."

He grinned. "Does pine make you gag, as well?"

"No, it makes me sneeze," she said, a bit through her nose for the proper effect.

He shook his head. "And to think I almost bought one of those little trees to hang from my rearview mirror." He *tsked*.

"And spoil your new-car smell? Blasphemous."

He looked at her plate. "Were you finished? You didn't eat much."

She'd lost her appetite during their discussion, but she couldn't very well tell him that. "It was a lot of food," she said. "I just couldn't finish it."

He didn't look convinced. "So you're ready, then?"

She nodded and reached to grab her purse. Madigan's was located a block off the little town square. "Why don't we take a walk?" she suggested. "Do a little window-shopping."

"It would have to be window-shopping," he said. "From the looks of things, they roll the streets up at five."

Will left enough money on the table to cover the bill and a generous tip, then stood. He literally towered over her. She'd noticed before, of course, but it never failed to send a thrill right to her midsection. Seemingly without thinking, he reached out and took her hand.

Feeling his against her own made her heart do that funny thing in her chest, but the rightness of his fingers threaded through hers quickly calmed her down. She wasn't used to being soothed, and had to admit the sensation was quite pleasant.

They walked past a five-and-dime, a beauty

parlor, a formal dress-wear shop, a shoe repair store—she hadn't seen one of those in a long time—various antiques stores and a little shop that boasted nothing but dollhouses and assorted accessories.

The only store still open was an ice cream parlor, and they ducked in and each got a scoop of pralines and cream in a waffle cone, then walked to the middle of the square and sank down on a park bench, where they could enjoy the fountain gurgling happily in front of them. It was twilight and the gas streetlamps sparkled to life, casting an orange glow. Kids zoomed along on their skateboards, ladies power walked in pairs and several people were taking their animals for their evening adventure.

Rhiannon sighed and licked her cone. "This is very Norman Rockwell," she said, giggling.

Will chuckled. "I keep waiting for Barney Fife to walk up and give us a citation for loitering."

She gasped delightedly. "I love Andy Griffith! I've got every season and special on DVD and am especially proud of my Fife Nip It in the Bud T-shirt."

He inspected his cone, looking for where it was melting the fastest. "You're joking."

"About what? The DVDs or the T-shirt?"

"The T-shirt," he said. "I'm with you on the DVDs, but the T-shirt is a no."

She rolled her eyes and snorted. "This coming from a man who wears the same T-shirt every day."

"It's not the same shirt. It's a clean version of the previous shirt."

"Yes, in black," she said. "Why don't you just print *Badass* in capital letters across the front? That would get the point across better." She took another swipe at her cone.

He leaned his head back and guffawed. "If you think I need a shirt to get that point across, then clearly I am not intimidating enough."

"You don't intimidate me at all," she told him, knowing that it was a lie. The things he made her feel scared the hell out of her and he damned sure didn't need a T-shirt for that.

Come to think of it, he was much more daunting when he was naked.

Another laugh sounded in her ear. "I'm not the least bit surprised about that. You don't scare me, either."

Ah…so she wasn't the only one who was lying, Rhiannon thought, feeling his sudden uneasiness. Because she'd lost any sort of perspective at all, she was almost giddy with the insight.

She nudged his shoulder. "I haven't tried to yet."

He slid her a wary glance. "Yet?"

She popped the last bit of ice cream cone into her mouth and smiled at him. "I'm going to scare the hell out of you tonight."

"How so?"

"With that length of rope we picked up at the hardware store today."

He stilled completely and a slow smile spread over his lips. "That's for you. You said you were intrigued by a little light bondage."

"Yes, but I never said *I* was the one who was going to be tied to the bed, did I?"

12

"THERE'S NO WAY IN HELL I'm letting you tie me to that bed," Will announced as Rhiannon twirled the length of rope in her hands.

Her face fell into a deliberate pout. "Damn," she said. "There were things I wanted to do." She waited a beat and then peeked up at him from beneath her lashes. "To you."

A cold sweat broke out across his shoulders at the innuendo and missed opportunity in her voice, but...*no*. She seriously couldn't expect to tie him up. He would readily own his control issues. He had them, he knew. And yet the promise of those things she'd wanted to do to him hung in the air between them, taunting him.

"One arm," he said, offering a compromise.

She shook her head. "Where's the fun in that? I want you completely at my mercy. I want to be able to explore and play and drive you crazy without fear of retribution." Another tragic sigh. "I wanted to be completely...uninhibited."

That was all it took to make him rock hard. She didn't so much as have to touch him. She didn't have to smile or let her eyes go all soft and wicked. She just had to make a few vague references and his dick acted as though she'd called it forward, her own devoted familiar.

He leveled his gaze at her, wavering. "You're not going to do anything terrible like leave me here for the hotel staff to find, or dress me in your underwear and take pictures and post them on the Internet, are you?"

Her lips curled into an indulgent smile. "Have you given me any reason to do that?"

"None that I can think of, no." But it still made him nervous. Surrendering control. As she'd said, being at her mercy.

She sidled forward and wrapped the rope sinuously around his wrist. "I promise you I won't do anything to you that you don't like." Her warm breath fanned against his arm. "I actually think you'll be pleasantly surprised."

Just like that, his will faltered. "In that case," he told her, holding out his arm, "bind me."

Her eyes twinkled. "You'll be my slave?"

He gloomily suspected he already was. "Yours to command."

"Then get naked."

He chuckled.

"And lie down."

He shucked his shorts and had the pleasure of watching her gaze droop in satisfaction. "And you have the nerve to say that I'm bossy?"

She grinned at him. "And shut up."

Minutes later he was sprawled across the bed, his arms stretched out over his head and securely fastened to the bedposts. A commingled sense of unease and anticipation made for a weird cocktail of sensation coursing through his blood. He couldn't believe that he'd let her talk him into this, that he'd actually allowed himself to be tied up. Though he trusted her not to do anything embarrassing or horrid to him, there was still the niggling inkling of being powerless, of being exposed.

Rhiannon stood at the foot of the bed and tapped her chin thoughtfully as she looked him over. Her gaze lingered on his dick and it instantly nodded a salute. A laugh that sounded dangerously hysterical erupted from his chest.

"Where to start?" she murmured. She shrugged out of her shirt, shucked her skirt—did the woman ever wear panties?—then coolly popped the front clasp of her lacy pink bra. The fabric sagged away from her breasts, catching on her nipples. With a casual lift of her shoulders, it fell off, leaving her just as bare and open as he was.

He felt marginally better.

"Would you like me to make a suggestion?" he asked.

"I thought I told you to be quiet." She crawled like a cat up along his body and rubbed her erect nipples across his chest. A hiss slipped beneath her teeth, straight into his blood.

"Ah," she said, letting her lids flutter shut. "Nice."

Without warning, she moved up and suckled his neck right beneath his jaw, then ran her hands down his chest and carefully slid her nails over his nipples.

Sensation bolted through him and he bucked slightly beneath her. He turned his head and kissed her neck, nipping her jawline, but before he could catch her mouth, she slid down his body, pausing to lick his chest, outline his ribs with her tongue and fingers, mapping every muscle, ridge and bone. Her hands kneaded him, insistent and greedy on his skin, and when her hair slid over the tops of his thighs he thought he was going to tear the posts away from the bed.

"Untie me," he said hoarsely. "I want to touch you. I need to touch you."

She took him in hand, then peeked up at him from between his legs. "Sorry," she said. "I'm busy." Then she deliberately took the whole of him into her mouth. There was no timid touching with the tip of her tongue, no tentative lick along the side of his dick.

She ate him.

And he'd never seen anything so profoundly sexy in his life.

Will's breath left in a startled whoosh and he groaned from deep in his throat. She sucked him, working the hot, slippery skin against her tongue, then wrapped her hand around him and used both to drive him crazy. In and out, up and down, a deliberate swirl of her tongue over his head, then she suckled the sensitive spot—unbeknownst to him—just below his head on the underside of his penis and he came dangerously close to coming right then.

"Rhiannon," he growled as the orgasm built force in his loins. "If you don't stop that, I'm going to—" She cupped his balls, took another long deep pull, simultaneously working her tongue against him, and he completely lost it. *"Come."* The word ripped from his throat as the release rocketed from his loins.

And just as if he was the ice cream cone he'd watched her eat earlier, she licked him up, savoring his essence on her tongue. If anything, she looked as if he tasted better, and the satisfaction of knowing that called to his inner caveman, made him want to drag her by the hair back to his cave and never let her go.

"Mmm." She sighed as she finished him off. "That was very good."

His laugh bordered on frantic.

"I hope you don't need a lot of downtime," she said as she slowly stroked him again. "Because I'm not finished with you yet."

He instantly hardened once more and shot her a self-satisfied smile. "I'm g-good," he told her, though it seemed like a vast understatement. He was *so* much better than good.

He was fucking fantastic.

Rhiannon snagged a condom and swiftly rolled it into place, then scaled his body once more. She winced with pleasure as the head of his dick bumped her clit and she slid back and forth along the ridge, coating him in her own juices. She was hot and wet and he set his jaw so hard he could have sworn he felt it crack.

His eyes almost rolled back in his head and once again the desire to touch her, to taste her breasts made him pull against his restraints. But something about the restriction heightened the experience. She set the pace. She was in control.

And she was brilliant at it.

Her dark hair slithered around her shoulders, down over her breasts, playing hide-and-seek with her nipples. Her lips, soft pink and swollen, rose in a sensual half smile and the dark thatch of hair between her thighs as it rested over him was quite possibly the most incredible thing he'd ever seen.

Gorgeous, he thought, thunderstruck with awe.

She lifted her hips and then slowly sank onto him, her breath leaking out in a long, slow hiss as though his invasion into her body was somehow pushing it out of her. Her heat completely engulfed him. He instinctively flexed beneath her, pushing up.

The slight movement made her grin and she rocked forward on him again, up and down, up and down, then bent forward and laved his nipple with her tongue while clamping tightly around him. *Who knew?* he thought as a flash fire flared down his middle and landed in his groin.

She leaned back once more, her hands on his chest, and she rode him hard. His arms strained against the bindings as he pushed up into her, bucking to meet her downward thrusts. A low purr built in the back of her throat and he watched her face as she caught the first spark of climax. She chased it, her hips undulating wildly against him, then she reached down and massaged her clit. A mere sweep of her fingers sent her flying over the edge and a low, keening cry ripped from her lungs.

She tightened hard around him, triggering his own release, and though he wouldn't have thought it possible, this orgasm was even more powerful than the last. He bucked and shuddered beneath her, every muscle clenched and spent.

Rhiannon collapsed on top of him, boneless and sated, and he felt her lips press a tender kiss against his chest.

It was that kiss—that small gesture—that propelled him over the edge of reason, and he felt himself fall, quite irrationally and against his better judgment, in love with her.

"ARE YOU GOING TO LET ME GO now?" Will wanted to know as she curled up against his chest.

She smiled against him. "I thought you were my slave."

"Yes, but even love slaves need to attend to necessary business."

"Damn." She sighed. "Can't you just hold it?"

He chuckled. "Rhiannon."

She loved the way he said her name in his low and husky voice. "Oh, all right," she said, sitting up reluctantly. "Any chance you'll let me put you right back?"

She freed his left arm first and he winced as he stretched it out. "No."

"I thought as much." She worked to free the second wrist. "But you seemed to enjoy yourself. I mean, if multiple orgasms are any indication," she added wryly.

The minute he was released, he flipped her over onto her back and pinned her to the bed, stretching her arms up and over her head. "How do you like it?"

"A little rough, as you know," she said silkily, reaching up to lick his throat.

"No," he admitted, then shuddered. "Jeez, woman, you're going to be the death of me."

"Let's hope not," she murmured. She lifted her hips suggestively against him. "That would be a tragedy."

Another gratifying growl vibrated against her lips. "Let's shower," he said. "I want to lather you up and watch the soap bubbles slide over your ass."

"I like the way you think."

He nuzzled her neck, then nosed his way down until he could pull her nipple into his mouth. Wicked sensation whipped through her. "I like the way you taste," he said. "I could easily get addicted. Or become a glutton."

She could, too, Rhiannon thought as her toes

curled into the sheets. And it utterly terrified her. She'd never had any interest in light bondage before, in tying anyone up, and yet she'd wanted control over him, had wanted him to bend to her will and let her have her way with him. There was more going on here than she was willing to admit, most especially to herself. She would acknowledge only that she was seriously besotted with him.

Besotted was a safe word. Anything else…was not.

He tugged her toward the bathroom, adjusted the tap and then followed her in.

Hot water, equally hot man, wonderful naked wet skin…

"Mmm, this is nice," she said as Will filled a washcloth with her soap and rubbed it over her shoulders.

"I love the way this stuff smells," he said. "I'll never look at another orange and not think of you."

She grinned, then turned so that he could wash her chest. "I'll never look at another piece of rope and not think of you."

"You're wicked."

"Yes…but you like it."

"I do." He sighed as though he found the knowledge mystifying.

He turned her around and carefully placed both

of her hands on the shower wall. "I don't have any rope in here, but do you think you could just stand here like this for me? Without moving?"

A breath stuttered out of her lungs. "I'll try."

He ran his hands down her arms, then slowly over her rib cage, casually brushing the sides of her breasts. He continued downward, licking the flute of her spine along the way.

Her legs shook.

He palmed her rump, kissed the twin indentations above her rear, then slowly skimmed her thighs. On the return trek, he pushed his hands around to her front, slipping his fingers over her mound, dipping between her folds, then upward until he held both of her breasts.

Her hands fisted against the shower wall, but she didn't move them. He bent his head and nipped at her neck, the sensitive place where throat met shoulder, and she felt a rush of longing sweep through her. The air was heavy with steam and he was hot and warm at her back and suddenly nothing else mattered. Everything in her world seemed to shift until everything past, present or future was tied to this moment.

He nudged her legs farther apart with his foot, then ducked beneath her arms and kissed his way down her body. He stopped at her sex and though she knew what was coming, she was not prepared for the shock of sensation that burst through her when his fingers parted her curls and his hot tongue laved her clit.

Another tremor made her knees quake and her hands slipped farther down the wall, but didn't leave it.

Then he buried his mouth in her sex, suckling, laving, licking, tormenting her until she was certain she wasn't going to be able to remain on her feet, much less stay anchored to the wall. He slipped a finger deep inside her, hooked it around and massaged a secret spot.

She gasped and locked her knees to keep them in place.

"Will, I can't—"

"Oh, but you will." He chuckled against her. "I did for you. You can for me."

"It's not that I don't want to. I don't know—"

He tented his tongue over her clit and pressed hard, stroking it back and forth, then wrapped an arm around her waist to keep her from falling down. Melting. Disintegrating. Flying apart.

Another skillful sweep of his tongue and a bit of pressure deep inside and she was beating the shower wall with her fist as the orgasm swept her under. She cried out, her voice hoarse and mangled, then literally sagged against him.

Before she could catch her breath, he was suddenly behind her, nudging her folds.

Then he froze and a hot oath fired from between his lips. "I left the condoms in the bedroom."

Oh, hell, no. She needed him inside her. Felt as if she couldn't breathe unless he filled her up again. "I'm clean and on the pill. You?"

"Yes."

"Then what the hell are you waiting for? Get inside me."

The exquisite sensation of him—*just him*—inside of her made unexpected tears prick the backs of her eyes. He felt so good. So perfect. So unbelievably right.

He growled a low purr of masculine satisfaction and his hands bit into her hips. "You are—" He released a shuddered breath as he stilled inside her, seemingly prolonging the moment, observing the event for what it was—flawless. "There aren't words to describe how good you feel to me right now."

He withdrew, then pushed back in.

"I know that f-feeling."

Pushed again, withdrew, a mindless seek and retreat that impossibly made her quicken again. She could feel the tension building in her sex with every skillful stroke of him deep inside her and she lifted her foot and set it on the lip of the tub to give him better access.

He growled and rubbed his hands greedily over her ass, thrust again and again, then carefully pressed his thumb against the rosebud of her bottom.

The sensation was so incredible she heard a loud gasp hiss through the shower and realized it was her own.

"That's...wicked."

"But you like it," he said, tossing the words back at her, and she could hear the self-satisfied smile in his voice.

He pressed harder, upped the tempo and angled deeper. Three crushing plunges later, she shattered. Sound receded, everything went black and white, then suddenly flared into Technicolor focus. She screamed and her nails scraped down the shower wall. A moment later he joined her, his guttural groan alerting her to his impending climax as he pushed in one final time and locked himself in place as though he wanted to permanently cement himself there.

And as the final vestiges of release pulsed through her, she let her hands fall away from the wall...and she let go of that figurative cliff face she'd been clinging to, as well, allowing herself to plummet into that terrifying place she'd never wanted to be.

In love.

Will pressed a kiss to her temple. "Sleep with me," he said.

She did.

13

"You're the second person who has come by today and wanted to see those old records," the petite lady told them when Will asked to look at the microfiche. "They're still out," she complained, frowning. "The gentleman—who told me he was a librarian, as well—didn't even bother to put them away. He rushed out of here as if his pants were on fire and hollered an apology."

Will's gaze swung to Rhiannon's and before he could utter a word, she was already firing questions at the woman. "What was he looking at? How long ago did he leave?"

The librarian flinched back at the intensity in Rhiannon's voice and darted a startled look in his direction.

"It's important that we find him," Will said. "He's unwell."

Not exactly a lie. He was diabetic.

She frowned knowingly. "Yes, I could tell that," she told them. "Had to get him a glass of water. The poor man had broken out into a clammy sweat."

The panic in Rhiannon's eyes tore at him.

"Oh, Will," she moaned, her voice cracking. "I knew this. I knew something was wrong. I've had a terrible feeling about it for days now."

"I thought you said you weren't psychic."

"I'm not, but I know when something is wrong," she repeated impatiently. She leaned across the counter to the woman. "How long ago did he leave? This is really important."

The librarian glanced at the clock and fretted as she tried to work it out. "A couple of hours ago," she said. "Maybe longer."

"Can you show me what he was looking at?"

"Right this way," she said. "Follow me."

They were escorted to another dim airless room, where a single book lay on the table. Rhiannon crossed the room quickly and scanned the documents, her gaze darting across the page. It suddenly stopped and she gasped.

"Here it is," she breathed. "Winston Watson. Oh, he was only three," she said, her voice breaking.

"Where was he interred?"

"Creekside Cemetery." She glanced up at the older woman. "Do you know where this is?"

She shook her head. "Your friend asked the same question and I gave him the same answer, honey. I'm sorry."

Will quickly nodded at the woman and propelled Rhiannon toward the exit. "We'll stop and ask until we find it," he told her.

Neither clerk at the first two convenience stores was helpful, but they finally got lucky when they stopped at a local feed and seed store. A couple of old-timers argued over the exact whereabouts long enough to make Rhiannon's face flush with irritation, but finally agreed on the location and passed along the directions.

"How long should it take to get there?" she asked them.

"'Bout fifteen, twenty minutes," one said. "The sign is gone and it's a far piece off the road, so you'll need to keep your eyes open. That's an old one. Not too many people buried there, either."

"I'd like to be buried there," the other one remarked.

"Oh, shut up, Marvin. Charlene's already bought your plot at Morningside."

Marvin frowned. "How do you know that?"

The other man grinned. "Because I sold her the burial insurance."

Marvin harrumphed. "Didn't know she had any."

While they continued to discuss their impending funeral arrangements, Will and Rhiannon hurried back to the Jeep. She tapped her toes impatiently against the floorboard and her mouth was set in a flat, worried line.

"We'll find him."

"Something's wrong," she said. "He would have called me by now."

"He might not have a signal."

She gazed out the window, a line of worry furrowing her brow. "He's had time to get back into town, Will."

He silently agreed, but was playing devil's advocate to try to distract her. "His battery could be dead."

"Stop it," she said. "I know what you're doing. You're worried, too. Don't try to pretend with me, please." She softened her statement with a wan smile.

He reached over and took her hand. "Forgot. Sorry."

And though it seemed bizarre, he *had* forgotten about her talent. Had she picked up on his feelings last night? Will wondered. Had she been able to tell that she'd gone from someone he couldn't resist to someone he suspected he couldn't live without?

A sense of dread settled in his chest as he raced toward what he instinctively knew was the end of this mission. They were going to find Theo today, if not right now, and for the first time Will stopped to consider the impact that was going to have on their present situation.

Mission accomplished. Rhiannon would no doubt insist on driving Theo home, so there would be no point in him hanging around. He would go directly back to Atlanta.

Without her.

To a job that might or might not be his when he told them what had happened.

And he would have to tell them. His conscience wouldn't permit anything less. Regardless of what would happen with her, they still had the right to know that he'd done more than step over the line—he'd ignored it completely.

He peeked at her and wondered what she was thinking. Had her thoughts turned to their inevitable goodbye or was she so preoccupied with finding her mentor that she hadn't even considered what this would mean for them?

For the first time in his life he wished he had some sort of special psychic ability, because he would dearly love to know what was going on in her head. She had to have picked up on how he felt about her—he knew it. She was too perceptive to have missed the change. To have missed his revelation.

But did that affect her? Did she still want something casual? Was she still happy with the status quo? Or like her, had he become her exception?

Tension coiled in his muscles with every rotation of the tires against the pavement, with every mile that put them closer and closer to the end of this journey.

"This is the turnoff," Rhiannon said.

He smoothly wheeled the vehicle onto the small, rutted dirt road. "A mile in, right?"

"Yes." Her tense gaze scanned the road ahead and she nervously wound a lock of hair around her finger.

"He's here," she said. "I can feel him." She closed her eyes and concentrated. Her forehead knotted. "Euphoria and…fear."

Theo must have found the treasure, Will thought. But why was he afraid?

She gasped and leaned forward. "There's his car!"

He'd seen it. The car shot forward as he quickly accelerated down the lane, then jerked to a stop behind Theo's sedan. Rhiannon was out of the car and running toward the graveyard before he could even get the gearshift in Park. He snagged the orange juice he'd been carrying in the cooler from the back, then bolted from the car and ran after Rhiannon.

The cemetery was untended and overgrown with weeds and the weathered headstones—those of them that were still standing—listed sideways as though the effort to remain upright was almost too much to bear.

"Here!" she called, then dropped to her knees, disappearing from sight.

When Will reached her, she'd gathered the old man into her lap and was hugging him tightly. "Theo!" she cried. "Can you hear me? Are you okay?"

A weak smile faltered over his lips. "You know the answer to that, child."

She laughed, but it held a slightly hysterical edge. "Don't toy with me," she said. "Tell me what's wrong!"

"I fainted," he said, his voice low.

Will uncapped the juice and held the bottle up to the older man's mouth. "Drink," he said. "You need the sugar."

Rhiannon's eyes rounded with astonishment, then appreciation. "I wondered why you never drank that," she said absently.

"It wasn't for me." He helped Theo take another drink and was relieved to see a bit of color come into the older man's face. The panic he'd felt when he'd seen Theo unmoving in Rhiannon's arms had been eerily familiar. Terrifyingly so.

"Thank you, young man," Theo rasped. "That's definitely helped. I feel much better." His eager gaze swung to Rhiannon. "But did you see?" he asked her. "Look," he said meaningfully. "It's here, Rhi. *It's here.*"

Her gaze swung to the little headstone that marked Winston Watson's life. Will followed her gaze.

Winston Watson
July 2, 1861
February 19th, 1864
My son, my heart

Ah, Will thought. Theo had been right.

Rhiannon's astonished gaze found his, then Theo's. "Oh, Theo!"

"You've got to dig," he told her. "My tools are right there. I don't have the strength quite yet."

"We've got to get you to a hospital first," she said, her expression clouding. "We'll come back. We'll—"

"Rhiannon," he said. "I've been looking for this for most of my life and have endured years of ridicule over believing in its existence. Do you really think I'm going to leave now without it, when I'm so close? Would you really take this from me?"

"Theo—"

Will picked up the shovel. "Where do I dig?"

Theo's shrewd eyes caught and held his for a minute. He instantly knew what Rhiannon meant about Theo being much better at reading people than she was. He could practically feel the old man excavating his brain. After an interminable moment, Theo smiled up at him. "No time for proper introductions," he said. "We'll do that later." He gestured toward the metal detector. "Hand me that and I'll show you how to work it."

Less than thirty seconds over the grave, the little beeping noise that heralded a find went nuts and Rhiannon marked the ground with the shovel. Will tossed the metal detector aside, snatched the shovel out of her hand and put the blade in the ground. A satisfying thump sounded when the edge of the metal hit something solid.

Theo was able to sit up now. His eyes lit up.

Will quickly removed the earth, then hauled a small metal trunk from the soil. Anticipation chugged through his veins, pushing a smile onto his lips. He walked over and carefully put the box into Theo's withered hands.

The older man slid his fingers lovingly over the box, then withdrew a pocketknife from his khaki pants and used it to pry open the lid. A single torn page lay on top of a blue velvet sack, curiously preserved despite its age.

It was a page from the Bible, the book of Matthew, chapter six.

Theo's hands shook as he carefully handed it over to Rhiannon for her inspection, then he lifted the little pouch from the box.

Diamonds, emeralds, pearls, amethysts, rubies, some in settings, some not, emptied into his open hand and he chortled with glee. "Rhi," he said. "Do you see this?"

Her eyes sparkled with tears and were much prettier than any of the stones in Theo's palm, Will thought.

"I do," she choked out. "You found it." She paused. "And I found you."

"Ah, but I'm no treasure."

"To me you are," she said, wrapping her arm around his shoulders. "Now, let's go."

RHIANNON STEPPED OUT into the hall where Will had patiently waited for hours and an overwhelming sense of loss washed over her before she'd taken the first step in his direction.

It was over.

Though she'd known this moment was going to come and that every step closer to Theo had put her one step closer to their farewell scene, she nevertheless was not prepared for the anguish that felt as if it was shredding her soul.

This was precisely why she hadn't wanted this, Rhiannon thought. Love made you weak. Love made you stupid. And while she knew it was going to hurt now, she was taking a page out of Barney Fife's book and nipping it in the bud.

Time for a clean break.

It would be easier if she knew he wanted it, but…he didn't.

There had been many times in her life when she'd wished she couldn't feel other people's emotions, and last night, when she'd felt Will's attraction and affection shift into something more—something frighteningly significant—she had never been more touched.

Or more miserable.

She could not do this. Didn't want to feel it. She didn't want the roller coaster her parents had. Didn't want the misery that went along with the joy.

Her hands shook as she started toward him and she made herself smile.

Will pushed away from the wall as she approached. She could feel the wariness hovering around him. He knew what was coming. She probed his emotions and mentally gave a sigh of relief when she felt his resignation.

He would not fight.

Because, ultimately, he was a gentleman.

"You didn't have to wait," she said, spying her suitcase at his feet. "We've been back there for hours."

"I wanted to wait," he said. "Wanted to make sure he was going to be okay."

"He's almost fully recovered," she said. "He's been properly frightened, so I think he'll take better care of himself in the future." She smiled at him. "You were great back there. Without the orange juice and hard candy, he might not have been so lucky."

"But he's going to be fine?"

"Yes," she said. "Insulin dependent, much to his horror, but fine."

He released a pent-up breath. "That's a relief.

"You know I'll have to give Tad an update," he added, darting her an uncertain look. "Does Theo want him to know about the jewels?"

"Oh, yes." Rhiannon felt her smile widen. "Since he never believed they existed, Theo is making sure he doesn't get them."

Will chuckled. "Can't say that I blame him."

"Tad's in for another surprise, too," she said, chuckling. "Theo's made a few changes in his will that are certain to enrage his son. But the city council will be *very* happy."

"Serves him right," Will said with a grimace. "Greed makes people mean and stupid."

Rhiannon couldn't agree more. She crossed her arms over her chest, trying to hold it together. "So...you'll be heading back to Atlanta, right?"

His guarded gaze tangled with hers. "That's the plan. I'm assuming you'll be driving Theo back to Begonia?"

She nodded. "I will. We should be able to leave in the morning."

"Good."

The silence lengthened between them and she swallowed, preparing her heart for the break. "Thank you so much," she said shakily. "Particularly for letting me come along with you."

He merely shrugged and that smile she'd come to love tugged at the corner of his mouth. "It's a good thing you did. I couldn't have found him without you."

She nodded primly. "I told you I would be helpful."

"A helpful distraction," he corrected, and it seemed like a lifetime ago that they'd had this argument. "But a—" his gaze drifted over her mouth "—very welcome one," he finished, his voice curiously rusty.

And it cleaved her heart in two. Rhiannon actually thought she felt it break.

She grabbed her bag. "I'm actually going to go try and clean up a bit," she told him, gesturing toward the restroom. She leaned forward on her tippy toes and gave him an awkward, one-armed hug. His own familiar arms twined around her waist and squeezed.

"I'm going to duck in and tell Theo goodbye, if that's all right."

She nodded, swallowing thickly. "I'm sure he'd like that."

He hesitated. "Rhiannon—"

"It's okay," she said before he could finish. "The status quo, remember?"

His face was grim, but he nodded all the same. He walked around her, thankfully without saying goodbye—unbearable—and soon disappeared into Theo's room.

Rhiannon looked heavenward, hoping to stem the tears that suddenly stung the backs of her eyes.

"This is for the best," she muttered quietly. "Really."

Too bad she wasn't convinced.

14

"Ah, Mr. Forrester," Theo enthused as Will walked into his hospital room. "Rhiannon tells me you're the security expert my son hired to find me."

Will nodded, still trying to process what had just happened out in the hall. He'd known it was coming, of course. But knowing it and being prepared to accept it were two entirely different things.

But he didn't have a choice.

She didn't want him.

He'd known that going in and had been fine with it until his feelings had changed.

He nodded at the older gentleman, a sense of pride swelling in his chest that he'd actually helped him, that he hadn't been too late. A curious sense of redemption lightened his heart, making his shoulders feel a little less heavy. "I am, sir. But

I couldn't have found you without Rhiannon," he told him. "You really gave her quite a scare."

"I know and I truly regret that. I'd meant to call her later and let her know what I'd found, but I forgot to pack the charger on my cell phone and didn't want to call collect. That would have been rude."

Will started to point out that she would have been much happier with a collect phone call than being left in the dark, but didn't. What was the point? A thought pricked.

"What exactly was it that you did find?" he asked. "Rhiannon didn't think you knew about Mortimer's first family."

His faded eyes lit up. "A photograph of the three of them," Theo told him. "Tucked in one of Mortimer's old Bibles. It was probably the only one that Sophia never destroyed. On the back was the inscription 'My love and my heart.'"

Will inclined his head. "Very clever."

"It was worth it," Theo said, nodding. "Not because of the jewels, you understand, but because of the mystery and the history behind them."

"They're probably worth a fortune."

His eyes sparkled with mischief. "My son will salivate."

Theo pulled the little bag from beneath his hip

and emptied it onto the tray table, and Will was struck again by how lovely the jewels were.

The older man plucked a single diamond solitaire from the pile and held it up for Will's inspection. "Rhiannon will like this one."

He wouldn't know, Will thought, swallowing.

"When were you planning on telling her you're in love with her?"

Will blinked and his startled gaze found Theo's. He laughed uncomfortably. "I'm sorry?"

Theo's brows formed a bushy line. "Don't play coy. You're talking to a master. I'm sure you know that."

He did. "Does she know?"

"Probably."

Damn.

"Has she given you that rubbish about being content in her own company and how love makes people stupid and how she doesn't want any part of it?"

Will laughed at the distaste in Theo's voice. "In a manner of speaking, yes."

Theo frowned. "Hogwash," he retorted. "Rhi's so used to feeling the bad things that come along with love that she's afraid of it. She focuses so much on how the emotion tears one down that she's ignored how it can build you up." Theo's gaze burned with intensity. "It's the most powerful, humbling emotion of them all. She calls it the Boss."

She would, Will thought with another weak chuckle. He rubbed the back of his neck. "She knows where I am if she wants to find me," he said. "I'm not going to force her."

Theo grew thoughtful. "No, she'll have to come around on her own. But she will. She loves you, too, you know."

Hope flared pathetically. "She does?"

"Yes, she just hasn't fully admitted it herself yet. But when she does—" he pressed the solitaire into Will's hand "—you're going to need this."

Will's mouth opened, but he couldn't get any words to come out. He cleared his throat. "Sir, I can't accept this. It's—"

"It's yours. For *your* treasure."

Will shook his head and silently pocketed the stone. "I'll return it if you're wrong."

Theo merely smiled. "I'm never wrong."

He certainly hoped so, Will thought. He had a lot riding on the outcome.

"This is ridiculous," Elizabeth said two weeks later as Rhiannon continued to mope around her house. "You can't keep on like this. It isn't healthy."

"I know," she said glumly. "Love sucks. This is why I didn't want it."

"Whether you wanted it or not, Rhi, you've got it." She scratched Keno behind the ears. "I wish I could understand why you don't simply call him."

"Because that would change the status quo, the one I told him I wanted."

"But isn't he in love with you, too?" Elizabeth asked, seemingly confused.

Rhiannon flinched at the word. "I think so. Theo says definitely and has been lecturing me about how fabulous love can be and how I've just got a terrible attitude." She grimaced. "Can you believe he actually told me he was disappointed in me?"

Liz snorted. "Yes, I can. He's an opinionated old fart."

"He is not," Rhiannon admonished, even though her friend was only kidding. "He's just looking at everything through Sarah-colored glasses. He had a wonderful, healthy relationship with her and doesn't understand why I'm reluctant to hand my happiness over to another person."

"Your parents were pretty screwed up," Elizabeth conceded. "But that doesn't mean you and Will would be. History isn't doomed to repeat itself. Just look at how different Theo and Tad are."

Tad, Rhiannon thought sourly. She absolutely couldn't believe him. Now that his father had found the Watson treasure, he was determined to get back into her good graces in order to get her to convince Theo to leave the jewels to him.

Er…no. When hell freezes over. Idiot.

But it was an interesting turn of events, one she had to admit she was enjoying.

And to a degree, logically, Rhiannon knew Liz was right. But she was still terrified of falling in love only to fall on her face. To have it backfire. She didn't want to be one of those bitter old people she saw consumed with the one who had gotten away, or the one who had broken their heart, or the one who had died.

It inevitably ended in disaster, even in Theo's case, which she had, in a fit of irritation, pointed out. Her old friend's eyes had softened and he'd taken her hand. "Rhi, there isn't a day that goes by that I don't miss my Sarah. But even knowing what I feel now, I would walk through hell for the simple pleasure of getting to hold her hand again. You don't know what you're missing, and it pains me that you're too afraid to try."

Was he right? Rhiannon wondered. Was she being a coward? Was fear what was holding her back?

All she knew was that it felt as if a huge part of

her chest was missing and it was all she could do to put one unhappy foot in front of the other every day.

Initially she'd told herself it would get better. That time was the ultimate remedy. That she would be fine. But she was increasingly afraid that this hole in her middle was getting bigger, the edges becoming more raw. She'd looked at her toothpaste yesterday, thought of him and stood in her bathroom and squalled.

She was falling apart.

Will, undoubtedly, could put her back together. But would he keep her that way? Or would he break her heart? That was what terrified her. That was what held her back.

"Go to him," Elizabeth said. "Tell him you want to change the status quo." Her eyes twinkled. "Then tie him to the bed again."

Rhiannon blushed and rolled her eyes. "Why in the hell did I tell you that?"

"Because we don't have any secrets," her friend said. "Trust me, Rhi. This is right. Don't waste it."

"But what if it ends badly?"

"But what if it doesn't end at all?"

An image of Will, shorn hair, pale gray eyes and that endearing smile, rose in her mind's eye, tormenting her with its perfection. She ached for him. Still burned for him. Dreamed of him every night.

Rhiannon released a pent-up breath and stood. "Okay," she said. "Time to change the status quo."

And she was going to need to stop by the hardware store on her way out of town.

"RHIANNON PALMER just came into the office, asking about Will," McCann informed Payne and Flanagan with a huge smile on his face.

"What did you tell her?" Payne asked, his antennae twitching. Will had been a dozen kinds of miserable since his return and had owned up to the relationship with Rhiannon. That took courage, character and a sense of right and wrong that wasn't always a part of every man's makeup. And Payne could hardly criticize Will for it when each and every one of them was guilty of the exact same offense.

"I pointed her in the direction of his apartment, of course," McCann said. "She lives close enough that he can commute. If she'd been any farther out of Atlanta, though, I might not have been so helpful. We can't keep losing our help."

Jamie laughed. "What's she look like?"

"Not half as beautiful as my wife," McCann said

dutifully. "But she's gorgeous. Pretty eyes. Violet-blue."

"You going to write a poem about her?" Jamie teased.

"Go to hell," McCann said, chuckling.

"I hope this ends well," Payne said.

"She's here, isn't she?" Jamie pointed out.

"She is," McCann said. He frowned. "And she had a length of rope sticking out of her purse."

MAYBE HE'D GET A DOG, Will thought as he sat in his silent apartment. The television was on, tuned to a baseball game, but he hadn't so much as looked at the score. He needed a companion of some sort. Granted, the Triumvirate had realized he'd sunk into a terrible funk and had been trying to jar him out of it—and he genuinely appreciated it—but at the end of the day, both McCann and Payne went home to their wives, and Jamie went to his apartment to talk on the phone half the night with his.

Though Will had had work over the past couple of weeks, it had been nothing that had taken him out of Atlanta and nothing that had required he use more than half his brain.

Which was good, because the other half was always consumed with Rhiannon.

Even thinking her name made an ache build up his chest. Maybe she had it right about the Boss, he thought, chuckling at her nickname for love. Maybe love did make people stupid and reckless and weak. Maybe she'd been onto something with her status quo.

And maybe this was all bullshit and he was just miserable, Will thought, rubbing the bridge of his nose.

But it had to get better. He couldn't possibly feel like this forever. As if he'd left a part of himself in Virginia and it had migrated south to Begonia, Georgia.

A brisk knock sounded at his door, which was odd because McCann and Flanagan typically just walked in. Must be Payne, Will thought, pushing up from his recliner and making his way to the door. He pulled it open and drew up short.

Rhiannon.

He blinked, wondering if his pathetic imagination was playing tricks on him.

"Hi, Will," she said, smiling tentatively. "Are you busy?"

He cleared his throat and marveled at the joy just looking at her made him feel. He felt a smile drift over his lips and hoped he didn't look like a fool.

But he was her fool.

"No," he said, opening the door wider. "Come in."

She walked by him, bringing the scent of

oranges with her, and his mouth instantly watered. She wore a red sleeveless top and another one of those little flippy skirts that had made it so easy to take her wherever he'd wanted. If she didn't have on any panties, he was going to have a stroke.

She settled on the side of his couch and waited for him to resume his spot in his recliner before she finally spoke.

"How have you been?"

"You read me the minute I opened the door," he said. "I'm sure you know."

"Depressed, lonely, miserable?" she asked, wincing.

He chuckled darkly. "That about sums it up."

"I can help you with that," she said, and there was a hint of uncertainty behind the bravado, which alerted him to how much this was costing her.

But it had to be her move. And he'd be a liar if he said he wasn't enjoying watching her make it.

He quirked a brow. "You can?"

She lifted her chin. "Definitely. And I would be more than willing to distract you, as well. It's just part of the services I offer."

His lips twitched. "What about the status quo?" he asked, letting her know that this wasn't going to be on some trial basis. She had to give him all or nothing. Anything less would result in him being in a padded room devoid of sharp objects.

She shrugged as though it didn't matter. "Time to change it, don't you think?"

"I was ready to change it before we left Virginia."

She smiled sadly. "I was afraid, Will. But I'm trying to be brave now. Is that going to count for anything?"

"You off your game?" he asked. "Surely you know the answer to that already."

She smiled and ducked her head. "I have an idea."

"Then why are you still sitting over there?"

She launched herself at him. The breath whooshed out of his lungs and into her mouth and her fingers were suddenly in his hair, kneading his scalp, then lovingly—reverently—tracing the lines of his face.

"I've missed you so much," she said, straddling him.

Will slid his palms over her bare ass and smiled against her lips. "No panties."

"No point in wearing them around you." She kissed him again, pressing her sweet breasts against his chest, and it took all the strength he possessed to push her back. He had to do something first.

"I've got something for you," he said, reaching into his pocket. He withdrew the ring and held it up for her inspection.

Her eyes rounded and she gasped. "Will." She looked closer. "That looks awfully familiar. Where have I—" Another sharp inhalation. "The Watson treasure? But how did you— Theo," she said meaningfully.

"He gave it to me for you," he said. "Because he wasn't the only person who found his treasure on that trip. I did, too. I'm in love with you, Rhiannon. And I don't care if it scares the hell out of you." He chuckled softly. "Welcome to my world."

"Are you going to put it on my hand?" she asked.

His chest felt as if it would explode with pride. "Happily."

She admired the stone on her finger. "I've got something for your hand, too," she said, and there was a hint of something wicked in her smile. She reached into her purse and pulled out a length of rope, then wagged it at him significantly.

He laughed, astonished, and offered his wrist. "Bind me," he said. Because he was always going to be her love slave.

She wrapped the rope around his wrist, then around her own and held it up meaningfully. "We're bound."

"Ah." Will sighed as he freed himself from his jeans and pushed into her. *Home,* he thought. "I like this better." He nuzzled her neck. "It's got endless possibilities."

She laughed. "I didn't know you were psychic."

"I knew you'd be back, didn't I?"

"That confident, were you?"

"No," he corrected. "Just hopeful…."

* * * * *

HOT-BLOODED

BY
KAREN FOLEY

All the characters in this book have no existence outside the imagination of
the author, and have no relation whatsoever to anyone bearing the same name
or names. They are not even distantly inspired by any individual known or
unknown to the author, and all the incidents are pure invention.

First published in Great Britain 2011
by Mills & Boon, an imprint of Harlequin (UK) Limited,
Eton House, 18-24 Paradise Road, Richmond, Surrey TW9 1SR

© Karen Foley 2010

ISBN: 978 0 263 88067 0

14-0611

Harlequin (UK) policy is to use papers that are natural, renewable and
recyclable products and made from wood grown in sustainable forests. The
logging and manufacturing processes conform to the legal environmental
regulations of the country of origin.

Printed and bound in Spain
by Blackprint CPI, Barcelona

For my friends and colleagues, Storme, Greta,
Kelly, and Gladys—the fearless women
who have volunteered to serve and sacrifice.
You are amazing. Thank you for your support!

Dear Reader,

I was so excited when my editor proposed the It Takes a Hero series. What could be better than a story that involves a tough, capable, totally hot guy in a uniform? Especially when he's willing to put everything—including his heart and his life—on the line?

My day job with the Department of Defense provides me with some unique opportunities to work alongside our men and women in uniform, including those who take voluntary deployments to Iraq and Afghanistan. While I've never found the courage to do this myself, several of my female colleagues have done so. For the most part, these women have been assigned to the larger bases with nice living quarters, fitness centers, etc. But I couldn't help thinking…what would happen if a woman suddenly found herself in a remote outpost that contained none of these amenities? What if she had to depend on a tough, capable, irresistibly sexy guy for everything? And what if he found himself tempted to throw protocol and training out the window in order to meet her *every* need?

I hope you enjoy Chase and Elena's story…and that it meets *your* every reading need.

Enjoy!

Karen

Prologue

Anbar Province, Iraq

THE SPIT of machine-gun fire and the acrid stench of
burning oil and scorched metal filled the air. First Sergeant Chase McCormick surveyed the battle through
a pair of high-optic binoculars from his perch atop an
armored Humvee. He and his special ops team had just
extracted a pair of Marine snipers from a site twenty
miles away when they'd received reports of a large U.S.
supply convoy traveling through the dangerous Anbar
province. They'd immediately made a detour to intercept the convoy and escort them through the region, but
they'd arrived too late.

Insurgents, hidden in an orchard on one side of the
dusty road and in a crudely dug trench on the other, had
attacked the convoy, which was now taking heavy fire
from both sides. Chase had to give the truck drivers
credit; along with their security detail, they were some
tough sons of bitches and were holding their own.

Despite the fact the insurgents had managed to destroy
two Humvees and the lead supply truck, their small-
arms fire was mostly inaccurate and ineffectual. Chase

had seen enough combat to know that this battle would be over shortly, but the entire scenario had him pissed off on a level so deep that he had to shut that part of himself down or risk losing his focus on the immediate mission.

While Al-Qaeda had, for the most part, been neutralized in the Anbar province, there were still pockets of rebellion and several attacks on the U.S. troops had occurred in recent weeks. Chase had received intel reports that the insurgents were hiding twenty miles to the north, where the sniper team had been conducting reconnaissance for the past five days. But in reality they had been here, digging their damned trenches and stockpiling their IEDs and rocket-propelled grenades.

As he watched, a driver exited one of the supply vehicles. Chase saw she was female, and she was aiming her weapon at the tree line, focused on some hidden target that even Chase couldn't see. In the next instant a second soldier, who up until that moment had been manning a fifty-caliber gun mounted on top of one of the convoy's gun trucks, abruptly abandoned his position and swung to the ground, apparently intent on intercepting and protecting the woman.

"Son of a bitch," Chase muttered beneath his breath, and swung his gun around to cover the man. Didn't he realize his best option for protecting the girl was to stay with his weapon?

As the soldier sprinted toward the woman, he took a direct hit from the assailant hidden in the trees, and went down on his knees before pitching face forward onto the ground. Chase swept the tree line with machine-gun fire, but was forced to stop when the female soldier stepped directly into his sights. She shouldered her weapon and

Get 2 books Free!
Plus, receive a FREE mystery gift

If you have enjoyed reading this Blaze romance story, then why not take advantage of this FREE book offer and we'll send you two more titles from this series absolutely FREE!

Accepting your FREE books and FREE mystery gift places you under no obligation to buy anything.

As a member of the Mills & Boon Book Club™ you'll receive your favourite Series books up to 2 months ahead of the shops, plus all these exclusive benefits:

- FREE home delivery
- Exclusive offers and our monthly newsletter
- Membership to our special rewards programme

We hope that after receiving your free books you'll want to remain a member. But the choice is yours. So why not give us a go. You'll be glad you did!

Visit www.millsandboon.co.uk for the latest news and offers.

Mrs/Miss/Ms/Mr .... Initials ....

BLOCK CAPITALS PLEASE

Surname ....

Address ....

....

....

.... Postcode ....

Email ....

K1FIA

NO STAMP
NEEDED!

MILLS
& BOON®
Book Club

FREE BOOK OFFER
FREEPOST NAT 10298
RICHMOND
TW9 1BR

bent to drag the wounded man to safety, and Chase reluctantly admired her guts even as he cursed her lack of self-preservation. She was completely vulnerable, and it seemed he was the only one who realized it.

Well, not the only one.

A shadow moved in the trees behind her, but before he could lock his sights on the target, the girl blocked his shot. Cursing, he shifted to a better position, when he saw the flash of a muzzle blast from the trees. The female soldier jerked once and then fell forward, covering the other soldier's body with her own and providing Chase with an unobstructed view of where the insurgent hid.

Only the man was no longer there.

Peering through the scope on his gun, Chase surveyed the area and saw the target lying in the grass beside a tree. He'd taken a direct hit, and Chase could see that he no longer posed a threat to anyone. He didn't need to guess who had eliminated the target; only the sniper team on the far ridge could have made such a difficult shot.

He swept his rifle scope over the two fallen soldiers to see that the female had risen to her knees. After briefly examining a wound to her shoulder, she bent over and began doggedly dragging her unconscious buddy across the ground to the relative safety of the trucks. Chase continued to provide cover, although he knew the sniper team was probably covering her, as well.

As much as he admired the woman for her bravery, Chase could have cheerfully shaken her. If she hadn't left the safety of her truck, then the gunner wouldn't have felt the need to abandon his own post in order to protect her, and neither of them would now be injured.

Women. He snorted in disgust.

He came from a long and distinguished line of military service, but there was one main reason he'd opted to join the Marine Corps special-operations command: they didn't allow females into their ranks.

He'd always maintained that women had no place in combat, an opinion that had less to do with their ability to do the job and more to do with the inability of their male counterparts to handle them doing the job. He'd seen hardened soldiers go soft and throw years of training and protocol out the window in order to protect a female soldier, or help her to complete a task that she could have handled on her own.

He had no idea if the gunner and the female soldier knew each other, but suspected there was some kind of romantic involvement. There usually was. The only thing worse than fighting alongside a female was fighting alongside one that you were also screwing, especially if you were fool enough to let it become about more than just sex. Nothing worse than letting a woman get under your skin.

The behavior he'd just witnessed only reinforced his belief that women shouldn't be placed in combat situations. He was convinced that if the female soldier had been a man, the gunner never would have abandoned his post. He'd have used his turret gun to cover her, the way he'd been trained to do.

Chase couldn't imagine losing control simply because a soldier was female. He prided himself on his ability to remain focused and make sound decisions, even under adverse conditions. If there was one thing he was sure of, it was that he'd never let a woman make him drop his guard on the battlefield. Or in the bedroom.

1

"IF YOU ASK ME, sex is overrated. I'll admit that it's pleasant, but earth-shattering? Not even close. Frankly, I don't know what all the fuss is about." Elena de la Vega arched a challenging eyebrow at her sister before taking a sip of her white wine.

"That's because you haven't had sex with the right guy," Carmen replied with a secretive gleam in her eyes. "Yet."

"Oh, c'mon," Elena scoffed, telling herself she didn't feel the tiniest bit jealous of the self-satisfied smile on Carmen's face. "Am I really supposed to believe that every time you and Nick get it on, he makes your toes curl with lust?"

Carmen set her martini down and leaned across the small table they shared, glancing quickly around to ensure none of the other patrons at the cozy sidewalk café could overhear their conversation. "Let's just say that Nick has a talent for making each time seem like the first time. You know, incredibly arousing. Exciting. Like I'm the hottest thing he's ever laid eyes on. The way he looks at me, and the things he does " Her expression took on a dreamy quality.

Elena rolled her eyes. "Yeah, well, I'll take your word for it. Nick may be great in bed, but he's also incredibly jealous. I couldn't be with a guy like that."

Carmen's smile grew wider. "Nick just wants other guys to know I'm with him. So what if he glowers a little bit, or likes to stay close to me when we're out together? At least he doesn't ignore me. I'm a happy, satisfied woman. Can you say the same?"

Elena thought of her own boyfriend, Larry, and a small sigh escaped her. He wasn't physically impressive, like Carmen's Nick was, but he was smart and considerate. They'd worked in the same office together for three years and Elena had a lot of respect for him. Larry was a conscientious man who took his job as a cost auditor for the Defense Procurement Agency seriously. He was brilliant when it came to numbers. Elena told herself again that she didn't mind if he worked long hours, or that he chose to spend most Saturdays in the office rather than with her. He treated her well, and when they did go out, he was a pleasant companion. Their typical routine was to catch a movie or a bite to eat, and then return to her apartment where he could be counted on to give her a very nice orgasm. Not an earth-shattering, body-clenching, toe-curling orgasm, but a nice one all the same.

"Larry is reliable," she finally said, but didn't meet her sister's knowing eyes. Instead, she trailed the tip of her finger around the edge of her wineglass. "I know what to expect with Larry. We get together on Wednesday and Saturday nights, and if our love life is a little…predictable, then who I am to complain?" She raised her gaze to Carmen's. "I actually prefer it that way."

"What way?" asked Carmen archly. "Flat on your back, making all the right noises so that he feels like a real man, while you just wish he'd hurry up and finish?"

Elena stared at her sister, amazed. "How did—? No, wait. It isn't like that."

"Isn't it? Don't forget, you're the one who dubbed him Old Faithful. As in…he's predictable and lasts less than two minutes."

Elena groaned and took a hefty swig of her wine. "That's not fair. I was a little tipsy that night and said more than I should have. You're taking it out of context. I dubbed him Old Faithful because he's, well, dependable. Trustworthy. *Faithful.* All good traits for a man to have."

"Or a dog," Carmen muttered. Then, seeing Elena's expression, she was instantly contrite. "I agree with you. Absolutely. Those are all good qualities for a man to have, but they shouldn't be his only qualities. He should make your insides turn to mush and your pulse quicken just thinking about him." Her expression grew earnest. "Please tell me you're not going to marry this guy, Elena. You deserve so much more. Every woman should have one great passion in her life. Don't settle for mediocrity."

"He hasn't asked me to marry him yet," Elena grumbled. "And I said our love life is predictable, not mediocre."

"Oh, come on," Carmen scoffed, and sat back in her chair. "Your boyfriend is boring. Your *life* is boring. When was the last time you did something exciting?

Something that made your heart pound and your mouth go dry?" She leaned forward again. "You're almost thirty, Elena, and yet you've never done any of the wacky things that most people do when they're in their twenties. Nick and I had sex on the roof of his building last night, under the stars. It was amazing."

"Nick's rooftop garden is amazing," Elena said drily, ignoring her sister's jabs. "I'm sure you're not the first girl he's brought up there."

Carmen narrowed her eyes. "So what if I'm not the first? I'll be the last."

Elena shrugged. "Well, it's your heart. Risk it if you want to."

"See? That's my whole point. You're not willing to take any risks, Elena. You'd rather settle for safe and boring than take a chance on something exciting. Something that could change your life." She shook her head in mock sadness. "You have no idea what you're missing."

Elena dabbed her mouth with her linen napkin before folding it neatly beside her plate, silently counting to ten. She refused to be baited.

"I don't feel as if I'm settling," she finally said, hoping that she sounded convincing. "And not everyone wants that kind of excitement in their life, Carmen. I've watched what great passion has done to Mom and Dad, and even to you." She fished in her pocketbook for some money and carefully placed several bills on the table. "I don't want that kind of chaos in my life. Larry is kind and considerate and I always know exactly what to expect from him. I'm happy with what I have." Seeing the disbelief on her sister's face, she stood up. "Really, I am. Look, I have to go. Thanks for lunch. I'll call you tomorrow."

As she walked to her car, Elena refused to feel guilty for prematurely ending their lunch. The whole thing was Carmen's fault, anyway. It seemed every time they got together, the conversation turned to Elena's love life. Neither of her two sisters could understand Larry's appeal, but they didn't know him the way Elena did. Admittedly, he wasn't adventurous in bed, but so what? Not everyone was into *that kinky stuff,* as Larry put it. And any therapist worth his salt would tell you that a successful relationship should be based on trust and mutual respect. Not sex.

Never sex.

All she had to do was look at her family for proof. Given the choice between a life of calm predictability or the blood-pounding, roof-raising drama that seemed to accompany her parents and her siblings wherever they went, Elena preferred the former.

She always would.

Even so, her sister's words rankled, partly because Elena knew that on some level, they were true. But she'd chosen her path with careful deliberation. Sure, there were times when she felt that she was meant for something bigger and more exciting, but she simply had to spend time with her parents and sisters to remember exactly why she'd opted for the conventional life she now led.

Her family might boast about the hot, Spanish blood that flowed through their veins, claiming it was the reason for their unpredictable and often volatile behavior, but Elena wanted no part of it. She'd watched her parents divorce and remarry each other twice; she'd spent countless nights with each of her sisters, lending both an ear and a shoulder as they'd wept and wailed about the failure of yet another relationship. Her younger sister, Sarita, actually enjoyed dating two, even three men at a time and then watching the fireworks when they found out about each other. That kind of excitement she could do without.

Granted, Nick Belcastro seemed like a decent guy, and he was both gorgeous and financially independent, but Elena wondered how long he'd tolerate Carmen's mood swings before he decided he'd had enough.

Elena glanced at her watch as she pulled out of the restaurant parking lot. Nearly one-thirty. Was Larry still at the office? They had plans to go out to dinner and a movie later on, but Elena suddenly had an urge to see him, if only to reassure herself that he wasn't as mediocre as Carmen claimed. She could picture him in his office, surrounded by papers, with his hair sticking up from where he'd combed his fingers through it in frustration. Deciding he could use a break, she swung the car in the direction of the federal building where they both worked. Even if he'd already left, there was some paperwork she could collect from her own office and bring home with her.

Twenty minutes later, Elena passed through the security checkpoint and walked through the darkened corridors toward Larry's office. The Defense Procurement Agency oversaw the purchase and delivery of goods and services for the military. Elena and Larry worked in the agency's headquarters, an impressive four-story structure of limestone and sleek marble, located on the outskirts of Washington, D.C.

After obtaining her law degree, Elena had spent the first few years of her career negotiating and administering contracts for the military, everything from nuts and bolts to major weapons systems. She was good at what she did. So good that she'd been offered a promotion to the DPA's legal department, writing policy and procedure manuals for the agency's contracting center. There was very little that Elena didn't know about contracting, both from an administrative and a legal perspective.

Her parents might be disappointed that she hadn't chosen to use her law degree in litigation, but striding up and down a courtroom while making impassioned speeches to a judge and jury held little appeal for Elena. Nope, she enjoyed researching regulations and statutes, and then applying them to how the agency did business. She didn't mind sitting through oversight meetings and briefing senior leadership on changes in federal procurement policy. She told herself yet again that what she did mattered. She was making a difference.

Elena stopped briefly at the mailroom and checked her box, flipping through the assorted envelopes and papers for anything that might require her immediate attention. Most of the mail was routine correspondence, including a letter from the Director's office requesting civilian volunteers—especially those with contracts and legal experience—to work in Iraq for six months, negotiating and monitoring the defense contracts there. According to the memo, such volunteer deployments were the agency's number-one mission.

Elena snorted. As if *that* would ever happen. This was the third such call for volunteers in as many months, and while most folks who did volunteer had only positive things to say about their deployment experience, Elena couldn't imagine working in Iraq or Afghanistan. While she had an extensive background negotiating military contracts, the agency couldn't pay her enough money to go over there. She disliked being hot, and having mortars lobbed at her wasn't a huge incentive, either.

Carrying her mail in one hand, she walked toward Larry's office. His door was closed and she had a moment's regret that she'd missed him, when she saw a shadow pass beneath the crack at the bottom. Just then, a crash sounded from behind the closed door and Elena heard Larry give a pained groan.

"Larry!" She thrust the door open so hard that it slammed against the wall, and then she stood there, speechless at the sight that greeted her.

Larry stood at the side of his desk with his pants and underwear crumpled around his ankles, his shirt open and flapping loosely around his pale buttocks and thighs. Sprawled facedown across his desk was a woman, her black skirt pushed up around her waist. Her legs were splayed wide, the stiletto heels on her shoes lending them extra length. Larry gripped the woman's hips as she bent forward over the desk, thrusting himself into her. His head was thrown back and the cords in his neck stood out in a way that Elena had never seen when he'd been with *her*.

The crash she'd heard had been Larry's alabaster paperweight falling to the floor as the woman swept it from the surface of the desk in her frenzy. The paperweight Elena had given to him on Valentine's Day last year.

In the instant before they both turned toward her, Elena recognized the other woman as one of the new interns they'd hired in the legal department. Her reddish hair fell forward over her face, and her eyes were hazy with pleasure. Her full lips were parted and moist as she gripped the edges of the desk and arched her back to give Larry better access. When she raised herself to look toward the door, Elena saw her pink blouse was open at the front and her bra was pulled down below her breasts, which had left a damp mark on the glossy veneer of the desk.

For a moment, the three of them stared at each other. Larry's harsh breathing was the only sound that broke the stunned silence, until he muttered an oath and snatched himself from the woman's body.

Elena didn't wait to see more. She turned on her heel and walked blindly back the way she'd come, unable to dispel the erotic images she'd just witnessed. She tried to recall when the woman—Claire—had first begun working at the agency. Five months ago, maybe? Six? How long had she and Larry been having an affair? Was this what he did every Saturday when he told her he was going into the office?

"Elena, *wait.*"

Larry trotted down the corridor after her, shoving his shirt into his waistband. Elena stopped and watched him approach, noting his flushed features and disheveled hair. She'd always thought he was attractive, but now all she could see were his white legs and thin buttocks, pumping furiously into another woman.

"What do you want, Larry?" She glanced at her watch, ignoring how her hand trembled. "I really can't stay. I only came by because I thought you needed a break from work." She gave a bitter laugh. "Little did I know."

Larry swiped a hand through his hair, looking both embarrassed and defiant. "You should have called. You always call first."

Elena gaped at him. "I should have *called?* Excuse me, but I work here, too. I don't need your permission to come by the office after hours, Larry." She ran a scathing eye over him. "It figures that the first time I do, this is what I find. You, in a sweaty clutch with the office intern. It's so cliché that it's actually pathetic. What if someone else had seen you? You both could be fired for this."

"I think I'm in love with her," he blurted, then swiped a hand across his face. "I mean, I know I'm in love with her. I *am* in love with her."

Elena's mouth fell open, but no words came out. She stared at him, speechless.

"I'm sorry," he muttered, clearly uncomfortable. "I didn't mean for you to find us—to find out like this." He rubbed the back of his neck and glanced toward his office where he'd left Claire. "It's just that—"

"What?" Elena asked sarcastically. "I wasn't willing to spread myself across your desk? To fulfill your naughty little fantasies? Maybe I would have done it, Larry. Maybe all you had to do was ask, but now you'll never know what I might have done, will you?"

To Elena's dismay, Larry's face grew tight. "I never asked, because I already knew what the answer would be. You're not exactly Miss Excitement."

"What is that supposed to mean?" Elena gasped, but she had a sinking feeling that she already knew. His words sounded a little too much like the conversation she'd had with her sister earlier that day.

"I don't want to hurt you more than I already have," Larry began, "but it wasn't until I met Claire that I realized what I'd been missing with you."

Elena's eyebrows flew up. *What?* The numbness that had enveloped her when she'd first walked into Larry's office was rapidly vanishing, to be replaced with a slow, simmering anger.

"Oh, and what would that be?" she asked sweetly. "I don't seem to recall that you were missing out on anything. You had sex every week—and that was just with me. I always paid my own way when we went out. I never objected if you wanted to play golf with the guys, or head up to Atlantic City for a weekend. I never demanded anything of you, Larry, and I was always there when you wanted me. Basically, you had a perfect relationship."

Larry missed the sharp edge beneath the silken veil of her words. "Yeah, it was a perfect relationship all right. Perfectly boring."

"Boring? You think I'm boring?"

Larry made a sound of frustration. "No, that's not what I said, but since you brought it up, then yes! I think you're boring. Okay? Are you happy now? I said it!"

"Oh. My. God." Elena stared at him in disbelief. "You're serious."

Didn't he realize that in their relationship *he* was the boring one? He was the stereotypical accountant—detailed, meticulous and not given to extravagance or grand gestures. He was the kind of guy that you'd pass on the street and never look at twice. He appealed to her because he was ordinary and because she always knew what to expect from him. At least, she amended silently, she'd thought she always knew what to expect. And now, to find out that he thought *she* was boring!

"Listen, Elena, you're a beautiful woman, but you're too set in your ways. You need to be a little more flexible. You need to live a little."

Elena arched an eyebrow. "It certainly appears your

new girlfriend is flexible. Is that what this is all about, Larry? Having sex in forbidden places?"

Larry's face turned a ruddy shade. "No, of course not. But it does have something to do with spontaneity. Face it, Elena. Your entire life is about order and routine. You're a creature of habit, and you hate surprises. You're about as capable of spontaneity as a fish is of flying."

Later, Elena would not be sure what made her do it. She only knew that in that particular moment, the most important thing in the world was to prove Larry wrong. To show him irrefutable proof that she was as capable of being spontaneous and exciting as the next person. She snatched the director's memorandum from the sheaf of mail she clutched in her hand and waved it beneath Larry's nose.

"Oh, yeah? Well, here's a little bit of spontaneity for you. I've decided to do a six-month deployment to Iraq."

To her dismay, Larry's eyebrows flew up, and he gave a snort of disbelieving laughter. "Oh, come on. We both know you're bluffing. When did you decide this? Two seconds ago? We both know you'd never volunteer to go over there. You may not be a spur-of-the-moment girl, but you're not stupid, either. Besides, you enjoy your creature comforts just a little too much to go to Iraq for six months. I can't picture you sharing a B-hut with twenty other women, or eating in a chow hall every night."

"Oh, really?" Elena tossed her head. "Well, believe it or not, I'm going. And I understand there are battalions of healthy, young, hard-bodied soldiers who would do *anything* to keep me safe. In fact, I'm sure my deployment will be rewarding on many different levels."

To her satisfaction, Larry no longer looked quite so skeptical. "You're kidding, right? That's your damned sisters talking. You'd never actually do it."

Elena gave him a sweet smile. "Watch me," she purred, and turned on her heel and walked away.

2

Kuwait City, six weeks later

THWAP, THWAP, thwap.

The steady sound of helicopter blades cut through the air overhead, but Elena hardly noticed the noise. After three days spent sitting in a converted hangar alongside the U.S. military airstrip in Kuwait City, she'd become well accustomed to the sound of both helicopters and jets as they came in and then left again. The kicker was she should have been on one of those helicopters long before now.

She'd seen her orders; she was going to the Green Zone in Baghdad, where she would try to clean up the colossal mess that had been made of the military contracts there. She'd heard countless stories about how good the quality of life was in the Zone, and she'd actually begun looking forward to her deployment. In the six weeks since she'd volunteered to come to Iraq, she'd had plenty of opportunity to examine her life and had concluded that both Carmen and Larry were right—it was boring.

But that was all about to change. She was shaking things up in a big way. She'd embarked on an adventure and made a promise to herself to embrace each new and exciting opportunity as it came her way, no matter what. Now she stared at the woman holding the clipboard that contained her new orders, and silently counted to ten, willing herself to control her rising temper.

"What do you mean they've changed my assignment?" she demanded in dismay. "I've been sitting in this hangar for three days, waiting for a sandstorm to subside so that I can fly to Baghdad, Iraq. As in the Green Zone, complete with fitness center, modern plumbing and a fast-food burger joint. That's what I signed up for—" she broke off to glance at the front of the woman's uniform "—Major Dumfries. Not some remote outpost in northern Afghanistan."

The other woman didn't even have the grace to look apologetic. Instead, she met Elena's gaze unflinchingly. "Your deployment paperwork clearly states that your assignment can change at any time, depending on need. The Defense Procurement Agency has indicated they now need you in Afghanistan, and *you* need to be flexible, ma'am." She glanced again at the clipboard. "We have a helicopter departing for the outpost at 0600 hours tomorrow morning. I'll see you back here at the airstrip then."

Elena's mouth fell open. "Wait! That's it? Just like that, I'm now going to some hellhole in Afghanistan? How can you do this? Is it even legal?"

Major Dumfries smiled. "I don't make the assignments, ma'am. I just make sure the folks get there in one piece."

Elena took a deep breath and reminded herself yet

again that this was an adventure—a new opportunity—and she would embrace it wholeheartedly. She pasted a smile on her face.

"Fine. I'll go to this outpost." Reaching down, she lifted her rucksack onto one shoulder and then hefted her two duffel bags with as much dignity as she could manage, considering they weighed about a gazillion pounds each. She started to turn away, and then swung back toward the Major. "Just out of curiosity, what kind of facilities do they have at this place?"

"Facilities?" The other woman's eyebrow arched.

"Yes. As in dining hall, fitness center, recreation center…please tell me this outpost *has facilities*."

Major Dumfries's mouth twitched. "I understand they're still in the process of improving the post, but they do have toilets and showers."

Elena stared at her. "What about a dining hall? They must have that, right?"

"I believe there is a dining facility, yes."

Elena drew in a deep breath. "Are there any other civilians at this outpost?"

"Several, as a matter of fact."

Elena supposed she should be grateful for that. If there were other civilians at the outpost, then the living conditions couldn't be too primitive. But she'd heard horror stories about some of the forward operating bases located on the northern and eastern perimeters of Afghanistan, particularly in regards to their vulnerability. She hadn't planned on going to an area that was potentially dangerous. After all, she wasn't a soldier. She had no combat training. She was a contracts geek—a desk jockey, for Pete's sake. Her job was to meet with the defense contractors who were doing work on the various military bases and to negotiate terms and conditions for performance of that work. Aside from ensuring that the soldiers had the facilities and equipment they needed to perform their jobs, she had no military background.

"I've heard some of these outlying bases come under frequent attack by the Taliban," she ventured. "Is that the case with this particular base?"

Major Dumfries gave her a reassuring smile. "You'll be in safe hands, ma'am. We haven't lost a civilian yet. There's a special-operations detachment based there. They'll keep you safe."

Elena swiped a hand across her eyes. "I need a drink."

She wasn't aware she'd muttered the words aloud until she saw the amusement in the other woman's eyes. "Alcohol is prohibited in Kuwait City, ma'am."

"Great," she replied. "I can't even have a last drink before I leave civilization."

Major Dumfries tucked the clipboard under her arm and leaned forward, glancing around to ensure they wouldn't be overheard. "This is strictly off the record, but sometimes the U.S. embassy personnel have access to alcohol. I understand they're having a small send-off tonight over at the hotel for some of their aides who are returning to the States."

A party? At the hotel? That was the first positive bit of news she'd had since arriving in Kuwait City three days earlier. Since then, it seemed she'd done nothing but schlep her gear back and forth between the hotel and the military airstrip, waiting for transportation to her final destination. Which was supposed to be the Green Zone, not some scary outpost in eastern Afghanistan.

Oh, yeah, she definitely needed a drink.

"Do I need an invitation to get in?"

"No, ma'am. Just take the elevator up to the concierge level at 2000 hours and follow the noise. Nobody will even notice you're there. But don't overdo it. The only thing worse than flying in a helicopter is flying in one with a hangover."

ELENA STEPPED OUT of the elevator and paused. Major Dumfries had been right about the noise; she could hear the festivities from down the hall, and it sounded as if the party was in full swing. She hesitated, hoping she'd dressed appropriately. Nothing worse than standing out in a crowd when all she wanted to do was blend in. While she'd brought five sets of agency-issued uniforms with her, she'd been restricted on how much civilian clothing she could bring from home, and had settled on several pairs of pants and tops, and some comfortable workout gear. The crimson blouse she'd chosen to wear with her jeans wasn't dressy, but it would have to do. She wore her dark hair loose around her shoulders, allowing it to wave naturally around her face, and had opted for just a touch of mascara and some lipstick.

She drew in a deep breath and smoothed her palms over the seat of her jeans. Crashing a party of strangers was totally out of character for her, not to mention bad manners. She wasn't sure she had the courage to go through with it.

But then she remembered that by this time tomorrow, she'd be hundreds of miles away from here and nobody would even remember—or care—that she'd been at this party. She'd never even see these people again. Really, what did she have to lose? This might be the last night she had to enjoy herself for the next six months.

Straightening her spine, she followed the sound of music and laughter. If this was going to be her last night in civilization, she was going to make it one to remember.

As soon as she stepped into the function room, Elena realized she needn't have worried. There were dozens of people inside, all of them talking or laughing together in small groups, and none of them paid her any attention. Several even smiled at her in a friendly, offhand manner. The lights had been dimmed to a pleasant glow, and a bar had been set up along one wall. The music was loud and upbeat, and a cloud of cigarette smoke hung suspended near the ceiling. Most of the people were men of varying ages and although all of them wore casual clothing, it wasn't difficult for Elena to distinguish the active-duty military from the civilians. If their haircuts didn't set them apart, their physical conditioning did.

Elena skirted the crowd and sidled over to the bar, where bottles of alcohol were lined up alongside plastic cups and an ice bucket. When she didn't see a bartender, she looked around, uncertain.

"It's an open bar, hon, so help yourself."

Elena turned to see a woman approach the bar beside her and liberally pour herself a glass of white wine from an uncorked bottle. She was older than Elena, probably in her forties.

"Are you sure? I mean, who provided all of this?"

The woman smiled and gave Elena a friendly wink. "You know the old adage—don't ask, don't tell. All I can say is drink up, because you never know when we'll have this opportunity again."

That was the truth, Elena thought bleakly. Just thinking about what lay in store for her in the days and weeks ahead made her unaccountably homesick for her cozy little apartment back home. Despite the fact that she'd volunteered for this deployment, right now she couldn't think of a single good reason for being here. Most people who volunteered did so because they had some patriotic calling or felt the need to support the troops in some way. Others did it for the money, which was in itself a huge incentive. But not her.

Nope.

She'd come because she'd had something to prove. Because she'd wanted everyone—her sister and cheating ex-boyfriend included—to see that she could be spontaneous and adventurous. She'd wanted to kick-start her life back into gear, but right now she just felt out of place and oddly alone, even in the midst of the party. She'd been excited about going to Baghdad, knowing she'd be just one of hundreds of civilians, and that the quality of life there was pretty good. But the prospect of spending six months at a remote outpost in the wilds of Afghanistan was another matter altogether. Quite frankly, it scared the hell out of her. She recalled Major Dumfries' assurance that they hadn't lost a civilian yet, but found little comfort in her words.

"I haven't seen you around before," the woman continued. "Where are you stationed?"

"Oh, I just came in from the States three days ago," Elena explained. "I've been waiting for transportation to Baghdad, but just found out this morning that my orders have been changed."

The woman nodded sympathetically. "That happens a lot. Where are they sending you now?"

Elena squinted, trying to recall the name of the base where she was headed. "Some forward operating base in Afghanistan. Shangri-la?" She laughed. "No, that's not right, because I'm pretty sure this place isn't paradise."

"Do you mean *Sharlana?*"

"Yes! That's the place."

The woman's face grew sober, and she took a long swallow of her wine, avoiding eye contact.

"What's wrong?" Elena asked, dread uncoiling in her stomach. "Do you know something about Shangri-la that I don't?"

The woman lowered her cup and sighed. "Didn't you hear? The Taliban attacked a U.S. base just forty miles north of Sharlana last night. Eight civilians were killed."

What?

Elena stared at the woman. "Are you sure?"

"Oh, yeah." The woman gave a bitter laugh. "There are no military stationed there. Rumor has it that the civilians who were assigned there—including the ones who died—had ties to the CIA, so the base is probably only used by intelligence personnel."

Elena blew out a hard breath. "That's awful." She hesitated. "Has anything like that ever happened at Shangri-la, er, Sharlana?"

"Not that I know of, but then again, there's a Marine expeditionary unit stationed at Sharlana to deter any attacks." She smiled at Elena. "You'll be perfectly safe."

That was the second time that day she'd heard those words, so why did she have trouble believing them? With a groan, she grabbed the nearest bottle and proceeded to pour several fingers of a pale green liquor into a plastic cup. She tipped it back, swallowing the entire contents in a single, long gulp and then gasped as the alcohol burned the back of her throat and made her eyes sting.

"Whoa, take it easy," admonished the other woman, watching her with a mixture of astonishment and admiration. "That stuff'll knock you on your ass."

"Oh, good," Elena gasped, as warmth seeped through her body. "I'm actually in need of a little technical knockout."

The woman laughed. "Suit yourself. Just remember that you've been warned. Good luck, hon."

Elena watched the woman saunter away before she poured herself another glass of the green liquid, this time filling the cup. The alcohol had left a pleasant taste in her mouth, a sweet mixture of black licorice with minty undertones. She took a hefty swig, swirling the liquid around on her tongue and enjoying the flavor. She never drank anything other than wine or the occasional glass of beer, and now she wondered why. This stuff was delicious.

"Careful there. You know what they say about the Green Devil."

The voice was deep and amused, and something inside Elena quivered in response. She turned to see a man leaning negligently against the bar, watching her. A broad-shouldered, lean-hipped man with a face that could have graced any number of different magazines, from guns and hunting, to high fashion. The appreciation in his eyes, combined with his lazy smile, caused a rush of heat to slide through her veins that had nothing to do with the liquor she'd just consumed.

He wore a black T-shirt and jeans, and her first thought was that he had a body designed for battle—or a woman's pleasure—honed to masculine perfection and sculpted in a way that she'd read about but had never actually seen up close. He had impossibly chiseled cheekbones and a mouth that would put a Renaissance angel to shame. In the indistinct light, she couldn't tell what color his eyes were, and his dark hair was cropped close in a distinctly military style. He was altogether delicious.

Elena wanted to bite him.

The thought came out of nowhere and shocked her so much that she started, sloshing the alcohol over her fingers.

"Green Devil?" she repeated lamely, sucking the liquid from her fingers and trying not to stare.

He nodded toward the cup she held. "Another name for absinthe." Reaching out, his hand closed around the cup, his fingers brushing against hers and sending a quicksilver thrill of awareness through her. "Did you know this stuff was banned in the U.S. until just a few years ago?"

"No, I had no idea." Elena watched as he swirled the cup in contemplation. "Why was it banned?"

He raised his gaze to hers, and one corner of his delectable mouth lifted in the barest hint of a smile. "The government believed it contained hallucinogenic properties, and could cause a person to lose their sanity."

Elena had absolutely no doubt that it was true. In fact, she was certain that she was hallucinating at that exact instant. What other reason could there be for the vivid images that were flying through her head? Images of this man, naked and gleaming with sweat as his body moved with purpose and strength over hers, his muscles flexing as he drove into her. She could actually *smell* him, a mixture of pure, male sex and something subtle and spicy, and the combination made her feel intoxicated.

Oh, yeah. She had definitely lost her sanity.

She passed a hand over her eyes and gave a shaky

laugh, trying to dispel the erotic imagery. "Wow. I had no idea. I guess I owe you a big thank-you for saving me."

"Chase McCormick," he said, extending a hand. "Always glad to be of service."

Oh, if only!

Elena reached out, and his fingers closed warmly over hers. Hardly realizing she did so, she stepped closer to him. The only thing she was conscious of was a slow heat building low in her abdomen, and how her breasts felt full and tight.

"Elena de la Vega." Was that her voice that sounded so husky and breathless?

He smiled, and the floor shifted beneath Elena's feet. The man was more gorgeous than he had any right to be, but when he smiled…sweet mercy!

"Easy," he said, and set the cup aside to grasp her beneath her elbow. He dipped his head to look into her eyes. "You okay? For a second there, you looked as if you were going down."

Now *there* was an idea.

How long had it been since she'd pleasured a man with her mouth? On that score, her sister Carmen had been right. Her sex life *had* been boring and predictable, and as much as she'd like to put the blame fully on Larry, he'd had no trouble trying something risqué with his new girlfriend. Which meant Elena must be the one with the problem, and it was way past time she did something about it.

Now she looked at Chase McCormick, and just the thought of tasting him…of having him in her mouth… caused ribbons of lust to unfurl low in her belly. In fact, just thinking about touching this man caused her heart to beat faster. She had no idea who this guy was, and yet here she was, contemplating doing risqué things with him that she'd never done with Larry.

Her eyes slid over Chase again, admiring the broad thrust of his shoulders and the way his T-shirt hugged the contours of his pecs and his flat stomach. She wanted badly to touch him.

She'd worked with dozens of military guys over the years, and while several of them had made their interest in her clear, Elena had never been tempted into a relationship. For the most part, they'd been too masculine, brimming with testosterone and confidence. She'd known instinctively that a man like that could overwhelm her, both physically and emotionally. The last thing she needed—or wanted—was to be dependent on another person for her own happiness. She'd seen what that kind of neediness had done to her parents and had vowed she wouldn't make the same mistake.

But as her gaze drifted over Chase's leanly muscled physique, she couldn't help but wonder what it might be like to be with him, to let him overwhelm her.

To lose herself in him.

He was the sort who would take his time with a woman, ensuring her pleasure before reaching his own. He would be assertive, playful and maybe even a little kinky. For one wild instant, her imagination surged. Images of Chase, wearing nothing but his dog tags, played through her head as she envisioned all the things they could do.

Then she remembered that after tonight, she would leave for some godforsaken outpost in northern Afghanistan where there was a real possibility, however small, that she would be killed. In that instant, she regretted every wild, crazy, impetuous thing she had never done. For instance, she'd never had casual sex, and had never engaged in a one-night stand. Instead, she'd deluded herself into believing she was happy having mediocre sex with Larry Gorman.

But she still had tonight to make up for all those years of self-denial, and somehow she had a feeling that this guy could make it all worthwhile. Withdrawing her hand from Chase's, Elena deliberately picked up the cup of absinthe.

"I'm fine," she assured him, smiling. "In fact, I'm better than fine, and if this stuff makes a person insane, then I want more." Without taking her eyes from his, she tipped the cup back and drained the contents, willing herself not to cough on the strong alcohol. When she'd swallowed it, she delicately licked her lips and gave him what she hoped was a seductive look. "Because tonight, I intend to go a little crazy. Wanna come along for the ride?"

3

CHASE SWEPT HIS GAZE over the woman, trying not to
let his surprise show, trying not to let her see how much
he wanted to accept her offer. She'd caught his attention
the moment she'd walked through the door, alone and
looking a little apprehensive. He was certain she didn't
work at the embassy; she lacked the self-important swag-
ger so common among the State Department personnel.
That meant she was a Department of Defense civilian
or a contractor, either just coming into the Middle Eastern theater or leaving it. He hoped like hell it was the
latter.

She appealed to him on a primal level, from her lus-
trous dark hair and suggestive smile, to her full breasts
and shapely ass. He wanted to do things with her that
he had no business doing, not when he was leaving for
a yearlong deployment. What could he offer her, or any
woman for that matter, beyond a single night? Then
again, if he were to take her proposition seriously, it
seemed that was all she was interested in. A single
night.

The prospect was tempting. More than tempting,

especially considering he was looking down the loaded gun barrel of enforced celibacy. Twelve long months of it. Even if the military lifted the ban on sex during deployments, he wouldn't be doing the horizontal tango with anyone. Females in uniform were off-limits, end of discussion.

But this particular female was something altogether different. He'd stake his life on the fact that she wasn't in the military, so technically he wasn't prohibited from getting involved with her. Besides, he was more or less off duty until dawn, when he'd board an Apache helicopter and fly to the forward operating base that he'd call home for the next twelve months.

"Dance with me," he commanded softly and caught her hand, pulling her toward him.

She came willingly into his arms, and he slid one hand to the small of her back, holding her just close enough that he could feel the heat emanating from her body and smell the fragrance of her hair. There was no dance floor, so he simply swayed with her where they stood, enjoying the sensation of just holding a woman in his arms. Of holding this woman. Her breath fanned his neck, and he had to resist the urge to pull her even closer. Her scent filled his head and made him want to bend her over his arm and bury his face against her skin.

"Well, this is nice," she drawled, tipping her head back to smile at him, "but not quite what I had in mind." Her voice was rich with suggestion. As if to emphasize her meaning, she sidled closer, so that her breasts pressed against his chest.

Chase's body responded instantly to her nearness, tightening until he was uncomfortably aware of his own arousal pressing against the zipper of his jeans.

He laughed. He couldn't help himself. It was just too freaking unbelievable that he should meet this gorgeous woman in the middle of Kuwait, the night before he was due to deploy. Didn't it figure?

"What's so funny?" she asked. Her eyes were liquid dark pools in the dim light.

"Nothing," he answered. "So tell me something, Elena de la Vega. What the hell are you doing here?"

She shrugged. "I heard there was a party, so I decided to check it out. Now I'm glad I did." She swayed unevenly and did a quick shuffle to steady herself, leaning heavily into him. "Whoa," she laughed. "I'm feeling a little dizzy."

"That would be the absinthe," he remarked drily, holding her secure. "It has a way of sneaking up on you, especially when you guzzle it by the glassful."

"Mmm, but it feels so nice," she said, sliding one hand over his chest, ostensibly to support herself.

Chase had to agree. Everything about her felt nice, but he hadn't yet reached the point where he'd take advantage of an intoxicated woman, even as his lower body urged otherwise. He had three younger sisters, and he'd kill any guy who tried to do with them what he was contemplating doing with this woman. Even if he hadn't been outnumbered by females growing up, his parents had raised him to treat them with respect. His father, a career military man, had drilled one adage into his young head: women were weak and it was a man's job to protect them. Mostly, though, Chase just avoided them whenever possible. Women were a complication he didn't need at this point in his life. Maybe one day, when his combat days were over, he'd allow himself to get serious about a woman. But not now.

He shouldn't let this woman affect him, shouldn't let himself feel such a primitive desire to possess her. He knew enough about the human psyche to realize it was perfectly normal to crave sex on the eve of battle, so to speak. It was a way to reaffirm life. But Chase had no intention of dying, and as much as his body desired release, he wasn't interested in a one-night stand.

"How long are you staying here in Kuwait?" he asked. Except for the embassy personnel, the hotel usually served as a temporary staging area for Americans while they waited for transportation to their final destination. Most people only stayed for a night or two before they moved on.

"Hmm?" She was leaning against him, and now she tipped her face back to gaze dreamily at him. "Oh, I leave tomorrow."

"Are you heading back to the States?"

She smiled. "I'm going to Shangri-la."

Chase frowned. Shangri-la?

"Paradise on Earth," she continued. "I can hardly wait."

"Okay, you know what?" Chase tucked her against his side and steered her through the crowd toward the door. "I think you need to go to bed."

"Ooh, I like that idea." She giggled and would have tripped if he hadn't been holding her. "Are you going to tuck me in?"

Chase gritted his teeth against the erotic images that swam through his head. "I meant that you need to get some sleep," he clarified. "But yes, I'll walk you back to your room."

"So what do you do for a living, Mr. McCormick?"

she asked, as he led her into the hallway. "You're not an accountant by any chance, are you?"

He glanced down at her with an arched eyebrow, but couldn't suppress a grin. "Sorry, no. Er, what floor are you on?"

She stopped, pulling him to a halt beside her. The lights were brighter in the corridor, allowing Chase to get a good look at her. Her Spanish heritage was evident in her fine bone structure and flawless skin, and he saw that her eyes weren't dark as he'd originally thought, but a light shade of brown that reminded him of caramel, the irises thickly ringed in black. She was striking.

She pushed a hand into the pocket of her jeans and pulled out a room key. "Aha, here it is," she exclaimed in triumph, holding up the key. She pushed her hair back and peered at it. "Room number six."

Chase took the key from her fingers and turned it upright. "That would be room number nine," he corrected. "C'mon, the elevator's this way."

"So, you're a soldier," Elena mused when they reached the elevator, leaning against the wall as she considered him.

"How could you tell?"

"You have that look." Her gaze drifted over him, lingering on his shoulders and chest before meeting his eyes. "Tough and serious. Your motto is probably something like Duty, Honor, Country."

The elevator doors slid open and Chase indicated Elena should precede him into the small compartment. "Actually," he said wryly, "my command motto is Always Faithful, Always Forward."

"I like that motto," Elena said with a smile, as the doors closed. "Especially the faithful part." She shook

her head in mock sadness. "So many men don't understand the importance of that particular trait."

The significance of her words wasn't lost on Chase.
So she'd had her heart broken. He shouldn't care, but he
found himself wondering what kind of guy would cheat
on a woman like Elena de la Vega. He reminded himself
that it was none of his business, but couldn't help thinking that whoever the guy was, he was a complete ass.

"So where're you from, soldier?" she asked, giving
him a look that could only be described as *hot*. Chase's
body reacted immediately to the implicit promise in her
eyes, and he struggled to think coherently, to remind
himself that he was so not going there. No matter how
much he might want to.

"I grew up all over the place," he replied. "My dad
was in the military, so we moved around a lot. But his
last assignment was in North Carolina, and I did most
of my high-school years there."

"Ah. Fort Bragg or Camp Lejeune?"

He smiled. So she knew something about North Carolina's military bases. Why did he find that so appealing?
"Camp Lejeune, actually. You know it?"

"Only by reputation. Do you still live in North Carolina?"

"I'm based out of Camp Lejeune, and my folks still
live in the area."

"Like father, like son."

"I hope so," he said seriously. His dad had been a
career marine who'd retired after nearly thirty-five years
of distinguished service. He was a tough son of a bitch,
but he'd always made sure his family knew how much
he loved them. Nothing had made him prouder than the

day Chase had been accepted into MARSOC, the elite Marine Corps Special Operations Command.

He'd redeployed back to Camp Lejeune six months ago after spending a year in Iraq, and had been glad for the opportunity to spend some time with his parents and sisters. But when his team had been called up to Afghanistan, he'd been happy to go. Too much time in the States made him feel as if he was going soft.

They reached her floor, and now Chase guided her out of the elevator with one hand at the small of her back. He could have simply let her find her own way, but told himself that he had an obligation to see her safely to her room. He also knew he was full of shit. He simply wasn't ready to say goodbye to this woman.

They came to her room much too quickly.

"Here you go," he said gruffly. He inserted her key into the door, pushing it open for her and then stepping back.

Away from temptation.

She didn't go in. Instead, she leaned against the door frame and considered him. The silky fabric of her blouse stretched taut across her breasts, emphasizing the thrust of her nipples. Chase swallowed hard. He could easily spend hours exploring her lush curves, but it was the expression in her eyes that made it impossible for him to move away. She was looking at him as if he were the most desirable man she'd ever seen, and his own body pulsed hotly in response.

"I wish I wasn't leaving tomorrow," she finally said. "I'd have liked to get to know you better."

Chase gave her a rueful smile, feeling her regret. "Just bad timing, I guess."

She laughed softly. "You're not kidding. I'm the queen

of bad timing." She glanced into the open room and then back at Chase, and he knew what was coming before she said the words. "We could get to know each other tonight...if you want to. It's still early."

Chase blew out a hard breath and rubbed a hand across the back of his neck, hoping she didn't see his body's instant response to her words. Visions of her, lying across the sheets, her skin warm and smooth, filled his head. His cock swelled as he imagined himself filling his hands with her breasts, kissing her softness. Did he want to stay? Hell, yes. The problem was, he knew he wouldn't want to leave, and he had an 0430 bird to catch.

"Forget it," she said quickly, misinterpreting his gesture. She crossed her arms defensively around her middle and gave him an overly bright smile. "Not such a great idea, I get it."

"No," he said roughly, stepping toward her. "That's not it at all."

He had a thing about honesty, sometimes to his own detriment. The only time he lied was when he absolutely had to, like when he was on a mission. Then, he could lie so beautifully that his own mother wouldn't doubt he'd told the truth. And he had no problem with small white lies if they were harmless, like telling a woman that no, those pants did not make her ass look big. But he had a sinking feeling that now was going to be one of those times when he'd look back and regret his own inability to completely dupe a woman. It was important to him that she understand his reasons for turning her down.

"You're a beautiful woman," he continued. "Being with you tonight would be...amazing, but it couldn't be anything more than just one night. I leave at dawn for a twelve-month deployment, so anything more would be impossible. I wouldn't want either of us to have regrets about it tomorrow. Especially when one of us has had too much to drink."

She pushed herself away from the doorjamb, and Chase could see the resignation and regret in her luminous eyes.

"I understand, and I think you're really sweet." She smiled at him. "Leave it to me to find the one guy in the world with scruples."

Scruples he'd rather do without, Chase thought grimly. He had to be the biggest idiot on the face of the planet to turn down what she was offering, but he knew from experience that casual sex never made him feel better, either about himself or the woman involved. Nope, better to let her go now and keep his fantasies about whatever might have been.

"Nobody has ever described me as sweet," he said sardonically, to cover his own conflicting emotions. "If any of my men overheard you say that, you'd completely destroy my reputation as a hard-ass."

"It will be our secret," Elena promised, "so please don't change." Standing on tiptoe, she pressed a kiss against his cheek. At least, Chase suspected the kiss was meant for his cheek, but he instinctively turned his head to follow her movement, bringing his lips into direct contact with hers.

She stilled for a moment, and Chase realized his hands were resting loosely at her waist, while hers were pressed lightly against his chest for balance.

"I'm sorry," she breathed, just before she pressed her mouth fully against his.

FOR AN INSTANT, Elena thought he would either pull back
or push her away. He held himself so rigidly still that if it
weren't for the warmth of his lips beneath hers, he might
have been carved from stone. Elena knew she'd had too
much to drink, but she hadn't consumed so much that
she didn't know exactly what she was doing. The alcohol
only blunted the sharp edges of her self-restraint and allowed her to loosen her tightly laced inhibitions. When
he didn't immediately move to end the kiss, Elena softened it, shaping the contours of his beautiful mouth.

A shudder went through him, and he made a sound
like a half groan. Emboldened, Elena slid her hands
along his rib cage and angled her mouth ever so slightly
across his, enjoying the sensuality of the kiss. There was
something erotic about being the aggressor, especially
when she knew Chase could easily overpower her.

He didn't resist when she backed him up against the
open door of her room and delicately stroked her tongue
along the seam of his lips, humming her approval when
they parted for her. As if helpless to withstand her sensual assault, he began kissing her back, a soft, moist
fusing of their mouths that made Elena go weak with
desire. She couldn't recall the last time she'd felt this
hot, sweet yearning for a man.

His arms came slowly around her, holding her captive
as he plundered her mouth, his tongue sliding against
hers with expert precision. Elena welcomed his heat and
strength, and she could feel her body blossom beneath
his touch, as if anticipating their joining.

She was unprepared when Chase dragged his mouth
from hers. "We can't do this," he muttered, trailing his
lips over her cheek until he found the soft juncture of her
throat and pressed his lips to her hammering pulse.

"We can't *not* do this," she whispered back. "Please… I really need this."

She needed to feel connected to someone, to be touched and held and reminded that she was a desirable woman. It had been so long since she'd felt wanted by a man. Maybe that was partly her own fault for holding herself so rigidly in check, but the prospect of spending the next six months alone was almost too daunting to contemplate. Just for tonight, she wanted this physical bond. She needed it. She needed this man, with his amazing physique and heart-stopping smile, to want her as much as she wanted him.

His breathing was uneven in her ear. "We might never see each other again."

Elena arched her neck, granting him better access. "I understand that, I really do. But you'd be doing me a huge favor if you stayed with me tonight. Please…" She threaded her fingers through his short hair, enjoying the velvet texture and feeling the warmth of his scalp beneath her fingertips. "Stay."

She was glad he didn't ask if she was sure.

She wasn't.

She'd never done anything this reckless or bold in her life, but there was no way she was going to stop. She wanted to experience this man and everything he had to offer, even if it couldn't last for more than one night. She would never say so to Chase, but there was a part of her that was grateful she wouldn't see him again after tonight. If she didn't see him again, he could never disappoint her.

"Please," she repeated.

He didn't argue. He simply swept her into his arms before she could utter another word and carried her into the room, kicking the door closed behind them. Elena had never before had a man pick her up so effortlessly, and there was a part of her that thrilled in his strength and the way it made her feel.

Feminine.

Fragile.

He set her on her feet next to the bed and without giving her a chance to move an inch, cupped her face in his hands and slanted his mouth across hers.

"I could kiss you like this all night," he murmured. "You have the softest lips…"

Tilting her head back, he worked his way down her throat, planting soft kisses and gentle bites against her flesh, until Elena shivered with need. His fingers unhurriedly worked the buttons of her red blouse, until she felt cool air waft against her bare skin. She didn't object when he pushed the shirt from her shoulders and drew her sleeves down, letting the garment drop to the floor until she stood before him in just her bra and jeans.

"Let me look at you," he said, his voice husky. Stepping back, he leaned over and flicked on the bedside lamp.

Elena blinked against the sudden intrusion of light in the dark room, and then blushed as she realized Chase was staring at her. Only he wasn't just looking at her, he was devouring her with his gaze, and the expression in his eyes made Elena feel both excited and nervous.

"What's this?" he asked, and reaching out, he touched the necklace that nestled between her breasts, his fingertips brushing against her sensitized skin and sending jolts of awareness shooting through her.

"Something my sisters gave to me," she said breathlessly, showing him the tiny silver angel charm that dangled from the chain. "It's a guardian angel, to watch over me."

"He'd better do his job," he said huskily, letting the little charm drop back between her breasts. "Lucky little angel."

"I've, um, never done anything like this before," she admitted. Her bones felt deliciously weak, and although she suspected part of it was a result of the absinthe, the major cause was the man who stood looking at her with pure, male appreciation.

"You don't have to do anything now," he assured her. "We could just—" He broke abruptly off with a laugh. "Hell, I don't know…we could just *cuddle*. You don't have to do anything you don't want to."

"But that's just it," she said. "I *want* to do this."

Elena realized it was the truth. And not just because she was leaving in the morning for some remote base whose name she couldn't even pronounce. She wanted this beautiful man and the promise of pleasure that lurked in his eyes. She'd never felt this kind of gnawing lust before. Ever. Her gaze dropped to his lush mouth and a sharp stab of desire speared through her. His lips were too tempting.

Keeping her eyes locked with his, Elena reached behind her and unfastened the clasp of her bra. She didn't miss how Chase swallowed hard. Elena didn't immediately let the undergarment go, but held it pressed against her breasts.

"When I first saw you back there at the party, I wondered…" Her voice trailed off as his gaze sharpened on her.

"What?" His voice sounded hoarse. "What did you wonder?"

"…what you would taste like in my mouth."

"Oh, Christ," he groaned, and in the next instant Elena was in his arms.

She half expected him to pick her up and toss her onto the bed. Instead, he stroked his hands over her bare skin, his fingers finding the dips and curves of her body with infinite care. His turned his face into the arch of her neck and pressed his mouth against her throat. Then he tugged the bra free from her fingers and let it fall to the floor.

Elena didn't have time to feel self-conscious before he covered one breast with his big hand, gently massaging her pliant flesh. She could feel the hard calluses on his palms and gasped at the sensations his touch created, unfamiliar with the cravings rising in her body.

She tipped her head back enough to see his face, and realized his eyes were a mix of browns and greens with flecks of pure gold, surrounded by thick lashes. With his eyes, cheekbones and delectable mouth, the only thing that kept him from too being perfect was his nose, which showed evidence of having been broken at some point.

As he cupped her breast, Elena pushed her hands beneath the hem of his T-shirt. He reflexively tensed, and her fingers skimmed over ridges of muscle across his abdomen. Larry had been a runner, and while he'd been lean, his body had lacked true definition. But not this man; he was sculpted in ways that Elena had never experienced before. She slid her hands higher, reveling in his warm, hard flesh.

He watched her the entire time, and the only indication that her touch affected him was the way his breathing hitched when her fingertips stroked over the small nubs of his nipples.

"Take this off," she said softly, and he complied instantly, reaching behind his head to grab a fistful of shirt and drag it upward.

Elena couldn't prevent a small indrawn breath.

Her first impression had been right; his was a body designed for a woman's touch, and she was helpless to stop herself from running her hand over his chest. She took note of the small scars and imperfections, realizing she knew nothing of him or what he had experienced.

"I was right," she murmured, tracing a long, thin scar that slashed over his ribs. "You're tough."

To her surprise, he laughed. "Oh, yeah. I'm real tough. That's why I have absolutely no willpower where you're concerned."

Elena slid her arms around his waist until they were skin to skin, absorbing the feel of him. "I'm glad. I don't want you to have any willpower tonight."

With a rough sound, Chase lowered his head and caught her mouth in a kiss so deep that she felt it all the way to her toes. She didn't object when he backed her up to the bed and pushed her gently down across the coverlet, following alongside her.

The bedspread was cool against her bare back, but Chase's skin was hot against her breasts. Dragging his mouth from hers, he worked his way unhurriedly down her throat and over her chest, nuzzling her breasts with his mouth. Elena watched him, spellbound by the sight of his dark head against her pale skin, and feeling the rush of heat and wetness between her legs. When he took a nipple into his mouth and drew deeply on the stiffened tip, she gasped and arched upward, clutching at his shoulders.

He tormented first one breast and then the other,

ignoring how Elena twisted beneath him, her hips shifting restlessly against his. He used his mouth to worship her body, moving from her breasts to her stomach, where he teased her navel with his tongue. His fingers moved to the waistband of her jeans and released the fastening in one easy flick of his fingers.

"Yes," she panted, as he slowly drew the zipper down. She lifted her hips, and Chase dragged the jeans down the length of her legs until she lay on the bed wearing nothing but her panties.

"Oh, man," he breathed, "you are so damned pretty."

If Elena had worried that she might not meet his expectations, those doubts vanished beneath the heat in his gaze. Reaching out, she caught him by the waistband of his jeans and tugged until he came over her on all fours, with her fingers still tucked into his pants.

"Take these off," she urged, needing to see him. "Hurry."

Dawn would be here before they knew it, and Elena felt a sudden urgency to meld with this man, to own him and belong to him before it was too late. Even now, her duffel bags lay on the floor by the far wall, packed and ready to go. She suspected that if she were to visit Chase's room, she would see the same.

"I'll take them off," Chase breathed, "but I want to go slow, okay?"

"Okay," she agreed, too eager to see him to tell him that she had no intention of going slow. She was past ready for him. Even now, her panties were soaked with desire, and her sex throbbed with need. She'd listened to her sisters describe lust often enough, but she'd never understood the meaning of the word until now.

Leaning back, Chase unfastened the snap on his jeans, and Elena helped to push them down over his hips. Her breath caught as she saw his erection tenting the material of his cotton boxer shorts. As he stood and kicked his legs free, Elena sat up on the edge of the bed. Reaching out, she laid her hand over the hot ridge of flesh beneath the cotton, thrilling at how he jumped beneath her touch.

"I want to see you," she said, and slid her fingers beneath the stretchy waistband to take him in her hand. His breath hissed in through clenched teeth as she curled her fingers around him, and her body pulsed hotly in response.

"You're gorgeous," she breathed, pushing his boxers down to stroke his length. Glancing upward, she saw Chase watching her through half-closed eyes, his face taut. "You know what I want to do."

"Yeah." His voice came out on a raspy groan.

Elena smiled. She'd never felt so sexy or powerful before in her life. This guy was the embodiment of masculine strength and beauty, and yet she literally held him trembling in the palm of her hand. The effect was an aphrodisiac.

She cupped his weight from beneath with one hand as she trailed her fingers along the velvety shaft with her other. The head of his penis was like a ripe plum, and Elena's mouth watered with the need to taste him. Leaning forward, she ran her tongue lightly over the blunt tip.

"Mmm," she murmured. "You taste delicious." Then she took him fully into her mouth.

Chase made a rough sound, a mixture of surprise and arousal. His hands came up to frame her face, his fingers massaging the tender skin behind her ears. Emboldened, Elena took him deeper, swirling her tongue around him as she used her hand to stroke and caress his length. She pressed her thighs together, squeezing against the sharp throb of arousal between them.

"That's enough," he gasped and eased her away, his breath coming fast. "I won't last if you keep that up, and I'm not ready for this to be over."

Reluctantly, Elena released him and let him push her back onto the mattress. Bending over her, he pressed his mouth against her abdomen. The faint stubble on his jaw abraded the tender skin in a way that made her squirm in delicious anticipation.

"You smell great," he murmured, and hooked his thumbs into the elastic waistband of her panties, pulling them down in one smooth movement. His lips drifted over the arch of her ribs and over the swell of her breasts until he reached a nipple and drew it into his mouth. Elena struggled for breath against the erotic sensations of his tongue and teeth, and she threaded her fingers through his hair, urging him closer.

His warm hand skated over her stomach and lower, urging her legs apart so that he could cup her intimately. Elena's thighs fell open and she pressed upward against his palm, wanting more of the delicious contact.

"That's it," he rasped against her breast, and swirled a finger over her slick flesh, parting her folds and finding the small rise of flesh that thrummed with need. "Oh, man, you're so wet."

He circled a finger over her clitoris, but it wasn't enough. Elena's skin went hot and her sex clenched hungrily. Someone moaned and she realized with a sense of shock that it was her. She needed more. Now.

"Soon," Chase promised, as if reading her mind, and knelt between her splayed knees. He stroked a hand along her inner thigh, urging her legs wider, before he bent down and covered her with his mouth.

Elena gasped and her hips came off the mattress, but Chase held her firmly in place as he laved her with his tongue and lips, alternately sucking and licking until she writhed helplessly. When he began tormenting the tiny bud of her clit, she pushed weakly at his shoulders.

"Please," she finally managed in a strangled voice. "Stop. I can't take any more."

Chase laughed softly, but reached down and grabbed his pants from the floor, fishing through the pockets until he produced a small foil packet. He covered himself quickly, but Elena noticed that his hands seemed unsteady.

He came over her again, bracing himself with his hands on either side of her. "You're sure about this?" he asked. His voice was level, but his breathing was shallow. He wanted her. "If you want me to stop, you have to tell me now, because once I'm inside you, I don't think I can—"

"I'm sure," Elena breathed, and slid her hands along his back to cup his lean buttocks and urge him closer. She felt him nudging against her most private spot, and she opened her legs wider, arching upward to meet him.

"I'm sorry," he grunted. "I can't go slowly—"

He surged forward in one powerful movement, stretching and filling her until he was fully seated inside her. He didn't move for a long moment, his head bent to hers, his breathing ragged.

Elena squeezed experimentally, the walls of her

channel tightening around his flesh. Pleasure lashed through her.

Then he began to move, withdrawing slowly and then sinking back into her in a series of bone-melting strokes. His heated flesh dragged at hers, creating a delicious friction that made Elena arch upward to meet him. The muscles in his arms flexed as he dipped his head and covered her mouth with his, feasting slowly and sensuously on her lips. Elena heard herself whimper softly, and she drew her knees back and hooked her feet around his waist, meeting his thrusts eagerly.

She wanted more.

Chase complied, sliding one arm beneath her to press her more intimately against the hard drive of his body. Elena shivered and clutched at his back.

"Oh, God," she gasped. "You feel so good."

Which was a huge understatement. Had she really told her sister that sex was overrated? If this was what other women experienced with their partners, it was a wonder any of them ever left their beds.

"Damn straight," Chase said, his voice low and rough.

Elena could feel the start of an orgasm building and pushed at his chest.

"Wait," she panted.

Chase raised himself up just enough to look into her face, his own expression taut. "Really? You really want to stop?"

"No. Yes." Elena struggled to think coherently. "I'm getting close, and I don't want this to end yet. I want to try something else."

Chase gave a disbelieving laugh, but his movements slowed and he began to pull back. Elena gritted her teeth and her body followed his, reluctant to release him. She was so close, and she sensed that he was, too. If they continued, he could take her to heaven in a matter of seconds. But suddenly, she wanted to be the one to take him there, to do things that would make him lose control.

She pushed at his shoulders and with a bemused smile he rolled away from her. But Elena didn't give him a chance to question her, covering him swiftly with her own body.

"What? Hey—" He laughed uncertainly, but when Elena dipped her head and traced the whorl of his ear with her tongue, he groaned and collapsed back against the pillows. She pushed his hands up above his head, and slid her own hands down the sensitive undersides of his arms, admiring the impressive bulge of his muscles. Her fingers continued downward, and she scooted backward until she straddled his thighs.

Sitting up, she looked down at him. Her breath caught at the sight he made. He was the embodiment of every fantasy she'd ever had. He lay prone beneath her, but there was nothing remotely relaxed about him. His entire body was rigid and his eyes glittered as he watched her through half-closed lids.

"Now it's my turn," she whispered. "I've always wanted to do this."

She leaned forward until her breasts brushed against his chest, and her angel charm necklace pooled in the depression between his pecs. She traced her lips across his. He cupped the back of her head and drew her down for a more thorough, satisfying kiss. Elena had intended to tease him, to maintain control of their love play until he begged her to release him. But when he smoothed his free hand along her flank and then reached between them to touch her intimately, she knew she was lost.

She gasped into his mouth, and settled more fully against him. He used his hands to splay her thighs even wider where she straddled him. Then there he was, hot and thick, moving into her bit by little bit, until Elena made an incoherent sound of need and pushed back, thrusting him fully into her.

"Ah," he groaned. "That almost feels too good."

Elena silently agreed, and slowly raised herself up until he was nearly free of her body, before pushing herself down once more, burying him to the hilt. The hot, throbbing sensation increased as she moved on top of him, gripping him tightly. His fingers were on her hips, guiding her, and he watched her face through pleasure-glazed eyes. When he slid his hands upward to cup and knead her breasts, Elena closed her eyes in mindless bliss.

"Yes," she breathed. "Oh, yes."

"Look at me."

The words were soft but insistent. She opened her eyes and stared down at Chase, seeing the raw, masculine need and pleasure on his face.

"I want you to look at me when you come," he rasped. His expression had tightened, and the tautness of his body told her he was close to losing control. Seeing his desire mount only served to fuel her own. and his words were enough to send her over the brink. Her orgasm slammed into her, and the only thing anchoring her to Earth were Chase's hands, holding her. She might have closed her eyes but for his soft command.

"Look at me."

As he reached his own climax, their gazes were locked

on one another, until with a last shudder of pleasure, he smiled into her eyes and tugged her down until she lay replete against his chest.

He pressed his lips against her hair, and his hands stroked soothingly down her body. When she turned her face up to his, he kissed her sweetly, and even in the faint light, she could see the softness of his expression. He tucked her closer against his side, and one hand traced lazy patterns on her shoulder and arm. "Hey, you okay?"

A reluctant smile tugged at her lips. "More than okay. I'm great."

"No regrets, then?"

Elena raised herself on her elbow to look at him. He lay against the pillows like a big, sleek cat. "Absolutely no regrets. You've actually fulfilled a lifelong fantasy of mine."

Chase chuckled. "Do you have any other fantasies you'd like to fulfill? Like I said, I'm here to serve."

"As a matter of fact," she murmured, tracing his lower lip with her thumb, "there are a few I'd like to explore."

Chase's eyes sharpened on her with interest. "Oh, yeah? Tell me."

Elena bit her lip, and then leaned forward and whispered softly in his ear. When she drew back, she looked at him with apprehension in her eyes.

"Oh, man," Chase said with a soft groan, pulling her down so that she lay sprawled across him, her breasts flattened against his chest. "We have about five hours before dawn. I may just die trying to do all those things, but I promise you I'm going to go out a happy man."

4

MAJOR DUMFRIES had been right about one thing—
flying in a helicopter while nursing a hangover was no
fun. At least, not after the first ten minutes, when the
initial thrill had faded and Elena found herself painfully
conscious of the cold. Before long, her bottom started to
ache from the weight of the armored vest that she was
required to wear. The constant whir of the rotor blades
was deafening, until she was no longer sure if they were
coming from the helicopter or inside her head.

Elena wasn't even sure if the total exhaustion she felt
was a result of the absinthe she'd consumed, or a combination of too little sleep and too much unaccustomed
physical activity. Her body felt deliciously tender from
her night with Chase, and each small movement brought
back memories.

She couldn't stop thinking about him, or about what
they'd done together. Last night had been an anomaly.
She'd acted completely out of character, but then again,
she'd never met a man like Chase McCormick before.
With Larry, she'd always tamped down her own desires
and contented herself with their standard missionary-

style sex. At least, she'd thought she was content with the routine coitus, but now she knew differently. She'd been going through the motions, and while she'd had some pleasant orgasms with Larry, none of it could compare to what she'd experienced with Chase.

The man was a master, and Elena had come alive under his expert touch. She hadn't known she was capable of such uninhibited passion. After that first amazing hour, they'd slept briefly. Elena had woken to find Chase propped with his head on his hand, watching her. The heat in his expression had made it impossible for Elena to feel embarrassed. Instead, an answering warmth had bloomed low in her abdomen. Without a word, he'd circled his thumb over her nipple and they'd both watched the small bud tighten beneath his touch. Finally, unable to stand it any longer, she had rubbed herself against him, sliding her leg over his hips and letting him know she was more than ready for him again.

Afterward, Chase had pulled her into his arms and she'd again drifted into sleep to the sound of his heartbeat thumping steadily beneath her ear. But when her alarm clock had finally gone off, she had found herself alone. While she'd told herself it was for the best, she couldn't deny feeling bereft at Chase's absence. He'd told her he'd have to leave before dawn, but even knowing that he had his own flight to catch hadn't been enough to keep her from feeling abandoned. She'd wanted to savor every bit of their short time together. If she closed her eyes, she could still feel Chase's warm body and his lips against her temple. Being with him was the closest to heaven that she would ever get.

And now she'd never see him again.

Elena looked around at the other occupants of the

helicopter. They were a group of fifteen civilians, with just one other woman besides herself. The woman was quite a bit older than Elena, in her early fifties at least. Dressed in the DPA uniform of black cargo pants and fleece jacket, she seemed frail and nervous. Her gray hair stuck out at odd angles beneath her baseball cap, and she continually smoothed it with her fingers, tucking the strands back in. Elena felt a rush of sympathy for the woman, wondering what had prompted her to volunteer for this deployment and if she had also been destined for a different location.

When Elena had arrived at the military airstrip, she'd been surprised to learn they wouldn't be flying on one of the military helicopters, but on a commercially chartered one. But they'd had to wait awhile before the helicopter had been ready to depart, giving Elena plenty of time to think about the previous night.

She'd had a one-night stand with a complete stranger.

She'd thought she'd feel cheapened and used. Guilty. But she felt none of those things. Instead, she found herself smiling each time she recalled the previous night. Chase had made her feel incredibly sexy, and she couldn't bring herself to regret the pleasure she'd shared with him. He'd been so attuned to her, anticipating the needs of her body before she did. He'd been tender and masterful, and they'd fitted together as if they'd been made for each other.

Casual conversation was almost impossible on board the helicopter, given the noise of the engine and the rotors, so Elena contented herself with looking out the window at the changing view. They flew high for several hours, the land beneath them turning harsh and rugged.

As they began to descend, Elena could just make out a compound in the distance. The base looked small and vulnerable in the vast openness that surrounded it, and only the distant mountains gave any relief to the stark landscape.

As the helicopter drew closer, Elena couldn't help but stare openmouthed as the base came fully into view. Even by military standards it was heavily fortified, surrounded by walls of sandbags and razor-wire fencing. She could see row after row of small huts, and then an area of hangars. More than half of the base was occupied by military vehicles of all sizes.

They landed on a helicopter pad on the far side of the base, and when the doors finally swung open, Elena was greeted by a blast of hot, dry air. A soldier, dressed in full battle gear and helmet poked his head into the passenger compartment where Elena sat with the others. His mouth creased into a smile, revealing white teeth in his tanned face.

"Welcome to Forward Operating Base Sharlana!" He had to shout to be heard over the engines as they wound down. "I'm Staff Sergeant Mike Corrente. I hope you had a pleasant flight. If you'll disembark and grab your gear, I'll show you to your quarters."

He spoke rapidly, and with such a strong Boston accent that Elena had a difficult time understanding him. She struggled into her backpack and climbed down, clapping a hand over her head to keep her hat from flying off from the downward wash of the rotors. She refused the sergeant's proffered hand, but she didn't miss how his blue eyes sharpened on her with interest as she stepped past him. She waited with the others while he and a second soldier began unceremoniously tossing their duffel bags out of the helicopter and onto the dusty ground.

Elena took the opportunity to survey their surroundings. Everything—from the helicopter and the nearby fleet of military vehicles, to the surrounding plains and distant mountains—was a uniform shade of dull brown.

After several moments of searching for her bags, Elena grunted with effort as she slung her first duffel over her shoulder and then hefted her second with her free hand.

"Okay, folks, listen up," Corrente called. He spoke with authority and Elena found herself wondering what position he held on the base. "I'll show you where you'll be staying, and you'll each have a couple of hours to rest before dinner. After that, we'll head over the rec center for orientation and a quick tour of the facility. The sooner you understand the battle rhythm here at Sharlana, the quicker you'll be able to adapt to life on a forward operating base, but don't expect any preferential treatment. Everyone on this base is responsible for their own quality of life. So grab your gear and follow me."

"How far is it to our quarters?" asked the older woman, looking across the expanse of tarmac to the hangars and tiny, plywood huts. There wasn't a single building in sight that resembled a dormitory or other living quarters.

"Not far," the sergeant said cheerfully. "See those buildings over there? Your quarters are just on the other side."

Elena saw the other woman's face blanch and felt sympathy for her. Her own head was pounding and the helicopter trip had left her feeling slightly queasy. That, combined with the oppressive heat, made even the slightest physical exertion a supreme effort. Under different conditions, she would have offered to carry the other woman's baggage for her, but it was all she could do to manage her own.

"I can carry that duffel bag for you, ma'am," Corrente said to the older woman, correctly interpreting her expression of dismay.

"Well, I don't know," the woman demurred. "If you're sure…"

"Absolutely, ma'am," he said with a grin. "It keeps me in shape."

She relinquished her bag to the younger man with a grateful smile. "Thank you so much. Maybe it's the flight, but I'm feeling a little peaked."

"Probably the altitude," the sergeant replied. "You'll get used to it."

Elena doubted it. She walked behind the two soldiers and the other civilians, hoping she didn't embarrass herself by passing out. She hadn't eaten anything all day, and she was starting to feel a little shaky. Sweat popped out along her brow and her shirt clung damply to her skin. The helicopter churned up clouds of dust, and her mouth felt thick and dry.

"Ma'am, can I take those bags for you?"

Elena looked around in surprise to see the second soldier speaking to her. He had reddish hair and a good-natured expression, and Elena found herself smiling back at him. He indicated her duffel bags. "Those look heavy."

"Oh, no," she said quickly, recalling the sergeant's remark about not receiving preferential treatment. "I can manage."

His quick grin and raised eyebrows clearly said, "Yeah, right." But instead of voicing his skepticism, he reached out firmly and took one duffel bag from her.

"I insist," he said. "I'll catch hell from my C.O. if I let you pass out before you've even checked in. Besides, it's easier to carry your gear than to have to carry you *and* your gear if you collapse."

Elena knew enough military jargon to know that C.O. stood for Commanding Officer, so she gave him another smile and let him take her other bag.

"Thank you so much," she said, falling into step beside him. "It must be the heat that makes me feel so tired. I'm Elena de la Vega, by the way."

"I'm Corporal Cleary, but you can call me Pete. Where're you from?"

"Virginia. I work for the Defense Procurement Agency."

He nodded. "We have a bunch of DPA folks on the base. What kind of work will you be doing?"

"I'll be working at the contracting center. I'll be overseeing the construction projects you have on base, as well as working with the contractors to ensure everything gets done on time." A breeze wafted across her face, bringing with it a putrid stench that made Elena recoil and clap a hand over her nose and mouth. "Oh, my god," she gasped. "What is that smell?"

Pete grinned. "I'd say that's your first project. We've been trying to install a waste water treatment facility on the base, but without too much success. We're having trouble getting the parts needed for the plant. What you're smelling is the cesspool at the back of the base. Nice, huh?"

Elena looked at him in disbelief and horror. "You're kidding, right?"

"Nope," he said cheerfully. "You get used to the smell. Well, mostly you get used to it. Sometimes it's so bad that it wakes me up from a sound sleep. We're almost there."

They passed a group of four men wearing ragged clothing and traditional Middle Eastern headgear. They sported beards and shaggy hair and as they drew alongside Elena and her companions, they deliberately averted their gazes.

"Who are they?" she asked, keeping her voice low. Because really, they looked a lot like the pictures of terrorists she'd seen so many times on the six o'clock news. And while she'd known she would have contact with the local people on some level, she hadn't been prepared for her own reaction of mistrust.

"Those are some of the locals. We have a dozen or so who come to work on the base each day. Task force Peacemaker also runs construction workshops for local men. Each man learns basic wood, concrete and masonry construction techniques, and at the end of the workshop we provide them with tools that they can bring back to their villages. The men we just passed are all graduates of the workshops."

Elena glanced over her shoulder at the retreating men. "How do you know if they're...you know..."

"Trustworthy? We do a background check on everyone who comes onto the base. Those are the good guys. But they're still funny about interacting with women, so don't take it personally if they steer clear of you."

So he had noticed how the men had studiously avoided acknowledging either Elena or the other woman.

"Trust me," she assured him. "No offense taken. I'd be freaked out if any of them looked twice at me. Should I cover my hair or something?"

She was half joking, but Pete didn't laugh. He looked deadly serious. "Not here on the base, but if you go outside the fence I'd recommend you wear a head covering under your helmet. Just to keep from offending anyone."

Elena digested this information, wondering how often she would be required to leave the base. She'd be just as happy if she never ventured beyond the fence.

They were walking between rows of the huts that she had glimpsed from the helicopter. There were dozens of them, side by side. Constructed of simple plywood, each had a door and two tiny windows, and were identical in appearance.

"What are these used for?" she asked. "Storage?"

Pete glanced at her with a quizzical smile. "Kinda. They're called *chews*."

Elena laughed. "Okay, I give up. Why are they called chews?"

"It's an acronym for containerized housing unit. You know…CHU…*chew*. One of these will be your home while you're at Sharlana. We bunk eight to a CHU. Under ideal conditions, civilians get to bunk with other civilians, but we just had a special ops team and two light-infantry units arrive this morning, so we're tight on housing. You'll have one other civilian and six military females in your CHU."

Elena stared at him in disbelief. "I thought I'd have my own housing unit."

Pete laughed. "Sorry, but that's a luxury we can't afford around here. Maybe that's the case in Baghdad, but out here only the big guns get their own units. We're building more, but it's doubtful that civilians will ever have their own private quarters, and the showers will always be open bay. But it's a hell of a sight better than the tents we used to live in."

They were walking past an area that was cordoned off from the rest of the base. A wire fence had been draped with camouflage netting, effectively preventing anyone from seeing what lay on the other side. As they walked past, Elena thought she could glimpse buildings and movement through the netting. She eyed the signs that hung from the fence that read No Admittance.

"What's this area used for?" she asked. "Detainees?"

Pete followed her gaze. "This is where the special ops guys hang out. Due to the sensitive nature of their jobs, they mostly work here or over at the Tactical Operations Center. Sometimes you'll see them at the dining facility." He shrugged. "Not that you'd be able to tell them apart from the rest of us, unless they grow their beards out."

"Oh." Elena peered through the netting as they passed, curious in spite of herself. She'd heard about the special ops guys, of course. Who hadn't? They were the unseen heroes of the war on terror, going where angels feared to tread, and getting out again without anyone realizing they had even been there. She pictured them as bearded and hard-eyed, dressed in clothing that would permit them to blend in with the local population.

From behind the fence, she could hear masculine whoops and shouts, and then a surprising cheer went up.

"Doesn't sound like secret work to me," she commented.

Pete shrugged. "A new team of guys just arrived this morning, and the team that's been here for the past year is getting ready to head home. They'll spend a couple of days transitioning. But right now they have ten guys behind that fence, which is enough for a serious game of touch football." He glanced at Elena. "It's important to let off steam, especially with these guys."

Up ahead, a gate in the fence swung open, and a figure emerged. Even from a distance, Elena could see he was dressed casually in a pair of shorts and a T-shirt, with a baseball cap pulled low over his eyes. With his tanned legs and sandals, he could have been a tourist. Only the assault rifle slung across his back indicated he wasn't what he appeared. He glanced at the group before turning away, and then stopped and slowly swung back in their direction.

Elena heard Pete mutter a curse under his breath.

"What's wrong?" she asked.

"I'm not sure," he replied. "But when a special ops guy decides you're worth a second look, it can't be good."

Elena followed Pete's gaze and saw the man striding purposefully toward them. This guy was special ops? He was silhouetted against the setting sun, and Elena had to shield her eyes to see him. Despite his casual clothing, everything about him said he meant business. But what could he possibly want with a group of civilians?

"I told you I could carry my own gear," she said to Pete, apprehension tickling her spine. "Are you in trouble?"

"Nah. Like I said, it was that or carry you *and* your gear." He shrugged, clearly puzzled. "I have no idea what this guy wants. But it's obvious that he thinks he outranks us, which means he probably does. Which means we'll respectfully listen to whatever it is he has to say."

"Soldiers, front and center!"

Elena craned for a better view of the man who spoke in such authoritative tones, but the group in front of her blocked her. Still, there was something very familiar about that voice.

Pete dropped her duffel bags and made his way toward the front. Elena edged forward, too. She watched as both soldiers came rigidly to attention before the man in the shorts, who stood, arms akimbo, surveying them through grim eyes.

Elena barely suppressed a gasp and her heart exploded into action. There was no way…it couldn't be! But as she swiped the sweat and grit from her eyes and peered again, there was no doubt in her mind. The man was none other than the one she thought she'd never see again…Chase McCormick.

Adrenaline, hot and dizzying, buzzed through her veins. Her blood pounded in her ears, and her first instinct was to turn tail and run. To hide. Because there was no way she could face him, not after last night. Not when he hadn't even said goodbye, but had slipped out of her room while she'd slept.

What was he doing here? She'd been so certain she would never run into him again, and although she'd liked him—really, really liked him—she would have preferred it that way. She wasn't sophisticated enough to act as if nothing had happened. Already every cell in her body was reacting to seeing him. But last night he'd been a different man, warm and solid and safe whereas right now he seemed every inch a warrior. Beneath the ball cap, his eyes were hidden behind a pair of dark sunglasses, but Elena could feel the weight of his scrutiny and knew with certainty that *she* was the reason he'd turned around and intercepted them.

She blushed and stepped casually behind one of the other civilians, out of his range of vision, hoping that she was wrong, and that he didn't recognize her beneath the DPA cap she wore. Just seeing him again caused her body to thrum with recalled pleasure. What were the chances that he would be here, at the same forward operating base as her? It was almost enough to make her believe in fate.

In the next instant, she wondered how he would react when he realized she would be working in proximity with him for the next six months. Would he be horrified to see his one-night stand turn up on his doorstep? Or would he think their prior encounter gave him rights for future hookups? The sex had been off the charts, but no way did she want to become his go-to girl every time he had an itch that needed scratching. She wouldn't be used. Not by him. Not by anyone.

He was speaking to the two soldiers in low tones while they stood rigidly at attention. When he was through, they both gave a loud "Yessir!" and turned back to the group.

"If you'll follow me," Pete said to the group, "I'll show each of you to your designated quarters. You'll have several hours to unpack and rest, and then I'll return to escort you to the chow hall."

Elena didn't miss how he gave her a cheeky wink, but as she bent to retrieve her two duffel bags, a shadow fell over her.

"Not you, Miss de la Vega," said a cool voice.

Elena glanced up to see Chase standing beside her.

This was definitely not the same, user-friendly version she'd known in Kuwait. He didn't fool her with his casual, tourist clothing and day's growth of beard. With his set jaw and a seriously badass weapon slung across his back, he still looked like a tough, hardened soldier. He'd removed his sunglasses and Elena felt her insides quiver at the expression in his eyes.

"I'll see you in private," he said quietly. "Now."

Without waiting to see if she would follow him, he turned on his heel and began striding away, while the other civilians gaped at her. Under any other circumstances, Elena would have looked forward to the prospect of getting some private time with Chase. But the rigid set of his shoulders as he walked away told her that this encounter wouldn't be of a romantic nature.

"Who is that man? And how does he know who you are?" the other woman asked Elena. "Is he your new boss?"

Elena struggled beneath the burden of her two duffel bags. "We met last night in Kuwait," she explained hurriedly. "But I don't really know him. And he is definitely not my boss."

She averted her gaze from the knowing looks and followed Chase, feeling like a schoolgirl who'd just been called to the principal's office. She reminded herself that she'd done nothing wrong. She had no reason to feel so apprehensive about what he might say.

Even then, she couldn't help but admire Chase's legs as he strode away. They were muscled and tanned, and she recalled all too well how powerful they were.

He climbed the steps of a small hut that sported a small, curtained window on either side of the door. A sign over the doorway read Tactical Operations Center.

Dropping her gear on the dusty ground outside the building, Elena followed him inside. She found herself in a crudely furnished office, with a desk built out of plywood and two-by-fours, and shelving crafted from stacked wooden crates. Two soldiers sat working at computer stations in the small space, and they looked up as Chase and Elena entered, their faces expressing surprise and interest.

"Can you give us a moment?" Chase asked quietly, his voice brooking no argument.

The men got up, nodding politely to Elena as they passed. The space was crammed with state-of-the-art computer and radio equipment, and an enormous map of Afghanistan covered one wall. On the opposite wall was a row of photos of men dressed in traditional Middle Eastern garb, with their names in bold print below them. Elena realized these were pictures of terrorists that the military hoped to capture or kill. In that instant, the full impact of where she was hit her.

Chase slid the weapon from his shoulder and placed it on a nearby surface. As he looked at her, Elena could see that he wasn't just upset, he was furious. "What the hell are you doing here, Elena?"

"I could ask you the same question."

Chase arched an eyebrow. "This is my fourth deployment to Afghanistan and my second time at this particular base. I'm active-duty military. This is what I do. But you're a civilian, so I'll ask you again. What are you doing here?"

"I work for the DPA. This is where they've sent me."

He cursed and raked one hand through his hair. Elena

watched, mesmerized, recalling the silky texture of those strands.

"You told me you were going to Shangri-la. I thought it was a joke. At the time, I figured you were heading back to the States."

Elena arched an eyebrow at him. "Sorry to disappoint you. I couldn't recall the name of the base, only that it sounded like Shangri-la."

Chase made a gesture of frustration. "I checked the manifest this morning, and it said you were going to Baghdad, to the Green Zone."

He'd checked the manifest! That information wasn't available to just anyone, and Elena was warmed to think he'd cared enough to find out where she was going.

"Obviously you didn't go to Iraq," he continued. "So how the hell did you end up on my base?"

Elena frowned, not liking his tone. Was he implying that she'd purposely come to Sharlana because she knew he was here? "I don't know what manifesto you were looking at, but I can assure you that I am assigned to this base. Originally, yes, I was supposed to go to Iraq, but my orders got changed at the last minute." She hesitated. "Do you have a particular problem with my being here?"

"Damn straight I have a problem with it." He took a step toward her, his gaze raking over her. "This is no place for a woman, and certainly not a woman like you."

Elena bristled. "And just what is that supposed to mean?"

Chase made a growling sound of frustration. "Jesus, Elena, do I need to spell it out? Look at you! You have no military background, no experience with life on a forward operating base. This place is hard enough for men to deal with, without having the added burden of a civilian female to worry about."

Elena's chin lifted. "I can take care of myself, Chase. Besides, there's another civilian woman here. Why aren't you bitching at her, too?"

He frowned. "I am not bitching at you. I'm just telling you that Sharlana is not an easy place to live. Besides," he swept her with another cold glance, "I saw the other woman and I can assure you that she's unlikely to distract the men, whereas you…"

"Oh. My. God." Elena stared at him in dawning comprehension. "I can't believe this." She gave a disbelieving laugh. "You are such a male chauvinist!"

"I am not a male chauvinist," he protested. "I just happen to believe that there are certain places a woman doesn't belong, and here is one of them."

"Why?" she challenged. "Because you think I'll distract the men? That's ludicrous."

"Is it?" he asked drily. "The men on this base have explicit instructions not to give females—or civilians—preferential treatment. Yet there they were, carrying your gear like a couple of lackeys."

"I was tired. Pete was being a gentleman."

"*Pete?*" he repeated in disbelief. "Jesus, you just met the guy ten minutes ago and you're already on a first-name basis?"

"Why not?" Her tone was deceptively silken. "Look where you and I were after just twenty minutes."

His eyes grew hot, and if Elena hadn't known better, she might have thought he was jealous.

"He's not *Pete*," he ground out. "He's Corporal Cleary and he's on duty. This isn't a Virginia tearoom, Miss de la Vega, and there are no bellhops or doormen to do your bidding. Here, everyone pulls their own weight or they get sent home."

"I bet you'd like that, wouldn't you?" Elena asked, feeling equally hurt and angered by his manner. To think, she'd actually been excited to see him again.

"Damn straight I would. In fact, I may just insist upon it."

"You wouldn't!" Elena gasped, outraged. "I came here to do a job, and I'm not leaving just because you're uncomfortable having me around." She hesitated as a thought struck her. "If it's about last night…"

"It's not," he insisted. "I'd feel the same way if I'd never seen you before today. But since you brought it up, now is a good time to inform you that sex is not permitted on this base. Or any other military installation in the Middle Eastern theater, for that matter."

"Don't worry," Elena snapped, giving him what she hoped was a disdainful look. "There's nobody—*nobody*—here that I'm interested in having sex with."

"Good," he snapped back. "You might want to make that clear to *Pete*."

Elena narrowed her eyes. Could it be possible that he *was* jealous? She might have forgiven his obnoxious behavior if she thought that was the cause, but he'd made it clear that he was less than happy to see her. More likely, he was one of those old-school kind of guys who thought a woman's place was in the bedroom.

"I can't believe we're even having this conversation," Elena said. "Pete—Corporal Cleary—said that you're special ops, and I realize they don't let women into their ranks. But in case you haven't noticed, women have finally been accepted in the military."

"Oh, I've noticed," he said meaningfully.

"But you don't like it," Elena finished for him.

Chase made a growling sound and Elena was unprepared when he advanced on her. "You're not getting it. Out here, *this is a man's world*. I don't have a problem with women in the military. I have a problem with assigning women—especially civilian women—to troops that in the past have been designated as all male."

"And why is that?" she asked. She tipped her chin up, but took an involuntary step backward. "Because you think we can't handle it?"

"No," he snarled. "Because I don't think the *men* can handle it. Think about it. There are lots of young males and damn few females here. The men can't go outside the base to look for sex, so they look inside. The shortage of women creates competition and poisons the work atmosphere with distrust and animosity, not to mention lust. Even if the situation doesn't erupt into overt rape, it will always be disruptive and undermine the cohesion, morale and discipline that these missions require. Now do you get it?"

Elena's heart hammered hard in her chest. "Are you saying I'm in danger from your men?" she finally asked, swallowing hard.

"I'm saying that you need to think long and hard before you bat your eyelashes in their direction, or play the damsel in distress and have one of them come running to carry your gear." He swept her with a long look. "Nobody could blame them for getting the wrong idea. Some of these boys have been out here for a year or more, and any one of them would bend over backward for just a smile from you."

"But not you."

Even as the words left her mouth, Elena wished them back. She sounded bitter and jealous, and the last thing she wanted was for Chase to think that she wanted *him* to notice her in that way, or to bend over backward to please *her*.

"No," he agreed quietly. "Not me. There's a time and place for that, and it's not here. And while we're at it, you're to address me as First Sergeant McCormick or sir, is that clear?"

"Perfectly," Elena retorted, her voice as chilly as his.

"Try to understand. We're in a combat environment, Elena, and each person on this base has a responsibility to see to their own safety. You'll receive no special treatment from me or any of the other men," he continued, "so if you can't handle that, you should think about leaving."

"Not a chance," she snapped. "I'm here to stay, *sir,* and the sooner you get that through your head, the easier it will be for *you*. Are we done here?"

"We're done. Just remember what I've said, Elena. The rules are for your own safety."

Elena snorted her disbelief. "Just tell me where my quarters are so that I can go and clean up." She swept him with a scathing look. "And while we're at it, I'll ask you to address me as Ms. de la Vega or *ma'am.*"

She watched as his lips tightened. Had she really thought his mouth delectable? He was a bastard, through and through, and her only regret was that she'd actually enjoyed their night together. More than enjoyed it. Sex with Chase McCormick had eclipsed every other pleasure she'd experienced in her life.

This whole horrible encounter would have been so

much easier if he'd been terrible in bed, but the fact was he'd been amazing. All three times. And as much as she told herself that she was better off having nothing to do with him, a part of her desperately wanted a repeat performance.

5

FROM THE DOORWAY of his office, Chase watched Elena struggle to carry her duffel bags. Her slender shoulders bowed under their weight, and his hands clenched at his sides. Every instinct in his body demanded that he go down and help her. He'd seen the shadows under her eyes. She was exhausted, and he was largely to blame. She hadn't gotten any sleep because of him.

Memories of the previous night rushed back, and he ran a hand across his eyes to dispel the erotic images. He'd known it would be a huge mistake to sleep with Elena, yet he'd been unable to resist. She was too tempting. Too feminine. Too entirely appealing.

But as much as he physically wanted her, he absolutely didn't want her at Sharlana. The remote, mountainous region frequently came under attack from the Taliban, and current intelligence reports suggested another one could come at any time. The recent death of eight civilians at the hands of insurgents less than fifty miles away only served to emphasize the danger they were in.

What if he couldn't keep her safe?

More than six months had passed since he'd witnessed

the ambush on the supply convoy in Iraq, but he'd never forget how the gunner had abandoned his post to try and protect the female truck driver, and they'd both been shot by insurgents as a result. After the attack, Chase had made inquiries and learned that both soldiers would survive their injuries. He'd also learned that the two soldiers had been romantically involved.

The experience had only confirmed his belief that women had no place in combat. Most men of his acquaintance had been raised to believe that women were weaker and required protection. To expect those same men to let a woman fend for herself in combat was unrealistic. Better to keep the woman out of danger in the first place.

Just the thought of anything happening to Elena caused his chest to tighten and a sick sensation to unfurl in his stomach. He didn't object to civilians working alongside the military, but he seriously objected to civilian women—especially Elena—being sent to remote bases like Sharlana. The conditions were too harsh. Even if he could ensure her safety, she wasn't cut out for life on a forward operating base.

She was soft. Literally. Even now, he could recall the satiny texture of her skin, feel the lushness of her lips pressed against his. She wasn't a woman who was accustomed to physical exertion; the demands he'd made on her last night had left her weak as a kitten. He couldn't envision her lasting through an Afghan winter.

She'd been asleep when the alarm on his wristwatch had gone off, reminding him that he had less than forty minutes to change into his combat gear, grab his shit and make it to the airstrip. Not wanting to wake her up, he'd scrawled a brief note on the hotel stationery and had tucked it into her duffel bag for her to find later. He'd had just enough time to stop by the embassy and scan the most recent lists, where he'd been relieved to find her name among those scheduled to go to Camp Victory in Baghdad. Shangri-la, indeed. At the large military base, she'd have all the amenities of home, including fast-food restaurants, shopping opportunities and decent living quarters. Most importantly, she'd be well protected. He just hadn't realized that her orders had been changed since that list had been printed.

When he'd first caught sight of her walking across the base at Sharlana, he'd been stunned. He'd thought of her more than he cared to admit—even to himself—since he'd left her bed. At first he'd believed he was imagining things; that he wanted her so much that his mind was playing tricks on him. His next reaction had been a fierce pleasure at seeing her again, followed immediately by anger. What the hell was she doing here? For a brief instant, he'd wondered if she'd somehow learned where he was headed and had managed to follow him. But according to Elena, she was at Sharlana on legitimate business as a contract administrator, although he intended to find out why her orders had been changed at the last minute. And the hell of it was, he couldn't do a damn thing about it. He was special ops; he and his men only used Sharlana as an operating base for covert forays across the border into Pakistan. He had no authority over Elena, and even his threats to have her sent back to the States didn't carry any weight.

Only she didn't know that.

As he watched her from the doorway, Corporal Cleary approached Elena. He glanced in Chase's direction and almost defiantly reached out and took the duffel bags from Elena. Chase watched as Elena tried to argue with him, but Cleary shook his head and continued walking until Elena had no choice but to follow him.

Chase frowned, unfamiliar with the odd, clenching sensation in his chest. He wanted to be the one walking Elena to her new quarters. He wanted to be the guy who made life easier for her—but he wouldn't be a hypocrite. He firmly believed that women had no place on a remote base like Sharlana. Their very presence created a distraction that could prove dangerous, both to themselves and the men who sought to protect them. He wasn't unfeeling, and he'd do what he could to keep them safe, but he couldn't afford to let his men lose their focus.

Elena and Corporal Cleary stopped in front of a hut at the far end of the housing area, about five doors from the unit where Chase himself was staying with his team. He groaned inwardly. Bad enough that they were on the same base, but knowing she was so close would be a distraction that *he* didn't need. Chase blew out a hard breath. He had no clue how he'd stay focused, knowing Elena was just feet away.

ELENA OPENED THE DOOR of her living quarters and stared in dismay at the cramped interior. The space had been divided into eight tiny compartments, each one with a cot and a crudely constructed nightstand and shelf. Elena had expected austere living conditions, but she hadn't been prepared for this. She'd thought Larry was exaggerating when he'd said she'd be sharing a B-hut with twenty other women. Just imagining his smug expression if he knew the truth was enough for her to square her shoulders and step determinedly inside. Sharing space with seven other women would be a piece of cake. She might prefer privacy, but she didn't need it to survive. After all, she'd grown up with two sisters and a mother who had invented the word *drama*. This would be easy by comparison.

The farthest compartment was occupied by the older woman who had traveled with her on the helicopter, and Elena saw she was unpacking her duffel bags and attempting to make her little space homier. Only the tiny cubicle nearest the door was free of personal gear.

"Sergeant Corrente said we could take whichever compartments we wanted, and I didn't want to be near the door," the woman said in way of explanation. "I'm Sylvia Dobbs, by the way. I'm a quality inspector from the San Antonio DPA office. How about you?"

Elena dumped her duffel bags on the floor of the empty cubicle. "I'm Elena de la Vega, from the HQ office. I'll be working at the contracting center."

"It must be nice to actually know somebody here, and especially someone so handsome," Sylvia said, smoothing a small, brightly colored throw blanket over her cot, but Elena didn't miss the curiosity in the other woman's voice.

Elena sat down on the bare mattress of the narrow bed, frowning at the unyielding surface. "I don't really know him. At least not well. And I'm not so sure he's all that happy to see me." She didn't want to talk about Chase. "How long did the sergeant say we had before dinner?"

"An hour or so. Enough time to unpack and maybe catch a quick nap." Sylvia yawned hugely. "I'm wiped out, so I'm going to lay down for a little bit. The sergeant said to tell you that there's a supply office in the warehouse at the end of the road. If you need anything you can get it there. Otherwise, he'll come to get us for dinner, and then we have to attend a base-orientation class with the other folks who came in today."

"Did he say how long that might take?"

"Maybe an hour. He said we'll go over safety and security procedures, then we'll take a quick tour of the base and see where we'll be working while we're here."

"Who's sleeping in the other beds?" Elena asked, noting the photos and stickers that the occupants had affixed to the plywood walls.

"Soldiers," Sylvia said. "Female soldiers. With our luck they probably get up at the crack of dawn."

Elena slanted Sylvia an amused look. "I'm sure we're expected to get up at the crack of dawn, too. I was told we'll be working twelve- and fourteen-hour days, seven days a week. There is no sleeping late."

Sylvia stilled, then resumed smoothing the blankets on her bed. When she spoke, her voice was so quiet that Elena almost didn't hear her. "I hope I didn't make a huge mistake in coming here."

"Why did you come here?"

The other woman turned toward Elena, and hesitated before speaking. "I just went through a nasty divorce. Unfortunately, my ex made out better in the settlement than I did." She shrugged. "I needed a change of scenery, and the money was too good to pass up."

Elena felt a pang of sympathy for her. "I'm sure that being here will take some getting used to, but you'll be fine."

She bounced experimentally on the bed, wincing at the unforgiving surface. Standing up, she examined the cot, seeing that she'd only been provided with a box spring, but no mattress. There was no way she could sleep on the bed without a mattress. She tried to see what Sylvia had on her bed, but the other woman had already covered the surface with her sleeping bag and the throw blanket. The other beds were also covered with sleeping bags, so it was difficult to determine if they had mattresses, or not.

"Maybe I'll take a walk over to the supply office and let you get some sleep." She looked doubtfully around the hut. "He didn't say where the bathroom is located, did he?"

Sylvia grimaced. "Unfortunately, they only have open bay showers and latrines. They're located in the last building on the right, so we passed it coming in."

Elena pulled her baseball cap off and smoothed her hair back from her face. "God, I could use a shower. I feel so sticky. Maybe I'll do that now."

"Oh, Corrente said that they have a water shortage, so showers are limited to just five minutes, and only every other day."

"You're kidding."

"Nope, I'm not. He said that one of the projects they're working on is a well. If they can get the well operational, then we'll have plenty of water, but right now it's being rationed."

Elena stood up, clapping her baseball cap back onto her head. "Great. I'm going over to the supply office. Is there anything you need?"

Sylvia shook her head and stretched out on her bed. "Just some sleep."

Elena left the hut and headed in the direction Sylvia had indicated. Even this late in the afternoon, the heat was oppressive, stealing her breath and baking down on her shoulders. Two helicopters flew low over the base, the sound of their engines overpowering. Elena shielded her eyes to watch them pass, then immediately covered her face as eddies of dust swirled through the air, kicked up by the rotor blades. Swearing softly, she brushed the grit from her eyes and continued walking. She passed several groups of soldiers along the narrow street and although they stared at her with undisguised interest, they were polite enough in their greetings, addressing her with a nod and a curt "Ma'am."

With her DPA uniform of black cargo pants and boots, tan shirt and matching baseball cap, Elena knew she resembled a park ranger more than she did a soldier. Even without the words *DOD CIVILIAN* emblazoned across her breast pocket, there was no chance that anyone could mistake her for being military. She certainly wasn't the first civilian to arrive on the base, and yet she couldn't help but feel conspicuous as she walked past the rows of housing. When she drew alongside the Tactical Operations Center where Chase had dressed her down, she couldn't prevent a swift, sideways glance at the windows.

Was he still inside? A part of her wanted to go to him and try to apologize for their earlier altercation. She didn't like being at odds with him, not after what they'd shared. But then she remembered his scathing words, insinuating that she didn't have what it took to live on the base. Tipping her chin up, she strode past the office, her back rigid. She'd show him exactly what she was made of. She might not be a man, and she wasn't military, but she could certainly deal with the conditions here at Sharlana as well as any soldier, female or otherwise.

She stopped in front of a large hangar with a sign out front that read S-4 Supply. Opening the door, she found herself in a cool, dark warehouse with row after row of shelving that reached to the ceiling. Large bins were stacked along the walls, and hundreds of boxes marked with stenciled stock numbers rested on the shelves. Elena could hear the low murmur of masculine voices from the rear of the hangar and cautiously made her way toward them.

A small office had been built in a corner of the warehouse, and through the pass-through window, Elena saw a female soldier sitting at a desk doing paperwork. Seeing Elena, she stood up and leaned through the window, smiling in a friendly way.

"Can I help you, ma'am?"

Elena approached the window. "I hope so—" she broke off to glance at the front of the woman's uniform "—Specialist Ostergard. I was told to come here if I needed any supplies."

"That's right. What do you need?"

"Well, a mattress for starters. And bed linens. I just arrived today."

SPC Ostergard's expression was one of surprise. "You don't have a mattress on your cot?"

"There's a box spring, but no mattress. And no sheets or blankets."

The woman looked quickly away, but Elena could have sworn she was suppressing a smirk. "Ma'am, you do have a mattress."

Elena smiled sweetly back at her. "No, I don't."

"Yes, you do. What you're calling a box spring is actually the mattress."

Elena stared at her in disbelief. "But it's as hard as a rock, and only about four inches thick. How can you call that a mattress?"

"It's standard military issue to every person on this base, ma'am. Maybe you could ask a family member to mail you a foam pad or a mattress topper. That's what most of us do."

Elena blew out an exasperated breath. "Well, what about sheets and blankets?"

"We don't supply those. Everyone just uses their sleeping bag. I'm sorry, that information should have been made clear to you during basic contingency ops training."

Elena digested this, acknowledging silently that she might have missed that bit of information during the stateside orientation. But before she could reply, a voice spoke from behind her.

"What's the problem, Ms. De la Vega? Your living quarters not up to your usual standards?"

Elena whirled around to see Chase and two other soldiers standing several feet away. Chase held a clipboard in one hand, and the soldiers were each pushing a hand truck loaded with supplies they had pulled from the nearby shelves. Elena realized it must have been their voices she'd heard when she'd first entered the hangar. How much of her conversation had Chase overheard? She'd die before she let him know that she'd mistaken her mattress for a box spring, or that she'd actually requested sheets and blankets.

"No," she assured him with a smile. "My living quarters are great. I was just, um, becoming familiar with the base and thought I would check out the supply office."

"Uh-huh." Both his tone and his expression told Elena he wasn't buying her story.

"Actually," she said quickly, "I was wondering where

I might get some soap and shampoo. I left mine back at the hotel in Kuwait."

From the expression on Chase's face, Elena knew he was remembering the previous night. She doubted he had woken up with sore muscles as a result of their nocturnal activities. He was in perfect condition. And what did she really know about him, after all? He might be well accustomed to having one-night stands with complete strangers. The thought darkened her mood, and she found it difficult to maintain her smile as she envisioned him in bed with other women.

Chase turned to the soldiers. "Can you finish up here? I'll walk Ms. De la Vega over to the post exchange."

"Oh, no," Elena protested. "That's really not necessary. I can see you're busy. I can find my way there on my own."

No way did she want to spend any more time alone with Chase, not after their previous confrontation. She wasn't sure she could endure another tongue-lashing from him, at least not without losing her composure and subjecting him to one of her own.

"I insist," Chase said. "Besides, there're a few things I need to pick up myself."

Elena could see that he wouldn't take no for an answer, and there didn't seem any point in arguing further. Reluctantly, she followed him out of the warehouse. Earlier, he'd worn only a T-shirt and shorts. Now he wore standard combat cammies, with a flak vest and an accessory belt weighted down with various pouches and gadgets. He looked as if he'd just stepped off the cover of *Soldier of Fortune* magazine, all broad shoulders and lean hips and badass attitude.

Just seeing him made Elena's pulse quicken and her

stomach flutter. Why did he have to be so *hot?* It would be so much easier to maintain her feminine outrage if she wasn't always thinking about his masculine assets. He seemed taller than he had when she'd met him in Kuwait, and his battle gear made him look more imposing. He pulled a pair of sunglasses out of his vest pocket and slid them on, effectively shielding his eyes from her. Elena found she was actually a little in awe of him. They walked silently for several moments.

"Listen, I want to apologize for what I said earlier." He stopped and faced her. "I was out of line. I was just so—" He paused, obviously struggling for words. "I was shocked to see you, plain and simple."

Elena nodded. "I understand."

"No, I don't think you do. You see, I know what's out there." He stabbed a finger beyond the fencing that surrounded the base, toward the distant mountains. "Hiding in those hills is an enemy who would do anything— *anything*—to destroy us. And while the military on this base are trained to deal with that, you aren't."

Elena tipped her chin up, refusing to be intimidated. She stepped closer and tapped a finger against his body armor. "Well, I guess that's why I have you. To protect me."

To her astonishment, he gripped her by the shoulders and gave her a light shake. "You're not getting it. I can try to protect you, but I'm not always going to be here. My job takes me outside this base for long periods of time. Who's going to protect you then, Elena? Your little guardian-angel necklace?"

She stared at him. She couldn't see his eyes behind the sunglasses, but a muscle worked convulsively in his jaw.

"What makes you think I even need protecting? I already told you, I can take care of myself."

Chase made a growling sound of frustration and before Elena could guess his intent, one hand closed around her upper arm and he hauled her alongside him as he strode down the street. They stopped in front of a concrete structure reinforced on all sides with sandbags. Chase thrust her through the open door and into a concrete tunnel that led downward until they entered a small chamber.

"This is a bomb shelter," Chase said grimly. "If we come under mortar attack, the sirens will go off. You grab your helmet and your vest and you run as fast as you can to this shelter, you got that?"

Elena glanced around at the dark room, feeling claustrophobic despite the open doorway that allowed some light to enter. She nodded, "Yes, I understand."

"You don't stop to grab your pocketbook or your ID card or anything else. You just get your ass in here, understood?"

Elena stared at him. "Yes, I understand. Now let go, you're hurting me."

Chase snatched his sunglasses off and although he loosened his grip, he didn't release her. "I'm dead serious, Elena."

"So am I." She tried to disengage herself, but his fingers were locked around her arm. "Listen, Chase, I appreciate your concern, I really do. But just because we…" She broke off, not sure how to continue and then decided to just be blunt. "You're not responsible for me just because we spent one night together."

"I know that, damn it." He stepped closer, and Elena felt her breath catch at the intensity of his expression.

"But the fact is, whether you like it or not, we have a connection. Don't pretend that you don't know it's true."

They had a connection. Elena's heartbeat quickened and the air changed. She could almost feel the electric charge that crackled between them. But there was no denying that what he said was true. There *was* a connection between them.

"Yes," she finally acknowledged. "I know it's true. But you said yourself that you won't give me any preferential treatment, so why are you doing this?"

"Because I don't want you to rely on anyone else—not the female soldiers you bunk with, and not even me—to help you out if there's an emergency, okay? You need to know exactly what to do without being told and without freaking out."

Elena arched an eyebrow at him. "I assure you that I would not *freak out*."

"Let's hope we never have to find out."

His expression was inscrutable in the hazy light, and Elena was suddenly conscious of the fact that they were alone in the bunker. He was standing close enough that she could actually smell his scent, and it brought all the memories of the previous night rushing back. The feel of his lips. The texture of his skin.

The way he tasted.

"I—I should go," she said, aware of how breathless her voice sounded. Her gaze drifted over his face and lingered on his mouth. He still held her, but now his grip changed. His hand slid down the length of her arm and captured her hand, turning it over and stroking his thumb over her palm.

"So fucking soft," he muttered.

The expression on his face was so sensual that Elena's

breath caught, and she couldn't prevent her fingers from curling around his. "Chase..."

He made a rough sound of defeat and hauled her against his chest as he lowered his head toward hers. Elena had only an instant to register the unyielding surface of his protective vest and the hard jut of his utility belt when a voice interrupted them from outside the bunker.

"Sergeant McCormick, sir! You down here?"

Chase pushed Elena away from him just before a shadow appeared in the entrance to the bunker. The soldier came to an abrupt halt when he saw Elena.

"Sorry, sir," he said in a rush, and Elena saw it was Mike Corrente. "You're needed at tactical. Intel says a large force of Taliban fighters is congregating about six miles down the south road."

The transformation in Chase was immediate and a little alarming to watch. In the space of a heartbeat he went from warm and intimate to cold and professional.

Gripping Elena's elbow, he steered her toward the entrance, his strides long and purposeful. "I'll take my men and use the north road to circle around and position ourselves above them."

Elena had to trot to keep up with Chase as they exited the bunker, and her heart rate kicked up a notch at the thought of him in danger.

"Best we can tell, they're hoping to overrun the compound after nightfall. Charlie Platoon was in the one of the villages outside Spera to pick up this guy who the villagers say has ties with the Taliban. But now they're on their way to intercept these guys."

"Tell them to avoid the wadi," Chase said. "That entire riverbed is an ambush point." He pulled Elena to a halt outside the Tactical Operations Center. "Go back to your living quarters and stay there, understood? Mike'll have someone escort you to the chow hall, and then back to your hut. Under no circumstances are you to leave it without a military escort. And remember what I said. If those sirens go off, you get your ass into that bunker."

Elena nodded. "What about you?"

For just a moment, his face softened and he reached out to stroke her cheek. "Don't worry about me. This is what I do best. Just take care of yourself."

But as he turned and took the stairs to the operations center two at a time, Elena realized she wasn't afraid for herself at all.

All her thoughts were centered on Chase.

The knowledge that he might be killed caused her chest to constrict. She'd told herself that what they'd done hadn't meant anything. They'd been two strangers who had briefly taken pleasure in each other, knowing that such enjoyment might not be available to either of them again for a very long time. Whatever connection they shared went no deeper than a physical attraction. So why, then, did it feel as if he'd taken a part of her with him when he left?

6

"WE'LL JUST COLLECT your roommate and then I'll bring you both over to the chow hall now," Mike Corrente said as he and Elena walked swiftly back to her living quarters. "I'll have one of the engineers walk you back afterward. I think the orientation brief may have to wait until tomorrow."

Elena agreed. From the activity surrounding them, she understood that the troops on the base had more important things to do than provide a tour to the recently arrived civilians. They skirted groups of soldiers who were busy prepping their weapons and shoving their gear into rucksacks, and the energy level seemed to have ratcheted through the roof. Elena could almost feel the excitement of the young men as they prepared to confront the enemy and realized they were actually looking forward to the encounter. Beyond the housing area, Elena saw more men loading Humvees and armored vehicles with weapons and ammo.

"How long will Ch—Sergeant McCormick be gone?" she finally asked.

The sergeant shrugged. "Hard to say. He and his men

could be gone overnight, or they could be gone for a week."

"What is it that he does, exactly?"

Mike slanted her a quizzical look. "You really don't know? He and his men do recon, and they've actually taken out several key Taliban leaders."

Elena frowned. "But he just arrived this morning, right?"

They'd arrived outside the door to Elena's hut, and the sergeant paused to consider her. "This is McCormick's fourth deployment to this region. His was one of the first special ops teams to be dropped into this zone after the war began. Hell, he helped to establish this as a base when it was little more than a series of mud huts surrounded by stone walls. If anyone knows this region, it's McCormick."

Elena digested this information. She wasn't surprised that Chase was special ops; he oozed confidence and capability. It was just part of who he was, and Elena knew instinctively that she could trust him with her life.

But she also understood that a man who was on his fourth deployment to Afghanistan, after having spent a year in Iraq, was a career military guy. He didn't have the time or luxury for long-term relationships. She couldn't feel bitter about this, since Chase had told her up front that he couldn't offer her anything more than one night.

Now she understood why.

Opening the door to her hut, she saw three female soldiers inside, stuffing gear into their backpacks. The one nearest the door gave her a brief nod. She looked to be in her early twenties, with a freckled face and pale blue eyes.

"Ma'am," she said in way of acknowledgment, and bent back to her task.

The other two soldiers were slightly older, and they barely glanced up as Elena entered. At the far end of the hut, Sylvia sat on her bed watching them, her eyes wide with apprehension.

"Hey, Sylvia," Elena called. "Sergeant Corrente is going to bring us over to the chow hall."

One of the soldiers, a pretty girl with dark eyes and hair, looked up when Elena mentioned Sergeant Corrente. Her gaze moved beyond Elena to the door and without a word, she stood up and slung her pack over her shoulder. Squeezing past Elena, she left the hut.

"Perfect," muttered the other woman, shoving a pair of socks deep into her rucksack. "We'll be lucky if we get out of here today. Once those two catch sight of each other, nothing else matters."

The freckle-faced girl laughed. "Yep, got that right. Poor Mike. He doesn't know whether to be pissed off that Valerie got assigned to the same base as himself, or get down on his knees and thank his lucky stars."

The first woman snorted. "He'll be pissed until the first time she gets him alone and rocks his world. Then he'll be thanking his lucky stars."

Her interest piqued, Elena stepped into her little cubby and pretended to be absorbed unpacking her duffel bags. In reality, it took all her self-restraint not to peek out the window to see what was happening with Sergeant Corrente and the girl named Valerie.

She looked at Sylvia, who hadn't moved.

"Sylvia? Hey, you okay?"

"I think your friend is freaked out over the news that the Taliban is closing in," said the freckled-faced woman, extending a hand toward Elena. She spoke in a soft, Southern accent. "I'm Corporal Callie Linden. I told her it's no big deal, but I don't think she believes me."

"I'm Elena de la Vega." Elena frowned as the woman stood up. "You're not actually going out there to confront the Taliban, are you?"

"I'm a gunner, ma'am. If they send a convoy out, then I'll go with them." She jerked her head in the direction of the third woman. "Corporal Chapman here does house-to-house searches with the guys because only female soldiers can perform body searches of the local women." She shrugged. "Like I said, it's no big deal."

Elena hesitated. "What you said about your friend and Sergeant Corrente…"

"Val and Mike? What about them?"

"I know it's none of my business, but were you referring to them having, you know, sex?"

Callie grinned. "Val's been plotting to get that boy alone since she first laid eyes on him, and I don't think he'll put up too much of a fight."

"Okay, I know this sounds stupid, but I was told in no uncertain terms that sex is strictly forbidden. Is that true?"

The first woman, Corporal Chapman, gave a hoot of laughter. "They can try to forbid it, but it's happening whether the brass likes it or not. General Order One doesn't expressly prohibit having sex, but it's highly discouraged. Yeah, there are rules about how we're supposed to behave, like we're not supposed to be in each other's quarters with the door closed." She gave another snort. "Like that's going to deter anyone. Believe me, if two people want sex, they'll find a way."

"Those rules," Elena ventured. "Do they apply to *everyone?*"

Corporal Chapman sharpened her attention on Elena. "Why do you ask? Do you have your eye on one of our boys already?"

Elena couldn't prevent the heat that washed into her face. "Of course not. I was just wondering."

"Uh-huh. Sure." But when it became clear that Elena wasn't about to offer anything more, she shrugged. "Even if the rules don't apply to you, they apply to the soldier you're fantasizing about. But like I said, if two people want to be together badly enough, they'll find a way. We always have female soldiers turning up pregnant and trust me, they didn't get that way by themselves."

Elena watched as the women finished stowing their gear and left the building, before turning her attention back to Sylvia. She sat on the edge of her bed, twisting her blanket in her thin fingers.

"Hey, what's going on?" Elena asked gently. "There's nothing to be afraid of. We're protected by some of the best and bravest soldiers in the world." She adopted a brisk, friendly tone. "C'mon, let's go get something to eat. Personally, I'm starving."

But Sylvia only shook her head. "No, I couldn't eat a thing. My stomach is in knots. I think I'll just stay here."

Elena nodded in sympathy. "All right. I'll bring something back for you, then. Why don't you lie down and try to get some rest? I'll be back soon, I promise."

Sylvia nodded and at Elena's urging, lay woodenly

on the bed with her eyes open, as if she expected the Taliban to burst through the door at any moment.

Elena left the hut and stopped uncertainly when she saw Mike Corrente in a heated, hushed conversation with the dark-haired woman who had left their living quarters so abruptly. Mike wore an expression of extreme frustration and twin patches of color rode high on his cheekbones. Valerie looked defiant. As Elena closed the door behind her, both soldiers looked up, and while Mike was distracted, Valerie took the opportunity to turn and walk away. For a brief instant, Elena was certain that Mike would go after her, before he visibly restrained himself.

"Where's Ms. Dobbs?" he asked in a clipped tone.

"Not feeling well. Look, if you just want to point me in the right direction, I can find my own way to the chow hall."

"No doing," he answered, shaking his head. "I promised McCormick I wouldn't let you go anywhere alone and I don't intend to."

Elena sighed. "Fine. Let's go."

As they made their way through the housing area and past the latrines and showers, Elena was amazed at the level of activity on the base. The sound of diesel engines filled the air as a dozen Humvees and armored vehicles prepared to leave the base and patrol the surrounding area. Two helicopters stood on the landing strip, the downward wash of their rotors creating small sandstorms of dust that rolled across the base in billowing clouds.

Elena wondered what Chase was doing at that moment. Had he and his team already left the base? Were they making their way toward the spot where the Taliban forces had been spotted? She knew for a fact that he hadn't slept the previous night; would he get any sleep this night? Her mind whirled with all the possible scenarios. Her stomach was a knot of anxiety, and she didn't think she'd be able to eat.

"Here we are." The sergeant's voice interrupted her thoughts. They had arrived at the chow hall, and the delicious aroma of grilled burgers and French fries made her mouth water. Inside, rows of tables and benches filled a large room.

"Just grab a tray and move through the line," Mike instructed, nodding toward the hot food. "There's also a salad bar and a dessert bar and the drinks are over there. You can pretty much help yourself to whatever you want, as much as you want."

Elena stared around her, amazed by the selection. "I thought I'd be eating MREs," she marveled, referring to the prepackaged field rations that the military used in combat.

Mike smiled. "No way. We're the best-fed military in the world." He winked at her and patted his flat stomach. "The only problem is the food is almost too good."

Although it had seemed to Elena that every able-bodied person on the base was gearing up to confront the enemy, the dining area was about half-filled with people, both military and civilian. She saw several of the men who had flown in on the same helicopter with her, and one of them raised a hand in friendly acknowledgement.

Not feeling particularly sociable, Elena smiled but turned to Mike. "I'm just going to grab something and bring it back to my room. You don't need to wait."

Planting his feet apart, Mike crossed his arms. "That's okay, ma'am. I'll wait."

Giving him a dubious look, Elena nodded. "Fine. I'll be right back."

She quickly chose some sandwiches, fruit and bottled drinks and bundled them all in a paper bag. Despite Mike's determination to wait for her, she sensed that he was anxious to get back to his job.

The sun was setting behind the mountains as they made their way back toward the living quarters, and Elena could feel the temperature beginning to drop.

"Does it get cold here at night?" she asked.

"It can. We're in the desert, so the difference between day and night is pretty extreme. Best to wear layers, since you never can tell what the weather will do." He hesitated before continuing. "So, um, how're your living quarters working out?"

Elena shrugged. "I grew up with two sisters so I'm sort of used to sharing my space."

"Did you—did you meet the enlisted women?"

Elena glanced sharply at him. "Do you mean Valerie?"

To her amazement, twin spots of ruddy color appeared on his cheeks. "Yeah. She won't tell me if she's going out on patrol, or not. Thinks I'll freak out, or something."

"I don't know about Valerie, but the other two women said they were most likely going out."

They were approaching Elena's housing unit when they heard a shrill, terrified scream from inside. Elena barely had time to register what was happening before Mike broke into a run and flung the door to her hut open, disappearing inside. Elena followed, her heart hammering. She reached the open doorway and peered over Mike's shoulder to see Sylvia standing on top of

her bed, an expression of horror on her pale face. She
stabbed a finger toward the floor.

"There! Did you see it? Under the bed! It went under
the bed!"

Mike worked his way through the cubicles, crouching
down to check the floor as he went. "What is it? What
am I looking for? A snake? A scorpion?"

"Sp-spider," Sylvia managed in a choked voice. "A
huge spider."

"Damn," Mike muttered. "I hate frickin' spiders."

Elena stood in the doorway, poised to run, when she
saw a dark shape, easily as big as her hand, scuttle across
the floor. Only scuttle was the wrong word, because that
would imply the thing merely hurried, when in reality it
raced across the open floor. Directly toward her.

Elena couldn't help herself. She shrieked and flung
herself outside, her eyes scanning the ground in case
the thing actually decided to follow her. She was only
vaguely aware of several soldiers running in her direction, and from inside the hut, Sylvia squealing in
fright.

Strong hands gripped her by the upper arms and gave
her a slight shake. "Elena, what's wrong? Are you all
right?"

"Spider," she managed to gasp as Chase stared down
at her. "A huge spider!"

"Wait here," he said grimly and ducked inside the
housing unit.

Elena leaned back against the wall of the hut, listening
to the chaotic noises coming from inside. It sounded as
if they were overturning the beds in their search for the
enormous creature. She could just distinguish Chase's
voice speaking in low tones, presumably to calm Sylvia.

She jumped when Mike emerged from the hut, looking a little stunned.

"Ah, you might want to move away a little," he said when he saw Elena standing beside the door.

There was a collective gasp from the congregated soldiers as Chase emerged from the hut. Dangling from his gloved hand was a massive spider.

Elena recoiled in horror.

"It's okay," he assured her. "It can't hurt you now."

"Oh, my god," she breathed, staring at the creature in disbelief. "What is it?"

"The soldiers call these camel spiders."

"Is it alive?"

Before Chase could answer, the thing made a hideous noise and began to twitch in his hand. As one, the soldiers took a step backward.

"Damn, Sergeant," one man said, "you're either the bravest son of a bitch I've ever seen or the dumbest."

Chase held the spider up and considered it. "They're actually not venomous. This guy was probably just looking for a shady place to hide."

The spider was sand-colored and hairy, and each of its legs were easily six inches long. It jerked grotesquely in Chase's hand. Elena shuddered and looked away, repulsed by the thing. Her imagination conjured up horrible images of what might have happened had Chase not captured it. What if the spider had attacked her during the night?

"Somebody get me a box or a jar," Chase commanded. He turned to Elena. "You okay?"

She couldn't understand how he could be so calm while holding something so frightening. "I don't think

I can go back in there," she said, indicating her sleeping quarters. "What if there are more?"

"We checked everything and the hut is clear. There's nothing in there to be afraid of."

Elena gave a disbelieving snort. "Right. You couldn't pay me enough money to sleep in there."

A corner of Chase's mouth lifted and his eyes gleamed with humor. "I did warn you that the conditions here are different than what you're accustomed to."

She bristled. "If you even try to insinuate that I'm acting like a typical female, Chase, then take a good look around. Even your own soldiers are afraid to get near that thing." She grimaced. "Any human should be afraid to get near something that revolting."

Chase laughed. "Okay, I concede."

One of the soldiers came forward with a cardboard box, and Chase dropped the spider inside, quickly closing the top before it could escape. He handed the box back to the soldier. "Release it outside the wire."

The soldier blanched. "Me?"

Chase arched an eyebrow. "You have a particular problem, Corporal, that prevents you from releasing an insect?"

The man flushed and defiantly snatched the box from Chase's hands, although Elena noted how he held it at arm's length. "No, sir," he snapped. "No problem."

He strode away, and Chase turned to the remaining men. "Okay, show's over. Back to your posts."

"Speaking of which," Elena said quietly, "why aren't you at your post? Something about insurgents preparing to overrun the compound? What are you doing here? I thought you were against rescuing damsels in distress."

He glanced at her. "The intel was false," he said curtly.

"Ah. Well, that's a relief. I mean, if you'd been gone, who would have captured that little critter?" Elena peered into the hut to see Sylvia still standing on her bed, her face pale. "The spider is gone," she assured the other woman. "You can come down."

Sylvia gingerly climbed from the bed and came outside. Elena could see she was shaking. She held out the bag she'd carried from the dining facility. "I brought you a sandwich and something to drink."

Sylvia grimaced. "Thanks, but I couldn't eat a thing." She drew in a shaky breath and faced Chase. "Actually, I'd like to speak with whoever is in charge of the DPA folks."

Chase's expression didn't change. "That would be Colonel Vinson. I can walk you to his office, if you'd like."

Realization hit Elena, and she reached out to touch Sylvia's shoulder. "You can't leave. Not when you've just gotten here."

Sylvia turned around. "I can't stay. I'm sorry, but I completely underestimated what the conditions would be like out here." She glanced back into the hut and Elena saw a shudder go through her. "I can't sleep in there, or anyplace else where there might be those spiders. Or worse. I'm sorry."

"There's nothing to be sorry about," Chase assured her. "You're making the right choice."

Elena briefly narrowed her eyes at him before turning back to the older woman. "Sylvia, you don't have to do this. Granted, the spider was disgusting, but it wasn't poisonous. We really need you out here. The *troops* really need you here. I wish you'd reconsider."

Sylvia shook her head. "I can't. I'm going to ask if I can leave on the next helicopter out."

Reluctantly, Elena glanced at Chase. She fully expected to see an expression of triumph on his face, but his features were somber as he considered Sylvia. "I'll personally ensure that you're on a flight back to Kuwait first thing tomorrow." He shifted his attention to Elena. "Can I persuade you to go with her, Ms. De la Vega?"

"Not a chance."

"Fine," he said, clearly not pleased. "But next time there's an uninvited, eight-inch critter in your bed, don't expect the cavalry to come to your rescue."

Elena smiled sweetly and allowed her gaze to drift over him. "Trust me. The next time I have an eight-inch critter in my bed, it won't be uninvited."

7

ELENA SPENT a sleepless night tossing and turning on her hard pallet, and she knew Sylvia did the same. After the other woman had returned from Colonel Vinson's office, she'd confirmed that she would be leaving in the morning. Then she had repacked her duffel bags with the items she'd unpacked just hours before, and had slid fully clothed into her sleeping bag. The female soldiers didn't return that night, and it was just Elena and Sylvia in the hut. The temperatures fell and Elena shivered in her sleeping bag, her eyes wide open.

The base apparently didn't sleep, either. Elena listened to the sound of diesel engines throbbing to life, and the shouts of soldiers as they went about their work. She dragged the sleeping bag up over her shoulders and turned onto her side, thinking about the events of the day. Part of her understood why Chase wanted her to go home, but another part of her felt hurt and insulted by his eagerness to see her gone. She still had a difficult time reconciling the man she'd known in Kuwait with the hard-eyed soldier here in Afghanistan. She just wished she knew if his desire to send her home really had to do with her safety or his own discomfort at having her around.

She had just begun to drift off when a strident alarm snapped her into full awareness. Sylvia mumbled something incoherent and Elena heard her fumbling in the dark until finally, she hit the alarm and blissful silence ensued. But for Elena, there was no falling asleep.

With a groan, she sat up and pushed the sleeping bag back, shivering in the cool air. Reaching out, she groped for the light attached to the wall and snapped it on, illuminating her little sleeping compartment. She looked over at Sylvia, who was also sitting up and rubbing her eyes.

"What time is it?" Elena asked.

"About 4:00 a.m. Sergeant Corrente is coming to get me in ten minutes to bring me to the airstrip." Sylvia swung her legs over the edge of her bed and scrubbed her hands over her face. "God, I'm tired."

Elena agreed. She was exhausted to her very bones, but she knew she'd never be able to get back to sleep. "I think I'll go grab a shower and something to eat, and then head over to the contracting center," she announced. "Any chance I can borrow your shampoo?"

Leaning over, Sylvia unzipped her duffel bag and tossed Elena a small cosmetic kit. "You can keep it," she said. "I'm not going to need it."

Elena slid her feet into her boots. "Well, I guess this is it," she said to Sylvia. "I'm sorry this didn't work out for you."

Sylvia gave a huff of laughter. "I'm not. I'm glad I came, if only for the fact that I now realize how lucky I am."

"What do you mean?"

Sylvia shrugged and looked a little embarrassed. "I've spent the past year feeling sorry for myself. My whole life changed after my husband left me. Somehow, I believed that was a bad thing." She looked around the room they shared. "But coming over here and seeing how these young people live was a real wake-up call. They work in these horrible conditions, far away from their loved ones, and yet I haven't heard one complaint. It's a little humbling."

Elena knew exactly what she meant. She considered that this was Chase's fourth deployment to Afghanistan and that he was prepared to spend another year away from his family.

"It does make you reconsider what your priorities are," she agreed. "I'm sure none of these soldiers take what they have for granted, not when they know they could lose everything at any time. You figure out really quick what it is that you care about."

She wondered what Chase cared about. Who were his loved ones? He'd told her that he wasn't married, but did he have someone waiting for him at home? She realized she knew next to nothing about the man, other than the fact he was from North Carolina. If circumstance hadn't placed them on the same outpost together, she would never have seen him again, never known anything more about him than what she'd learned during that one amazing night.

The thought was oddly depressing.

Bending down, she unzipped her duffel bag to pull out a clean change of clothing and a towel, when something white fell from the folds of fabric and drifted to the floor. Elena picked up a slip of paper that had been folded in half, her name scrawled across the front. Her pulse quickened as she slowly opened the note, half afraid of what she might find. He'd only written two lines, but they were enough for Elena.

Didn't want to wake you up, but not ready to say goodbye.
Write to me, Elena.

He'd provided an e-mail address, and his signature was a bold slash of ink across the bottom of the note. The message was so much like him, direct and authoritative, that she had to smile.

He hadn't wanted to say goodbye.

The realization that he'd wanted to stay in touch with her caused a slow warmth to seep through her. She closed her fingers over the paper. *Write to me, Elena.* Which meant that his earlier hostility at seeing her on the base was from his own fears for her safety, and not because he didn't want her around.

"Elena, are you sure you want to stay here for six months?" Sylvia's voice interrupted her thoughts. "There's room on that helicopter for you if you think you'd like to go home."

Elena turned to the other woman with a smile. "Oh, no. I'm definitely going to stay. In fact, I'm really looking forward to it. But thanks."

She gave Sylvia a brief hug and then hefted her backpack over her shoulder. Stepping outside into the cool darkness of predawn, she made her way to the lavatory facilities, but her thoughts were on Chase. He'd written the note believing he wouldn't see her again, at least not so soon. But the fact that he'd given her his e-mail address and asked her to write to him was huge. She knew instinctively that he wasn't the kind of guy to give his personal information out lightly.

Lost in her thoughts, she made her way past the other living quarters. The base was mostly quiet at this hour, although she could hear the lazy *thwap-thwap* of an idling helicopter over on the landing pad, and guessed it was Sylvia's ride home.

She entered the showers and saw a row of changing stalls facing a wall of lockers. Beyond the locker room, she could hear the spray of water from the shower room itself, which meant she wasn't going to have the privacy she'd hoped for. With a resigned sigh, she set her belongings in the closest stall and quickly undressed. Wrapping her towel around her, she grabbed the bottle of shampoo that Sylvia had given to her and padded over to the open shower room.

And stopped dead in her tracks.

A man stood beneath the spray of a single nozzle, steam wreathing his body. A supremely muscled, supremely naked man.

Chase.

All the saliva in Elena's mouth evaporated at the sight of him. He stood with his back to her, his head bent as water sluiced down his body. He soaped himself, his hands moving over his chest and up under his arms, washing there before sliding lower, over his stomach. He was golden everywhere except for the paler skin of his hips and buttocks. Despite having seen him unclothed before, Elena greedily drank in the sight of him.

He was the most gorgeous man she'd ever seen, lean and hard, and his face…with his cheekbones and full, sensual mouth, he had a face that could make an angel weep. Elena just stood there, clutching her towel and staring. She couldn't drag her gaze away from him, devouring the play of muscles along his sleek back. His ass was perfect, his thighs hard and sinewy. She remembered all too well the feel of them between her own, and a hot burst of yearning spread through her abdomen.

He tipped his head back, exposing his strong throat and letting the spray hit him full in the face before he slicked it away with one hand. He turned slightly, and Elena saw the heavy thrust of his penis; he was semi-aroused. Heat swamped her, churning through her veins and making her feel a little light-headed.

The plastic bottle of shampoo slipped from her fingers and bounced on the tiled floor. His head snapped around and in the next instant their gazes collided. Elena couldn't move, couldn't breathe. Chase's eyes turned hot, and even from where she stood, she could see how every muscle in his body tightened at the sight of her, and his erection went from halfhearted to rampant in the space of a heartbeat. Her breathing quickened and with a mumbled apology, she turned on wobbly legs to flee.

"Elena." He moved fast. He caught her by the arm and spun her around, and she found herself hauled against his wet chest. Steam still rose from his skin in a fine mist, and his lashes were spiky with moisture.

"Elena," he said hoarsely. "What are you doing in here?"

She stared at him, mesmerized by the hunger in his expression. "I came to take a shower," she breathed.

"This is the men's shower. You can't be in here."

The sound of voices drifted toward them from outside the door. Glancing swiftly around, Chase dragged her into a changing stall and jerked the curtain closed.

Before Elena could protest, he lifted her onto the wooden bench and covered her mouth with his fingers, silencing her with a single look.

"Sergeant McCormick, you in here, sir?"

Elena recognized the voice as Pete Cleary's.

"Uh, yeah," Chase called back. His voice was rough.

"I just thought you should know the helo's taking off, but your girl's not on board."

His girl.

Elena didn't have to guess who Pete referred to, and her eyes snapped back to Chase's over the warmth of his hand. He was watching her intently, and twin patches of ruddy color rode high on his chiseled cheekbones. His eyes glittered, more green than hazel, and his breath came in short pants. He had a small, perfect mole on his collarbone and as Elena watched, a droplet of water fell from his hair and landed just above it, before trickling downward in a tiny rivulet. Her eyes followed its path, and she had an overwhelming desire to lap at the moisture with her tongue.

"Sir?"

Elena heard heavy footsteps enter the shower room.

"I understand. Thank you, Corporal," Chase finally responded. "I'll be out shortly."

The footsteps receded and Chase slowly removed his hand from her mouth. Standing on the bench, Elena towered over him. She realized her hands were resting on his broad shoulders, and her fingers spread across his skin almost reflexively. Her glance swept downward and she was reminded he was still naked, and still very much aroused. Beneath the towel, her nipples contracted. She moistened her lips.

"I thought this was the women's shower," she whispered, half in explanation, half in apology.

"Elena," he groaned, and his fingers tightened on her waist, bunching in the terry cloth and dragging it downward until the towel fell away and cool air wafted over her bare breasts and stomach.

She watched, entranced, as his eyes darkened. Then he leaned forward and very gently circled his hot tongue around one nipple. Elena gasped and her hands crept upward to clutch his head, her fingers burrowing into his dripping hair. He drew her breast into his mouth and suckled her, while his big hands cupped her bottom and pulled her closer, until she leaned fully into him.

He sucked harder and from between her thighs came an answering throb, sharp and sweet. He kneaded her bottom, and then his fingers dipped between her buttocks and found the secret spot where she pulsed hotly. He touched her intimately, one finger probing her slick entrance until Elena groaned and her legs buckled.

"Hold on to me," he said, his voice husky, before he crouched in front of her and began laving her with his mouth and tongue.

Elena groaned. Part of her knew she should stop him, but she was too far gone. Her blood pounded hot and insistent through her veins, until she thought she might spontaneously combust. She threaded her fingers through his wet hair, and when he urged her thighs farther apart, she complied, rolling her head back against the wall of the changing stall. She was completely unrestrained in her urgency; the part of her brain that still functioned understood that an entire platoon of U.S. Marines could come marching through the shower room at any moment.

She didn't care.

All that mattered was the man who knelt before her, pleasuring her with his hands and tongue. She glanced down and the sight of his dark head at the juncture of her thighs, combined with the erotic sensations he created, was too much. She gave a strangled cry as her orgasm crashed through her. Even then, Chase didn't stop, drawing her pleasure out until she thought she couldn't take any more and still survive. Her fingers were still tangled in his hair, and she didn't let go, even when he worked his way up her body, pressing warm, moist kisses along her heaving stomach and breasts. When he finally stood upright, he cupped her face in his big hands and slanted his mouth hard across hers, kissing her deeply. Elena could taste her own essence on his lips.

She wreathed her arms around his neck, boneless with release, and kissed him back. "Now it's your turn," she breathed into his mouth. She could feel him, hot and hard against her thighs, but as she slid a hand down to touch him, he captured her wrist, halting her.

"You have to go," he muttered. "Someone could come in."

Elena drew back just enough to search his eyes, but his expression was shuttered. "I don't *have* to go," she protested softly. "Not if you don't want me to. I could stay. I *want* to stay."

With a low sound of frustration, he stepped back and reached into a backpack that was on the floor, dragging out a pair of black boxer briefs and pulling them on in quick, jerky motions. Elena slid down the wall until she was sitting on the bench. She watched him fish through his gear until he found a T-shirt and hauled it over his head, yanking it into place.

"You're upset." She picked her towel up and covered herself with it, feeling exposed and vulnerable and defensive. "You were the one who dragged me in here, remember?" she said tightly. "I was leaving."

His head snapped up and his eyes blazed. "Listen, it was fun but it's not going to happen again."

Elena stared at him. The sexual buzz she felt from her orgasm was fading fast, to be replaced with a sense of confusion and the beginnings of a simmering anger. "Oh, that's right. I remember now—no sex on the base. Right?" Chase didn't answer, but she knew from the rigid set of his shoulders that she'd hit the mark. He had laid down the law and nothing would induce him to break it. "So that's how it's going to be, huh?" she continued, boiling. "Everything on your terms? You make the rules and I'm just supposed to obey them?"

"Damn right."

"Well, you can forget it. You're not the boss of me. I do what I want."

It was a childish retort, she knew, but the man infuriated her. He made her do and say things that were totally out of character for her. She'd always prided herself on maintaining her composure, but he completely upset her equilibrium.

Before she could guess his intent, he pinned her against the wall, his face inches from hers. "What, you think this is a *game?*"

Elena refused to be intimidated. "What am I supposed to think? One minute you're telling me that sex is strictly forbidden, and the next you're—you're—"

"Like I said, it was a mistake," he grumbled, releasing her shoulders. His voice was full of self-disgust. "This whole thing was my fault, not yours."

"What a relief. I feel so much better." Elena stood up, but the changing stall was so cramped that it brought her into full body contact with Chase. He flattened himself against the opposite wall as if she carried some contagious disease.

"Don't worry," she said with false sweetness, wrapping her towel around herself and securing it tightly over her breasts. "I'm not going to touch you." She let her gaze drop with deliberation to his crotch, where the fabric of his boxers molded to the impressive outline of his erection.

He still wanted her.

The knowledge pleased her. She knew what self-denial felt like; she'd spent most of her life denying her own desires and impulses. She wanted him to suffer, at least a little. "As much as I'd like to help you out, this looks like a problem you'll need to, uh, handle yourself."

Without waiting for a response, she yanked back the curtain of the tiny stall and stalked out. She paused only long enough to snatch up her own belongings, clutching them against her chest. Without waiting to see if he would follow, she made her way blindly toward the exit, where she saw the women's showers were directly next door.

She just managed to dump her stuff on a bench and turn the shower on before her tough-girl facade crumbled. Stepping beneath the spray, Elena turned her face into the water. She was close to tears. Even when she'd found Larry with that woman, she hadn't felt as miserable as she did right now. Then again, she'd never wanted Larry the way that she wanted First Sergeant Chase Mc-

Cormick. And she'd known Chase for just two days, so what did that say about her?

She'd thought she could have him for just one night, with no inhibitions, no complications and no regrets. And no chance of ever running into him again.

She'd been shocked to find they were both assigned to the same forward operating base, but had convinced herself that she could handle it. On some level, she'd even understood that his initial hostility toward her stemmed from his own concern for her safety. The knowledge had made her feel...special.

But now she had to acknowledge that they had no real relationship. What they had was purely physical, and now it seemed that Chase didn't even want that. She shouldn't feel so upset. She didn't even know the guy, so what did she care if he rejected her? He was probably a Class-A jerk, anyway. One of those arrogant, know-it-all alpha males who believed a woman's place was in the bedroom.

Which, if she was honest with herself, was where she wanted to be.

In *his* bedroom, in *his* bed.

Elena told herself again that the last thing she needed was the complication of a serious relationship, especially out here.

So why did she feel so disappointed?

8

TWO DAYS HAD PASSED since the shower incident. Two days in which Chase had studiously avoided going anywhere on the base where he might cross paths with Elena. If he closed his eyes, he could still see her face as he'd pushed her away from him. He'd hurt her. But Christ, what did she expect? That they'd be able to pick up where they'd left off? The worst part of it was, he desperately wanted to resume their relationship.

He'd known when he'd met her in Kuwait that she was the kind of woman he'd like to know better. Now he told himself that they both had a job to do, and he wouldn't let his libido get in the way of either of them doing that. But he wasn't able to ignore her. The base was too small not to know where she was and what she was doing at any given time.

She'd reported to the contracting center the morning that he'd found her in the men's shower. He'd watched as the contracting officer, Brad Carrington, gave her a tour of the base and took her out to view the waste water treatment facility. They'd spent about an hour talking with the men working on the project, until Carrington had walked her over to the dining facility, and then back to the contracting center.

Carrington was a good-looking guy, and he'd been at the base for over six months. He was career Navy and he was married. But Chase knew that didn't matter to some guys. He wondered if Carrington had tried to put the moves on Elena yet, and his gut twisted at the thought of her with the young officer.

As much as he'd tried, he couldn't stop thinking about that encounter in the showers. She'd been so hot. So incredibly sexy. He'd been unable to sleep, partly due to the time-zone change but mostly because he'd been thinking about her. So he'd risen before dawn and walked over to the showers, but even the cold water hadn't diminished his body's response to his memories of their night together. Then suddenly, there she was. In the shower room, her eyes turning from warm caramel to liquid amber as she'd devoured him.

He might have let her go if Corporal Cleary hadn't threatened to walk in on them. He'd lifted her onto the bench so that if the other man did come in, he'd see just one pair of feet beneath the curtain of the changing area. But that had put him on eye-level with her lush breasts, barely concealed beneath the terry cloth, and her skin had been so smooth and fragrant, and the heat in her eyes had been an invitation he couldn't resist. And the way she'd tasted…

"McCormick, did you hear a word that I just said?"

Chase snapped his attention to the two men who occupied the tactical ops room with him. Staff Sergeant Sean Brody stood next to an oversize map of the Paktika province, circling areas where the Taliban was suspected of having strongholds. He paused, hand poised over the map as a third man, Gunnery Sergeant Rafael Delgado, leaned back in his chair and considered Chase with barely concealed impatience. With his Antonio Banderas curly black hair, dark eyes and growth of beard, Rafe could easily pass for a local tribesman, which made him invaluable for the missions they conducted. More importantly, he spoke both Pashto and Dari, as well as half a dozen other languages. Now he looked at Chase, irritation written all over his face.

"What?" Chase asked, feigning ignorance.

Rafe snorted. "I knew it. You haven't been listening to a fucking thing we've said for the past fifteen minutes."

Chase frowned and pinched the bridge of his nose. As part of a five-man special operations team, he'd worked with Sean and Rafe on more missions than he cared to recall, both in Iraq and Afghanistan. He'd trust either man with his life, and he owed it to them to get his head back in the game and focus on their next operation. He squinted at the map.

"I'm listening," he lied. "We know that Mullah Abdul Raqid is rumored to be using the town of Surobi as his stronghold, but he has the locals so completely terrorized that none of the tribal leaders will give him up for fear of reprisals."

Sean tapped the map. "Until yesterday. Our guys were on patrol along the wadi, here, when they were approached by a local boy. His father had been injured in a fall and was airlifted to a hospital in Kabul."

"And?"

Rafe leaned forward. "And he was supposed to deliver a cache of weapons to Raqid, but now that's not going to happen. None of the other men will go without him, and he's afraid that Raqid will retaliate by coming after his family. He's asked us to protect them."

Chase knew the facts; he'd read the intel report. He and his team already had an approximate location for where Raqid and his men were hiding in the hills above Surobi. But those mountains were pockmarked with caves and crevasses, and Raqid could be in any one of them. Even with an approximate location it would take weeks or months to pinpoint the bastard's exact location. But with the information about the weapons transfer, they had a real shot at finally getting him. The special ops team would move into position, and when the local tribesmen delivered the weapons, Chase and his men would intercept the transfer and, with luck, capture Raqid. In return, the villagers would get a new school and a clinic, paid for with U.S. funds.

"We'll leave in three days. The recon team is already in place, watching the exchange point," Sean said. "We'll insert here," he tapped the map, "and work our way across this mountain range to approach from the rear. Once we're inserted, we'll have just eight hours to get into position."

Chase surveyed the map, noting the rough topography they would have to traverse. They'd managed worse, and so long as their position wasn't betrayed, there was no reason to believe the mission wouldn't be a success. If they succeeded in bringing down Raqid, they would eliminate much of the threat in the local area. Without Raqid, his followers would have a tougher time regrouping. The U.S. troops would ensure that they didn't retaliate against the villagers.

The door exploded open in a cloud of dust and heat,

and a man entered, sweeping the room with a cheerful grin. "Yo, whazzup?"

"Jesus, don't you ever do anything quietly?" Rafe asked, annoyed.

"What, were you sleeping or something, Gunny?" the man asked innocently, but his blue eyes sparkled.

As the newest and youngest member of the special ops team, Corporal Josh Legatowicz, or Lego as the team called him, was far more cocky than he had a right to be. But his personality was so engaging and his skill with a sniper rifle so flawless that the older members of the team put up with him.

"You're late," Sean said, looking pointedly at his watch. "I specifically said to be here at 1300 hours."

Lego grabbed a chair and spun it around, straddling it as he polished an apple against his jacket front and then bit into it with a loud crunch. "Sorry, I got held up. Hey, Sarge," he said, addressing Chase. "Any chance I can do a security detail tomorrow?"

Security details weren't something the special ops team routinely participated in, unless it was for somebody very important, like a general or a diplomat. The Tac Ops received a situation report every six hours, and Chase didn't recall that anyone was scheduled to visit the base.

"What kind of security detail?" he asked.

Lego's grin widened. "A most excellent female civilian needs to drive out to the drilling site, and I just thought it would be safer if she were accompanied by someone who could protect her. Someone like me."

Chase knew he was glowering, but he couldn't help himself. "This *most excellent* female wouldn't be Elena de la Vega by any chance, would it?" But he already knew the answer.

Lego brightened. "Ah, her reputation precedes her. That's awesome. And if you've seen her, then you know what I said is true." He tucked the chair under his armpits as he leaned forward. "Man, this chick isn't just desert hot, you know? She's the real deal. Even if I was back in the States, I'd try to nail her. I give her two weeks before she realizes she can't live without me."

Desert hot was a derogatory term used by the troops to describe female soldiers who achieved a certain level of hotness simply because they were female, and not because they were exceptionally attractive. At home, these women might not have earned a second glance from most guys; here in the desert, they were often the cause of intense rivalry between their male counterparts.

"You're not going to pull security detail for her," Chase said easily. "In fact, you're not going to accompany her anywhere."

"Why not, Sarge?" Lego asked. His face expressed both dismay and disappointment.

"Yeah, why not?" asked Sean, smirking.

"Because she's not leaving the base, that's why," Chase shot back.

Rafe frowned. "Now wait a minute, McCormick. First of all, she doesn't work for you. Second of all, you can't keep her from doing her job."

"She can damn well do her job from inside the fence," he retorted. "What reason does she have to go out to the drilling site? She's a desk jockey, not an engineer. Seeing the project isn't going to enable her to do her job better, and I'm not about to give up one of my men to accompany her on a nonessential mission."

"That's not your call, McCormick. Besides, the previous contract administrator visited the construction sites fairly regularly." Rafe paused. "But then, the last contract administrator was a man. And that's the crux of the whole issue, isn't it? You don't want her going because she's female."

"I don't want her going because we don't need anybody on this base taking unnecessary risks. I don't care if they're male, female or an alien from outer space. And for the record, the last contract administrator was sent home two weeks ago because he suffered a heart attack, which is why Ms. De la Vega was sent here to replace him. She doesn't need the added stress of visiting the construction site."

Even as he said it, Chase knew he was full of shit. Worse, his team knew it, too. But they were too well trained to let their skepticism show on their faces, and they tactfully said nothing. Except Lego, who hadn't yet figured out when to keep his mouth shut.

"Well, jeez, Sarge, she sure looks healthy to me. But that's all the more reason I should go with her," he argued. "As long as she's with me, she won't be at risk. I'll guard her with my life. And it's not like I have anything else to do, at least not until we move out." He followed this with another of his signature grins that made him look about twelve years old. But Chase knew better. The kid was a total chick magnet.

He also knew he had no valid reason not to let Elena leave the base. The construction site was a scant two miles outside the fence, and was as well guarded as the compound itself. Civilian contractors who were assigned to Sharlana traveled to the site without incident. There was no reason to think that Elena would be in any danger. And as much as he hated to admit it, he had little control over what she did in the normal course of her job—if she wanted to visit the drilling site, he couldn't prevent her from going. But he could damned well make it unpleasant for her.

"I'll go with her," he finally said.

"Yeah, you look real reluctant about it, too," Rafe said sardonically. "I can see it's the last thing in the world you want to do."

"Damn!" Lego flung himself out of the chair. "I knew it! I knew you'd take this one for yourself. Jeez. How come you always get the good assignments?"

Chase laughed. The kid looked so disappointed, he couldn't help himself. The thing Lego didn't know, and what he wasn't about to tell him, was that he'd already taken Elena for himself, and he'd be damned if he'd let any other guy move in on her. As far as he was concerned, she was already his.

ELENA WAS EXHAUSTED, both physically and mentally. She didn't mind the long work days, so maybe it was a combination of the altitude and heat, but by the time she returned to her CHU each night, she felt completely drained.

The extensive needs of those living on the base floored her, everything from supplying food and laundry services, to heavy drilling equipment and private security guards. The sheer volume of work was overwhelming, but the job was equally satisfying; what she did had an immediate and positive impact on the men and women assigned to the base. Here, there was no time for politics or red tape. The daily needs of the troops were real and urgent, and Elena found it a little daunting to know that she had the ability to authorize or deny those needs with a stroke of her pen.

She and Brad Carrington were the only contracts personnel assigned to the base. Brad had been friendly as he'd briefed Elena on the projects she would oversee, but he'd been all business. Elena was grateful for that, and she sensed that they would work well together. The last thing she needed was another overbearing soldier trying to tell her how to do her job.

After just two days of familiarizing herself with the projects she would be working on, Elena had decided to visit the construction site where a new well was being drilled. She'd heard plenty of horror stories about contracts being awarded for projects that were either unnecessary or bogus. While she doubted that was the case with this project, she wouldn't be satisfied until she saw the ongoing work with her own eyes. Part of her job entailed verifying the progress of the construction, especially since payments were made to the contractor based on the percentage of completion. She was not going to be the contract administrator who authorized millions of dollars for bogus or unnecessary work. When she'd announced her decision to visit the drilling site, Brad had tried to argue that it was unnecessary, but had admitted that he had not seen the project and had little idea how it was progressing.

Elena felt nervous about going out there, but if her job was to oversee the construction projects, then that was what she would do. Brad might roll his eyes and think she was being overly picky, but she sensed that he also had respect for her work ethics. As long as her signature was going on the paperwork to authorize continued performance—and continued payment—she would do everything by the book. At her insistence, Brad had arranged for her to visit the drilling site the following day. She would leave just after dawn and be back on the base by lunchtime.

The sun was setting as she made her way back to her CHU, and she hoped that none of the other women with whom she shared her quarters had yet returned. More than anything, she wanted a few minutes of total quiet. While the female soldiers were respectful to her, Elena felt like an outsider. Actually, she felt like the den mother to a group of rough-and-tumble, foul-mouthed Girl Scouts. The other women could be loud and boisterous, but they were also impossibly young and desperately homesick. They were truck drivers and maintenance technicians, and although technically they weren't in combat positions, they faced the same rigors and dangers that the men did.

Elena wondered how Chase McCormick felt about having them on the base. Just the thought of Chase made her toes curl with longing, even as her teeth clenched in frustration. She'd caught glimpses of him during the past two days and knew he was avoiding her.

Which was fine with her. He occupied her thoughts more than she liked, and the last thing she needed was to get into another confrontation with him. The man was a pigheaded misogynist and she didn't need him distracting her.

"Hey, Ms. De la Vega!"

Elena was just approaching her CHU when the voice interrupted her thoughts, and she turned to see Mike Corrente jogging toward her.

"Hey," she called, genuinely pleased to see him. "When are you going to start calling me Elena?"

He smiled, his teeth white in his dust-covered face. "Maybe when I'm not in uniform and I don't have some badass special ops guy breathing down my neck." He indicated the armful of folders and papers she carried. "Are you done for the day?"

"Yes, just a little nighttime reading. Why?"

"You're moving to new quarters."

"I am?" Elena couldn't keep the surprise from her voice. She knew the housing situation on the base was cramped, at best. Where could they possibly move her to, unless it was into another CHU with a different group of female soldiers?

"Yep. I'll wait here if you want to pack up your gear."

Elena laughed. "I'm not going anywhere, Sergeant. My quarters are fine."

To her surprise, he looked suspiciously smug. "Sorry, but you don't have a choice about it." He glanced at his watch. "I'll give you five minutes, and then I'm coming in to pack up your gear for you."

Her eyebrows shot up at his authoritative tone and he relented. "Trust me on this, okay? You're going to like it."

Elena wasn't so sure she believed him, but she was packed and back outside in just a few minutes, where he hefted her gear over his broad shoulders, leaving her no option but to follow him. He didn't ask about Valerie, although Elena hadn't missed how he stretched his neck to peer inside as she'd opened the door. Not that it would have done any good; the other women were still on patrol through the local villages, performing humanitarian visits.

"So we got a shipment of new CHUs about a week ago, right? And there was a lot of bickering about who was going to get these units, because they're pretty sweet, but there're only six of them. And one of them is yours."

Elena stopped walking. "Mine? As in mine, alone?"

Mike grinned. "Yes, ma'am. C'mon, we're almost there."

He stopped in front of a CHU that looked almost identical to the one she had just vacated, except it was obviously newer. The air-conditioning unit mounted in the wall hummed invitingly, and over the door someone had hung a placard with her last name on it.

Mike opened the door and motioned for her to enter. Elena did so, and stopped just inside the dark, cool interior to stare in amazement. The CHU was the same size as the one she had shared with the other women, but it was designed for just one person. The front part of the unit was a small living area complete with a table and chair and a small desk. Somebody had placed a brightly woven rug on the floor, and tacked a paper sign to the wall that read, "Welcome home, Ms. de la Vega." Standing neatly in a corner was a broom and dustpan.

A crudely constructed wall separated the living area from a tiny bedroom, which held a cot, built-in shelves and a small nightstand. A utilitarian wall lamp had been mounted over the bed for reading.

"What's through here?" Elena asked, indicating a doorway that led to the rear of the unit.

"Go ahead and look," Mike encouraged, dropping her duffel bags onto the cot.

Elena opened the door to a small bathroom. "I get my own shower?" She couldn't keep the amazement out of her voice.

"That's why these units are in such high demand," Mike said. "They're called wet chews, because they come with running water."

Elena turned around to look at Mike in astonishment. "Why do I get one? Surely there are senior military who deserve this more than I do? I'm just a lowly civilian."

Mike shrugged, but Elena didn't miss the color that crept into his cheeks. "We can't have you wandering into the men's showers wearing nothing but a towel. It's, um, distracting."

Elena stared at him for a full minute, until he finally looked away. "How do you know about that?" Her voice was no more than a whisper, and she knew all the color had drained out of her face. Had Chase McCormick said something? She'd been so sure he was above bragging about his conquests. What else did Mike know about that morning?

"Pete Cleary thought he saw your gear inside the changing stall the other morning, and then he saw you come out and go into the women's showers." He glanced at her. "For what it's worth, most of the guys on the base are a decent bunch, but you still have to be careful. Not to mention we have local nationals who work on the base, and if they saw you…" He let his voice trail off meaningfully.

Elena didn't have to guess what he meant. Seeing her come out of the men's showers clad only in a towel would undermine the progress the troops had made in gaining the trust and respect of the local men.

"It was a stupid mistake," she mumbled, brushing a

hand over her eyes. "I was tired, it was dark and I went into the wrong shower. It won't happen again."

"Right. That's why we gave you this unit. So you won't have to worry about making that mistake again."

Was it Elena's imagination, or did Mike refer to something beyond just walking into the wrong shower? Did he know that Chase had been in there with her? Worse, did he know what had happened between them?

Hot color flooded her face, and she couldn't meet his eyes. "Please tell the guys thank you. I love my new digs, and I appreciate the work they did in getting it ready for me."

"Great. I'll let them know." He turned to leave and then paused. "So you're heading out to the drilling site tomorrow, huh?"

Elena nodded. "I want to see the project firsthand and get an estimate on how far they are from completion. It can't hurt for the contractor to know that the project is being closely watched. Not for the kind of money they're getting paid."

"Do you have a firearm?"

"No, of course not. I'm neither trained nor authorized to carry a weapon." Apprehension snaked its way up her spine. "Why? Do you think I'll need one?"

"Who are you traveling with?"

Elena shrugged. "I'm not sure. I was told I'd travel with a security detail."

Mike's mouth tightened. "I'm sure you'll be fine. Just stay close to your men, okay? Don't even go to the bathroom without an escort. Promise?"

"Sure." As if that was going to happen.

But her assurance seemed to placate him, and with a muttered good-night, he left. She watched him leave, plagued with new misgivings about her decision to leave the base. Why would she need a weapon? To protect herself from possible insurgents? Or worse, from the very men who were assigned to protect her?

9

CHASE PAUSED in front of Elena's new housing unit, his hand poised to knock. He could still back out of this detail and give the assignment to Lego. As much as the kid liked to project an air of boyish enthusiasm for everything he did, Chase knew he took his job seriously. He hadn't been exaggerating when he'd said he would take care of Elena.

But while his brain told him that letting Lego handle the assignment was the smart thing to do, every other cell in Chase's body rebelled at the thought. He knew enough about himself to understand that while Elena was away from the base, he'd be unable to concentrate on his own work until she'd returned safely. He and his team were ready to move out, had gone over the covert operation countless times. There wasn't anything more they could do until the operation began.

Blowing out a hard breath, he rapped sharply on Elena's door. The sun had just begun to rise over the horizon, and he wanted to reach the drilling site early. He'd arranged for a convoy of three armored vehicles, each with its own gunner, to travel to the construction site.

He had no reason to expect an attack, but with Elena, he wasn't taking any chances.

He waited a moment and when nobody answered his knock, he rapped again, a little louder. Still nothing. With a muttered curse, he tried the handle, stunned when it turned easily beneath his hand.

"Jesus Christ," he muttered. The woman had absolutely no sense of self-preservation. A dozen different scenarios shot through his mind, each one more unpleasant than the last. Didn't she realize she was on a base with a couple hundred horny, sex-deprived men? While he liked to think none of them would cross that particular line, he'd heard too many horror stories about sexual harassment and rape to think it couldn't happen here.

Opening the door, he stepped quickly inside. A swift glance told him that both the living and sleeping areas were empty. Her bed was neatly made, her combat boots were on the floor and her helmet and flak jacket on a nearby chair. The room smelled of freshly brewed coffee, and he spied a small electric coffeepot on a nearby shelf, with a scant inch of the dark liquid remaining, next to a container of powdered creamer. On the lower shelf were a couple of paperbacks and a framed photo. Curious, he picked it up and studied the faces of Elena and two other women, obviously her sisters. They were almost identical in their dark, sultry beauty. But while one sister was laughing and the other copped a sexy pose for the camera, Elena stared unsmilingly at the lens, almost as if she were afraid to be caught enjoying herself. He placed the frame back on the shelf.

The door beyond the bedroom was closed, but he heard no telltale sound of running water or a flushing toilet. He was getting ready to call her name when the door suddenly opened and there she stood.

In nothing but a pair of black cargo pants and a lacy white bra, and the silver angel charm necklace nestled between her breasts. At the sight of her smooth, bare skin, Chase had to curl his hands at his side to keep from reaching for her.

She came to an abrupt stop when she saw him standing there, and in the instant before she composed her expression, he saw a myriad of emotions flit across her face—surprise, pleasure, apprehension and then embarrassment as she realized she wasn't wearing a shirt. Her face was still damp from where she'd washed it, and now she used the hand towel she'd been holding to cover herself. As if that could keep Chase's imagination from running rampant, recalling in perfect, Technicolor detail just how gorgeous she looked without her bra, her head back, eyes heavy-lidded and lips parted as he suckled her.

"Don't you knock?" she asked sharply, pushing past him to snatch a folded jersey from the shelf beside her bed.

Chase kept his back turned as she thrust her arms through the sleeves and dragged it over head.

"You should lock your door," he said over his shoulder. "Just because you're on an American base doesn't mean you're safe."

She snorted. "Obviously."

He did turn around then, both relieved and disappointed to see she was decently covered. She sat on the edge of the bed and bent over to pull her boots on. Every inch of her bristled with resentment. He knew exactly why she was pissed off. Chase didn't blame her for being angry with him, but he couldn't feel bad about ending their encounter in the shower.

If anyone had come in…

He told himself again that he'd done them both a favor by pushing her away. She'd never know how difficult that had been for him.

"So you're going out to the drilling site today."

She glanced up at him, her hair spilling over her shoulder in sleek, dark waves. "That's right, and don't even think about trying to talk me out of it. I have a job to do, and visiting the project sites is part of it. I have a military escort, so I'll be just fine."

She stood up and he watched, mesmerized, as she swept her hair back and secured it with a ponytail holder she'd had around her wrist. The DPA uniform should have given her an androgynous appearance, but the tan, cotton T-shirt only emphasized the feminine swell of her breasts, and she filled out the seat of her cargo pants in a way that could never be mistaken for a man. Even without makeup and with her stony expression, she was prettier than she had a right to be.

"I know you'll be fine," he replied smoothly.

Pointedly ignoring him, Elena grabbed her DPA cap from a nearby hook and jammed it onto her head, dragging her ponytail through the opening at the back. Picking up her helmet and vest she finally turned to Chase.

"If you don't mind, my ride leaves in a few minutes. I have to get going."

Chase nodded, keeping his expression bland. "Absolutely. That's why I'm here. Let's go." He indicated she should precede him out of the trailer, but she just stood there and stared at him. He knew the precise instant when she realized the truth.

"Oh, no," she said, laughing in disbelief. "You are so not coming with me."

Chase crossed his arms over his chest and gave her what he hoped was a bland smile. "Fine. Then you don't go."

"You don't even like me," she spluttered. "Why would you want to spend an entire morning with me?"

Didn't like her? Was that really what she thought? Didn't she realize that his problem had to do with liking her way too much? He wanted to peel her uniform from her body, lower her to the small cot and spend the entire day worshipping her with his hands and mouth. Since she'd shown up, he'd hardly slept, could barely focus on his own job and was swiftly becoming a joke among his own men. And she thought he didn't *like* her?

"Look," he said, striving for a reasonable tone, "I think we got off on a wrong foot somewhere." Like when she'd wanted to go down on him and he had pushed her away. Yeah, way to convince her that you really like her.

She watched him warily, and he blew out a hard breath. "I know we jumped the gun back in Kuwait, and it might seem like there's no place for our relationship to go from here, but..."

"But what?"

He hesitated. He desperately wanted to get to know Elena better. Hell, he wanted nothing more than to make love to her, right here and now. He wanted two uninterrupted weeks with her in this room. But he also knew Afghanistan was no place for a budding romance, and that he had no business encouraging her to have feelings for him. Soon enough, she'd return to the States while he'd still be here. And how difficult would that be? Not just for him, but for her, too.

He'd been thirteen when his father had left for the first Gulf War, and he'd seen the toll that his absence had taken on his mother. She'd tried to be strong for Chase and his sisters, but she hadn't fooled him. She'd gone through hell, not knowing if her husband was safe. Chase didn't want to put a woman through that uncertainty. Did he want to settle down and have kids? Sure. But not now. Not when he spent more time deployed than he did at home. But he'd be lying if he said he didn't want a relationship with Elena. Maybe, when his deployment was up…if she was still interested…

"Look, I'd like to get to know you, and I want you to get to know me, too." He laughed softly and pinched the bridge of his nose. "I don't blame you if you're not interested, because I've been kinda hard on you, but you have to believe that I meant it in the best possible way."

She narrowed her eyes at him, one hand on her hip. "What is it, *exactly,* that you want from me, Chase? You've been giving me mixed signals since I showed up, and I'd really like to know. Do you want to pick up where we left off? Or would you rather just pretend I don't exist? Because either way, I really don't care. It's your call. Just let me know so I don't end up making an idiot of myself, okay?"

Either way, I really don't care. He knew she was lying, giving him a show of bravado to hide the fact that she did care. Every fiber of his being wanted to shout, *Yes, let's pick up exactly where we left off, with you getting ready to make me go blind with pleasure.* Instead, he forced himself to smile at her in what he hoped was a platonic way.

"I think we could be friends," he finally said, knowing he was lying through his teeth and hating himself for it. The way he felt about Elena went way past friendship. A true friend wouldn't think about licking every inch of her skin, or about how she looked straddling his thighs as he thrust into her.

He watched as her mouth opened and then snapped shut. She stared at him as if he'd suddenly sprouted a third eye in the middle of his forehead.

"Friends." She repeated the word in disbelief, but her hazel eyes began to shimmer hotly. "You want to be *friends?*"

"Yeah."

"I see."

But he knew that she didn't.

She thought that he didn't want her, that he wasn't interested in her that way. The truth was, he wanted to possess her, to claim her as his own so that she would know it, and so would everyone else on the base. But he also knew that going public with their relationship would be a huge mistake. It was tough enough to be a female in a military environment without the added label of being an easy screw, and warranted or not, he knew that's how the soldiers would view her. He was doing her a huge favor by keeping their relationship platonic. And if that pissed her off, too bad. At least the other guys wouldn't bother her.

"Fine," she muttered, giving him a tight little smile. "Let's be *friends.*"

"Great." He forced a smile. "Now put on your helmet and vest."

"But we're not even off the base yet," she protested.

"Just put them on," he commanded, and watched as she struggled into the heavy gear.

"So what did you do to end up having to accompany me out to the drilling site?" she asked, glancing sideways at him and then away. "Forget it. I can see by your face that there was never going to be anyone but you."

And there never will be.

Whoa! Chase had no idea where that thought had come from. He had no room in his life for a permanent relationship, and he certainly didn't intend to tie himself down to a prickly, argumentative woman like Elena de la Vega. The woman was too hot-blooded. Too hot, period.

They made their way to the motor pool as the sun began to rise over the distant mountains. The air was still cool, but Chase knew that in a matter of hours the temperatures would climb back into the nineties and higher. He could hear the throaty, diesel rumbling of the engines before they actually reached the three heavily armored trucks, called MRAPs, that were lined up, ready to go. Chase nodded to the gunners who sat in round turrets on top of each vehicle, manning a 50-caliber machine gun. Small groups of soldiers stood talking, each dressed in full combat gear.

Elena stopped and Chase could see she looked a little stunned. "I thought we'd simply go in a single Humvee," she said, staring at the convoy of armored trucks. "Do we really need all these men?"

"We're in a war environment," Chase reminded her. "Each time we leave the base we need to be prepared for an attack. These vehicles are specifically designed to withstand that."

When she turned to look at him, he could see her face had paled and her eyes were huge in her face. She swallowed hard. Any second now, she'd change her mind and cancel the trip. He could see her weighing the options and calculating the risks. He knew exactly what she was thinking. So many men, so many resources being dedicated to her, just so that she could visit a construction site and verify that work was progressing to her satisfaction.

He knew that only a few of her predecessors had ever gone out to visit the project sites. Not even the chicken-shit Lieutenant Commander Carrington made any effort to visit the construction sites, preferring to remain within the perimeter of the base. Like most of the contract administrators who'd been here before him, he simply took the contractors' word that the projects were being done in accordance with the terms of the contracts and paid them accordingly. Which was partially why the government was losing its financial shirt to dishonest contractors, and paying for work that was either shoddy, incomplete or unnecessary.

She drew a deep breath. "Which vehicle do I ride in?"

He shouldn't be surprised that she was going to go through with it. Elena struck him as a woman who, once she made up her mind about something, followed through on it.

"The second one," he answered, and indicated she should climb inside. He followed close behind her. There was no way he was letting her out of his sight.

ELENA CLIMBED into the vehicle, glad that she didn't suffer from claustrophobia. The interior was relatively spacious, with two benches that hung along each wall, facing each other, but it felt a little like a sardine can. Behind the driver's seat was a tall platform for the gunner, who sat in a leather sling seat with his upper body protruding through a hole in the ceiling as he manned the turret gun.

Elena took a seat against one wall and noted the extensive digital electronics built into the interior. The vehicle was like something she'd imagine seeing in a futuristic sci-fi movie. Chase climbed in behind her and then pushed a button, raising and closing the pneumatic rear doors and sealing them into the small space.

"This is, um, pretty impressive," she finally said.

Chase sat down across from her, laying his weapon over his thighs. His knees almost touched hers. "You bet. These vehicles are designed to withstand a direct hit from an IED—an improvised explosive device. The hull is V-shaped to deflect the blast outward."

"Have there been many, uh, attacks in this region?"

His face softened fractionally, and Elena wondered if he could see her fear. "There've been a couple of attacks, but none recently."

Something in his expression said he wasn't being completely truthful, but she also instinctively knew that he'd never allow her to visit the drilling site if he thought she might be in danger.

"How long will it take to get there?"

"Not long. The site is just outside a small village about two miles from here. The road is pretty rough, which will slow us down a bit, but we should be there in under twenty minutes."

"I read that the villagers will also benefit from the well."

"That's right. Part of our mission is to win the hearts and minds of the local people, so anything we can do to improve their situation only benefits us."

The driver and a second soldier climbed into the cab of the truck, and looked back at Elena and Chase. "Everyone comfortable?"

"You bet," Chase answered. He looked over at Elena. "Hold on to something. The road gets a little bumpy."

He wasn't kidding. The loudness of the engines, combined with the swaying and tipping of the vehicle as it traversed the road, made conversation nearly impossible. Above her, the gunner rocked in his sling seat, his booted feet planted firmly on the platform as he surveyed their surroundings. Elena found her initial apprehension fading, and she felt a sense of excitement at being embedded as part of a military convoy.

All too soon, the vehicle began to slow, and Chase rose to his feet to lean through the opening into the driver's cab. He spoke in low tones and Elena couldn't make out what was being said.

"We're here," he announced unnecessarily as they came to a stop. He lowered the rear door, and Elena blinked at the sudden brightness.

She climbed out of the MRAP and realized they had driven onto what looked like a military compound, complete with razor-wire fencing, guards and temporary buildings. But dominating the small complex was a large, steel drilling machine, and its rhythmic pounding shook the ground and reverberated through her body. Stacked on the ground beside the drill were a dozen or more lengths of wide pipe, each nearly thirty feet in length. As she watched, two men in military uniform carefully inserted a pipe into the mechanism.

"What are they doing?" she asked.

"Drilling," Chase answered sardonically. "C'mon, I'll introduce you to the project manager." He glanced at his watch. "You have two hours to conduct your business, and then we're leaving."

The time passed swiftly for Elena. She and the project manager, a civilian contractor named Bill, took a tour of the compound and he explained the mechanics of drilling for water. Inside his trailer, they reviewed progress reports and charts, and Elena learned that pipe was being laid from the well site to both the forward operating base and to the nearby village. Even when the well was completed, they would need to maintain a security detail at the site to prevent insurgents from destroying it. But having a water source would enable the troops to be more independent and provide the villagers with a clean water source that they didn't need to pay for.

During the entire visit, Elena was all too aware of the big soldier who dogged her footsteps. Chase never let her out of his sight, taking his role as her personal bodyguard seriously. He didn't participate in her conversations with the workers, or indicate that he was at all interested in the papers that she pored over or that he even understood them, but she sensed that he missed nothing. All too soon, he indicated that their time at the site was up. She might have protested, but the implacable expression on his face said he wouldn't change his mind on this. Reluctantly, Elena said goodbye to the construction team and climbed back inside the MRAP.

"That was amazing," she said to Chase. "I have a whole new appreciation for the work being done over here. I wish my coworkers back home could see this."

The thought reminded her of Larry, who had scoffed

when she'd told him that she'd be deploying to Afghanistan. What would he think if he could see her now? In the next instant, she realized she didn't really care. Her relationship with Larry might have occurred in another lifetime. Even the thought of him with that other woman didn't cause her chest to tighten.

Sitting across from Chase, with his rock-hard body and unflappable attitude, she couldn't imagine what she'd ever found attractive about Larry. Chase was the most unapologetically masculine guy she'd ever met, but she also knew he had a softer side that he allowed few people to see.

Back in Kuwait, he'd been so honest with her about not wanting to lead her on. She'd even called him sweet. He hadn't appreciated her description, but she knew it was true. He could be both lethal and incredibly tender, and she found the combination completely irresistible. She knew he wanted her. She'd caught him watching her several times during the trip, when he didn't think she'd notice. The heat she'd seen in his eyes had brought her right back to the shower incident, and she'd had to press her thighs tightly together and try to ignore the sharp stab of arousal she'd felt.

He'd made it clear that he didn't want her in Afghanistan, but since she'd arrived at the forward operating base, she'd realized that she was a lot tougher than she gave herself credit for. Now she just had to convince Chase of that.

"You're smiling," he observed, watching her.

"Am I?"

His eyes narrowed fractionally. "What's going through that head of yours?"

But she just shook her head. "Nothing. Really."

She could see he didn't believe her, but she wasn't about to reveal her thoughts to him. Six months ago, she'd never have considered working in Afghanistan, or traveling to a construction site with an armed military escort. There were so many things she would never have considered doing six months ago, and having a one-night stand with a guy like Chase McCormick topped the list.

But she'd done all those things and more. She'd surprised herself with her own capabilities. She knew Chase didn't want her on the base, but she had to believe that she'd impressed him today, just a little bit, with her abilities. Now she was going to take it one step further.

He'd said he wanted to be friends, but Elena knew from the way he looked at her that he wanted more than just *friendship*. Six months ago—six days ago—she might not have had the courage to take a risk and go after what she really wanted. But not anymore. And she really wanted Chase McCormick.

She was going to show him that she could be effective, both on the base and in the bedroom.

His bedroom, to be precise.

10

IT HAD BEEN A MISTAKE to accompany Elena to the drilling site. He'd been okay as long as he'd been able to think of her in terms of a woman he'd like to nail, versus a woman he had to respect. Chase wasn't proud of himself for his Neanderthal attitude, but it was a hell of a lot easier to maintain an emotional distance when he told himself that she was just a pretty face without too much else going on.

But the morning's visit to the drilling site had shattered that illusion. The fact was, Elena de la Vega was both beautiful *and* brilliant. He'd pretty much glued himself to her side during the visit, ready to either whisk her to the safety of the MRAP or protect her with his own body if the need had arisen. Which, thank Christ, it hadn't.

But the downside of eavesdropping on her professional discussions was that he could no longer fool himself. She'd asked pointed questions of the project manager and the engineers and had been able to decipher their spreadsheets and charts within minutes. She'd pointed out inconsistencies, made recommendations for improvements and—much to his disappointment—had promised to return to the site to check on the progress.

But even more disturbing than her keen mind…she'd been personable and charming. She'd smiled and laughed with the men, and he'd known the instant that they'd each fallen under her spell, spilling their guts about the problems they were encountering, and even going so far as to admit that some of their invoiced costs were excessive. Through it all, she'd smiled and nodded and taken notes, and none of them had seemed to understand that she wasn't their friend. She had all the control, and she could tighten the purse strings to their accounts until they choked.

He'd tried to see her through their eyes and acknowledged that she must be like a tall, cool drink of water after enduring the dust and heat and threat of death for months on end. Even wearing a helmet and flak vest over her DPA uniform, she didn't resemble a soldier. She could have been a visiting dignitary or a celebrity on a USO tour, here to cheer up the troops. She'd certainly cheered up the guys at the construction site. At one point, the project manager had placed a hand at the small of her back to guide her into his work trailer. Even knowing that Elena couldn't have been aware of his hand through her flak vest, Chase had wanted to pick the man up and throw him across the threshold.

Now he watched her as she sat across from him, a small smile lifting the corners of her gorgeous mouth. He couldn't stop thinking about how her lips had felt against his own. Soft and lush. And when those lips had moved lower, across his torso and over his abdomen… oh, man.

He realized he was getting turned on and adjusted his rifle across his thighs to hide the evidence. In the same instant, he realized she was talking to him and he hadn't heard a word she said.

"Huh?" Oh, that was good. Way to impress the lady. He regrouped. "Sorry, I was thinking about something else and missed what you said. Repeat?"

Her smile widened, as if she knew exactly what he'd been thinking. "I asked if it's okay to take my helmet off, seeing as we're in an armored truck. I'm so hot, and my head itches."

"Sure, just hold on to something while we're moving." He indicated the low ceiling. He was back in control. "We've had guys whack their heads while going over rough ground."

Reaching up, she unsnapped her helmet and removed it, and placed it on the floor between her feet. Chase couldn't look away as she pulled her hair free from the ponytail holder and shook it out, then worked her fingers into the glossy strands to massage her scalp. She gave a blissful sigh and tipped her head back against the wall. Her eyes drifted closed.

Chase curled his hands onto his thighs. Even from where he sat, he could smell her shampoo, and his fingers itched to wrap themselves in her hair. He admired the slender column of her throat and the delicate line of her jaw, remembering how soft her skin had been beneath his fingertips. Beneath his lips.

And just like that, he was hard again.

"Hey, Sergeant!"

Chase jumped guiltily and leaned forward to look at the soldier sitting in the front passenger seat. "What is it, Corporal?"

"Looks like market day in the village. Wanna stop?"

Elena had opened her eyes and was sitting upright, straining to catch a glimpse of the village through the windshield. Her gaze swung toward Chase, and he already knew what she was going to ask.

"Can we do that? Is it safe?"

Chase hesitated. Normally, they would stop the vehicles and greet the villagers. They would exchange courtesies with the elders, pass out candy to the kids, purchase goods from the market stands, all part of their campaign toward winning the loyalty of the local population. But today he had to think about Elena. The responsibility of keeping her safe was a huge weight on his shoulders.

"Sergeant?" asked the corporal. "The lead truck wants to know if we stop or keep moving."

Chase made the mistake of glancing at Elena. He saw the excitement and hope in her eyes and knew he couldn't say no.

"We'll stop," he replied gruffly. "Twenty minutes, max."

Elena gave him a beautiful smile, and Chase felt something shift in his chest. "Thank you," she said.

Instead of acknowledging her thanks, he reached into a pocket and pulled out a camouflage bandana. He always kept several handy in case of sandstorms, and now he shoved it unceremoniously at Elena.

"Here, cover your head."

She took the cloth and stared at him, then shook it out and began to arrange it over her hair. Chase watched her struggle with it for several seconds before he made a sound of impatience. Setting his weapon on the bench, he crouched in front of her.

"Not like that," he admonished softly. "You need to cover your hair and your neck."

Taking the bandana from her, he shook it out and refolded it, and then draped it over her head. She was so close that he could feel the warmth of her breath against his face, and see the tiny pulse that beat frantically at the base of her smooth throat.

He swallowed hard, forcing himself to concentrate on his task. "Take the ends, like this," he said, "and bring them around the front. Then cross them at the throat and tie them like so, behind your neck."

He had to reach behind her to secure the ends of the cloth, and he didn't miss how her breathing hitched. He forced his hands to remain steady as he tied a knot and then rocked back on his heels to survey his handiwork. She looked like a beautiful peasant girl, or give her a pair of big, dark sunglasses and she'd look like a Hollywood movie star. Her cheeks were flushed and her eyes were focused on him with such intensity that his pulse tripped into overdrive.

"Here," he muttered, "your hair is still sticking out." He raised a hand to push the escaped strands beneath the cloth, then froze when she turned her cheek into his palm.

"Chase," she murmured, her gaze drifting over his face to settle on his mouth.

Jesus. He was going to kiss her; he couldn't stop himself. Nothing short of a direct rocket attack would prevent him from covering her mouth with his own, right there in the back of the MRAP, with two junior soldiers sitting just feet away.

He bent his head toward her. Her lips parted, but at the last second she pulled away and ducked beneath his arm to snatch her helmet from the floor. In the same instant, the pneumatic door at the back of the truck lifted open and two soldiers peered inside.

Chase sat on his heels for a moment, head down, fighting for composure. He'd come so close to losing it.

"Hey, Sarge, you okay?" asked one of the men.

"Yeah." Reaching out, he snatched his weapon from the bench and jumped down from the back of the vehicle before turning to assist Elena. But she had already taken the corporal's proffered hand, and he was leading her to the little village where children ran toward them in anticipation.

He watched as she bent down to greet the children, and within seconds she was surrounded by a sea of tiny arms, reaching up toward her.

"I gave her a box of candy," the corporal explained with a self-satisfied grin. "The universal icebreaker."

"Twenty minutes," Chase said gruffly, "and then I want her back in this truck."

As much as he wanted to be within arm's reach of Elena, he stood back a dozen or so paces. He didn't trust himself to get any closer. He followed her as the children took her hands and dragged her over to a tiny marketplace to show her the colorful array of handwoven scarves and tassels, tiny bells that hung from embroidered loops and strings of beads carved from stone. He knew he should back off and let a couple of the junior officers watch over her. He should be greeting the village elders and making nice with the tribal leader, but right now all he wanted was to watch Elena.

She lingered over a selection of hand-knotted rugs, and two local women, heavily draped in mustard-yellow cloth, shyly offered her a cup of Chai tea. She looked toward Chase for permission, and he gave her a barely perceptible shake of his head. He didn't want to be rude, but the drawn-out ritual of drinking tea would take longer than he planned for them to be there.

He watched as she pulled a wallet out of her cargo pants and began bargaining with the women, and even from a distance he could hear their soft voices and musical laughter. The children laughed, too, and Chase groaned. Great. Even with the language and cultural barriers, she did a better job of winning hearts and minds than his men did.

"Hey, Sergeant," called one of the soldiers, "we should get going. Looks like a storm's brewing in the east."

Chase looked to the horizon, where an ominous reddish cloud had formed, darkening the sky. A dust storm, by the looks of it. He knew from experience the damage that blowing sand and grit could do to an engine. No way would he risk breaking down out here. Neither would he let their convoy be overtaken by the looming cloud, which could reduce visibility to zero. They needed to get back to the base ASAP, and batten down the hatches.

"Elena," he finally called, "we need to go."

She nodded to the women, hugged several of the children and turned back to him, her arms spilling over with bright textiles and shiny beads.

"Look at all this," she exclaimed as she reached him. She was breathless with excitement. "These people made these beautiful things with their own hands."

"How much did you give them?"

Elena laughed. "I have no idea, but I don't care. It was worth every penny."

"Leave it to a woman to find a shopping opportunity, even in the middle of nowhere," he said wryly, but he couldn't help smiling at her enthusiasm.

Chase didn't relax until they were back inside the MRAP and rumbling along the road toward the base. Elena spread her purchases out on the bench beside her. He thought she would show each item to him, and found he was actually looking forward to seeing what she had bought. Instead, she smoothed a hand almost reverently over an embroidered shawl and grew quiet.

"What's wrong?" he asked. "I thought you enjoyed your shopping adventure."

He was teasing her, hoping to elicit another laugh. God, he loved to hear her laugh. But when she looked up, he saw a deep sadness in her eyes.

"I did enjoy it," she murmured, "but at the same time it made me so sad."

"Because you've suddenly realized that your wallet is empty?" he teased.

She gave him a half smile. "No. It's just that beauty like this should be shared and seen by many people, not just those stationed in Afghanistan. The people are so gracious and lovely." She gave a deep sigh. "Someday, I'd like to come back here as a tourist. When the country is safe, and I can visit these villages without an armed escort and accept an invitation to have tea."

Ah, man. Not just beautiful and brilliant, but sensitive and caring, too.

"Someday," he said softly, wishing it could come true. For her.

THE MRAP SHUDDERED to a stop. Chase was on his feet in an instant, peering through the windshield to see the reason.

"What is it?" he asked the driver.

"Looks like an accident up ahead, Sarge," the driver replied. "Ah, shit, that looks like one of our vehicles."

Elena stood up, peering over Chase's shoulders, but she couldn't see past the lead MRAP.

Chase hit the pneumatic doors and grabbed his weapon, preparing to jump down from the vehicle. He turned at the last minute and pointed a finger at Elena, and his voice was deadly serious.

"You. Stay. Here. Until we know whether this is an accident or something more, you're not to leave this vehicle, understood?"

She nodded, and watched as he sprinted toward the front of the convoy. She peered up at the gunner who was surveying the entire scene from his perch on top of the MRAP.

"Can you see what's going on?" she shouted up to him.

"Looks like an accident with a Humvee and a jingle truck."

"Is anyone hurt?"

"I can't tell, ma'am," he called down to her. "Wait! I see a kid! There was a kid in the truck and it looks like he's been injured."

Which meant this was an accident, not an ambush. At that instant, the radio in the cab squawked and she heard Chase's voice.

"Charlie Company, we need a medic ASAP. We have a child, possible broken bones and lacerations. Over."

"Roger that," replied the soldier sitting in the passenger's seat. Reaching down, he pulled a medical kit from beneath his seat and leaped from the vehicle.

Elena didn't wait to see more. She climbed down from the MRAP and ran toward the front of the convoy. A Humvee that had been driving in the opposite direction lay on its side in a ditch beside the road. The brightly decorated jingle truck, so called for the assortment of chains and pendants that swung from the front bumper, rested nose down in a ditch on the other side of the road.

Soldiers from both the Humvee and the MRAPs swarmed the area, assessing the damage and standing guard in case this was more than just an accident. Two of the soldiers carried a young boy from the truck and laid him carefully on the road. A man followed, dressed in a long white shirt and baggy pants, his head wrapped in a turban, his face creased in worry. The boy's father, Elena thought. She could see the boy's face was covered with blood.

Chase and another soldier bent over the child, speaking to him in soothing tones as they assessed his injuries. Elena crouched beside Chase, ignoring the dark look he angled at her. The boy was conscious, and she could see fear in his huge, dark eyes. Nearby, the father spoke rapidly to one of the soldiers, gesturing with his hands.

"Is he going to be okay?" Elena asked quietly, looking at the little boy. God, he was just a baby.

"I thought I told you to stay in the truck," Chase said between gritted teeth.

Elena watched as his hands moved with gentle skill over the child, checking for broken bones and internal injuries. She blew out a hard breath. "I couldn't stay in there and not know what was happening out here. How is he?"

Chase took the boy's arm in his big hands and deftly probed his wrist, which hung at an awkward angle. The child gave a sharp cry. "Broken wrist, and he'll need stitches for the head wound."

"Shouldn't he go to a hospital?" she asked.

"He should absolutely go to a hospital," Chase agreed grimly, "but there isn't one for several hundred miles. Fortunately, his injuries aren't life-threatening. We'll take him back to the base and patch him up there."

"Sir, I'm going to splint the wrist and put a bandage on the laceration," the medic said, but as soon as he tried to swab the child's head, the boy began thrashing in panic.

Without thinking, Elena moved to the boy, lifting his head and settling it on her lap. She stroked his hair, careful not to touch the nasty gash on his forehead.

"Tell him that everything's going to be okay," she said, speaking to Chase.

He stared at her for an instant, and then repeated the words to the child in a language that Elena had never heard before. The child stopped struggling, but still cried.

"Tell him he's a very brave boy, and he's going to have something to brag about to the other boys when he gets home." She listened as Chase translated for her. He must have added something else, because he grinned and winked at the child, and earned a quick laugh in return.

The medic swabbed the wound and quickly applied a bandage. "That will do until we get back to the base," he said, "but I still want to splint the wrist."

The boy cried out when the medic lifted his arm, and Chase held him down with one hand on the child's narrow chest to keep him from struggling. Reaching behind her neck, Elena unfastened her necklace and dangled the angel charm where the boy could see it.

"Tell him that this angel will keep him safe, and that there is nothing to be afraid of."

The child quieted as Chase repeated her words, his eyes fastened on the sparkling necklace. Elena continued to speak to the boy, soothing him until the medic finished fastening the splint.

"All set," he said. "No pun intended. We should move him to the MRAP and get him to the base."

While Chase went to coordinate uprighting the overturned Humvee and getting the jingle truck back on the road, Elena stayed with the child. He had pushed himself into a sitting position on the dusty road, and his father crouched beside him, talking gently to him and patting him on the head.

"Here," Elena said, fastening the necklace around the boy's neck. "I want you to have this. That way, you'll always have someone to watch over you and keep you safe."

She looked up as Chase translated her words to the child. She had thought he was out of hearing range. The boy looked down at the little angel around his neck and then at Elena, and said something to Chase.

"He wants to know your name," Chase interpreted.

Elena told him, and watched as the boy repeated her name several times. He pointed to himself. "Kadir," he said proudly.

"Kadir," Elena repeated. "It was a pleasure to meet you."

Kadir looked up at Chase and asked a question, and Chase solemnly replied in the boy's language. Kadir looked satisfied and didn't object as Chase lifted him up and carried him to the waiting MRAP.

Elena watched as he settled the boy inside and then helped the father climb in beside the child. When the door had closed, he banged on the side of the vehicle.

"Let's move out," he called. He turned to the soldiers who struggled to get the two vehicles back onto the road. "Step it up, boys! This storm isn't going to wait for us."

When they were back in the MRAP and moving again, Elena looked at Chase. "You were very good with the child. Are you a medic?"

"It's not my specialty, but I have field training. Any of the others could have treated him just as easily." His beautiful mouth lifted at one corner. "He was pretty taken with you. Another conquest, it seems."

Elena felt her cheeks warm beneath his regard. "I only did what his mother would have done. But you did a great job." She hesitated. "What did he ask you, just before you picked him up?"

He didn't pretend to misunderstand. "You gave him your guardian angel. He wanted to know who would watch over you and keep *you* safe."

"What did you say?" Her voice was breathless.

Chase's eyes glittered hotly. "I told him that's my job."

11

BY THE TIME they reached the base, the wind had kicked up, and great eddies of dust swirled around the low buildings. While the medics brought Kadir and his father to the base clinic, Chase walked Elena to her quarters but declined her invitation for a cup of coffee. Realistically, Elena knew he couldn't come in. Even if it wasn't the middle of a workday, there were rules against being alone with the opposite sex in your private quarters, and Chase had made it clear that he supported those rules. Leaving her door open for propriety's sake wasn't an option, either. Not with the crap that was blowing around outside.

"Thanks for coming with me today," she said, standing inside her doorway.

"No problem." His voice was brusque. Professional. "Listen, this storm is just going to get worse. If we lose power, don't panic. The generators will kick on and the lights will come right back up. Do you have a supply of water in your hut?"

"Not a supply, no. Just a couple of bottles that I use to make coffee with. I haven't really had a chance to stock up on anything. Except coffee." She laughed a little. "I have an addiction to the stuff."

Chase had removed his helmet and now he scrubbed a hand over his short hair. "Okay, I'll ask one of the guys to bring a case over to you. What about food? Do you have anything to eat inside?"

Elena shook her head again. "Nope. Nothing. But don't worry about me, Chase. You're not responsible for me. I can always walk over to the chow hall. It's not that far. Anyway, I should probably head over to my office to see if Brad needs a hand."

She watched his beautiful mouth tighten, but didn't know if it was due to her use of the lieutenant's first name, or out of concern for her safety.

"Absolutely not. Once this thing hits, we're going to lose daylight. Only essential emergency personnel will be permitted outdoors. You're better off remaining in your quarters. I'm going over to the chow hall myself. What can I bring back for you?"

Elena leaned against the door frame and considered him. Something had changed about Chase. She wouldn't exactly describe him as *softer,* but he was definitely more approachable than he had been just days earlier. More like the man she had known in Kuwait. More like the man who had completely rocked her world and then tucked a note inside her duffel bag that said he wasn't ready to say goodbye.

"Aren't you violating your own rules?" she asked softly. "I mean, this is beginning to sound an awful lot like preferential treatment, if you ask me."

To his credit, his expression didn't change. "Not at all," he said smoothly. "It's actually safer for me to bring something back to you than to have you get lost out here until the dust settles. Literally. Besides, you can't carry a case of water, and the DPA would have my ass if I let you starve to death in your trailer."

Elena smiled, not at all fooled. Whether Chase acknowledged it to himself or not, there was a part of him that wanted to protect her.

They had a connection.

"Okay, thanks," she said, relenting. "I'll just have whatever you're having."

He grinned then, his teeth a flash of white in his handsome face, and Elena recalled again why she had fallen so easily into bed with him. The guy was walking sex in combat boots. She watched as he jogged back the way they had come, and then closed the door.

The storm hadn't yet reached them and already there was sand everywhere. A fine coating had settled on every surface, and Elena spent the next thirty minutes wiping down the tables and shelves, shaking out her bedding, and sweeping the floor. Not that it really made a difference; the stuff was insidious, finding its way through the chinks in the doors and windows.

Once she had removed the worst of the dust, she used her new purchases to transform the stark interior of the trailer, draping an embroidered shawl over the table and covering the floor with brightly woven rugs. She hung another shawl on the wall in the living area, and used three more to create a hanging curtain around her bed, tying them back with the hand-knotted tassels.

When she was finished, she stood back to admire her handiwork. Nothing could really disguise the fact that she was living in a prefab trailer, and there was no way that the plywood and two-by-four construction could be described as cozy, but the addition of the fabrics was definitely an improvement. But now she felt grimy and uncomfortable. Glancing at her watch, she saw that nearly an hour had passed since Chase had left. Until the well was operational, even bath water was rationed and she didn't have enough water remaining in her storage tank for a nice, hot shower. Maybe a quick sponge bath, though.

There was a brief knock at her door, and then it just about blew open, bringing in a whole new load of sand and dust. Elena's eyes widened as both Pete Cleary and Mike Corrente stumbled inside. Mike kicked the door shut with one booted foot and then turned around, grunting under the weight of two cases of bottled water.

"Where do you want these, ma'am?" he asked. He wore a pair of clear goggles and his face was covered in grit, turning his eyebrows into fuzzy caterpillars. Without waiting for a reply, he set both cases of water down on her little table. "This should keep you for a while."

Pete carried two large brown bags in his arms, sealed at the top. He set them down next to the water and pushed his own goggles to the top of his head. Only the skin around his eyes was free of the red dust, giving him a distinct raccoon appearance. "McCormick sent this over," he explained. "Enough food to keep you going for a couple of days, at least."

The fact that he'd sent two soldiers to bring her supplies wasn't lost on Elena. He was still looking out for her reputation. But holy moley, she was just one person. Did she really need two cases of water and what looked like enough food to feed an army? Did that mean he wasn't planning on seeing her for a good, long time? That he intended for her to ride out the storm by herself?

"Where is Sergeant McCormick?" she asked.

Pete shrugged. "I couldn't say. He just asked us to make sure you had enough supplies to make it through the storm."

Mike was looking around the small living area, and now he whistled through his teeth. "I like what you've done with the place. Very homey. Very nice."

"Thanks." Elena hugged her arms around her middle and tried not to let her disappointment show. Why should it matter who brought her supplies? Realistically she knew that Chase had more important things to do than play delivery boy.

"Yep, I think it's safe to say that McCormick wouldn't have done nearly as nice a job decorating this place as you've done," observed Pete.

Elena stared at him. What was he saying? That the CHU she was living in had originally been meant for Chase?

"Nice job, asshole," muttered Mike.

Pete frowned and made a pretense of cleaning his goggles.

"Wait," Elena said. "Are you telling me that this is Chase's trailer?"

"Well, he never actually lived in it. We got a shipment of CHUs for the special ops guys, but Chase said he didn't want one. He said he didn't need all this space," explained Pete.

"So where does he sleep?"

"He bunks with a couple of his team members."

Elena digested this bit of information. Chase had opted to give *her* the unit that had been meant for him. Preferential treatment, indeed.

She was also sure that he hadn't wanted her to find out

about his grand sacrifice. Because then he'd be revealed as a complete hypocrite. A softy.

"Listen," began Mike, "I'm pretty sure he didn't want you to know…"

"I won't say anything to him," she assured the two men who stood in her living area, looking apprehensive.

Pete gave a huff of laughter. "Thanks. He'd have my ass if he knew I told you. Hey, if you, uh, want some company until this thing blows over, I'd be happy to stay with you. These storms can pass in a matter of hours, or they can sometimes last for days." He shifted his weight, but Elena didn't miss the hopeful look on his face.

"Oh, well, that's very considerate of you," she began.

"You bet."

"But completely unnecessary," she finished. "You see, I have, um, some paperwork to complete from the site visit today, and it will probably take me a while to finish. I won't even notice the storm."

"Maybe we should both stay," Mike countered, shooting a dark look in Pete's direction.

Elena laughed. "I'm pretty sure there are rules against that, and you probably both have a ton of work to do. I'll be fine." They looked doubtful, and Elena felt a flash of irritation. Did she really come across as being that helpless? "*Really* I'll be fine," she said more firmly. "Now go."

They did, but only reluctantly. Elena closed the door behind them and locked it, grateful to be alone. The knowledge that Chase had given her his housing unit still stunned her. What had prompted him to do such a thing?

She unpacked the food he had sent over, smiling at

the selection Chase had provided. He'd sent bread and fruit and a dozen snack packages of cheese and crackers. There were chocolate-pudding packs, and granola bars. And at the bottom of the bag, wrapped in wax paper, a thick turkey sandwich which she devoured, washing it down with a bottle of water.

She hadn't been lying when she'd told Pete and Mike that she had paperwork to do from her visit to the drilling site, and after stacking her food supplies neatly on the shelf, she sat down at her desk and began to work. It seemed only an hour had passed when she heard what sounded like a police radio.

Standing up, she pushed back the curtain on the window and peered outside. A Humvee made its way slowly through the housing area, and a voice spoke through a loudspeaker.

"Seek shelter now. Get off the roads. Emergency vehicles only. Seek shelter immediately. Over."

Elena could see the dust had thickened. Curious, she opened her door and stepped outside, throwing an arm across her nose and mouth. A dry wind whipped her hair around her face, and she could hear the flags near the Commander's office snapping against the metal poles. She looked toward the east and gasped. An enormous billowing cloud of dust rolled slowly toward her. The cloud towered over the base, at least sixty feet high, and the leading edge bloomed outward like a nuclear explosion in slow motion.

Elena stared, hypnotized.

"Ma'am, please remain indoors." The Humvee had stopped directly in front of her unit, and Elena could see a soldier in the driver's seat speaking to her through a handheld unit that broadcasted out of a speaker on the roof. Elena nodded jerkily and, with a last look at the advancing cloud, ducked back inside and closed the door.

It was just a dust storm, she reminded herself. There was nothing dangerous about it, yet she felt anxious and edgy. She stood at the window and watched the cloud advance until suddenly, the sun vanished and the entire housing area was swallowed up in a thick, reddish haze. In the space of a heartbeat, daylight turned to complete darkness.

Elena fumbled for the lights, switching on the small utility lamps over the desk and bed. Back home, she'd always enjoyed a good thunderstorm or snowstorm, but this was unlike anything she'd experienced before. The wind whistled past the door, and an occasional burst of gravel and sand rattled against the window. She almost wished she was still in her former CHU, where at least she'd have the company of the female soldiers. She could envision them joking and playing cards, or lounging on their cots listening to their iPods.

Knowing that she wouldn't get any more work done while the storm raged through the base, she gave up any pretense of doing so and lay down on her bed to read one of the paperbacks she'd brought with her. She'd barely gotten through the first chapter, however, when the lights flickered, and then went out altogether, plunging her small living space into complete blackness. The air-conditioning unit whirred to a stop, and the only sound was the wind.

Elena sat up, heart pounding, and waited. And just like Chase had promised, there was a mechanical snap, and the overhead utility light came on, casting the room in an eerie bluish glow. Elena had spent her entire adult

life living alone and she'd always enjoyed having her
own space, but now she would have given anything for
the sound of another human voice.

The emergency lighting was insufficient to read by,
so Elena flopped back on her bed and closed her eyes,
listening to the lonely sound of the wind. Before long,
she grew uncomfortably warm, and realized the air con-
ditioner had not restarted when the back-up generators
had kicked in. Which made perfect sense, since they
drew so much electricity. But the heat inside the trailer
was quickly becoming oppressive and Elena didn't even
have the option of cracking a window.

Standing up, she opened another bottle of water and
sipped it, but found no relief from the cloying warmth.
She wondered if it was possible to suffocate from lack of
air movement, and if she might not be better off trying
to make her way to the dining hall or the small recreation center, where at least there would be other people
around. But a quick glance out the window told her that,
if anything, the dust storm had only intensified. She'd
be lucky if she could see her hand in front of her face.
Finding her way to the street, never mind to the dining
facility, would be next to impossible.

There was no question in her mind that she was stuck
in her quarters for however long the storm lasted. With a
sigh she peeled off her uniform until she wore only her
bra and underwear, and then grabbed her iPod and lay
down on her bed to wait it out. At least with the strains
of Coldplay in her ears, she could shut out the lonely
sound of the wind. And if she closed her eyes, she could
almost imagine she was somewhere else.

What was Chase doing right now? Was he with his
team, planning his next mission? Did he think about

her? Her mind drifted back to that moment in the MRAP when he'd almost kissed her. She'd known he was going to, and the knowledge had thrilled her. Her heart had begun racing the second he'd crouched in front of her to help adjust the bandana. She'd wanted to inhale him, to absorb him through her skin. But she'd seen a small red light by the door begin to blink the second before the door had swung open, and she'd quickly moved away.

She knew instinctively that the reason Chase had asked Mike and Pete to bring her the food and water was because he didn't trust himself to be alone with her.

Smart guy.

While she'd been unwilling to compromise his reputation in front of his men, there would have been nothing to prevent her from completely seducing him in the privacy of her living quarters. But she also knew he wouldn't stay away. Eventually, he'd come by to make sure she was okay because that's the kind of guy he was. And when he did, she'd be waiting.

12

A SOFT WHOOSH, followed by a low, deep thump that shook the ground, had the men of the 2nd Marines Special Operations Battalion scrambling for their body armor.

"Holy shit," exclaimed Lego, tightening his helmet strap beneath his chin, "that sucker sounded like it hit the compound!"

Chase and the others had been waiting out the dust storm by scrupulously going over the upcoming mission and ensuring their backup plans were in place in the event it turned into a complete disaster.

Now Chase shot to his feet and flung open the door of the Tac Ops building, trying to see where the mortar had hit. The worst of the dust storm had passed, but the air was thick with a choking red haze that would linger for days, making visibility almost impossible. Night was falling, although it was difficult to tell, given the heavy fog of dust that enveloped the base.

Stepping outside, he could see a darker cloud of smoke and fumes from the area of the motor pool. "Looks like we took a direct hit on the eastern side of the base," he yelled over his shoulder. Even as he spoke, there came another low, howling whistle.

"Jesus!" shouted Sean. "Incoming!"

In the same instant, the mortar hit with an explosive thud, only closer this time, near the dining facility. The ground beneath Chase's feet trembled with the impact. Immediately, the sirens began to wail, and there was pandemonium as soldiers scrambled to get to their battle stations or to a bunker. The air was filled with the sound of voices as men shouted orders and directions.

Chase heard a low, distant *whoompf* and knew another mortar had just been launched. *Elena.* He had to get to Elena. She'd be terrified, alone in her trailer. He'd told her that if there was an attack, to get her ass to the nearest bunker, but with the choking dust, he wasn't sure she'd be able to find her way.

Without hesitating, he leaped down the steps and began sprinting toward the housing area, ignoring the shouts of his men to come back. The third mortar hit somewhere just outside the compound wall, but close enough that the impact made him stumble. Regaining his footage, he ran on, searching the faces of those who passed him in the other direction, hoping that he'd see Elena. But there were only soldiers, racing toward the bunkers and their stations. He reached Elena's CHU and tried the door handle, but found it locked.

"Elena!" he shouted, knowing the likelihood of her hearing him over the wail of the sirens was slim to none. "Elena!"

There was no response, and he wondered if she might actually have listened to him and already left for the bomb shelter. But she wouldn't have locked her door behind her, which meant she was still inside. Standing back, he used his foot to kick the door in and then he was inside her quarters, moving swiftly through the empty living area and into her bedroom.

"Elena, what the hell are you doing?" Relief at seeing her sitting uninjured on the edge of her bed washed over him, making his voice rougher than he'd intended.

She'd donned her protective vest and her helmet, and was struggling to pull her boots onto her bare feet. Now she looked up at him, her eyes enormous.

"I—I just need to get my boots on," she explained shakily, "and then I'm leaving."

"Too damned late for that," he growled, and bent to haul her to her feet. "You should have been gone ten seconds after those sirens sounded. Christ!"

To his astonishment she twisted her arm free and turned back to the bed. "I need to put my boots on," she said stubbornly. "I can't run in my bare feet."

"Then I'll goddamned well carry you," he all but shouted, "but we need to go *now*."

Before she could protest, he bent a shoulder beneath her and lifted her over his back, holding her in place with one hand across the back of her thighs and—*Jesus!* Beneath the armored vest she wore nothing but a pair of panties, and his palm rested solidly against soft, warm skin. He realized that she must have been sleeping when the attack occurred.

Now she struggled in his grasp, pushing herself upright as she clutched at his shoulders. "No, wait!" she panted. "I need my boots! I can't go out there without my boots!"

"Elena—"

"Put me down!"

He could carry her even if she struggled, but it

wouldn't be pleasant for her or for him, so he put her down, prepared to reason with her and yes, even let her put her damned boots on if that's what it took to get her to a bunker.

But the moment he set her on her feet, another whooshing sound came from overhead. Instinctively, Chase pushed Elena to the floor and covered her with his body. The impact, when it came, was dangerously close, rattling the windows of the little hut and shaking the walls. Almost immediately, the mortar was followed by the sounds of a counterattack as the U.S. troops fired back, launching their own missiles in the direction of the insurgency.

As Chase covered Elena, he became aware of several things at once. The first was that while Elena wore both a flak vest and helmet, he'd charged out of the Tac Ops building with neither. In fact, he was damn near as naked as Elena was, wearing only a pair of shorts and T-shirt. The air conditioning had quit when the power went out, and when the heat had become too oppressive, he and his men had changed into casual clothes. To have gone sprinting across the base during a mortar attack without his protective gear had been beyond stupid. Christ, he knew better!

In the next instant, he became aware of Elena, curled on the floor beneath him. She hadn't fastened her helmet and it had fallen off when she'd hit the deck. Now his nostrils were filled with the scent of her flowery shampoo. The armored inserts of her flak vest dug into his chest and stomach where he pressed her against the floor, but her legs her smooth, bare legs—were tangled with his.

The mortars had stopped although the sirens still

wailed. Chase lifted his head and looked down at Elena. Her eyes were tightly closed.

"Elena," he said, smoothing her hair back. "Elena, look at me."

She did, opening her eyes to stare at him, and he saw the fear in her eyes and for a split second he thought she was afraid of *him*.

"Oh, Chase," she whispered, and she flung her arms around his neck, clutching him as if she'd never let go. "I was so frightened."

"I know, baby, I know," he whispered back, emotion roughening his voice. He pushed into a sitting position with his back against her bed and pulled her across his lap, cradling her head against his shoulder. "But it's okay now. In a minute the sirens will stop, and this will all be over."

She shuddered and burrowed closer. "I wanted to leave, but I couldn't find my protective gear and you said I shouldn't leave unless I was wearing it, but then I was barefoot and I couldn't get my boots on."

"Shh," he soothed. "It's okay. You're safe now. Listen." He cocked his head. "The sirens have stopped."

Elena raised her head and as they listened, the sirens let out several short blasts.

"Hear that?" he asked softly, keeping his voice low. "That's the all-clear sign. It's over."

"Thank God," she breathed. "I never want to go through something like that ever again."

Chase pressed his lips against her hair, knowing this was a perfect opportunity to suggest she return to Kuwait or even the States, but he selfishly kept his mouth shut. He didn't want her to leave, even though he knew it was dangerous for her to stay. He tried to convince himself that he only wanted her near so that he could keep an eye on her, but that was a lie.

He wanted her near because he was a selfish bastard.

Because he just plain wanted her.

"Is the dust storm over?" she asked.

"Mostly. The wind has died down, but the air is still pretty thick. They should have the main power back on in a few hours."

"A sandstorm and a mortar attack, all in one day," she said, laughing a little. "They'll never believe this back home."

"I should have expected it," Chase said grimly. "The insurgents like to launch their attacks during bad weather. They know our options for retaliating are limited. Hey." He cupped her face and pulled back enough to look at her, smoothing his thumbs over her cheeks. "You okay?"

She drew in a deep breath and nodded. "I am now."

They stared at each other for a long moment until hot color seeped into her face and she looked down. "Oh, wow," she exclaimed in mortification. "I should put some clothes on."

"No, you're fine," Chase protested, reluctant to let her go. Reluctant to have her cover up all the warm, feminine flesh pressed against him.

She gave him a tolerant look. "Somehow, I don't think a flak vest falls under the category of *clothing*."

He released her and she braced her hands on his shoulders to push herself up, but then stopped. Her eyes traveled over him, taking in his T-shirt, shorts and bare legs, before flying back to his face.

"You're not wearing protective gear." Her voice was

filled with a combination of horror and wonder. "You came over here without even putting on your helmet."

He knew his expression was chagrined. "I didn't have time," he said carefully.

"But you're like the King of Combat Rules," she persisted. "The only thing that kept me from running, screaming, out of this building the second those mortars hit, was what would happen to me if you caught me without my helmet and vest, and yet you…" Her words drifted off.

"Like I said, I didn't have time." His tone was gruff.

"Because you were worried about me." Her gaze was filled with dawning understanding. "You broke one of your own hard, fast rules because you were worried for my safety."

Chase started to protest that he absolutely had *not* abandoned protocol because of her, but the expression on her face caused the words to die on his lips. She looked stunned. And awed. Like he was her own personal hero.

And just like that, he broke. "I couldn't get here fast enough," he admitted, his voice hoarse with recalled fear. He cupped her face in his hands, searching her eyes. "The thought of anything happening to you…"

"Oh, Chase," she breathed, and then she was kissing him. But Jesus, she wasn't just kissing him, she was *devouring* him. Chase resisted for about a nanosecond because as much as he'd dreamed of this happening, this was not the reason he'd raced across the compound during a mortar attack. He'd just needed to make sure Elena was okay and maybe stay long enough to comfort her. But this worked, too.

Elena raised herself up and straddled his thighs, holding his face in her hands as she angled her mouth across his. Her tongue swept past his lips, and Chase groaned. His arms went around her, and he realized she still wore her flak vest.

"Let's get this off," he managed, his fingers working the Velcro fastenings. She helped him slide it off, and then there she was, wearing nothing but a lacy white bra.

"Oh, man," he groaned, "you are so damned beautiful."

Elena wound her arms around his neck and he buried his face in her neck, breathing in her scent. She smelled like shampoo and soap and under that, a subtly feminine smell that was hers alone. The combination was a complete turn-on.

"Take this off," she demanded, tugging at his shirt, and he helped her push it up and over his head until finally—proof that there really was a God—they were skin on skin.

He wanted to consume her, to take her hard and fast and deep, until she acknowledged that she was his. The mortar attack, combined with the adrenaline rush of fear he'd felt for Elena's safety, had left him completely jacked. He couldn't remember the last time he'd ached so desperately for sexual release. Well, that wasn't completely true; he'd been in serious pain after he'd pushed her away in the men's showers. He was rock-hard for her, but there was a minuscule part of his brain that still functioned.

"Elena, babe," he managed, "we can't do this. There are rules—"

"Too bad, soldier," she breathed, shifting so that she

was in full, sweet contact with his erection. "Some rules were meant to be broken."

And then she kissed him, a hot, openmouthed kiss that made him forget his rule about no sex on the base. Jesus, he should stop, he knew that, but she made him forget everything except his need to be with her, inside her, hearing her gasps of pleasure as he pushed her over the edge.

She was fumbling with his zipper and he flicked the fastening of her bra open, filling his hands with her breasts. He stood up, pulling her with him, and helped her to strip off his shorts even as he pushed her panties down, and then they were both gloriously naked. He wanted to inhale her, to run his hands and mouth over every inch of her and reassure himself that she really was okay.

Chase lay back on the narrow bed, pulling her down on top of him, and she laughed as she kissed him again, their teeth scraping together before he swept his tongue into her mouth. She was liquid fire in his arms, her sleek, warm thighs pressed tightly against either side of his hips as she rocked against him, her fingers in his hair, her soft breasts crushed against his chest.

When she reached between their bodies and curled her fingers around him, he had to grit his teeth to force himself not to come immediately.

"Oh, God," she panted, lifting her head to gaze down at him, "you're so *hard*. And hot."

Oh, yeah. The things she was doing made his eyes roll back, but when she raised herself up to position him at the entrance to her body, he reacted swiftly.

"Whoa, babe!" Before she could lower herself onto his straining cock, he flipped her so that she lay beneath him on the narrow bed, her legs still curled around his hips. "I didn't exactly come prepared for this," he explained, seeing her confusion. "I don't have any protection."

She swallowed hard, and he could see indecision warring with desire in her shimmering eyes. "Well, I'm on the Pill," she finally admitted. "And I promise you that I don't have anything contagious or dangerous."

Chase might have argued that, since he was pretty sure everything about her, including her smile, was dangerous to his heart, but he wasn't a man to question good fortune.

"I just had a full battery of tests and all my shots before I came over here," he said, not adding that he hadn't had sex with anyone but her since before the *last* time he'd deployed, about eighteen months ago. "I'm squeaky-clean."

Elena searched his eyes and gave him a smile that caused his heart to turn over in his chest. "Well, except for the dust," she said, wiping a single finger along his jaw and showing him the reddish evidence on its tip. "Please, I don't want to wait anymore."

As if to emphasize her words, she arched upward, pressing herself against him. Chase groaned and she caught his face in her hands, covering his mouth in another soul-destroying kiss. But when she would have reached between their bodies to touch him, he pushed her hands over her head and held them there. He didn't know how long he could last if she touched him again.

He dipped his head and kissed one breast, then drew her nipple into his mouth. Elena gasped. Chase smiled and released her wrists to slide his hand down her body and along the back of her thigh, lifting her leg higher and hooking it behind his back, opening her to him.

He slid his aching cock against her, feeling how warm and slick she was, and wanted nothing more than to bury himself in her heat.

"Elena," he rasped, "I thought I could go slow, but I'm not sure I can…"

"I don't want you to go slow," she said, pressing her hips upward. "I want you inside me now."

Chase wanted the same thing, but his control was tenuous, at best, and he was afraid he'd lose it too soon. He eased himself into her, inch by excruciating inch, stretching and filling her, gritting his teeth against the overwhelming urge to thrust hard and deep and fast.

God. God, he could hardly stand it.

"Jesus, I've never done this without a condom," he said thickly.

"Me, either," she whispered, and arched upward, gasping his name, clutching his back and urging him closer. "Is this considered preferential treatment?"

"Oh, yeah," he groaned.

And then he was fully seated inside her, surrounded by her silky heat, and he could feel the walls of her sex gripping him. She began to move, rocking against him. Chase rested his head against her neck and pushed deeper, and she rose up to meet him. Elena made a strangled sound of pleasure and cried his name, and that's all it took for Chase to lose whatever restraint he had.

He thrust into her, harder, again and again, and the small sounds she made drove him over the edge, shattering his control, but it was okay because she was there, too, coming apart in his arms. His heart pounded like a jackhammer in his chest, and one coherent thought managed to surface in his lust-saturated brain.

They didn't make body armor tough enough to protect his heart from this woman.

13

ELENA LAY WITH HER HEAD on Chase's chest, listening to the heavy thump of his heart beneath her ear. She wrapped her arms tighter around him, never wanting him to leave. Lying with him like this, she could almost forget where they were, or that they'd just survived a mortar attack.

"Did you actually kick my door in?" she asked, recalling how he'd burst into her quarters.

"Hmm? What?"

He was almost asleep and now he came partially awake, his eyes reflecting his confusion.

"I'm pretty sure I locked my door earlier," she said, tracing a finger over his chest, "so I just wanted to ask if you really kicked it in?"

"Holy f—" He broke off abruptly and sat up, disentangling himself from Elena's arms.

She sat up, too, pushing her hair back and watching as he snatched his shorts from the floor and shoved his legs into them.

"What's wrong?"

"How long have I been here? Did I fall asleep? Shit,

shit, *shit!*" He searched the floor, found his T-shirt and dragged it on, then began looking for his sandals. "They'll be doing a head count, and I should be back at Tac Ops, and they'll be wondering where the hell I disappeared to and—*shit!*"

Elena had never seen him like this—out of control. Even when he'd been angry, he'd never used such foul language. She found her panties and pulled them on, and then grabbed a clean shirt from the shelf next to the bed.

"You didn't tell anyone that you were coming here?" she asked, incredulous. Even she knew that you didn't just disappear during an emergency. She'd assumed he'd told *somebody* where he was headed. "You just left?"

"Can you believe that?" he asked, laughing in disbelief. "I should know better. Jesus! I should be out there with my men, doing damage control and helping to launch a counterattack, and instead I'm in here—" He broke off abruptly. "Where's my damned sandal?"

Elena stood up, understanding that his anger was directed at himself and not at her. He'd broken another rule, again because of her. But she couldn't feel sorry for what they'd done. Bending down, she retrieved his sandal from where it lay beneath her flak vest and handed it to him.

He took it from her silently. She thought he would just go, but he stood there for a moment, turning the shoe over in his hand.

"Elena," he began.

She laid her fingers over his lips. "Shh. Don't say anything, okay?"

Because if he told her that he regretted what had just happened between them, she'd lose it. And she'd been working so hard to show him that she was tough and capable, and could handle being out here just as well as he could. But if he said that being with her was a mistake, she might just cry.

"I'm sorry," he muttered. "This has nothing to do with you." He turned away, rubbing a hand across the back of his neck. When he turned back to her, she could see that he was back in control. "Coming over to make sure you were okay was one thing, but taking advantage of you like that was another thing altogether."

Elena stared at him. "You think you took advantage of me?"

"I do. I did. You were scared and I only meant to reassure you, but instead I completely used your vulnerability to my own advantage."

Elena smiled. "You didn't hear me complaining, did you?"

Chase returned her smile, but it didn't reach his eyes. "Listen, I hate to do this, but I really do have to run."

"I understand."

"Elena…" He hesitated.

"I know," she said, not wanting to hear him say it. "This can't happen again." To her relief, she didn't cry. She wrapped her arms around her middle, hugging herself. "There are rules against this sort of thing. I get it."

"If there's another attack, I'll send one of the female soldiers to bring you to the bunker."

"There's no need," she said quickly, keeping her voice even. "I know the drill now. I know what to expect, and I'll be fine."

Boy, did she ever know the drill. She could have Chase for stolen moments here and there, but he'd never let his guard down enough to really be hers. Not on a permanent basis.

He looked uncertain, and Elena almost felt a stab of sympathy for him. God, next he was going to apologize, and she didn't know if she could handle that. Because she couldn't feel the tiniest bit sorry about what they'd done.

"Go," she said. "Just…go."

He did.

THE MORTAR ATTACK had done minimal damage to the base and there were no casualties, unless you counted the Humvee parked in the motor pool. Elena had seen the truck and there were so many ragged holes torn in the doors and roof that it resembled Swiss cheese.

But the attack had left the compound in a state of heightened alert, and even Corporal Cleary and Sergeant Corrente were too focused on their jobs to give her anything more than a cursory greeting in passing.

There was a surreal quality to the base in the days immediately following. The dust storm had passed, but the air was still heavy and thick with a reddish haze that even the sun couldn't completely penetrate. Routine patrols were on hold since visibility was so poor. As a result, most of the soldiers were confined to the base and kept busy doing maintenance and repair on everything from the buildings and fences to the vehicles.

Elena was busy, too. She spent the next two days in the contracting center with Brad, ensuring the minor damage to the dining facility was repaired, expediting delivery of the parts needed to complete the waste treatment plant and keeping needed supplies flowing into the base.

She didn't see Chase, although she found herself looking for him whenever she walked between her office or the dining facility and her housing unit. She didn't even know if he was still on the base, or if he and his men had gone out on patrol into the surrounding hills. She had sat in on the post-attack briefings, knew the Taliban were responsible for the mortar attack on the base, and that the U.S. forces had retaliated with enough firepower to smoke the entire mountain where the explosives had been launched from. During the day, she tried not to think about him or what he might be doing or whether he was safe. Or if he thought of her.

But at night, in her solitary living quarters, she couldn't escape her memories of their time together, both in Kuwait and following the attack. She'd been so certain when he'd been with her, loving her with his body, that it had been more than just a physical joining for him. She hadn't imagined the sheer relief she'd seen on his face when he'd found her alive and whole, or the desperation in his touch as he'd made love to her.

She knew he considered his attraction to her a weakness. He didn't bend the rules for anyone, and he'd said more than once that he wouldn't give her preferential treatment. Yet he'd gone out of his way to ensure her comfort and her safety. He'd personally accompanied her to the drilling site. He'd given her his CHU. Surely that meant something?

"Hey, why don't you call it a day?"

Elena looked up from her computer to see Brad Carrington standing in the doorway to her little office. He was handsome, in his own way, with red hair, blue eyes and fair skin that was perpetually sunburned. To Elena, he looked like a slightly older version of Prince Harry. His smile was friendly enough, and he worked just as hard as Elena did, even if he refused to go outside the fence to visit any of their projects.

"I'm a navy guy," he'd said more than once. "I don't play in sandboxes."

Elena understood that unlike her, the Defense Procurement Agency hadn't given him any choice about coming over to Afghanistan. He'd taken a three-year assignment with the DPA because he'd wanted to be at home with his wife and kids instead of having to be at sea for months at a time. But then they'd sent him to Afghanistan for a year and he wasn't at all happy about it.

"I'm just wrapping up this e-mail," Elena said, "and then I'm calling it a night."

"You've been at it for almost fourteen hours," Brad said. "Tomorrow is Sunday. You should sleep in."

Elena smiled at him. "Maybe I will." She wouldn't.

"It's dark outside. You want me to walk you back to your quarters?"

If the offer had come from anyone but Brad, Elena might have interpreted it as a come-on, but she knew without a doubt that the navy officer was completely devoted to the wife he'd left in San Diego.

"I'll be fine," she assured him. "But I did want to ask you if I could arrange to go back out to the drilling site?"

Brad frowned. "You were just out there. Why do you need to go back?"

"I want to check on the progress they're making laying the pipeline from the well to the base."

"Is that really necessary? Can't you just talk with the project manager about it? Going out there isn't safe."

Elena gave him a tolerant look. "It's less than two

miles from the base, and I'll only be gone for a couple of hours. I just received an invoice for more than a million dollars for the work they've done just this past month. The invoice states they've laid three hundred meters of pipeline, which I find hard to believe. Before I authorize payment, I'd like to verify the progress myself." She shrugged. "It's part of my job, Brad."

He sighed. "Well, okay, if you have to. I'll talk with Charlie Company and see if they can set you up with an escort. When did you want to go?"

"As soon as it can be arranged."

"I'll see what I can do. I'd feel a lot better if one of the special ops guys could go with you, like the last time, but that's not a possibility now."

He had Elena's full attention, although she tried to sound casual. "Why is that?"

"They're leaving tonight."

Elena felt her heart tighten. "Are you sure?"

"Yep."

Elena didn't ask him how he knew. As one of the few officers on the base, there probably wasn't much that went on that he didn't know about. She strove to sound natural, when inside she was freaking out. Chase was leaving on a mission that she knew would be dangerous. "How long will they be gone?"

"Until they've completed whatever mission they've been assigned. They're usually gone for a week or two, at least."

A week or two. Logically, she knew a couple of weeks was not a long time, but to Elena it felt like an eternity. Chase was preparing to leave and he hadn't even bothered to let her know or say goodbye. But what had she expected? A declaration of love? A promise of forever?

Not when their relationship had started as a one-night stand.

She felt sick. More than that, she felt angry. Angry at Chase for not caring enough to say goodbye, and angry at herself for caring too much.

After Brad left, Elena finished her e-mail and closed her computer. Glancing at her watch, she saw it was 8:00 p.m. Her chest felt tight and ached. She pressed her fingers against her eyes, trying to think rationally.

Chase was leaving.

She shouldn't feel so hurt that he hadn't told her, but when she recalled his face the last time she'd seen him, she wanted to cry. He might want her, but he resented the hell out of her, too. She represented everything he believed was wrong with the military—she was female and she was in a combat environment. Worse, she was a civilian. She didn't even have the benefit of a military background or training. He probably viewed his attraction to her as a colossal weakness in his character.

Sighing, Elena pushed away from her desk and retrieved her flak vest and helmet. She was completely wired, which meant she'd lie in bed tossing and turning, thinking about Chase and aching for him. She'd never been so attuned to the needs of her own body as she'd been since she met Chase. All she had to do was think about him and her body would begin to thrum with recalled pleasure. And unless she was engrossed in her work, she thought about him pretty much all the time.

Snapping off the lights in the office, she locked the door and turned to walk to her living quarters when a lone figure detached itself from the shadows and approached her.

Elena hesitated. While she hadn't heard of any women

being attacked on the base, she wasn't naive enough to think it couldn't happen. She stood uncertainly for a moment, torn between flight or fight, when the man stepped closer and she recognized Chase.

"Oh, my God," she gasped, her body sagging in relief. "You scared me there for a moment."

"Why are you walking back alone?" he demanded, grasping her by the arms and giving her a light shake. "It's not safe."

"Brad offered to walk with me, but I refused," she explained, trying to discern his expression in the indistinct light. Her heart had exploded into a frenzied rhythm as soon as she saw him, and now she strove to sound normal, as if seeing him didn't upset her equilibrium. "What are *you* doing out here?"

"I was waiting for you." He released her arms and took a step back, as if he didn't trust himself to get too close.

"Oh."

"And why aren't you wearing your protective gear?" He took her vest from her hands and held it out for her to slip into. "Jesus, please don't tell me you go outside without it, not after the other night?"

"I'm only going to my quarters and it's so heavy," she explained, knowing that was a poor excuse. "I hate wearing it."

"Well, get used to it," he said grimly. "Most mortar attacks occur between eight and ten o'clock. You should wear it whenever you're outside."

Elena wasn't in the mood to talk about what would happen if the base came under another attack; the last one was still fresh in her mind. And she wasn't the only one who was thinking about that night. She could see from Chase's expression that he was remembering what had happened, too.

"Is that why you're here?" she asked. "To make sure I'm wearing my protective gear? Jeez, Chase, I'm a big girl. I can take care of myself." Irritated with herself for being glad that he cared, that he had come to see her before he left, she pushed past him and strode in the direction of her living quarters.

He fell into step beside her and they walked in silence until they reached her door. He blew out a hard breath. "Listen, there's something I need to tell you. We can talk inside…or maybe that's not such a good idea."

A foot patrol of two soldiers turned the corner at the end of the road, walking toward them, and Elena made a quick decision. "No, it's okay," she said quietly. "Come in. I can make some coffee, if you'd like."

"I can't stay long."

He stood back while she unlocked the door and flipped on the light, and then followed her inside, closing the door behind them. Elena slipped out of her vest and dropped it onto a chair. Turning toward Chase, she got her first good look at him.

He looked dangerous.

His face was covered in several days' growth of beard, making his chiseled cheekbones stand out even more prominently. She realized he wasn't wearing the traditional desert camo fatigues that she'd become accustomed to seeing him in. Both his pants and his jacket were solid beige beneath his heavy vest, and he wore a black-and-white checkered scarf wrapped around his neck. A patch on one arm bore the initials *NKA*.

"Why are you dressed like that?" she asked.

"I'm leaving tonight."

She already knew, but hearing him say the words caused her heart to twist painfully. "Where are you going?"

"I'm sorry, I can't say. All I can tell you is that I'll be gone for a week or so, but I didn't want to leave without telling you."

He had come to say goodbye. And just like that, the hurt and anger evaporated. Was this what it was like for military wives and girlfriends each time their husbands or lovers deployed? She felt weak with fear for Chase. She was unfamiliar with the painful, clenching sensation in her chest, or the way she couldn't seem to catch her breath.

Unwilling to let him see her weakness, she turned away to open the Tupperware container of coffee and scoop some into the coffeemaker. Her hands trembled, and she finally dropped the spoon back into the container and braced her hands on the shelves, her head down. "I can't do this," she whispered.

"Elena." He was right behind her.

"Don't." She was only barely holding it together.

"Elena, look at me." His voice was low and insistent.

He turned her around, and she knew couldn't hide the tears that had welled in her eyes, so she tried to laugh them off.

"I'm sorry," she said, smiling as she wiped at her eyes, "You just took me by surprise."

"I'll be fine," he said softly, studying her face. "This is my job. It's what I do."

"I know." She nodded, trying to sound strong. "I do."

"Ah, babe, come here."

Before she could protest, he hauled her into his arms and she went willingly, winding her arms around his waist and pressing her face against his chest. She felt his lips against her hair, and then he tipped her face up so that he could look at her.

"You'll be okay while I'm gone?" he asked.

She pushed back and stared at him, letting her gaze drift over his face, lingering on his mouth.

"Listen to yourself." Her voice sounded strained. "You're the one going into a dangerous situation, and yet here you are, asking me if *I'll* be okay?"

"I can't be distracted by worrying about you," he admitted, "but I know I'll worry anyway. Just promise me that you won't leave the base, and that you'll wear your protective gear and do everything you're supposed to do to keep safe while I'm gone. *Promise.*"

Elena felt more tears well in her eyes. It wasn't a declaration of love, but she suspected this was the closest thing she'd get from Chase.

For now.

She stood on tiptoe and he cupped her face in his hands and kissed her so sweetly, so tenderly, that she prayed to God to keep him safe. Just watch over him and bring him back safely, and she would never, ever ask for anything more than this moment. Please, God, do this one thing, and when the time came—and she knew it would—she would let him go.

14

FROM THE HELICOPTER, Chase saw Forward Operating Base Sharlana come into view. He watched as a small convoy of vehicles left the base and wondered where it was headed. After ten days away, he and his team were finally back. The helicopter was coming in low, preparing to land, and he could make out every structure. There was the housing area, and there was the roof of Elena's CHU. The sun had barely risen; was she still sleeping, or had she already left for work?

He was impatient to get onto the ground. As exhausted and filthy as he was, he had just one driving need—to see Elena. He could try and tell himself that he just wanted to make sure she was safe, but he knew he was full of shit.

The woman had gotten under his skin in a big way. As much as he told himself that he didn't want her on the base, he had to admire the way she'd adapted. She hadn't freaked out during the sandstorm or the mortar attack, and she wasn't afraid to leave the protection of the base to visit the construction sites. Moreover, she'd shown herself to be adept at her job, and he'd overheard several officers speaking highly of her skills. All in all, he was pretty amazed by her tenacity and proud as hell of her courage.

He glanced away from the window to the other four members of his team, wondering if he looked as rough and weary as they did. After ten days spent crawling through the rugged mountains, they looked more like enemy insurgents than they did American soldiers. He hadn't showered, his beard had grown in and scratched uncomfortably against his skin, his uniform was soiled and torn in places, and he'd lost weight.

But they'd succeeded in intercepting the weapons transfer and had captured not only Mullah Abdul Raqid, but two of his top advisers, as well. The operation had been an unmitigated success, especially when Chase considered the information they'd found out from Raqid's men.

He just needed to get on the ground and brief the base commander so Colonel Vinson could prevent any troops from inadvertently traveling into the area where the Taliban was planning an ambush. They hadn't been able to convey that information over the radio for fear of giving away their position or having the enemy intercept the communication. He needed to tell the commander in person. Then he'd clean himself up and head over to Elena's quarters. There were no rules in existence that could keep him from spending the next twenty-four hours in her arms, and his body tightened in anticipation.

As soon as they landed, Chase jumped down from the helicopter, bending low beneath the rotors as he and his men jogged over to a waiting Humvee.

Climbing inside, he was surprised to see the colonel

sitting in the passenger's seat. Great. If they could debrief him on the way to Tac Ops, he could shave a few minutes off the time it would take to get to Elena's.

"Gentlemen," Vinson said, turning in his seat to face the team. "Welcome back and congratulations on a job well done. Your efforts reflect favorably not only on yourselves, but on the U.S. Marine Corps. Your last communication said you had information regarding a potential ambush. Tell me what you know."

"Thank you, sir," replied Rafe. "The detainees are on their way to Kabul under armed escort, but we do have information that we believe is reliable and may impact your operations here at Sharlana."

The prisoners had confessed that one of the nearby villages had been harboring a dozen or more insurgents and that these same insurgents were planning to ambush the next military convoy that traveled through the village. Chase couldn't help but think about the similar ambush during his last deployment in Iraq.

The memory of the female convoy driver getting shot still haunted him. Try as he might, he would never be comfortable putting women in harm's way.

Rafe was still talking to the commander, and Chase forced himself to concentrate on their conversation. The tiny village of Jani didn't exist on any map, and U.S. troops rarely passed through the hamlet. The route to the drilling site came close to Jani, but in order to actually drive through the village, a convoy would have to leave the main road and make a circuitous detour. And the only reason a convoy would use the detour would be if the main road became impassable—

Chase leaned forward. "Sir, I saw a convoy of

MRAPs leaving the base as we were flying in. Where is it headed?"

The men waited as the commander picked up the radio and spoke to the motor pool. The response made Chase go cold.

"Sir, convoy is headed to the southeast drilling site. Over."

"Find out if any civilians are with that convoy," Chase said tightly. "Ask if Elena de la Vega is in one of those trucks."

"Roger that," came the reply. "That's an affirmative. Over."

"Shit!" Chase wanted to punch something. He felt impotent. Elena was in one of those vehicles and if, as he suspected, the main road had been rendered impassable, the MRAPs would have two choices—they could turn back and return to the base, or they could make a detour through the village of Jani, where they could be ambushed by the Taliban.

He hoped like hell they decided to turn back. How long had it been since he'd seen the convoy leave? Ten minutes? Twelve, at most? Enough time to have reached the turnoff to Jani.

"Colonel, I'm going to need this vehicle," Chase said grimly.

The colonel nodded. "You can have my driver, as well I'll come with you."

"Sorry, sir," Rafe said, "but with all due respect, we can't allow that. We'll drop you off here, if that works."

The commander sighed. "I guess it'll have to. Be careful, boys, and good luck. I'll get you some backup and some air support."

They dropped the commander off by the motor pool, and then they were racing out of the base toward the drilling site. Chase couldn't believe that Elena had actually left the base after she'd promised not to. He should have anticipated that the Taliban would eventually try to attack a convoy traveling to the drilling site. Knowing that Elena was part of that convoy made his blood run cold. For once, he hoped the information they'd received was false. He hoped that they'd arrive at the drilling site to find Elena drinking lemonade with the project manager. The alternative was unthinkable.

Chase scanned the road as the Humvee sped along, taking the curves too fast, in danger of overturning if they miscalculated even a little. But the driver, a kid barely out of his teens, seemed imperturbable as he maneuvered the rutted road, and Chase eyeballed him with respect. "Nice driving," he murmured.

The kid flashed a grin without taking his eyes from the road. "Everything I know about driving I learned on the back roads of Alabama. Nothing like being underage with a trunk full of beer and three cop cars in pursuit to hone your driving skills."

"Very nice," approved Rafe, his eyes gleaming.

"There!" Chase indicated the road. "Slow down. The road is out up ahead."

A rockfall from the nearby hill made the road impassable, and the deep ditch on the other side made circling around the barrier impossible. Chase felt his heart come into his throat. There was no way the convoy could have gotten around the debris, and they hadn't encountered any trucks since they'd left the base. Which meant the convoy had taken the alternate route through the village of Jani.

Sean leaned forward to get a better look, surveying the hillside with critical eyes. "Natural or man-made?" he asked, referring to the fallen debris.

"We have to assume it's man-made, and that the insurgents are counting on that convoy taking the detour and passing through Jani. Back it up," Chase said to the driver. "The turnoff is just behind us."

They backed up and took the turnoff to Jani, and up ahead, Chase could just make out a low cloud of dust. "That must be them. Slow down, and keep your eyes open."

As one, the men readied their weapons. Chase surveyed the landscape on either side of the road, noting the thick copse of trees on one side and the steep hill, studded with boulders, on the other. Even now, insurgents could be hiding on either side of the road, aiming their weapons at the convoy.

The dusty road was narrow and deeply rutted, and as they rounded a curve, Chase had a clear view of the three MRAPs. They had come to a stop about a hundred meters from the village.

"Jesus Christ," he breathed, and his blood ran cold.

Elena and two soldiers had exited their vehicle and were walking toward the front of the convoy. And approaching them from the village was a group of men, dressed in long, loose traditional clothing. Clothing that could conceal anything from rifles to grenades. What the hell were Elena and the soldiers thinking? Didn't they understand the danger they were in? Chase realized he had stopped breathing as he braced himself for the sound of gunfire. He needed to reach Elena before that happened—to protect her with his own body, if need be.

In that instant, Chase realized he would do anything to keep her safe. Even die.

The Humvee skidded to a stop behind the last MRAP, and Chase had to force himself not to leap out at a dead run. The last thing he wanted was to startle the local men and inadvertently instigate a firefight before Elena was safely back in the MRAP. He'd have those soldiers' balls in a vice for letting her out of the vehicle in the first place.

Scratch that.

He'd have their balls for not immediately returning to the base when they'd realized the main road had been compromised.

Chase walked slowly alongside the convoy, aware that his team had taken up defensive positions that would enable them to provide cover if fighting did break out. As he came around the front of the lead MRAP, he saw Elena crouched down in front of a child, speaking to him. Beside her, one of the soldiers translated. At least the guy had his rifle out and in his hands, Chase thought bitterly, and not slung across his back as if they were at a damned church social.

"Elena," he called.

She turned and saw him, and for just an instant there was no recognition in her eyes. Then she smiled, and the relief and sheer joy he saw on her face made him go a little weak.

"Elena, get in the truck," he said, keeping his voice low as he walked slowly toward them.

"What?" She looked bewildered, her gaze flying from the weapon he held in his hands, to the convoy where she must have been able to see his team drawing down on them, back to his face.

"What's going on?" she asked, but she obediently rose to her feet and took several steps back, away from the villagers. "This is Kadir. Remember Kadir?"

Chase let his gaze flicker to the child, and recognized the boy they had treated for a broken wrist. He sported a cast on one arm.

"Yeah," he answered. "I remember Kadir. Now do as I say and walk slowly toward me. This is not a safe situation."

ELENA HARDLY RECOGNIZED the hard-eyed man who stood there as the same man who had left her just ten days earlier. With his scruffy beard and dirty clothes, he looked more like an insurgent than he did a special ops soldier. The expression in his eyes was one of cold intent, and she realized that if any of the villagers made a misstep, he wouldn't hesitate to shoot first and ask questions later.

For the first time, she understood the risk she'd taken in leaving the MRAP. The soldiers had tried to prevent her from approaching the villagers, but she had recognized Kadir and had wanted to see for herself that the child was on the mend. Now she realized that she had put herself and the villagers in very real danger.

Before she could retreat gracefully, however, one of the village men pushed his way forward. Elena didn't miss how Chase's hand tightened on his weapon. The man was elderly, with a long beard and deep wrinkles, but his dark eyes were shrewd. Elena didn't need to be told that this man was quite possibly the tribal leader. He didn't acknowledge Elena, but directed his attention to the soldier who stood tightly coiled, ready to spring.

As the old man began to speak, Chase visibly relaxed and reluctantly lowered his weapon.

"He says that Kadir is his grandson," he translated, "and that he's grateful to the American soldiers for providing medical treatment for his injuries."

The old man bent down toward the boy and reached beneath the child's tunic, withdrawing the angel necklace. The tiny charm winked against his wizened palm as he continued talking.

"He assures us that the American soldiers will be granted safe passage through these territories," Chase continued, "and that no harm will come to the woman who showed such kindness to his family."

Chase's gaze flicked briefly to Elena, but his expression was shuttered. He said something in return to the elderly man, and then held out his hand to Elena. "Let's go," he said. "Now."

Elena allowed herself one last glance at Kadir, who stood watching wide-eyed, before making her way past Chase to the MRAPs. She heard the whirring of a helicopter, and looked up to see a Black Hawk pass overhead, a gunner clearly visible in the open doorway, and her chest tightened in dread.

She climbed inside the MRAP, fully expecting Chase to follow her. *He had come back safely.* But to her dismay, he stalked past the convoy of armored trucks and climbed into the Humvee with his men. The two soldiers who had been assigned to escort her climbed into the MRAP with her, and as they closed the pneumatic doors, Elena was bitterly aware that Chase didn't give her so much as a second glance.

He was furious with her, and she couldn't blame him. She had no business leaving the MRAP, but had never guessed she might be in any danger. When they had come upon the rockfall, her military escort had suggested they return to the base. She might have agreed if the other soldier hadn't mentioned the detour through the little village of Jani. She had wanted to visit the drilling site, and the detour had seemed like a safe option. She still wasn't certain what had happened back there, but sensed she had dodged a bullet, both literally and figuratively.

When they arrived at the motor pool, she waited impatiently for the soldiers to open the rear door of the MRAP, intent on intercepting Chase. But by the time she climbed out, the Humvee was empty and Chase and his men were nowhere in sight. Frustrated, she began walking toward the contracting center when a voice called her name. Pausing, she turned to see a second Humvee driving slowly toward her. As it drew alongside, she recognized the base commander, Colonel Vinson, in the driver's seat. He didn't look very happy.

"Ms. De la Vega," he said coolly. "I'm glad to see you…alive. Climb in, please," he commanded. "You and I are going to have a little chat about protocol and the rules of engagement."

Elena blew out a hard breath, knowing this was one bullet she wasn't going to dodge so easily.

Two WEEKS, Elena thought in dismay, as she made her way across the base to her living quarters. Her soon-to-be ex–living quarters. Two weeks was all she'd managed to last before she'd been given the heave-ho.

She hefted her flak vest over her arm and let her helmet dangle from her hand. If Chase could see her, he'd give her hell for not wearing her protective gear, but why bother? She almost hoped a mortar would squash her flat. God, she'd never felt so embarrassed or ashamed.

She recalled the conversation she'd had with Colonel Vinson in his office and cringed. Despite the fact that he'd been courteous and even kind, he'd made it clear that she had put both herself and his men in danger by leaving the safety of the MRAP. Worse, he'd suggested that the soldiers who'd made the decision to detour through the village of Jani, rather than return to the base, might receive a reprimand for their actions. Elena had tried to explain that she was to blame, not them; she'd been determined to visit the drilling site and prove that she could do her job.

She swiped angrily at her damp cheeks. She'd known that taking the detour was a foolish decision, but had she cared? No. She'd actually encouraged the soldiers to ignore protocol and do whatever it took to get her to the drilling site. And they had, because they'd been young and stupid and had wanted desperately to impress her. If she'd been a man, they probably would have held their ground and insisted on returning to the base. But because of her misguided priorities, she'd nearly gotten them all killed.

Colonel Vinson had explained to her, in excruciating detail, about the planned ambush. She'd been shocked, and then horrified by her own role in the morning's events. No wonder Chase hadn't wanted to see her. He must be as disgusted with her as she was with herself. But the colonel hadn't seemed angry with her. In fact, if she hadn't known better, she'd have thought he was actually amused. He'd told her that while she had disregarded protocol by leaving the MRAP, he credited her with actually averting a firefight as a result of her kindness to a little boy. He'd gone on to suggest that he was doing her a favor by sending her away. As if leaving Sharlana—and Chase—was some kind of reward.

No doubt Chase would be thrilled to hear that she was leaving. Her heart clenched painfully at the knowledge that she wouldn't see him again. She would board a helicopter in the morning that would take her to Bagram Air Base, where she would work for the remainder of her six-month deployment. Bagram wasn't that far from Sharlana, but it might as well have been on the other side of the world.

Colonel Vinson was right; she should be thrilled with the relocation. Two weeks ago, she would have been. Bagram Air Base was known for its amenities, including an indoor swimming pool and an ice-skating rink. As far as recreation and support services went, the base was second only to the Green Zone in Baghdad. She'd have her own small apartment and access to a state-of-the art fitness center. She should be delighted.

She wanted to cry.

Just the thought of leaving Chase, of never seeing him again, made her inexplicably depressed. She could care less where they assigned her because without Chase, none of it mattered.

She opened the door to her living quarters and dropped her vest and helmet unceremoniously onto the floor.

"I thought we agreed you would wear your protective gear whenever you left your quarters," drawled a deep voice.

Elena spun around. Chase leaned negligently in the doorway to her bedroom. He had showered and shaved, and wore a black T-shirt and a pair of clean camo pants.

His face was leaner than she remembered, and sun-burned, but his hazel eyes glowed as he watched her. A tornado of emotions whirled through her.

"Chase." His name came out on a croak. "What are you doing here? I got the distinct feeling you were avoiding me."

"Damn straight I was avoiding you. Hell, I practically sprinted from the motor pool to avoid seeing you." He grinned, his teeth startling white in his tanned face.

Elena stepped over her vest and approached him, drinking in the sight of him. Alive. Vital. She wanted to touch him and reassure herself that he was really there. But something was so not right with this picture.

"If you didn't want to see me, then why are you here?" she asked carefully.

"Correction," he said, shoving his hands into his pockets. "I didn't want *you* to see *me* when I looked like an animal and smelled like a goat. Especially not when I couldn't trust myself around you."

A tiny bud of hope bloomed in Elena's chest.

"Is that why you didn't ride back with me in the MRAP?" she asked. "Because you couldn't trust yourself?"

He gave a huff of laughter. "I couldn't trust myself not to shake the living hell out of you." He pulled his hands out of his pockets and straightened. "Jesus, Elena, what the hell were you thinking to do something so stupid?"

The bud of hope shriveled and curled in on itself, and Elena covered her face with her hands and turned away. "I don't know!" she cried, not able to face his censure. "I didn't think there would be any harm in taking the detour, and then I saw little Kadir by the side of the road, and I just wanted to make sure he was okay. I'm sorry. I screwed up!"

"Elena, don't cry," he groaned, and then she was in his arms. "Please don't cry, babe."

And then, amazingly, he was kissing her as if he couldn't get enough of her, his hands roaming over her body and burying themselves in her hair, tilting her face so that he could deepen the kiss, sweeping his tongue past her teeth and devouring her. Elena clung to him, kissing him back with her entire heart and soul.

When he finally pulled away, they were both breathing hard. Chase tipped his forehead to hers.

"I thought I was going to lose you," he said, and his voice cracked.

Elena smoothed her palms over his freshly shaven cheeks, cradling his face. "I'm leaving Sharlana. Tomorrow morning."

Chase turned his face into her palm. "I know."

"What?" Elena frowned, not understanding.

"Whose idea do you think it was to have you transferred?"

Elena gasped and snatched her hands away. She stared at him. "You? I'm losing my job because of you?"

"Elena—" He tried to catch her hands, but she held them up, warding him off.

"What right do you have, Chase?" Her voice was incredulous. "I know you think I can't take care of myself, and that women have no place in your dangerous world, but this is my job, Chase. My job, and my choice. Not yours."

God. She didn't want to leave Chase, but she didn't want him thinking that she was some kind of wimp who couldn't handle life on a forward operating base.

"I'm going to Bagram, too," he said quietly. "My team is being transferred, and I couldn't leave you here, Elena. Please understand."

She swallowed hard. "But you still think I need you to protect me, right?"

"I think you do just fine on your own," Chase smiled. "If it weren't for you—and your little guardian angel—those men might have been killed today."

Elena grimaced. "You don't have to be so nice to me, Chase. I was the reason those men took that detour."

Chase made a sound of frustration. "If it wasn't for you, that ambush would have killed the next bunch of guys who drove through that village. You prevented that, Elena. You did more to win the hearts and minds of the local people in just two weeks than the men on this base have been able to accomplish in two years. Do you get how huge that is?"

"Really?" Elena glanced at him. "So you don't think I'm a distraction to the men, and that I have no business being on a forward operating base?"

He searched her eyes. "I think you're a serious distraction, both to my heart and my peace of mind. Because of you, I've become exactly the kind of soldier I used to condemn."

"What kind of soldier is that?" she asked, needing to hear him say it.

"The kind who puts the safety and well-being of the woman he loves above everything else."

He loved her! Elena felt her heart swell until she was certain it would explode out of her chest.

Chase drew her close. "You've changed me, Elena. And while I know you'd do fine here at Sharlana for the next six months, I won't be fine at Bagram without you.

Besides, I think the other guys are onto us." He smoothed his thumb over her cheek. "I need you, Elena, and if that makes me weak, then so be it."

Elena laughed, her fingers closing reflexively over his muscled arms. "*Weak* isn't exactly the word that comes to mind when I think of you."

He tipped his head down to look at her. "And it's not the word I'd use to describe you, either. You're one of the strongest, most passionate women I've ever known. Please say you'll come to Bagram. My team and I will be based there for the next year. We'd have more opportunities to spend time together, and it's a big enough base that we wouldn't be under a microscope."

""Do I have a choice?"

"You always have a choice, Elena."

"What happens when my six months are up and I have to return to the States? Will you stay at Bagram?"

"Yeah, but I'll have two weeks of home leave that I can take, maybe more. I know you'll want to spend time with your family, but I thought maybe we could take a week and—"

"Yes," Elena interrupted.

"Yes?" Chase laughed. "You didn't let me finish. I was going to say that we could take a week and check into a romantic, oceanfront hotel somewhere. Sort of load up on what we'll need to make it through the last six months of my deployment. That is, if you're interested."

"Six months apart?" To Elena, it sounded like an eternity. How was she going to get through six months without Chase?

"I know it sounds like a long time, but it'll go by quickly," Chase assured her. "I'll call you as often as I can, and I'll have access to e-mail. I know we can make this work."

"Or I could extend my own deployment."

Chase leaned back to look at her, and Elena could see the flare of hope in his eyes that he quickly hid. "I wouldn't ask you to do that, Elena. I'd consider myself lucky just to have you at Bagram for the next six months."

Elena smiled, wreathing her arms around his neck. "I don't know…six months at Bagram? My life was pretty boring before I came to Sharlana. I mean, where else can a girl experience giant spiders, sandstorms, mortar attacks, close encounters with Taliban insurgents and the most incredible, amazing sex of her life?" She arched an eyebrow and gave Chase a challenging look. "How can Bagram possibly compare to that?"

Chase grinned and drew her closer. "I can't promise you that there won't be any sandstorms, but I can assure you that you'll be safe from spiders, mortar attacks and Taliban insurgents. As for the sex, keeping it incredible and amazing won't be a problem, I promise." He lowered his mouth to hers. "Let me show you."

Epilogue

North Carolina, one year later

ELENA STOOD by the baggage-claim carousel at Raleigh-Durham Airport and watched the passengers as they came through the security doors. She sucked in a deep breath, willing her nerves to calm down. She was a bundle of anticipation and anxiety, and it was all she could do to stand calmly and wait. She'd been waiting for three months, and now she just wanted to move on with her life.

She'd extended her deployment at Bagram by three months, both to spend more time with Chase and because she'd genuinely enjoyed the work she'd done there. After nine months together, leaving him in Afghanistan had been one of the hardest things she'd ever done. But she'd had work to do back in the States, too. Things she'd needed to take care of before Chase returned.

The security doors swung open, and suddenly there he was. Elena stopped breathing. He didn't immediately see her, and she took the opportunity to drink in the sight of him. He wore his desert camo uniform, and he looked lean and dangerous and altogether delicious. Then he looked across the crowded terminal and saw her, and Elena was struck again by how gorgeous he was. He shouldered his way through the crowd, his eyes fastened on her, until finally she was in his arms and he was kissing her with all the pent-up passion and frustration of three long months apart. When he finally pulled back, they were both breathless.

"What are you doing here?" he demanded, his voice filled with amazement. His eyes devoured her as if he couldn't believe she was really there, and his hands stroked up and down her arms. "I wasn't expecting this. I was going to fly up to D.C. this weekend to surprise you."

Elena grinned foolishly at him. "Now you don't have to. I don't live in D.C. anymore. I live here."

His expression turned into one of astonishment. "You *what?*"

"I sold my condo and moved down here about a month ago. I rented a little apartment in Morehead City. I've been interviewing for a job at the contracting center at Fort Bragg, and it's beginning to look like they might make me an offer."

"You're going to be working at Fort Bragg?" His tone was incredulous.

"It's a lot closer to Camp Lejeune than D.C., and… well, let's just say I really needed a change."

Chase stared at her for a moment, and then he began to laugh. Elena studied him uncertainly.

"You don't mind, do you?"

Chase hauled her against his chest and buried his face in her neck. "No," he said roughly against her skin, "I don't mind at all. I've been considering my options and trying to figure out how we could be together. You just solved that problem for me. How long is the lease on that apartment?"

Elena leaned back in his arms and searched his eyes. "Why do you ask?"

"Because I have a little house on the water near Camp Lejeune, and I think you'd really like it."

"Are you asking me to move in with you?"

"Lady," he growled, "since you left Bagram, the only thing I've thought about is how much I was looking forward to getting you alone for a solid month."

"Only a month?" she teased.

"That'll do for starters," he replied. "And four weeks is how much free time I have before I need to report back for duty."

"You're serious."

"Absolutely. I said I'd do whatever it takes to make this thing work, and I meant it. But I never guessed that you'd leave your job...your family..." He looked a little dazed.

"I'll do whatever it takes, too, Chase. We have something special, and I won't risk losing that." She cupped his face in her hands. "And if it means stepping out of my comfort zone and taking chances, then I'm willing to do that."

Standing on tiptoe, she kissed him, a moist, sweet fusing of their mouths that left her trembling with need.

"Christ," Chase said against her lips, "I've missed you so much. I've been thinking, too, that if we're going to make this work then I can't be disappearing from your life for months at a time."

"What do you mean?"

"I mean that I don't intend to do any more deployments. I'm going to request a transfer to the Marine

Special Operations School as an instructor. I was invited to do that when I returned from Iraq, and I declined. But things have changed. *I've* changed."

Elena caught her breath. "Are you sure?"

"Absolutely. Now let's get out of here and go home. We have a lot of catching up to do, if you get my meaning."

She did.

And nothing had ever sounded so perfect.

* * * * *

UNDER HIS SPELL & TAKING CARE OF BUSINESS
(2-IN-1 ANTHOLOGY)

BY KATHY LYONS

Under His Spell

Nicky Taylor is a driven executive. And magician Jimmy Ray has loved her forever. When he spots her in the audience, he realises he finally has a chance to fulfil his lifelong fantasy.

Taking Care of Business

Sam Finn, undercover multi-millionaire, has been watching Julie indulging her fantasies via the office security cameras...and now they're having a secret fling.

DELICIOUSLY DANGEROUS
BY KAREN ANDERS

The man Callie's dealing with is sexy-as-hell, ruthless and has his own agenda. So inevitably, the sensual games must come to an end. Her mission is an *undercover* seduction...with a delicious side of danger!

HEROES WELCOME
BY JILL SHALVIS, RHONDA NELSON & KAREN FOLEY

Three deliciously sexy soldiers come home and get a very special welcome from three very special women. These men have it all—on the battlefield and in the bedroom!

**On sale from 17th June 2011
Don't miss out!**

*Available at WHSmith, Tesco, ASDA, Eason
and all good bookshops*

www.millsandboon.co.uk

0611/14

Polo, players & passion

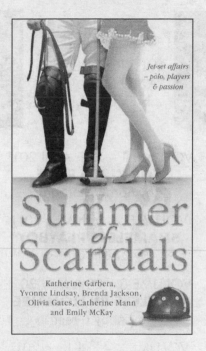

Jet-set affairs
– polo, players
& passion

Summer
of
Scandals

Katherine Garbera,
Yvonne Lindsay, Brenda Jackson,
Olivia Gates, Catherine Mann
and Emily McKay

The polo season—the rich mingle,
passions run hot and
scandals surface…

BAD BLOOD

A POWERFUL
DYNASTY,
WHERE SECRETS
AND SCANDAL
NEVER SLEEP!

VOLUME 1 – 15th April 2011
TORTURED RAKE
by Sarah Morgan

VOLUME 2 – 6th May 2011
SHAMELESS PLAYBOY
by Caitlin Crews

VOLUME 3 – 20th May 2011
RESTLESS BILLIONAIRE
by Abby Green

VOLUME 4 – 3rd June 2011
FEARLESS MAVERICK
by Robyn Grady

8 VOLUMES IN ALL TO COLLECT!

www.millsandboon.co.uk

BAD BL∞D

A POWERFUL
DYNASTY,
WHERE SECRETS
AND SCANDAL
NEVER SLEEP!

VOLUME 5 – 17th June 2011
HEARTLESS REBEL
by Lynn Raye Harris

VOLUME 6 – 1st July 2011
ILLEGITIMATE TYCOON
by Janette Kenny

VOLUME 7 – 15th July 2011
FORGOTTEN DAUGHTER
by Jennie Lucas

VOLUME 8 – 5th August 2011
LONE WOLFE
by Kate Hewitt

8 VOLUMES IN ALL TO COLLECT!

www.millsandboon.co.uk

SIZZLING HOLIDAY FLING...OR THE REAL THING?

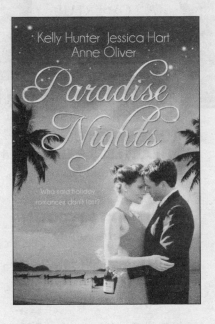

Who said holiday romances didn't last?
As the sun sets the seduction begins...
Who can resist the baddest of boys?

Intense passion and glamour from our bestselling stars of international romance

Available 20th May 2011

Available 17th June 2011

Available 15th July 2011

Available 19th August 2011

Royal Affairs – luxurious and bound by duty yet still captive to desire!

Royal Affairs: Desert Princes & Defiant Virgins

Available 3rd June 2011

Royal Affairs: Princesses & Protectors

Available 1st July 2011

Royal Affairs: Mistresses & Marriages

Available 5th August 2011

Royal Affairs: Revenge Secrets & Seduction

Available 2nd September 2011

LATIN LOVERS COLLECTION

Intense romances with gorgeous
Mediterranean heroes

Greek Tycoons
1st July 2011

**Hot-Blooded
Sicilians**
5th August 2011

Italian Playboys
2nd September
2011

**Passionate
Spaniards**
7th October
2011

**Seductive
Frenchmen**
4th November
2011

**Italian
Husbands**
2nd December
2011

 MILLS BOON™

Collect all six!
www.millsandboon.co.uk

Dating and Other Dangers
by Natalie Anderson

After being trashed on Nadia Keenan's dating website, Ethan Rush faces three dates with her! *He's* determined to clear his name. *She's* determined to prove him for the cad he is...

The S Before Ex
by Mira Lyn Kelly

World famous celebrity Ryan Brady's secret wife is filing for divorce! Unfortunately for Claire Brady, her soon-to-be-ex is *still* the only man her body wants...

Girl in a Vintage Dress
by Nicola Marsh

Lola Lombard, 1950s style siren, is petrified: she's got to organise a terrifyingly glam hen do! Worse still, the bride's gorgeous brother seems interested in the shy woman behind the red lipstick...

Rapunzel in New York
by Nikki Logan

When a knight in pinstripe rushed to the aid of this damsel, she declared she didn't want saving, even by a billionaire! *Yet sometimes even modern Maidens secretly need rescuing...*

On sale from 1st July 2011
Don't miss out!

Available at WHSmith, Tesco, ASDA, Eason and all good bookshops

www.millsandboon.co.uk

2 FREE BOOKS
AND A SURPRISE GIFT

We would like to take this opportunity to thank you for reading this Mills & Boon® book by offering you the chance to take TWO more specially selected titles from the Blaze® series absolutely FREE! We're also making this offer to introduce you to the benefits of the Mills & Boon® Book Club™—

- **FREE home delivery**
- **FREE gifts and competitions**
- **FREE monthly Newsletter**
- **Exclusive Mills & Boon Book Club offers**
- **Books available before they're in the shops**

Accepting these FREE books and gift places you under no obligation to buy, you may cancel at any time, even after receiving your free books. Simply complete your details below and return the entire page to the address below. You don't even need a stamp!

YES Please send me 2 free Blaze books and a surprise gift. I understand that unless you hear from me, I will receive 3 superb new books every month, including a 2-in-1 book priced at £5.30 and two single books priced at £3.30 each, postage and packing free. I am under no obligation to purchase any books and may cancel my subscription at any time. The free books and gift will be mine to keep in any case.

Ms/Mrs/Miss/Mr_____ Initials _____

Surname _____
Address _____
_____
_____ Postcode _____
E-mail _____

Send this whole page to: Mills & Boon Book Club, Free Book Offer, FREEPOST NAT 10298, Richmond, TW9 1BR.